LET
ME
TRY
AGAIN

LET
ME
TRY
AGAIN

(a novel)

MATTHEW DAVIS

Arcade Publishing • New York

Arcade Publishing books may be purchased in bulk at special discounts for sales promotion, corporate gifts, fund-raising, or educational purposes. Special editions can also be created to specifications. For details, contact the Special Sales Department, Arcade Publishing, 307 West 36th Street, 11th Floor, New York, NY 10018 or arcade@skyhorsepublishing.com.

First Edition

Arcade Publishing® is a registered trademark of Skyhorse Publishing, Inc.®, a Delaware corporation.

Visit our website at www.arcadepub.com.
Please follow our publisher Tony Lyons on Instagram @tonylyonsisuncertain.

10 9 8 7 6 5 4 3 2 1

Library of Congress Cataloging-in-Publication Data is available on file.
Library of Congress Control Number: 2024016259

Jacket design by David Ter-Avanesyan
Cover image by Jon Rafman

Print ISBN: 978-1-64821-074-7
Ebook ISBN: 978-1-64821-075-4

Printed in the United States of America

LET
ME
TRY
AGAIN

One

Oh, I was all set to blow my brains out and throw them directly into the nearest East River. Well, not "all set" per se, but I was miserable. I was suffering from this horrible cucking sensation. It was terrible. *Inimical.* Pointed and harrowing. I'm feeling sick just thinking about it— the agony, the irony, my many losses and humiliations, etc, etc, etc, etc. Sorry, sorry. Let me go back a bit. I'll explain everything.

It was my fault. I had broken up with my Lora Liamant after nearly a year together. Not because I didn't love her (I still did), or because she wasn't beautiful anymore (her attractiveness was trending *upward*, with no plateau in sight), but because I thought it (the breakup) would shock her, stun her, make her realize how good she had had it (with me, Ross), and inspire her to stop smoking weed and drinking alcohol (I couldn't stand to see her hurting herself like that) so we could get married (like *adults*) and have children together. It was a tactic, a scheme, I'll be the first to admit.

Despite my initiating the separation, I was prepared to take her back (with arms ajar) as soon as she came to her sober senses. I waited for weeks. Chatting intermittently with her, forwarding her links to interesting articles, sending her poems, etc, etc, without any signs of progress. And then, a few nights before Flag Day, three months into the breakup, I was roused out of bed, out of my dogmatic slumber, acutely aware of the aforementioned cucking sensation.

Heaving and hawing, I scuttled to the bathroom and knelt within a few scoots of my toilet, mistaking this cucking sensation for a more simple bodily biliousness (it should be understood that I'm prone to bouts of nervous vomiting).

And then, as if placed there by some kind of supernatural daemon, the thought occurred to me, with great clarity and certainty, that my Lora had entered into a newfound tryst of sorts. And after checking that app that people use to send each other money, and finding a number of Lora's recent transactions with memorandums like "Vino" and "French Fries," my suspicions were confirmed, with great clarity and certainty, that my Lora had entered into a newfound "tryst" of sorts, with the thirty-year-old brother of network-TV-actor Kiefer Sutherland. Oh, you should've seen me rolling around my bathroom floor, pounding my fists, mourning my loss; I wanted to blow my brains out and throw them directly into the nearest East River. I couldn't sleep all night. Every time I closed my eyes all I could see was Lora and . . . no, no. I won't say it. It's too upsetting.

This was . . . *calamitous*. Particularly because I had actually *met* this gentleman—this network-TV-actor's thirty-year-old brother—once, four months earlier, at a party commemorating an important annual American football game, hosted at Lora L's cousin's apartment in Clinton Hill, Brooklyn. And he was not at all impressive to me. He seemed really very bitter. He accused me, in his lispy monotone, of being "a straight-up psychopath," all because I said *American Beauty* (1999) was one of the biggest "pieces of bull" ever made and was "a movie for people who have never had an original thought in their lives." Lora sided with him and told me I ought not to be so "negative" about things that people "worked hard on." They then smoked "weed" together on Lora's cousin's front stoop later in the evening, making eyes at each other, musing romantically about "life," or something stupid else that has no wrong answers, I'm sure. Who knows how long she waited to see him after we'd broken up? Certainly not long enough. (It was a slap in the face, how swiftly I was replaced.) Everyone knows it's *cheating* to take on a new partner within the same calendar month of a breakup.

So I was hurt. Terribly hurt, and terribly confused.

The adult response, to this discomfiting cucking sensation, was to do some *moving on* of my own. The next morning, I downloaded *All Work*

MATTHEW DAVIS

and All Play, a new dating app that requires you to submit two recent paystubs and possess a LinkedIn account with over one hundred "connections" in order to sign up. This seemed fitting, as my professional life was at a nine, while my personal life was at a two. In my application, I selected the app's "The New Classic" mode, which gave me access to a pool of women whose salaries lay between seventy-seven and ninety percent of my own, which I figured would make for a nice power dynamic.

Once I was "in," I found it was mostly disgusting, filled with ghastly looking women, desperate to meet a man with a purpose. None of the women on there could compare to a Lora L, but in the spirit of revenge, and of *moving on,* I reached out to a twenty-eight year old Senior PowerPoint Associate at ViacomCBS, whose interests included "books," and whose bio read: "Diehard defender of the oxford comma!" which at the time I had assumed was some sort of wry, ironic-type of joke, or even something that was genuinely clever when she was my age. But since meeting her, I'm not really sure what she could've possibly meant by it. She (her profile) looked sane, very standard—tanned skin, blonde hair, photos of herself drinking wine, wearing dresses, loitering around islands, etc, etc.

Naturally, she was charmed by my advances, and so we arranged to have an after-work dinner together at the *Emeril Lagasse 360° VR Experience* restaurant in New York's Times Square.

It was a relief to have found someone so quickly, but hardly a surprise, as I've never seemed to have much trouble appealing to women on apps of this nature. Not because of any immediately obvious evolutionarily desirable traits, but because of some more subtle qualities that I think women of the twenty-first century can't help but appreciate (although I've been told I resemble a young Andrew Garfield). What's most notable is how there's nothing frightening or alarming about how I look. No piercings, tattoos facial hair, or ostentatious musculature indicative of excessive exercise. I simply look normal. Jewish and nonthreatening. It cannot be said enough that I have the body and face of a non-rapist. My features scream safety. Just by looking at me, you can tell that I'm financially secure, not at all violent, and eager to commit.

~

It was around 5:00, warm, still sunny; I was hanging around "midtown," by myself, and I had so much time to think. I liked to be early for this sort of thing. Demonstrate discipline by budgeting for unexpected delays.

I sat anxiously, tapping on a bench, wearing noise-cancelling wireless earphones, somewhere around 44th and 7th, let's say. I was waiting for the appearance of this twenty-eight-year-old woman whom I'd met on an app on my phone. This was the night before my twenty-third birthday, three months and a week (or so) after I had broken up with Lora Liamant.

She came out of her building dressed in black, with a big bag on her shoulder, holding in her hand a second, smaller bag, one of those tiny purses that women seem to find fashionable. "Ross! Happy Birthday!" she exclaimed, as she gave me a hug and a kiss on the cheek. It occurred to me that she was overdressed, that she must have been wearing her Date Night Outfit to work all day, or, more sadly, even, she had just changed in the bathroom of her office. She was mature, physically, and I thought that was a noble thing for me to desire.

"Hey! Thanks!" I replied, "But my birthday isn't until midnight," I raised my eyebrows playfully, as if to say *I'm pedantic, but at least I'm aware of it!* "You still have a few hours to wish me a happy *Bloomsday*, though!" I said aloud.

"What's that?" she said with a smile.

"Oh. Nevermind. It's stupid. Sorry. Are you going to change before we have dinner?"

"Change? Why?"

"Oh," I said, "I'm just kidding. You look lovely."

On the walk over, I talked about my job, about stocks, about bonds, about how computers aren't all that smart, but they're very powerful.

4

"They're like big dumb brutes that can do exactly what you tell them to do. And the only problem is, they do *exactly* what you tell them to."

"That's hilarious," she said.

Inside I gave my name ("Hi uh, I have a reservation for Mathcamp?"), and we were seated at a booth labeled "Adult Party" and instructed to place Oculus Quest virtual reality headsets on ourselves, which would transport us to the simulacrum of Emeril's chefside table.

"BAM! Welcome to Emeril Lagasse's Times Square Virtual Reality experience! BAM! Now who's already to eat? Are you two lovebirds ready to eat?"

I heard the grown woman across from me say "Yeayuh, Emeril!"

"Now I got three specials for you tonight. BAM!" Emeril said, "We got Emeril's Chicken Gumbo—melt in your mouth chicken topped with Emeril's signature filé powder, tossed in Emeril's Louisiana hot sauce, all on a bed of ghost white rice and baby bella mushrooms. BAM! Second, we got Emeril's Cajun Style Lasagna—suicide-free pork, grass-fed beef, buffalo mozzarella, and the same KICK you've come to expect. BAM! And last but not least, we got Emeril's Stir Fried Vegetables—for all those *vegans* out there!" Emeril, very predictably, rolled his eyes at the *v word*. "So BAM! What's it gonna be?" Emeril said, as he pointed his large silver pepper shaker at Ross (me). "Use your virtual pin-pad to select from these options!"

I chose the Mixed Vegetables—which my mother used to have waiting for me after school as a small child—paired with an appetizer of Emeril's Jazzy Jambalaya. After you order, you're treated to VR video of Emeril preparing your appetizer and entree, although of course, the real meal is being microwaved in the back by someone who has tattoos and smokes cigarettes.

The presentation was dizzying, uncanny. I found it terribly unsettling, to be unable to see my date. I let my mind think of Lora, of the last time I'd talked to her. I told her quote "I love you" on the phone that night, and she replied, "I don't think I should say it back. I don't think that would be fair to you," which at the time I didn't find terribly discouraging, as men are constantly told they can do whatever they want to women and always be taken back, eventually. But as I watched Emeril slam a fistful of parsley onto my plate of pixely Po' Boys (and smelled what seemed to be an artificial New Orleans scent being spritzed into our booth), I placed that conversation in the context of my discovery of Lora L's new "tryst," and felt horribly humiliated and emasculated. Like an undignified little bug.

As Emeril finished plating everything, a real-life waiter (or waitress) placed real ("real") versions of our ordered meals in front of us, and Emeril signed off saying, "Thanks for coming! And remember, if you want to eat like Emeril at home, treat yourself to Emeril Lagasse's Power Air Fryer Pro, now available at Bed Bath and Beyond. *BAM!*"

My date looked excited to eat. In addition to her food, there was also a glowing green drink in front of her. "It's an *appletini*, Ross," she said to me. This woman was definitely not fat but had pretty clearly gained some nontrivial amount of weight since taking her older younger dating app photos. "Can I ask you something, Ross?" she asked.

I swallowed a 500-mg activated charcoal pill from my backpack, to help handle any impending gluten. "Sure. Why not?" I replied.

"How'd you know I loved Emeril? That'd it get me so hot being here?"

"What?"

"Oh yeah!" she said, as she took a big ecstatic bite of Emeril's Chicken Gumbo, "He was my first crush! I used to *jay off* to his show on the Food Network all the time when I was in first grade! Of course, I didn't know what I was doing . . . at the time . . ."

"I've heard of that actually," I told her.

Oy . . . this made me sick. Thinking of this woman, (now nearly thirty and unmarried) at age six (before I was even *born!*) grinding against her couch cushions, bellyside down, getting off to the sight of the Food Network's *Essence of Emeril* (1994–2007).

"Yeah, just thought I'd share that with you," she said, "so you'd, you know, know what kind of *mood* I'll be in for the rest of the night."

Now this was just wrong. I felt terrible. I mean, I'd always intended to *go home* with this woman, but I wanted to have to *work* for it, really have to show off my many amazing qualities. But this, this was just unrewarding. It felt like getting attention from a *dog*. Whereas Lora was always cultured and elusive, having descended from a prominent 19th century New York family.

Trying to change the subject, "So you said you liked books, on the app."

"Oh yeah. Definitely. I've always been, like, a ferocious reader. Here." She proceeded to pry an off brand "eReader" out of her tiny purse, pressed some horrible combination of buttons on its side, and handed it to me.

On the screen, I found not, as I'd hoped, some classic, some novel, some epic feat of female fiction from the likes of Woolf, or Didion, or Ng, but instead, the recently released smash hit self-help manifesto: *HOW TO BE A MOTHERF*CKER WITHOUT F*CKING YOUR F*CKING MOTHER: A step-by-step instruction manual for kneeing life in the balls* (2018) by Juliette Smink.

"I've seen people reading this on the train. I think I saw it won the PEN/Dale Carnegie award. Is it any good?"

"Oh, it's *amazing*, Ross. I'm only halfway through, but I'm trying to really savor it, you know? Make sure I really grasp every last word. Like there's this part I've been reading all week, it's so smart, Ross. She says you have to take what you want. But first, you have to take what you *need*. One handful at a time, Ross."

"That makes sense."

I looked around at the rest of the restaurant. It was full of fellow young people, all seemingly there for some silly sardonic experience. This was regressive. I felt like a horrid cliché, one of thousands of pale cynics having an ironic meal at a "theme" restaurant, laughing at the "tourists"—as if there's something so funny about people living in places that aren't New York City. There must have been seven or eight other Jewish-American Zoomers on the premises, with their cocky collegiate chums, Asian lady-friends, etc, etc, paying top dollar to yuck it up at Emeril's expense. Is it that funny? Is this all they had to laugh about? I felt childish. I felt terrible. I was no better than these people, really. Reaching into my backpack, I took another 500 mg activated charcoal (for my guts) and 200-mg L-Theanine (for my kishkas). "I uh . . . take a lot of pills, especially around dinner time ha, ha" I said to her.

"That's weird, but cute, ha ha," she replied.

She told me some more about her work. "I just published a new infographic today. For Pride Month. It was *soo* cool to do, you know, like working with characters that I've loved for so long. Let me see if I have it on here." She scrolled through her phone (the same phone everyone has, but with a *BET* branded case on the back), made a frowny face, sighed, then said, "Oh, well, I guess it's on my work computer. But basically, it's SpongeBob explaining Crohn's Disease to Patrick!"

"That's cool . . . Hey," I said, before inviting her back to my home to watch ("watch") Joel Schumacher's *The Number 23* (2007), starring Jim Carrey as a deranged man who becomes obsessed with the number twenty-three.

"Oh that's funny, 'cause tomorrow's your twenty-third birthday!"

"Exactly. Isn't that hilarious?" I added, but actually, it wasn't funny at all, now that I think about it.

We left the restaurant without paying (the menu was, as they say, *prix fixe*, and I had already given a credit card when I made the reservation), then took the F train to my luxury apartment on Roosevelt Island. At the platform she said "Race you up the escalator!" and I shook my head no, as I thought it would be unbecoming of a man my age. Despite all my rage, and all my contempt for this Senior PowerPoint Associate, I was desperate to impress her. I had to feel like I was earning something, that I'd *convinced* someone of something. I had to make her respect me before I could feel comfortable seeing her nude.

I held the door for her as we walked into my building's lobby. Inside, I showed her my view of the water and glimpse of the "Pepsi" sign in Long Island City, Queens ("so cool! I love Pepsi!"), my laundry closet ("so convenient!"), my many air purifiers and robot vacuum ("so *that's* why it's so clean in here!"), my Juicero ("so yummy, and healthy, too!"), and finally my library, my wall-mounted IKEA "BILLY" stuffed neatly with assorted "classics." Each shelf more impressive than the last. Heirlooms like my mint-condition autographed Jacob Epstein novel (1980). Trilogies like *White Noise* (1985), *White Teeth* (2000), *and White Fragility* (2018). My Belloc, my Bellow. My Barthes, my Barth, and my Barthelme. My Thomas Aquinas, my Thomas Pynchon. My Leonhard Euler, My Lauren Oyler. My John Stuart Mill, my Jon Stuart Leibowitz. Etc, etc, etc, etc.

"This right here," I told her, "is *America: The Book* (2004), it came out around the peak of *The Daily Show* (1996—), when he was really *giving it good* to Bush and his cronies night after night. Of course, I didn't read it until high school . . ." I don't know why I was saying this to her, but she nodded along as if it were interesting, then climbed onto my bed and took off her socks, stretching and sprawling all over the covers with an unsexy grin on her face. I sat down beside her and ran my left hand through her tawny blonde hair, cleared my throat, and said "uh, *The Number 23* (2007)" into my voice-activated Chinese TV remote.

Within seconds, she was groping my torso and kissing my neck as if that's what I *wanted* from her. Well, I suppose it was, but perhaps now it feels embarrassing to act like I was really enthused by it in any meaningful way, even though I almost certainly was.

I pulled away from an extended series of snogs. "Do you want to take a shower first? I think that would expand our *Overton window* of . . . available acts, you know?"

"Oh . . . *oh*! Yeah, for sure. I was going to say your shower looked really cool."

"Yeah it's nice. I like that there's a sliding door. My last apartment had a bathtub, but it seems like you have to choose between a door and a bathtub. And I can't stand shower curtains. I think they're disgusting."

She laughed as she walked over to the bathroom and began removing her clothes.

"Oh, and just scream for me when you're done. I'm putting a towel in the dryer on the 'Keep Warm' mode, so it'll be hot when you're done. I used to have a heated towel rack, but I think those things might just do nothing. I think they're just useless. So just scream, just start yelling and screaming at me when you're done," I told her.

While she was in there, helping herself to my array of fancy organic soaps and shampoos, I ran over to the kitchen table and began digging around through her bags. Toothbrush, underwear, progestin-only birth control pills, Dentyne Ice, Starbucks gift cards, etc, etc. Her phone had a notification that the latest episode of *Girls Talking About Having Premarital Sex* (2018–) was available on her podcasts app.

On my own phone, I noticed a few missed calls from my sister Emily, and a voicemail from a number with an 818 area code. But of course, I was far too focused on invading the privacy and well . . . *privacy* of this woman to worry about that sort of thing. I took out her "eReader" and started snooping through it. In a queue called "Next Up" she had the following books: *The Da Vinci Code* (2003), *The Slippery Slope* (2003), and *Dude, Where's My Country?* (2003). I looked at the list of authors in her "library," and for a small second was excited by the name "Roth," but it turned out to be the name of a children's science-fiction writer named Veronika Roth, born in 1988.

"Ross? Ross! I'm all clean now!"

I've often wondered if I were destroying some sort of tension or mood or mystery by making these women shower first, but what is the alternative? Just being filthy? After a day of trains and restaurants, just denying that we were covered in sweat and smut? What would separate us from wild animals if we didn't have rules about this sort of thing?

I brought her a towel and she let out a number of moans and remarks ("ooah . . ." "aah . . .") re: the warmth and comfort it gave her. She dried fairly quickly (that's the point!) and climbed atop my bed where we began to engage in increasingly impure acts. A real gentleman (such as I) doesn't kiss and tell, but what I will say, is that she behaved in a way that would make it difficult to have any real-world respect for her afterward. I could only imagine what sort of stunts she'd be willing to pull on a second, third, or even fourth date. She did abominable things to a total Jewish stranger. Most of all, I was stunned by her obsequiousness on bed (obviously I wouldn't let her *in* it). I mean, she simply did not know me. Why was she doing these things?

For what it's worth, I too, I'm willing to confess, gave one of my more effortful performances. (Breaking my back just to know her name, etc, etc.) But did any of that make this more pleasurable? Certainly not for me. It was disgusting—all of it. We simply did *not* know each other. Don't you think there's something wrong here?

As we lay in my shame, side by side, I wished desperately ("I wish I had an honest excuse to get this woman to leave!") for an honest excuse to get this woman to leave. I wanted her gone. I wanted her to get her arms off of me. I needed Lora Liamant back. I robed myself (I didn't want this weird woman seeing my nude body walking around upright!) and went to take a shower of my own, grabbing a handful of raspberries and a 50-mg tablet of 5-HTP (to replenish any serotonin I may've accidentally ejaculated) out of the refrigerator on the way in, where I noticed she'd sorted my array of fancy organic soaps and shampoos into a neat little grid, which I actually found sort of charming and thoughtful.

While she was taking her second, I spent a minute listening to the hour-old voicemail, from our family lawyer, Robert B Shapiro: "Hi Ross, uhh . . . [extended pause] it's Uncle Bobby, call me back as soon as you can, it's uh . . . [extended pause] pretty urgent."

And since he said it was quote "pretty urgent," I pressed the button to call him back right away.

"Hello?"

"Hi, Uncle Bobby? It's Ross."

"Oh, *oy gut,* Ross. Have you got a minute? You'll want to sit down."

"Is everything okay?"

"Oh it's going to be fine. Long story short, your parents are dead, Ross. Helicopter accident, in Turks and Caicos. Emily's fine. She didn't go. I already called her, Ross. The good news is, I think we have a case against *Sandals Resorts International,* Ross. They'll settle. I've worked with them before, Ross. People die at their hotels all the time. They have insurance for this sort of thing. They're flying the bodies in for a funeral the day after tomorrow. Are you standing up, Ross? You'll have to do your *kriah,* Ross, you know, tear a piece of your clothing. It's a Jewish tradition, Ross."

A terrible feeling of regret came over me. Clearly my parents' death was my punishment for fornicating with this dating app idiot and then wishing for an excuse for her to leave. Punishment from some cosmic force of justice (karma, G—d, etc, etc), either for having sex without love, or sex outside of a relationship, or loveless sex outside of a relationship for the sole purpose of getting revenge on someone I *did* still love from a previous relationship. Something like that. It couldn't have been anyone's fault but my own—my parents' untimely death.

Try to imagine the panic I felt in this moment. What was I supposed to tell people when they asked where I was when I heard my parents were killed in a helicopter accident in Turks and Caicos? How was I supposed to respond to my family's lawyer, Robert B. Shapiro? "I'm uh . . . nude, Uncle Robert."

"You're nude? Why are you nude, Ross?"

"Well, I just got out of the shower, I'm wearing a towel."

"Okay, Ross. So here's what you do. You go to your kitchen drawer, grab a pair of scissors, kitchen shears, and give about an eight-centimeter snip into that towel you're wearing."

"What is this obsession with Jews and snipping things?" I asked as I walked over to the kitchen drawer.

"Oh, that's a good one, Ross. Oh that's real good. That's real funny. I'm gonna tell everyone at the office you said that. What a great sense of humor you got, Ross. Clever as a whip. You've got that *yiddisher kop*, Ross."

"Okay, I did it," I said as the blonde-haired dating app woman came out of the shower and did a goofy little dance, trying to be funny, or cute, or sexy. I felt terrible. Terribly alone in her unLoralike presence.

"See, now don't you feel better, Ross? It's tradition, Ross," said Robert Shapiro.

"Yes. I'm going to go now. I'll see you in California in a day or so, Uncle Robert."

"Who was that?" she asked.

"I just got some terrible news and you really must go now. I don't want to talk about it, but it's terrible. It's the sort of thing that means you have to get out of here as quickly as possible."

"Is everything okay? You can tell me, don't be shy, Ross." She put her hand on my shoulder as if that could somehow comfort me.

"No. No! Get off." I threw my hands into the air. "Get out! You have to leave. Can you just leave? Can you just go? *Please!*"

Two

I was up late into the night, contemplating my loss. Frantically penning a thoughtful eulogy, the thought of which has always excited me. Dazzle everyone in attendance with my wry wit and eloquent reading voice. It would also make a sexy and sympathetic moment to record and send to Lora (my ex-girlfriend whom I miss desperately) later. Let her see how thoughtful and solemn and *mature* I was capable of being now that I'd undergone such a tragic loss. It's worth noting that I had *wanted* to give a eulogy when my Bubbe died two years ago, but for whatever reason, I wasn't asked to speak at the service. But this time, *I* was the son, the boy bereaved. Now no one could take away my right to free speech.

The sad thing about my parents dying so unexpectedly was that I didn't have anything prepared for this big moment, so it would have to be written hastily—and with help.

At exactly midnight New York time, my Watch buzzed with an email from my parents, a prescheduled birthday note with a one-thousand-dollar Best Buy gift card attached. It read:

> Happy early birthday, son! Remember, nobody likes you when you're 23. Just kidding! This is going to be your best year yet, Ross. We are so proud of you for living in New York City all by yourself.
>
> Love,
> Mom and Dad

I printed it out and left it on the desk in my bedroom, the last thing my parents would ever say to me. The last Best Buy gift card they'd ever email me.

After redeeming the one grand gift card, I took 10-mg amphetamine salts, looked up the rules for discounted airfare for funerals, booked a 9:08 a.m. JetBlue flight from LaGuardia to Burbank, and scribbled down a two-thousand-word eulogy draft into my Moleskine, a thirty-three-hundred-word rewrite into my Muji, and a five-thousand-word final draft into my MacBook Pro. It was brilliant. My prose masterpiece. Every syllable accounted for, every reference highbrow, each anecdote more decorous than the last. I sent it over to Emily (my sister) for line editing around 4:00, then used an app on my phone to schedule a car to bring me to the airport around 7:00.

Between 4:00 and 6:00 I lay in bed, pretending to sleep, but my body remained full of residual amphetamine energy. Slumber was out of the question. A minute before my alarm was set to go off, I barked at my voice-activated smart-speaker ". . .cancel the six o'clock alarm!" then jumped out of the covers and began preparing my Morning Drink—one tablespoon of cacao powder blended in eight ounces of boiled water mixed with a tablespoon of caprylic acid triglycerides.

In my research, I've found that consuming a high-fat, high-temperature beverage early in the morning keeps my mind clear for the next several hours.

After the drink was finished and its mug washed (by hand), I packed a few things into a tiny suitcase, showered, dressed, took my vitamins (D3, B6 (P5P), K2), waltzed into the elevator, and turned on the Blink XT2 Outdoor/Indoor Smart Security Camera with cloud storage included, facing my front door, just in case someone tried to rob me while I was away in Los Angeles.

Downstairs, a black 2017 Volkswagen Passat was waiting to take me to my JetBlue flight. The driver, a slightly balding half-Hispanic-American named Victor, hopped out of the driver's side seat to load my bag into the trunk. "I got you boss," he told me.

"Thanks, again, for taking the bags," I said from the back as I watched him place his huge phone into its magnetic stand affixed via suction-cup to the windshield.

"You hungry? You want something to drink? Snapple? Miniature 3 Musketeers? Phone charger?"

"I'm okay, thanks, Victor."

He sped out onto Main Street, scratching his head confusedly. "No offense bro, but what is this place?"

"My apartment building?"

"No like this whole island. Like this place is crazy. I never even heard of this place. What's it called again?"

"It's uh . . . *Roosevelt* Island."

"Yeah, see. I heard of like *Riker's* Island, *Governor's* Island. *Randall's* Island."

"Long Island."

"Yeah that too. I heard of all these islands, but I never heard of Roosevelt Island."

"Not a lot of people come here," I told him. "It's actually one of the city's *best kept secrets*. They have a tennis club, a hospital, and a prestigious Ivy League engineering campus. Plus you're surrounded by river. I love it. I love Roosevelt Island. It's like my own private island that no one knows about, and even if they did know about it, they wouldn't know how to get here, and even if they knew how to get here, it would be too hard for them to get here."

"Yeah, yeah. That's cool bro. When the app told me I had to take this bridge I was mad confused, you know?"

"Oh, I bet you were," I told him.

There was silence for a few minutes until eventually Victor looked back at me and said, "I had a crazy night dude. You had a crazy night?"

"No. Not really," I started. "Actually, wait, yes, I did. I actually *did* have a 'crazy' night. But I usually say no to that question, because I don't drink alcohol or do drugs, so my nights usually aren't very crazy, you know?"

"Oh I feel that. I had these two Russian girls staying with me, and they were like mother and daughter, you know? Do you know what I'm saying?"

"That they were mother and daughter?"

"No, well, they weren't actually like mother and daughter. Just one was old and the other one was young. And *hot*. And I picked them both up from the airport and they had *no bags*. Like what's that about? So I'm just thinkin' like *what are they doing here with no bags*, right?"

"Yeah. You'd think they would have bags, if they were coming from the airport, Vic."

"Yeah exactly. So I ask them, I say 'What are you two doing with no bags? Are you two stupid?' you know, kinda like flirting with them."

"Sure."

"And they start telling me they're models, or whatever. Whole time I'm just thinking: what kind of model doesn't have bags? Don't you need bags to model? What kind of modeling are they doing? So I told them I was a cop, that their phone got flagged for human trafficking when they requested the car on the app, and that they're gonna go to jail, for thirty years, blah blah blah, you know?"

"You tell them you're a cop?"

"Yeah I even got this badge from the Spirit Halloween store," he said as he showed me a patent leather prop badge, with a plasticky gold sheriff's star and a photo of himself printed on unlaminated computer paper.

"And you show them this?"

"Yeah and then I tell them they're gonna go to jail for life if they don't come back home with me. So I brought them back home and we did some," and then he honked the horn of his Jetta two times close together like *beepbeep*.

It wasn't clear what exactly he meant, but I got the gist of it. "So you just lied to these women and told them you were a cop and that they were in deep trouble? That you were going to lock them up and throw away the key?" I asked.

"Yeah, why not? You never lied to impress a girl bro?"

"No, I guess I have. I guess that's a fair point."

I watched as Victor navigated expertly through the tangled mess of cars that constitute the so-called "rush" hour. Leaning back in his driver's seat, fiddling with blinkers and turn signals, narrowly avoiding collisions, etc, etc. I've always thought there was something masculine about being able to operate a car well.

My father, may he rest in peace, was an intimidatingly masculine figure. Oozing machismo. Much taller and stronger than I could ever hope to be. And he loved to drive. He loved to own and operate motor vehicles. "Do you see this, Ross," he would ask me, "this is called *cutting the wheel*, Ross. You have to learn how to cut the wheel, and that's the trick. That's the trick to getting this Expedition into the garage, Ross. Put that book down, Ross! And watch your father! Don't you want to be a man some day? A real *man's man*? Then watch your father back his Eddie Bauer Edition Ford Expedition into the garage," he would shout as I stood there, in awe of his ability to manipulate that behemoth backward and forward, contorting it until it slid orthogonally into our home's slim orifice. Vic, negotiating the Astorian traffic was similarly impressive. I was always too scared to drive in New York. It seems terribly stressful. Like a real opportunity to make a mistake and get yelled at and have to deal with all sorts of pain.

Feeling sentimental, I let my head collapse against the seatbelt and texted Lora Liamant: "hey, just so you know my parents died in a helicopter accident at the Sandals resort in Turks and Caicos."

As I fell asleep, my Watch buzzed to notify me of an email from JCPenney, announcing their upcoming sale in celebration of National Schizophrenia Day weekend.

When I awoke, we were already deep into Queens, and Victor had tuned his Jetta's stereo to an FM radio station playing contemporary rock music featuring frightening motifs of blood, suffering, servitude, and love.

"What is that?"

"What's what?" he said.

"What are you playing on there? That's horrible. It sounds horrible."

"It's worship . . ."

"What are you talking about?"

"It's K-Love radio, dude. Their mission is to help *everybody* have a personal relationship with Christ."

"You're a Christian?" I asked him.

"Absolutely. A hundred-fifty-*THOUSAND* percent, bro. Jesus is my savior."

"But you were just telling me how you impersonate a police officer to fornicate with confused Russian women."

"Yeah, but you know . . . I can do that. Because I'm saved."

"What do you mean, you're *saved*?"

"Martin Luther says I'm saved by faith. Alone. I can do whatever I want. Jesus died for my sins."

"And you believe this? You really think you can do whatever you want?"

"Martin Luther said you can commit murder and fornication a thousand times a DAY, bro. And still go to heaven. Isn't that awesome? It's so amazing what Christ did for us . . ."

"That doesn't sound good at all. Why would you want to commit murder and fornication a thousand times a day?"

"Well . . . what do you believe? Are you saved, bro? Do you want to become Christian? Like me? You just have to say this prayer: 'I accept Jesus as my savior, thank you Lord.' You just say it one time and you're saved forever. You can do whatever you want and never go to hell, as long as you say that one time. That's what Pastor Jeff told us."

"You really think you can just do whatever you want as long as you say those words once?"

"Well, you gotta really *mean* it, or else it doesn't count."

"Well I probably wouldn't mean it then. Maybe another time."

"So if I may inquire, sir," he said, adopting what he thought was an impression of an "English" accent, "what are your personal religious beliefs, then, indubitably?"

I contemplated explaining my position of rationalist deism, giving a brief cosmological argument, that since the universe had a beginning, it must have had a cause, and there necessarily ought to have been some Creator, first mover, etc, etc, but that we have no way of knowing whether this Creator cares about us, or whether it has a gender, or a Son, or a consciousness, but this all seemed terribly complicated for Vic. So instead, I just told him, "I'm like, Jewish, I guess."

"Oh that's cool," Vic replied. "So are you like from Israel? Pastor Jeff says we have to protect Israel. That's like . . . God's land."

"No, I'm from Los Angeles."

"Oh but you're Jewish, right?"

"Yeah."

"So you know like a lot about money, right?"

"Well, I guess I do, but I don't think it's just because I'm Jewish. I think you just got lucky guessing that. I know a lot of Jews who don't know very much at all about money."

"You gotta help me bro, with this money stuff. Here, put your number into my phone," he grabbed his huge phone out of its holster and tossed it back to me. I sent myself a message from his device saying "Victor," and handed it back to him.

"Thanks dude. And if you ever need anything let me know, I do like private security, private investigator detective type stuff, on the side, and I, I got these sick binoculars, night vision goggles, paintball guns, you know, gear. So just let me know if you ever need anything." He handed me a small manila business card that read:

VICTOR "VIC" BOWFLEX
BRONX, NEW YORK

PROTESTANT YOUTH MINISTER,
DRIVER, PRIVATE INVESTIGATOR

"Thanks, Vic."

When Victor dropped me off at LaGuardia, he told me I absolutely needed to try a restaurant he loved called Au Bon Pain. But there was no need for me to do that, as I was already smiling and satisfied from my homemade high-fat beverage.

In life, I've found it to be helpful to do the same thing every day. Having the same breakfast, wearing the same shoes, shirts, etc, etc, can help minimize *decision fatigue*. It's a trivial mathematical fact that with each decision a person makes on a given day, the likelihood of making a *bad decision* increases, but research from top social scientists like Jonathan Levav has shown that this concept of *decision fatigue* is a psychobiological reality. That our brains run out of gas as the day goes on. And so I try to stick to routines, and have a strict rule against eating at airports. This helps minimize my daily decision count.

I skipped through security rather painlessly, as the only person in Terminal A's Unexpected Funeral line, and it occurred to me that most people don't really travel by air very often. Maybe once a year if they're lucky. We're accustomed to seeing depictions of airports constantly in TV and movies, because the megarich freakshows who control our narratives are constantly jetting back and forth—from New York to Los Angeles, from their wintertime orgy-sex islands to their summertime orgy-sex islands, etc, etc—and they're so self-absorbed that they think their awkward little encounters with security agents and stewardesses are brilliant and literary and worth portraying On Screen. But aside from a small snide comment uttered as my backpack slid through the X-ray baggage scanner ("Damn, why this boy got so many pills?"), my airport experience was entirely uneventful.

On the plane, I sat in an assigned aisle seat, stretching my legs in all sorts of directions, as the rest of my half-row was empty. A few feet away from me, a man excitedly told his wife that the plane's in-flight entertainment system had the entirety of *The War At Home* (2005–2007) available on-demand.

Before we took off, I opened the *Find My Ex-Girlfriend* app and saw that Lora was still at the strange (and by that I mean, it belonged to some man who wasn't I) address that I'd seen her at the night before. I sent her another message: "hey I wasn't being ironic or anything before. My parents really did die. The funeral is tomorrow. I feel really weird about it all . . ." and then turned my phone off so that if she did reply, I wouldn't be able to see it and reply for another five hours, making me seem sort of busy, and less obsessive, I'd hoped.

On my iPad, I quickly jotted down a sixteen-line ballad about the agony I was experiencing:

Lora left me all alone
Her humble Ross, her heart of stone
Another man, she'll be his whore,
Because his bro's on 24
That love will fade, grow stale and sick
A foolish fling, all over quick
That man, he'll drink; he'll spurn his liver
While my brains float down the East River
Is there something that I lack?
A famous fam, with Bauers, Jack?
Just normal people, normal jobs,
Not descended from heartthrobs
We don't kill Muslims on TV,
Do drugs, get drunk on Chablis . . .
This alcoholic gets rewarded,
While I feel like I'm waterboarded . . .

I stared at it for a bit, found it to be raw, honest, and most of all, true, but didn't think it was compelling enough to be able to change Lora's mind, at least not yet. Even though any rational high-IQ person would be able to tell that I was clearly a better catch than this ridiculous geezer she'd shacked up with. Out of my backpack, I grabbed a green banana (high in prebiotic-resistant starch) and ate it slowly, taking deep breaths between bites to assuage my anxiety about being cucked by Kiefer Sutherland's thirty-year-old brother, and also, I suppose, the anxiety re: my parents dying in a helicopter accident in Turks and Caicos.

Still on the iPad, I started reading the Wikipedia pages for "Bereavement in Judaism" and "Shiva (Judaism)" to see what sort of weird rituals I'd have to do now that my parents were dead. From what I could tell, Wikipedia wanted me to go a week without leaving my home or looking in the mirror, sitting on a tiny stool, lighting candles and eating hard-boiled eggs.

I clicked around a bit until I got reading about the Jewish afterlife, you know, *sheoul*, *gehenna*, etc. And from what I could tell, the expert opinion of most rabbis was that even in the worst case scenario, the maximum time a sinful Jew would have to spend there was only one year, and at that point, any game theorist could tell you it's just not worth spending seven days of literal suffering to avoid a year (at the most!) of theoretical (let's say twenty-five percent chance?) purgatory. The expected value calculation was pretty unambiguous about what the smart move was. And it seemed unlikely I'd have to do the whole year, right? I mean, why would *I*, of all people, get the whole year? If I got the whole year, what would Roman Polanski, Brett Ratner, Charles Kushner, etc, etc, get? Well, the maximum punishment is a year, so *they'd* get the year, and *I'd* also get the year. So *Hashem* would basically be saying I'm just as bad as those guys!

I got angry at G-d and fell asleep for the rest of the flight, waking up only occasionally to decline ("Uhh . . . no thanks") the silly snacks and sodas the stewardesses kept coming around to offer.

Three

My teenaged orphan sister Emily was waiting for me at the airport, chauffeured by her interim intern Handler, Daniel, a tallish USC pre-law rowing scholarship recipient who was working over the summer at our deceased parents' law firm, *Shapiro, Rubin, Sullivan + Weiss, Attorneys at Law.*

In a private message to me, Emily described Daniel as quote "one of those athletic types who acts like he's in the army, even though he's really just on a sports team." The two of us (Emily and I) agreed that this military posture is a neat side effect of spending your formative years under the influence of various "coaches" and "trainers."

I paused to give Emily a sizable hug while Daniel loaded my bags into the trunk of the firm's Lincoln Continental.

"Mr. Mathcamp, sir," he said to me, as Emily and I climbed into the backseat of the American-made luxury sedan, "please, let me extend my sincerest condolences to you for the recent loss of your parents who got blown up in that helicopter. And let me also say, that it has been a privilege to work with your sister this morning. I hope everything went well with your flight, sir."

"Oh yeah, it was great," I told him, "my ears didn't do any of that horrible *popping* in the air this time. I don't know what the pilot did differently to prevent it, or whether that's even something in the pilot's control, but I'm going to send an email to JetBlue to tell them the pilot did a great job. I started a clap when we landed. Everybody joined in."

We pulled out of Burbank's Bob Hope Airport, past palm poplars, through the Hills, down North Hollywood Way, through Magnolia Park, etc, etc, etc, etc. The sun ("el sol") was brightly beating down onto the all-black exterior of the car, forcing me to squint and press certain buttons that made cool air blow out of tiny holes in the leather backseats of the car.

I found Los Angeles terribly unsettling, haunted, even. The home of my most pathetic teenaged moments, I could feel myself becoming weaker after just a few minutes there.

"So Ross, I mean, uh, Mr. Mathcamp, sir," Daniel began, "I was telling your sister on the way to the airport, about what's been going on lately."

"Yeah?" I replied, "Something's been going on?"

"Well you know, with all this crap they're doing."

"What crap?"

"Like all these pedophiles running the world, and now they're getting scared, because patriots, like me, we're finally starting to catch on to what they're doing. That's why they're pushing this new thing, with the bio-chip implant."

"The what?"

"It's been all over the news, I'm sure you've seen it. How they're going to try to put that chip in our arms. It's basically a computer, and they're putting it inside of us so they can track our every move, control our thoughts, and give us new DNA, and then fluoride. After the election, that's when it's going to get really bad."

"And they're pedophiles?" I asked to clarify.

"Yeah, pedophiles. And a lot of them are Je—I mean, uh, um . . . Je. . .—Je—Junior pedophiles! They're junior pedophiles which means they go after like *really* young kids. Like babies. And they eat them, they put the blood of these babies into their . . . unleavened bread. It's really sick, the kind of stuff going on. I'm sure you've read about it. So if you need like . . . any private protection, Mr. Mathcamp, I'd be happy to keep working with you. When things get really bad."

"Okay, thanks," I replied.

"Thank you so much," Emily added.

We found ourselves stalled in a buildup of cars, a block or so north of Hollywood Boulevard, on this miserable alleyway that my Watch's maps app identified as "Yucca Street," filled with diverse groups of young people taking turns smoking things, playing loud music, etc, etc. Daniel asked us if we wanted to stop at Panda Express, but I told him I was "fine." Emily said she wasn't hungry either; she was remarkably mature. Much more composed than I would've been under the circumstances, although we're quite similar, even sharing the same birthday, but ten years apart, obviously.

It took us another near hour before we were at our parents' SoMel (South of Melrose) house. Daniel kept saying things like "it would be faster to walk, right?" and "We could just be *WALKING*, right now. And we'd get there faster," and "I can't believe this . . ."

At the house, Daniel carried my bags to the door, saluted us, and made his way back to the car. Inside I asked Emily how she felt about the whole thing, her newfound orphanhood, etc, etc.

"I cried a lot last night," she told me.

"I haven't cried yet." (I had, quite a bit, but I had to appear strong for Emily.) "But I think it's sad. It's certainly not good."

"Well, Ross," she picked up a stapled stack of paper from the top of our kitchen table, "we need to talk about this ridiculous eulogy you sent me last night. I can't let you read this at the funeral."

"What? I *have* to read that. Those are my sincere grievous convictions!"

"It's ridiculous, Ross. The first sentence, alone, I mean, what does this even *mean*? Whom are you trying to impress with this?"

She handed me my own tome, and I looked at the line in question.

As The Very Reverend Jonathan Swift so brilliantly put it, "I shall be like that tree; I shall die from the top."

"Well, I can see why that might need to be edited out," I conceded.

"And these, Ross." She flipped to the second page and pointed at another few howlers of mine, circled in red.

*. . . Growing up, my sister and I certainly heard a lot more about **bagels** and lox, than **Hegel** or **Locke** . . .*

*. . . while other people would stand in the shower, practicing to sound like their favorite singer, I would stand in there, practicing to sound like my favorite, **Peter** Singer . . .*

"This is barely even *about* Mom and Dad, Ross. It's just sick. It's fellatious. With a 't'. Why are you talking about yourself so much? Why are you making all these puns and references? And the alliteration . . . I just . . ."

"Well what sort of references would you have preferred that I made?"

"There shouldn't be *any* references, Ross. It's a *eulogy*. And why would anyone in our family—or in California—know or *care* who these people are? It's totally inappropriate for the funeral of such a young couple in such a sudden, gruesome death. The tone of this thing is much better suited for someone dying at a hundred than two people dying in their forties. It's pretentious. It's smut disguised as tribute, Ross."

Looking it over a few more times, she was right. It was a horrifying showing. Overwrought and unaffecting. If it weren't for Emily, I might've made a real arse of myself up there. She had done me a great service. It was nice to enter into a house with such a *culture of critique*, where we felt free to be honest with each other about that sort of thing. And Emily, as my protege, a girl after my own heart, was more qualified than anyone to point out when I was in the wrong. "You're right," I told her.

"And another thing," she added as I was walking upstairs, "the writing came off as, like, vaguely sexist. And you know that I'm really not into complaining about that, and it doesn't offend *me*, but I know you're a big fan of the so-called 'Great Male Narcissists' and that a lot of this is ironic. I mean, I know you're not a misogynist, you're my brother. But I just want you to be careful, Ross. You're writing stuff like this thirty, forty, fifty years after the other guys, and audiences are going to be less forgiving of that stuff, just naturally. Especially at a funeral. Really, Ross, writing like that is just totally inappropriate for a eulogy."

"I know, I know. I already said you were right. I already said it. So stop. Just drop it now."

Upstairs, in my room, I looked over at the Hästens Mustang bed my father bought me for my sixteenth birthday. Thought about how excited he was to show it to me. "This cost me fifteen grand, Ross. It's a luxury bed. And I figure, you loved that new Mustang so much, why not have *two* new Mustangs? It's a man's bed, Ross. I know you might be thinking it's for kids, but believe me, this is a luxury bed. It's made out of real carbon fiber on the outside, real horsehair on the inside, Ross. It's not a race car bed. *Those* are for boys. It's a muscle car bed, for *men*. You're a man now, Ross."

Everything was very clean, dustless and organized. My mother, a homemaker, in every sense of the word, loved to clean. She would dust and mop and sweep and stow, tidying up the place multiple times a day, room by room, corner by corner. And in the spirit of thoroughness, she also had a whole sick crew of Guatemalan women come clean the house once weekly, just to be safe, just in case she was systematically missing any spots. Now this is something I find very admirable, especially in women— cleanliness. So many "modern" women think their alleged "liberation" is also permission to be liberated from tidiness. It's terrible. It's really just a lack of self respect. They think they can go home with whoever they want, face no consequences, and then go back to their *own* homes, throw- ing Poland Spring water bottles all over the floor, leaving pizza boxes on their coffee tables, neglecting even to *own* a Swiffer, etc, etc.

It occurred to me how lucky I was to have been raised by a mother who cared about cleanliness, who never claimed to be too depressed to do dishes, or too "busy" with "weed" to be able to scrub our toilets, who put her family first. Oh, it's terrifying, where things are headed. These new New York women would rather . . . would rather . . . have horrible things done to their bodies (by men) than cook a nutritious meal for a family. Even Lora, the love of my life, never cooked, never cleaned for me. Not that I really needed her to; I liked being the thoughtful grown-up in the relationship, chopping zucchini and sautéing broccolini for us while she sat on the couch contemplating how good of a boyfriend she had. I shut my bedroom door and sobbed for a moment, realizing I no longer had anyone to cook or clean for, and no longer had anyone to cook and clean for me.

I felt a great longing for mommy, for Lora, for no one in particular. And quickly decided (told myself) I was just hungry.

"Em?" I called out from my desk chair, where I was fiddling with some heinous ceramic contraption I'd crudely molded in a middle school art class. A miniature teacup, if I'm recalling correctly.

"Yes?" she shouted back.

"Can you just come in here? So I don't have to yell?" I yelled.

After a few seconds she appeared in my doorway, standing cross-legged, looking impatient. "Do you want to go to Erewhon?" I asked her.

Erewhon—by far the most redeeming asset Los Angeles has to offer with its lovely neighbor, The Grove, coming in a close second. Their website includes the following promise:

> No synthetic additives or preservatives. No artificial colors or flavors. No hydrogenated or solvent extracted oils. No refined flour or sugar. Only natural sweeteners such as honey, maple syrup and molasses.

They sell all sorts of potions priced in the double digits of dollars, and foods that won't kill you. And it's kind of classy, you know what I mean? Unlike any place you can find in New York, where any sort of "healthy" store is either owned by oligarchs or staffed by satanists, falling apart, poorly lit, confusingly organized, cramped (etc, etc). The name (Erewhon) is also a sneaky nineteenth-century literary reference. Not that anyone in "LA" knows that, but it's a nice nod to people like me. Smart people, like me.

"Yeah, I can go. I haven't been in a while," Emily replied, then turned around, leading the way downstairs.

"Good," I got up and followed her. "Let's go now. I was on a date with this ridiculous woman last night, at a virtual reality restaurant, and I ate a plate of mixed vegetables that almost certainly had canola oil in it. So we need to get some milk thistle and Vitamin E." I grabbed the keys to Mom's Ford Edge out of the little wicker bin in the mud room and held the garage door open for Emily on our way out.

On Fairfax Avenue, I looked over at some of the new businesses that had opened since I was last in town. Places with names like *The Gelato Skank*, *Mammon's Pizza (& Wings)*, *Smoke Weed Infinity*, etc, etc. None seemed interesting enough to warrant a stop.

In the parking garage at Erewhon, I saw a familiar face and ducked down behind the steering wheel to conceal myself.

"What are you doing?" Emily asked.

Panicked, struggling to breathe, "We can't go in yet. We have to wait here for a while."

"Why?"

"I just saw Leona Richeda go in. It's definitely her. I can't see her. We have to wait for her to leave."

"Who is that?"

I unbuckled my seat belt and climbed into the back seat, behind the darkly tinted back windows. "She was the most beautiful girl at John Burroughs Middle School, because well, you know, she'd sort of like, *developed*, early, if you know what I mean."

"Uh huh."

"And you don't know about this, but I was actually very popular in middle school. I don't want to say I peaked; I think that would be silly to say because it implies my life was better then, even though it really wasn't at all. You know, because I was a child. But certainly my popularity with fellow young people was peaking, mostly because I had the nicest cell phone at the time. This was before everyone had the same phone. Did you know that people used to have different phones? And then certain kids would be cool based on whether nor not they had cool phones or not?"

"You've mentioned that to me before."

"So in the weeks leading up to Leona's bat mitzvah—her dad is Latinx, but her mom is, well, you know . . .—everyone was talking about the big dance, you know, who was going to dance with Leona Richeda, now that she was a *woman*. And the favorite, the sort of obvious choice, was me, as I was still very cute at the time, my nose bump hadn't grown in, and the other boys hadn't yet stumbled into any sort of pubescent progress vis-à-vis height or shoulder breadth. So while my body was pathetically tiny relative to adult men, compared to the other tweens I was somewhere around the middle of the pack. And fashionable, of course. Thanks to Mom. Just try to imagine, twelve-year-old Ross wearing nice black slacks, dress shirt, dress shoes. Remember my hair was very long, down to my shoulders, but *cute*, I was *cute*. I really was."

"I believe you."

"So at the bat mitzvah, all the other kids, Leona included, went to smoke weed with the valet drivers by the loading docks in the back of the Beverly Hilton. We were all back there, everyone was taking puffs, except me, because Mom and Dad always told me how disgusting they thought smoking was, and I never wanted to do anything to disappoint them. I still don't. Anyway . . . what was I saying? Oh yeah, all the other kids were smoking weed with a couple of the valet drivers at the Beverly Hilton, which was just insane, now that I'm thinking about it. I mean, we were in seventh grade, why were those valet drivers giving us drugs? And why were the adults at the party letting us sneak around in the back with those valet drivers, most of whom were on a prison work release program? It's sick. It makes no sense. Sorry, sorry, let me get back to the story. So after they're all done smoking, we go back into the ballroom, and 'Tik Tok' (2010), you know, the song, it was the name of a song from 2010 by Kesha—but the 's' was a dollar sign back then—is playing extremely loudly. That got everyone really riled up. And when that's over, the DJ announces something like 'alright, now this next song is for all the *love birds*,' and he starts playing 'Hey, Soul Sister' (2009) by Train. Are you paying attention?"

"Yes."

"Almost immediately the floor clears out, and there's a lot of space all around, and then it's just me and Leona in our little quadrant. Sorry. *Leona and I.* Did you know about that? It sounds weird, but the verb 'to be' is intransitive so you end up having to say things like *it is I.*"

"I know about that."

"Okay, good. So Leona signals for me to come over to her, and I do. I take her hand and we begin waltzing crudely to 'Hey Soul Sister' (2009). My hands were sweating profusely, oozing slime, etc, etc. And Leona was pretty clearly out of her depths, but I did a nice job leading, since Mom had given me a number of dance lessons as a young boy, because she wanted me to be able to dance with girls. But still, even with all the preparation I was a wreck, a *trained* wreck, but a wreck nonetheless, feeling Leona's . . . buxom body pressing up against mine."

" . . ."

"As the song was nearing its end, the other kids broke into a chant. 'Kiss her!' 'Kiss her!' 'Kiss her!' they were screaming. And poor Ross, what was he to do? I'd never kissed anyone before. I was terribly nervous. My mouth felt filthy and dry. I didn't want it anywhere near hers. At first I tried ignoring them; they only grew louder. 'No,' I finally said. 'She's a girl under the influence! It wouldn't be right for me to kiss her. She can't even consent! She's high on *pot!*' And everyone starts *roaring* at this. They're *dying* of laughter at me, Em. They start calling me 'Faggot Ross' and chanting it, 'Fagg-ot Ross, Fagg-ot Ross!' just like

32

that. Falling over laughing. All because I wouldn't kiss this girl who was *stoned* on drugs! And the nickname, so hurtful, right? Kids used to be terribly homophobic. I don't know if you know about that."

"They're doing that again actually."

"Oh, really? They all stopped doing it like a year later."

"Yeah they just started doing it again. But they claim they're doing like two levels of irony. A lot of gay kids are doing it. Calling things gay to mean stupid or bad. It doesn't really make sense for it to be ironic though since they weren't really around for when people did it sincerely."

"Oh, well anyway, I was mortified. Everyone thought I was a gay nerd. And then the other boys became bigger and stronger than I, and the good phone that everyone likes stopped being an AT&T exclusive, and soon I was irrelevant. Not cool anymore, all because I respected women so much. So now, I'm sure you can tell, she's like the *last* person I would ever want to see at Erewhon."

"But Ross, didn't you keep going to school with her for like four years after that?"

"Well, that's different. I mean, you have to see people at school. It's not weird to see people at school since you do it every day. There's no weird dynamic, really. You know how you're supposed to act in school. You don't have to say *hi* to people at school because you're there with them every day. It's not a surprise, Emily. But when you see someone at Erewhon five years after graduation, it *is* a surprise. It's a novel event. You're expected to say hello, stop and chat, it's terrible. We can't do that. We have to wait. We have to wait until she comes out and leaves."

We waited until she came out and left.

∿

Inside the store I grabbed a cart and filled it with bone broth, Belcampo beef, eighty-five-percent cacao dark chocolate, and various supplements I'd been meaning to try. Mostly mood enhancers and nootropics, meant to make me the smartest possible Ross. Nice sounding things like *lion's mane, rhodiola rhodesia,* and *Alpha-GPC*, that have been shown to reduce symptoms of autism in certain Israeli mice.

"I just got this American Express Gold Card, Em. That means I get four points for every dollar we spend at grocery stores. So get whatever you want, as long as there's no CBD in it. Be careful and make sure you don't accidentally get something with CBD. They have all these cool looking eighteen-dollar drinks but when you look closely, they have CBD in there. And I don't know what that would do to us if we ingested it. It's basically weed."

"Thanks, Ross."

Emily got herself some sushi (they have California rolls with real crab (instead of surimi), a low-carb bovine collagen protein bar, and a low-carb gluten-free dairy-free sugar-free birthday cake to add to our basket (totaling $286.71), which I then handed to an attractive blonde-haired cashier.

"Did you find everything you were looking for?" she asked me.

"Yep," I squeaked out in the pathetic, neutered voice I use when I'm talking to low-skill employees. Just barely getting the sounds out.

"And did you need me to validate your parking?"

"Yep." I meekly handed her my little parking ticket for her to stamp.

"And would you like to donate $1 to help fight white supremacy?"

"What?"

"Would you like to donate $1 to help fight white supremacy?"

"No."

"Why not?"

"What do you mean *why not*?"

"Why wouldn't you donate just one dollar?"

"I just don't want to. I don't want to give you a dollar for that."

"So you don't *care* about fighting nazis?"

Aha! Now she was trapped. Now I was really prepared to give her the business. My real voice came out in full force. "I just don't think giving you a *dollar* is going to help with that. So please, madame, if you

34

could just hand me my items, I need to get home. My parents, who were *Jewish*, I might add, just *died* in a tragical tropical helicopter accident. So my *sister*—whom I *love*, and have an obligation to care for—and I really need to get home to prepare for their funeral."

Oh, I sure showed her. I really got her. I bet she felt awfully silly when she found out I was not only a *Jew*, but an *orphan*, and a *feminist* (I have a sister), to boot!

∼

At the house, Emily and I sat down at our kitchen breakfast island eating our Erewhons. Emily sliced an avocado for me to add to my cedar plank seared salmon (sockeye, wild caught). On my phone, I was reading an article titled "How To Safely [sic] Remove A Snake From Your Home."

"Ross?" Emily asked, waving her hand in front of my phone.

"Sorry, I was just . . . reading something," I replied, then put my phone back into my pocket and looked up at her. "Hey Em, do you think we should've gone to the Los Angeles Museum of the Holocaust? I mean, we were right across the street and didn't even think to go."

She swallowed a slice of sushi and replied "No, I don't think so. You don't think we're already experiencing enough grief?"

"Well, that's the thing. This just doesn't feel very real, does it? There's something fake feeling about it. So I was thinking it would be nice for us to feel as sad as possible right now, I mean, this is the saddest thing that'll ever happen to us, right? We should try to get it all out of our systems. I heard the LAMH (Los Angeles Museum of the Holocaust) has some Jew shoelaces on loan from the Washington, D.C. Museum that they're displaying until the end of the month."

"What do you mean *fake* feeling?" she asked.

"I guess, it feels . . . not real? Like a dream, or a cartoon. That they died in a helicopter crash, for example. It just feels sort of silly. And then, I flew into Burbank from LaGuardia. I didn't even know they had

JetBlue flights between Burbank and LaGuardia. I always thought they didn't have those. But I'm surely not dreaming. It's pretty obvious that I'm awake right now. You always know you're awake when you actually are. It's only when you're dreaming that you're not sure."

"Yeah."

"So this is all real. Our parents don't exist anymore. But it doesn't feel that way. Which is why I wanted to go to the Holocaust museum . . . You know, since everyone agrees the Holocaust was a real thing that happened and feels sad about its having happened."

"Yeah. I think I know what you mean. There's something shocking and hard to believe about this situation. It's hysterically real." She put her hand on my shoulder. "You also don't seem to have slept since you heard the news."

"That's fair. I might be freaking out more than I realize, just based on that horrible eulogy I wrote."

"Yeah."

"Why didn't you go with them?" I asked as I elevated a forkful of crispy salmon skin (wild caught) and mashed cauliflower up to my mouth.

"They didn't even ask me, actually. They were taking a quote 'getaway.'"

She put sardonic air quotes around "getaway," a mannerism she surely learned from me. "And now, I'm glad I didn't go, because I probably would've died in that helicopter crash."

"Well, if you went, they probably wouldn't have gone into that particular helicopter. But I'm not very interested in hypotheticals, they can get terribly tiring."

"I agree that it's not really worth thinking about. Not falsifiable in any meaningful way." More Rossian language from her. "Maybe if I'd gone, we would've been eaten by sharks or kidnapped by pirates, or something even more whimsical than a helicopter crash."

I noticed she was already done with her food. She was a quick and efficient eater, but tiny. Not a big girl, really. But if she's anything like me (which I think she is), she has another half decade before she'll really be considered beautiful.

"Have you been reading lately? What are you reading in school?" I asked her.

"We've been reading *The Giver* (1993) by Lois Lowry for the past two months. We just got to page a hundred out of two oh six. And we have like a week left of school, so I don't think there's any way they're going to finish it. At this pace . . ."

"And how about on your own? Anything grownup?"

"Yes. I'm going through your list. I just read *Zooey* (1957) yesterday, and *Franny* (1955) the day before that."

"What did you think of those two?"

"I liked how they talked to each other. He does a nice job with that. You forget that he's venturing into *literature of ideas*, at certain points, because the talking is fun."

"That's true. I do hate it when a book is trying to give you some Big Idea instead of just being a nice story—full of imagined debates, Socratic dialogues jammed in for no reason. Or when a book has a bunch of hidden symbols that you're supposed to look for. Or when a book is being all *meta*, preemptively critiquing itself, half-ironically, in an attempt to be 'smart' or 'self-aware' or something."

"Yeah, that is a cheap trick." She took a sip of a sugar-free seltzer.

"But I *really* roll my eyes when he starts getting into that eastern 'Everyone is one!' business. He was suffering from that twentieth-century George Harrison–style delusion. I don't have much patience for that. The *zen this* and the *reincarnation that*—it's all mishigas, let me tell you, all invented by peasants to keep from blowing their brains out directly into the nearest South China Sea. This obsession with mystical enlightenment, I mean. There's no such thing!" I found myself getting wound up, "and if there *were* such a thing, a central truth to the universe, why would it be so simple, so comprehensible to *us*? Why do we think *we're* so important?"

Emily got up to clear the table and wipe it down with a Mrs. Meyer's paraben-free eucalyptus scented wipe. "Well, I don't see why you think we *aren't* special, Ross. I mean, we're the universe becoming aware of itself. Like, spacedust and atoms studying other spacedust and atoms."

"You're talking like a bumper sticker now," I told her.

"Well, what I mean is, we're the only living things in the universe that *knows* stuff. That knows that there's a universe, that has reason and consciousness, the only life forms that know they're life forms. You don't think that's important?"

"You can try to make that argument, as a materialist, that we're the *soul* of the universe, the universe becoming 'aware' of itself, like you said. But if you admit we're just a bunch of atoms, you would have to agree there's no such thing as 'important' or 'consciousness' or 'awareness' anyway, that it's all just a chemical phenomenon caused by atoms inside our eonically evolved monkey minds."

"I'll have to think about it some more, Ross."

I don't really know what point I was trying to make. Maybe that it was dumb to care about things? Because we're all just monkeys made of atoms? No, no, that doesn't sound very good at all. I may have just been saying things for no reason. "I'm going to go try to lie down for a bit, Em. After that, do you want to watch Nickelodeon's *iCarly* (2007–2012)? I used to really enjoy it when I was your age. It's about a teen girl who lives with her much older brother. So you might like it. It's on Hulu now."

"Sure. And then we have to go to bed early. For the funeral."

Four

My parents were both born in Orange County, California (Huntington, Laguna) during the second Brown's first administration. After they graduated from high school, they separately signed up for an automobile entrepreneurship *kibbutz* outside Haifa, where they met one another, and almost immediately began a romantic relationship. Within a few months my teenaged mother was pregnant (with me, Ross!), and out of some secular pro-life sentiment, decided to keep the dammed thing (smart!). My father, smitten (if you could've seen her, you wouldn't have blamed him), married her swiftly, and returned to California to found Mathcamp Motors: Ford, Lincoln, and Subaru (formerly Mathcamp Motors: Ford, Lincoln, and Mercury).

Some version of this, with a less incriminating chronology (not revealing that Ross was conceived out of wedlock), was recited by the rabbi as we gathered and sat in the Hollywood Temple Beth El. Before the service, a crowd of relatives and goyish family friends ambushed my sister and me in a show of support, hugging us as we stood in the little lobby, I in my kippah, suit, and tie, next to Emily in her black dress and veil.

"Oh, it's *awful* what happened, Ross! You better sue that Caribbean resort for every penny they have!"

"How are you, darlings? Are you holding up alright? Are you eating? Have you eaten? You need food?"

"Your father was a great man, Ross. He just sold me a certified pre-owned 2016 Ford Flex for two grand under the *Blue Book* value, Ross. I'm gonna miss that guy. He knew how to take care of a friend."

As we sat in our jaundiced wooden seats, listening to the cantor scream at the top of his lungs some prayer, some ancient Semitic song, I felt something resembling disgust for the ceremony, and for my forced participation in it. No one in the room really believed in the efficacy of these silly religious recitations; they were just trying their best to hold on to the traditions they were taught as children, afraid of what might occur if they were to stop. I mean, this was a seriously sad event, like objectively, the saddest thing that could ever happen to me. I wanted to be alone, but the Rules (the Law) demanded that my sister and I sit in the front of a carpeted room while an obese bearded stranger standing in front of a microphone led us through a litany of joyless gibberish.

Discreetly, I fished my phone out of my trousers, hid it under a flimsy pamphlet of Hebrew threnodies, and searchengined the name of that actor's brother whom Lora had been "seeing" as of late. A frothy mixture of pride ("he's so much worse than *I*!") and rage ("he's so much *worse* than I!") stewed in my noggin. All my suspicions were totally confirmed. His LinkedIn, "portfolio," and DUI-arrest-mugshot revealed that he was the archetypal Thirty-Year-Old Loser (a term I coined for a familiar phenomenon). One of these guys who spends eight years after college acting like it's his first month after college. Bouncing around between freelance copywriting "gigs," occasionally appearing in the background of an "indie rock" "music video." Never getting a serious job, never accomplishing anything. Drinking and smoking himself to sleep every night. Stealing girl-friends from nice Jewish boys, etc, etc. Simply some rich and famous New York City man who's squandered every advantage in life. This is a real generational problem, you know. There are *tons* of guys like this who've had their developments arrested by drugs, precocious handsomeness, and the vague promise of an eventual family fortune. Guys like this doing *nothing* all day, creating *nothing*, contributing *nothing*. Renting apartments in Brooklyn with other TYOLs, sleep-ing on mattresses directly on their floors, collecting allegedly vintage leather jackets, listening to Lou Reed, talking about "Bukowski," etc,

etc, etc, etc. There's just nothing cool about these guys. The Thirty-Year-Old Loser will call himself a "writer." But if you were to ask him what he's written, he would have no choice but to say *nothing*. It cannot be said enough that the Thirty-Year-Old Loser has done *nothing* with his last eight years. His net worth is *nothing*. And still, I was being replaced by one. Why? I'm no woman, but if I were, I wouldn't want anything to do with this guy, as he's pretty clearly a Thirty-Year-Old Loser. But perhaps his cool last name and chiseled cheekbones more than make up for that.

I exhaled forcefully and put my phone back into my pocket. I felt terrible; I had thought I had distracted myself, in the permanent sense of the word, from worrying about her (Lora) and the affection she used to give me. As I lay in bed the night before, my mind felt free from all Lora-related anxieties (she didn't even appear in that last chapter, did she?). I had felt at ease knowing that, just like, as a mathematical certainty, I'd be able to find a multitude of other beautiful women who could appreciate my many amazing qualities. But sitting there, in the Temple, sweating, *schvitzing,* staring at my parents' death, it occurred to me how much of a fool I was for having just thrown out the love of my dreams (etc, etc). That there could never again be a new romantic interest of mine who was approved of by my mother. And in that moment, all the pining ("I miss Lora Liamant. I need Lora Liamant!") came pouring back into my orphan heart. Such is the nature of these things. Love has a nasty habit of reappearing overnight, etc, etc.

She was now in the loose grip of a Thirty-Year-Old Loser. What was there to be done? Wait for that to fizzle out? Utterly debase myself? Grovel and beg to be welcomed back between her arms and her . . . *legs*? Would it be that humiliating? Were things really that unbalanced, given that we've both "spent evenings" with opposite-sexed geezers? Although, if I were really seeking "revenge" or "equity" in an attempt to make her (Lora) feel how I felt, I would've sought out an attractive seventeen- (the age of consent in New York) year-old girl and publicly posted photos of us canoodling together—but of course that's disgusting, I'm well aware. It's all so wrong—I'm just saying that that would rectify some perception, re: my own post-breakup patheticness. Since everything seems to have to be so autistic and transactional, as of late. It's terrible, this obsession with revenge. It's a symptom of a lack of sincerity, a lack of maturity. This desperate need to repair my cucked Jewish ego. This fear of being vulnerable. Etc, etc. Something to think about.

I grabbed a Holy Basil ("may help inhibit melancholic and introspective thoughts") chewable tablet out of my backpack and popped it into my gob without much concern for who might've been watching.

~

At the cemetery, the shammes let us toss handfuls of dirt (two per person, one per corpse) onto the lowered caskets containing my parents. Rabbi Shmuley said some additional kind words ("The Mathcamps were true pillars in our community, I couldn't be more saddened by their untimely demise"), offered pithy aphorisms ("If the rich could hire the poor to die for them, the poor would make a very nice living," etc, etc.), and read Psalm 91 seven times twice.

In accordance with the written instructions left by my parents, a Ford Raptor was parked alongside the trail near their graves, and over the truck's speakers, Lifehouse's "Hanging by a Moment" (2000) and Hoobastank's "The Reason" (2003) played back-to-back. There was not a dry eye in the house, let me tell you.

I was relieved to feel rather feelingless after having that Holy Basil tablet. Emily took one of her own on the car ride over to the *Shapiro, Rubin, Sullivan + Weiss, Attorneys at Law* offices, where we were scheduled to celebrate the Jewish-American tradition of the reading of my parents' last will and testament.

In Robert Shapiro (Esquire)'s office, a four-thousand-square-foot space in Robertson Plaza (just slightly east of Beverly Hills, in terms of its official zoning, but most people would say, erroneously, that the office and I were in Beverly Hills, even though we technically weren't), Emily and I sat in a brightly sunlit glass conference room, sipping bottled water, waiting patiently for our bequeathments. Robert Shapiro came stomping in after a few minutes with a thick orange envelope tucked under his arm and sat down across from us. "Sorry, kids. I'm so sorry. Do you want anything? Anything to drink? A little snack? Snapple? Miniature 3 Musketeers bar?"

"No. I'm fine, thanks."

"Well then let's not waste too much time beating around the bush here, am I right, kids?"

"Sure. That makes sense."

"Well let's open this bad boy." He used a mail opener to slice open the envelope and pulled out a laptop computer. "All digital, these days, heh, heh," he said as he opened it up and frustratedly pressed one of its buttons repeatedly. "What the . . . the thing's dead. I mean uh . . . the battery . . . has lost its . . . charge. *Daniel?!* Would you get me the charger for this thing? *Please!?*" he called out.

After Daniel arrived with the charger, Robert Shapiro connected the computer to the wall, put on his reading glasses, and pressed some combinations of buttons under the table that lowered the room's blinds. "Ah, that's much better, isn't it?" he asked.

Emily and I smiled nervously at him as he stared at the screen, occasionally subvocalizing its contents. "*We, the Mathcamps,* blah blah blah, *stipulate that in the event of our combined death,* yadda, yadda, yadda."

"Can we read what it says?" I asked.

"You know, it's a lot of *legalese,* Ross. Heh, heh," he wiped his forehead. "Trust me, you don't want to read this. Just let me explain it to you two. Okay? Okay, Ross?"

"Okay."

He pulled his glasses back down to eye level. "Uh-huh, uh-huh. Oh . . . oh, wow! That's right. I'd forgotten about this," he was saying as he skimmed his findings.

"Well, kids, the good news is, you're gonna be rich. As long as you're not totally mentally retarded with this money, you'll never have to work a day in your lives."

Emily and I both nodded.

"So, first of all, your father, the bastard, heh, heh, bless his heart, had about eleven million dollars split across five different life insurance policies for himself and your mother, Ross. And that's to be, uh, split evenly between you and Emily, with you acting as her *custodian* until she turns eighteen. Now that also includes the $38,913 she took home after taxes from *Jeopardy!* (1964–1975, 1978–1979, 1984–) *Kids Week* (1999–2014), Ross. Which has accumulated two percent in interest from the Ally Bank Penalty-Free Certificate of Deposit your parents put it in. Meaning, Emily will be inheriting . . . oh hell, I don't know, some small percent more than you, Ross. But don't be so jealous, Ross. She earned it. And you're both still very wealthy." He lowered his glasses and made firm eye contact with me. "Very wealthy, Ross."

I can distinctly recall, that on multiple occasions I begged my dad not to put so much money into life insurance. "It just doesn't keep up with inflation, Dad. Ray Dalio says not to get too much life insurance, Dad. This policy is two million dollars, but you don't get it until you die. What if you live another fifty years? That's going to be the equivalent of like, five hundred grand in today's dollars. You're better off putting it in the market and letting it—"

"Dammit, Ross! It's *guaranteed*. The market has *crashes*, it has *fluctuations*, it's unstable. At least with this we know what we're getting."

"Sure, but you're going to live another fifty years, probably. The market will almost certainly gain an average of eight percent per year until—"

"Just stop it, Ross. You never know when to stop, do you? With all of your whining, all of your intellectualizing. Just be happy I'm taking care of the family. How am I supposed to know that I'll live that long? You're just . . . rude, you know that, Ross? Don't you know affable, educated people don't talk about these things? Personal things! Like politics, religion, money, sex, or death? It's not polite, Ross," he would tell me. Which was some of the worst advice ever, as those are basically *the only* things smart people ever want to talk about.

I could even more clearly and distinctly recall, my Bubbe, who'd lived with us before she died with us, pleading with me not to expose myself to Market Risk. "Oh, Ross! Don't go to New York for college," she would tell me. "They'll kill you there. They'll take one look at you and kill you. They'll see your phone, and they'll kill you on the subway, Ross. They'll cut a big hole right into your face and steal your phone, keys, and wallet. Oh, it's terrible in New York, Ross. Why do you think we left when I was pregnant with your father? It wasn't *safe*, Ross. Oh, you're gonna kill me. You're gonna make me take so many tranquilizers that I'm going to fall asleep and never wake up, Ross. Why would you do this to your Bubbe? Your Bubbe who never did anything but love you? . . . Please, Ross. Promise me you'll never get a motorcycle. I don't know what I would do if you ever got on a motorcycle and cracked your head wide open . . ." And suddenly, it became very clear why my Dad thought it would be wise to wager on a premature meeting with his maker.

Emily chimed in with a rather important question. "And what about me? Do I have a guardian?"

"Your parents were clear that in the event of their death in any sort of freak flying accident, *after* Ross's twenty-first birthday, that Ross be given custody over you," Robert Shapiro said.

"Well, that makes sense," I replied.

Robert Shapiro went on to tell us about other small morsels of wealth our parents had accumulated over the years, a few hundred grand in 401(k)s, which Emily and I would have five years to withdraw money from before incurring all sorts of fees, Dad's dealerships and their land, the house, the cars, the gold coins, the gadgets, the action figures, everything, left to the two of us. He was clear, however, that the most exciting part of it all, was the quote "beauty" he'd pulled off with the life insurance, which was exempt from any taxation (estate, income, federal, local) for some silly reason that only Shapiros are capable of understanding. But for me, it meant I would soon have a seven-figure net worth at age twenty-three.

Robert Shapiro attempted to get up from his chair and broke into a geometric series of moans and yelps. "Ahh . . . oh, just shoot me now, dammit! Just shoot me! I want somebody to shoot me, Ross. My body's turning to crap, Ross," he was saying, "never get old, Ross. Enjoy being young while you still can. Before your body turns into a sack of dogcrap like mine did, and you wake up every morning hoping an armed robber is going to be standing over you, ready to pull the trigger and put you out of your misery. Because the pain is so bad you just want it to stop at any cost. I used to have *hair*, like *you*, Ross. And now I wake up every morning praying that I'll just get *shot*—by an armed robber. I'm just in pain all the time, Ross. And there's no hope of it getting any better, of course not. It's just going to get worse. It's only just getting started for me. Never get old, kids. Just stay young."

"You should try turmeric pills," Emily told him as we walked out of the conference room and into the elevator.

At home, I found myself in a rather foul mood, despite the exciting news about my upcoming millions of dollars. Just terribly pissed to be in the structure that housed me during my most pathetic and least productive years. Now, I *owned* half of this ridiculous house and was responsible for taking care of it. It's a nightmare. Far too big. Built during the peak of the early 2000s Big House Boom. I can clearly and distinctly recall our first week there, sitting in the kitchen, my parents watching the May 1, 2003 "Mission Accomplished" speech George W. Bush gave aboard the USS *Abraham Lincoln*. "The war's over, Ross. We won, our boys will be back home any day now, Ross," my dad said to me as he ate his soft-boiled egg that morning.

But now, even though I've undergone considerable growth, the house is no less a monstrosity. Just to get a glass of water you have to go down seventeen steps to our Berkey water filter, and then back *up* seventeen steps carrying the glass, and once you've finished climbing the stairs, you're too tired even to read or sit upright or do any serious work. So you just end up lying down listlessly on one of the many upstairs couches, lounging languorously, catching your breath after that surfeit of stairs. And by the time you finally feel good enough to get something done, and feel some productivity coming on, some genuine moment of focus, it becomes time to refill your cup of water (I recommend drinking ten fluid ounces of water per hour) and the whole sick cycle restarts itself.

Fed up, I set up shop in my dad's downstairs office, a room I'd formerly been too frightened to enter. In there, I brushed off some muck from his desk, mail, checkbooks, a CD case for Bush's *Sixteen Stone* (1994)—that, when I opened it, had the DVD for *The Wedding Singer* (1998) inside, which I moved over to its proper case on his media shelf next to *The Wedding Planner* (2001)—, his Palm Pilot, his Tino Martinez bobble head, etc, etc. I moved it all to a box in the back of the room to give myself a nice clean workspace.

At the sliding glass door on my left, a gray feral cat appeared and began pawing at the glass. I recalled that my dad (before he died) mentioned that he had been feeding a group of feral cats and raccoons in our backyard and recording videos of them on his night-vision camera, but I didn't have any cat food for this particular feral cat to eat, so I just closed the curtains and hoped it would go away.

Already feeling productive with my clean catless workspace, I sat down in Dad's polyurethane (but almost as nice as genuine leather, really) upholstered chair and got to work on my first adult assignment. Robert Shapiro had given me a printed list of my parents' internet usernames and passwords from their "1Password" account and encouraged me to use these credentials to begin closing out their many accounts and services. TJ Maxx credit cards, *USA Today* subscriptions, cable TV, satellite TV, Facebook TV, cell phones, home phones, Anti-Defamation League automatic recurring donations, etc, etc—so many things to call and cancel. I appreciated my parents' password hygiene, though—they'd made it extremely easy for me to comb through a list of their monthly expenses, one item at a time, severing the relationship with every corporation they'd loved while they lived. No one could say they were unprepared for death.

After a taxing experience with the woman from my mother's Pilates studio ("Hi I'd like to cancel my mother's membership." "Are you the account holder?" "No, my mom was the account holder, but she's dead now." "What do you mean she's dead?" "What do you mean, *what do I mean she's dead?* She died. People die all the time. She can't call herself because she's not alive anymore. So just let me cancel it." "Sir, please do not use that tone of voice with me."), I saw something seriously shocking.

On my dad's Citi Double Cash credit card transaction history, I spotted a $500 charge from a few weeks earlier to a website that's primarily used to purchase lewd photos and videos of attractive women, which initially I assumed was the result of a credit card-stealing-related incident—why would my dad even know about this website that's primarily used to purchase lewd photos and videos of attractive women? But then, when I searched for the site in the list of his passwords (just to be safe, right?) I found a bona fide entry: username: mathcamp motors@aim.com / password: Cjv8:&k5m_b]QeT>. And when I logged in, I was shocked to see this was a *shared* account, used by *both* of my parents, to purchase "amateur" pornography produced by socialist sex workers in New York and Los Angeles. On their account I found all sorts of horrible messages they were sending to a particular blonde-haired e-stripper ("Spank dat ass," "Wow." "Keep up the good work," etc, etc). It was sick. What kind of world was I living in that my own parents were perverts? That *anyone's* parents could still be perverts. That any adult could be indulging in such smut. I really thought my own generation was particularly demented, afflicted by e-lust, but no, grown-ups, too, are horny and vile, it turns out. Luckily, I found no evidence that my parents were smoking weed. That seems to be a problem unique to my generation. But they were definitely perverts, that much was clear.

Most recently, the day before they died in that helicopter crash, their account sent a message to a woman named Rachel (also, isn't it unsettling that this new generation of pornographers is so unabashed? Whatever happened to ridiculous "sexy" pseudonyms like "Jasmyne" or "Stormy"? What's going on with this real name business? There's no shame anymore? We just have Rebeccas and Leahs and Rachels getting nude online now? Oy. . . vey iz mir . . .). They wrote to her:

> Hi Rachel,
> We are a youngish couple (early 40s, but wealthy) who really enjoy [sic] your videos. We're currently on a sexy vacay in T&C (Turks and Caicos), but we would love to meet up with you when we're back. Let us know how much that would cost us. :)

Now this was just sick. Sick, sick, sick. What a terrible thing for a son to have to see. It was a great relief to me that they died in a helicopter accident before getting a chance to meet with this internet hooker. In a moment of sincere courtesy, I started typing up a follow-up message:

> Hi Rachel,
> Ignore that previous message. That was from my parents, but they recently died in a terrible accident and so you won't be able to meet them. However, I've just inherited a great deal of wealth from them, so if you'd like to meet up (I'm in LA right now) with an intelligent, nice, handsome, (and rich) guy and stop making pornography I can—

And then I realized this was ludicrous. Why would *I* want to meet up with this woman? She was a literal *whore!* So, I deleted the message and their account and instead, drafted an email, attaching the evidence of my parents' perversion, and scheduled it to be sent to Emily on the date of her eighteenth (and my twenty-eighth) birthday. Because why should an innocent little girl like Emily have to see her parents in that light at such a young age?

Five

A few weeks later, I woke up a real millionaire, although I didn't realize it right away. It started off a very normal Adult morning. I rolled out of bed at 7:15 (Pacific Time), stumbled into the bathroom, relieved myself, and headed downstairs to guzzle eight ounces of purified ice water with a teaspoon of pink Himalayan salt mixed in (I've seen great results from drinking water with moderate amounts of salt mixed in, especially first thing in the morning. It seems the sodium-induced hypertension helps me think more clearly by forcing more blood up to my brain), peruse the news (*WSJ*, plus the latest Bret Stephens op-ed (it's a shame we can't get these in the same place anymore . . .)), and drink a high-fat beverage (ceremonial grade matcha green tea with coconut oil mixed in). And when I went to check my credit score (760, good, but not great) in the Capital One app, I noticed an eleven million dollar (plus the five or six grand I had been keeping in there to pay my rent) checking account balance. One would think this creates a fun feeling, or would be a nice, relaxing thing to see, but it really just looks stupid in there. Not at all convincing. I rolled my eyes at it on my phone. But the real problem, which I recognized right away, was that bank accounts only provide Federal Deposit Insurance Corporation (FDIC) insurance for up to $250,000 in deposits. Meaning I was way over the limit of what any smart adult would responsibly keep in his big-bank bank account. When you consider the paltry point two percent annual percentage yield paid by the crooks at Capital One, I was actually *losing* money to inflation every second my millions lay there. It was criminal. Don't even get me started on the Federal Reserve, on their criminal rate-cutting addiction (I looked it up and the APR on a one year CD in 1984 was eleven percent!), but to keep it short, as all the experts will tell you, buying equities is the only way to beat inflation, and put your money to work for *you*.

Almost no one is smart enough to know about compound interest. People think they know about it, but they're always blown away when you actually show them how powerful it really is. Take five and a half million dollars, and put it in the S&P 500, which has grown at about ten percent a year for the last hundred years (I think). Do you know what five and a half million dollars earning ten percent interest, compounded annually, is worth after forty years (Retirement Ross, age sixty-three)? I just calculated it, and it'll be worth $248,925,905.62. That's called basketball player money. That's how much money you make if you play basketball for money in America. But no one is smart enough to realize you can get the same amount of money by putting your parents' life insurance payout into something called "stock." Most people would leave their five and a half million dollars in their checking accounts for forty years, and what would it be worth there? Earning a puny point two percent? $5,957,602.88. That's just no money. Imagine being sixty-three years old and not even having six million dollars to your name. I mean, *six million* is a huge, almost unbelievable, number . . . for some things, but for dollars for someone born in *my* generation to have at *retirement*, it's not very impressive at all.

So I went upstairs to my bedroom, took a shower, brushed my teeth a few times, and transferred my money into a Vanguard brokerage account, buying several thousand shares of the NTSX WisdomTree 90/60 US Balanced Fund, which was an ETF (exchange-traded fund) which used ninety percent of my money to buy US equities, and the remaining ten percent to buy leveraged Treasuries futures, meaning ninety percent of my money would be in stocks, and sixty percent would be in bonds.

In some backtesting that I found on bogleheads.org, this strategy of putting ninety percent of one's money into stocks and sixty percent into bonds consistently outperformed a one hundred percent stock portfolio

since 1980, due to the inverse correlation of stocks and bonds, etc, etc.
This will someday be worth hundreds of millions of dollars, as long as
previous performance predicts future results.

Emily's half, we'd have to see about, I wouldn't want to make any
decisions without asking her, even though I could, legally. Oh, I felt so
smart putting it in the exchange-traded fund. Not a lot of people would
do that. They wouldn't have the guts or the brains.

The one thing I refuse to do is enter into business with any of these
hedge funds. That's what they don't tell you on the news, that hedge
funds don't even outperform the S&P 500. You just lose money when you
put money in a hedge fund. And then you lose even more when Misters
Asness and Soros and Simons and Mercer take their "two and twenty"
from you. My Vanguard has none of that. When I buy the exchange
traded "NTSX" I pay a teeny twenty bip (basis points) "expense ratio."
On an eleven-million-dollar balance that comes to twenty-two grand a
year. Chump change compared to what those ghouls at the hedge funds
would charge. Only a moron or a narcissist would ever get himself
mixed up with a hedge fund.

I popped a 30-mg Lisdexamfetamine and a 500-mg acetyl L-carnitine
(ALCAR) for my brain and went for an outdoor walk. Past trees, green
lawns, black-dressed wig-wearing women herding their kids into and out
of their many Chryslers Town and Country, out into the smoggy morning weather phenomenon commonly referred to as "June Gloom." I was
enjoying myself, taking in the gentleness of the coolish spring air, when my
left wrist alerted me of a message from my massive (he's maybe 6'5", 350
pounds) Dominican-American (not that I see color—I don't) closest male
friend (I just get along better with women, what can I say?), André Abalos.

> Can you come to Swinger's Diner in thirty minutes. Yes or no?

André and I have known each other for years, since we were children,
actually. We first met at my dad's company picnic (André's dad has

worked at my dad's (now mine, I guess?) Lincoln dealership in Encino for nearly two decades) and became fast friends. I liking André because of his incredible size and strength (so useful during the company picnic field day athletic events!), and he liking me because . . . well, I guess because I had a cool house with a pool and lots of video games and snacks.

I paused to deliberate, on the sidewalk, and then it seemed very obvious that I had nothing better to do than to see my black friend, and treat him to a nice meal with my newfound wealth. So I turned around toward home, grabbed my helmet out of the garage, and followed the map on my phone toward the nearest cluster of freestanding "e-Scooters" that littered the LA sidewalks.

I much prefer riding the Los Angeles electric scooters to driving cars, especially when I'm alone, and don't have to transport any important groceries or electronics. After clicking together the straps of my helmet, I tuned my wireless noise-cancelling earphones to *transparency mode* (a clever auditory illusion that lets you monitor music and hear honking cars simultaneously, as if your ears were totally unplugged) and hopped on one of the app-activated electric standing scooters, sailing through the streets, inhaling whimsy, listening to silly love songs (The Turtles, The Monkees, The Rascals, The Zombies, etc, etc), as I narrowly weaved between traffic and bikers and pissed off pedestrians. Now this was fun. Just lovely. Good clean fun. This was a real cultural advantage that was nowhere to be found in New York—these VC-subsidized brittle battery-powered Chinese scooters. As I zoomed south and west toward the diner, I spotted directly in front of me, on the sidewalk (which I wasn't really supposed to be riding on), a really rather mild pothole, and I saw it from pretty far away, and because I was riding in the new "Model Two" (with sealed tires for higher traction and decreased vibration) scooter from the top electric scooter company in California, I thought this pothole would be relatively easy to conquer, with no need to slow or swerve to avoid it. Oh, but I was wrong; I was horribly wrong.

Within seconds the front tire of my micromobility device was dunked head-first into the ground's chasm at the full fifteen mile per hour top speed. My body (so innocent, so fragile), flipped over the handlebars, continuing to fly at fifteen mph long after the vessel carrying it was held back by the snag in the pavement. The world and I are very lucky that my head had a helmet on (imagine how sad it would've been if something were to have happened to my beautiful mind?), but my hands (slightly scraped and covered with dirt), earphones (the left one fell out of my ear and into a nearby sewer grate), and ego (two beautiful, large-breasted human women were standing a few feet behind me when I fell) were each less lucky. I lay there in a panic, sprawled on my back like a stoned ape, unsure whether to get up and pretend nothing ever happened, or instead to exaggerate my injury and earn some attention from nearby women. I decided it was best to act as if I were tough and resilient, as if I weren't in any pain whatsoever. And so I stood up, slapped my hands together (to shake off any large chunks of asphalt), and remounted my steed.

Unfortunately, I seemed to have triggered one of Model Two's "self-reporting damage sensors," because for the remainder of the trip, the machine seemed unable to move at any rate faster than two miles per hour, meaning it was faster for me to kick and pedal the thing as if it had no motor or battery to speak of. Oh, it was awful. Oh, I must've looked terribly pathetic in front of those two women . . . and any others who might've seen me with dirt all over my body, riding slowly on a scooter through the streets of West Hollywood with a shiny white ornament dangling from my right ear.

~

By the time I got to Swingers, André was already sitting in a booth, waiting for me, wearing his fanny pack and Chicago Cubs fitted cap.

"Hold on," I said as I walked past him and into the bathroom to wash my hands.

"Why did you do that? That's just weird," he said when I came back to the table. "You're just weird, Ross. You walked right past me and went straight to the bathroom. Ross. That is *only* acceptable, if you were about to—"

"Yeah, yeah. I know. I know what you're about to say," I said as I sat down, "but I had all this mud and dead skin on my hands because I fell on an electric scooter in front of two women on my way over here."

"See, I don't ride those scooters. I'm big. I'm too big for them, Ross. But even if I could, I wouldn't ride them. What kind of *man* gets on that thing?"

A white male waiter with no pen or paper came over to take our orders, "Hi, can I take your orders?" he said.

André, refusing to look up from his menu, "Yeah I'll have the All American Special. Scrambled. Whole wheat toast. Turkey bacon. French toast. Orange Juice. And the Edwin's Pasta." The Edwin's Pasta was two organic eggs, scrambled and tossed with farfalle pasta, applewood smoked bacon, pork sausage, parsley, and Parmesan cheese. He looked up from his menu, "Ross, did you want wings?"

"No, I'm okay." I turned and tried my best to make eye contact with the white male waiter, "can I have the uh . . . Steak and Eggs, but with no bread or potatoes or anything, just the steak and the eggs, and uh . . . I guess, if you could, also a side dish of steamed broccoli, if you could. Thanks."

After the waiter left without writing anything down, André looked at me and said, quite seriously, "I hate diner food, Ross. It sucks. It's only good late at night, or early in the morning."

"Well you're the one who invited me here, so I don't know what to tell you. We could've gone wherever you wanted."

"Ross, I'm kidding. Relax. I'm trying to cheer you up. You must be sad, right?"

"Well, I'm going to try to see her when I go back to New York."

"What? What are you talking about?"

"Oh, you mean my parents. Yeah sure. That's sad. I thought you were talking about Lora."

"What about Lora?"

"Well I've been miserable. Without her. Thinking about what she's up to."

"I told you at the time. I told you your little strategy of breaking up with her and waiting for her to come back was one of the most cucked maneuvers in the history of cuckkind, Ross. Didn't I tell you that?"

"I don't remember you saying that at all."

"Well what did you *think* she was going to do? You had to expect that you were going to get cucked at least once."

"Well at first I thought she was just dating this guy, this actor's brother. A famous actor whom you've heard of. I don't want to say which. And I thought she was just dating *that* guy, because of some sleuthing I'd done, digitally. But I think that's over now. Her little whirlwind romance with this alcoholic brother of a famous TV actor. Which you would *think* would be a good thing, but it's actually terrible. I've been checking her location on the *Find My Ex-Girlfriend* app like crazy. And she's really Living Single, if you know what I mean. You know what I'm talking about, right André? *Living Single* (1993–1998)? Is that what that show was about?"

"We were *babies* when that show ended, Ross. But no, I don't think it was a show about women being whores. But I have no idea. Why would I know what it was about?"

"I just thought that you, well, you know . . ."

"Oh, I get it, so because I'm half black, you thought I would know what *Living Single* (1993–1998) was about?"

"Kind of, yeah. I did think that. That's exactly what I thought."

He shook his head at me. "I have *never* in my life seen an episode of *Living Single* (1993–1998), Ross."

"Well she's running all over town with who knows whom, really enjoying herself. She's spent the night at like five different addresses in the past two weeks. She's just getting absolutely *run through*, André."

The waiter came back to give André his orange juice and me my tap water. I took a 225-mcg potassium iodide pill to help neutralize any fluoride in the tap water.

"You see," he took a sip of OJ, "that's where you're thinking like a real cuck Jew faggot, Ross. You think you're so smart, with all your little books and your gadgets and your pills, but you're looking at it all wrong. You shouldn't be *mad* that your ex-girlfriend is acting like a whore."

"Why?"

"See, you *want* her to be acting like a whore. Sex is terrible the first time. With anybody. The *last* thing you want, is for her to find a new boyfriend. Think of the stuff your girlfriends let you do to them. To their mouths, to their faces and bodies, think of that stuff. Really, I want you to think about it."

"I don't want to think about that. We're *eating*."

"Well it's sick, Ross. That's the last thing you want. For her to get a new boyfriend. With a boyfriend it's the sickest stuff, and it's night after night after night." He took a packet of Splenda from the table, mixed it into his juice, and sipped, smacking his lips and nodding approvingly, then continued, "but with a stranger, when it's one time only, you know, the food is *terrible* and with such small portions. Maybe two or three times a month. You should *definitely* prefer that."

"Well, I would *prefer* if she were doing none of it at all!"

"Look, I'm trying to cheer you up. I'm trying to give you perspective. If you're going to be so uptight, just remember there are beautiful Brandy Melville employees turning eighteen every day. Is that what you want? Some child to do exactly what you want?"

"No, I don't really want that."

"Exactly. What you need to do, is you need to be honest, no more games, no more schemes, strategies. All of that has to go. You just need to be honest. Be direct. Tell her what you want. That's how I've been in my relationships. And I've found that they're going a lot better."

"What do you mean *relationships*?"

"I didn't tell you? I'm seeing these two girls."

"And they know about each other?"

"We met at the same party, Ross. Yes," he sighed, "the conversation has been had. We discussed it. What kind of guy do you think I am? Of course they know about each other."

"And they're fine with this?"

"They're *bi*, Ross. It's all just casual."

I looked at him incredulously.

"I know what you're thinking," he said. "And no. We haven't, you know, gotten together, the three of us, all at once, but we might. I'm going to ask them soon. And I'm going to be *direct* about it. And just say what I'm thinking. That's what men do. That's what a mature relationship looks like."

"You think dating two women at once is mature?"

"Why wouldn't it be? You have to be a grown man to manage what I'm managing right now, Ross."

"I guess you're right."

The waiter came over with our plates of food, carrying no noticeable mistakes. I guess he was able to remember everything because all of the menu items had cute and memorable diner names. But really, I think it's almost always a bad sign when a waiter doesn't even pretend to write down what you're telling him. I mean, if he were really smart enough to remember these huge orders, why is he a waiter? Why isn't he working for the NSA? Putting his *incredible* memory to use for the benefit of our national security.

André, filling his fork with all sorts of food and putting it into his mouth for a single large bite: "So you're fine then? You're not that sad about your parents? You're just sad about your own cuck mentality?"

"I don't know. Am I *fine* about it? I don't know if that's fair to say. There's just not very much I can *do* about it right now. I'm Emily's legal guardian now, so I guess that's a new grownup responsibility for me."

"Mhm. Mmmhm," he chewed and nodded.

"Oh, if you want to see something stupid. Look at this," I took out my phone and showed him my Capital One 360 Checking checking-account balance.

Shocked, he spit his bolus of bread and egg and potato and pasta back onto his plate. "That's for the bit, the spitting part," he said, "but seriously, Ross. You are a bad guy. You are a bad person for having that much money. Get rid of that."

"What do you mean, *get rid* of it?"

"You need to give that away, Ross. No human being should have that much money."

"Do you really think it's that much money? There are houses around here that cost double this."

"Ross, those aren't normal people. *You* don't get to have as much as much money as those people. You were never on TV. You never played a sport. You're just some guy. You're just some guy whose parents died in a helicopter accident in Turks and Caicos. That doesn't entitle you to a life of luxury. If you keep that money, you're cursed, Ross."

"Why am I cursed? Why would I be cursed now?"

"You just are. You are cursed now, Ross. Until you get rid of that money."

"I'm not going to get rid of it. Just because *you* tell me I'm cursed. Whom would I even give it to?"

"I don't know. That's not my problem. That's your problem."

"Well I really don't appreciate you telling me I'm cursed now. I don't like that. It's my money and I'm keeping it."

"You see, this is what you people do. This is what people *like you* do any time they get any criticism. Do you know what they did to the Ethiopian refugees in Israel? Here let me—" He reached for his phone.

"Yeah I've seen that. You don't have to show me. Please don't show this to me again."

"No, no. Look at this," he tapped his phone for a bit, and then placed it in front of my eyes. It was that article "Israel Forcibly Injected African

Immigrants with Birth Control, Report Claims" that everyone is always trying to show me. "This is what people like *you* do, when they're given power, Ross. And if you don't see that, we're done," he wiped his hands on his cloth napkin and stood up from the booth.

"Are you actually mad at me for this? I didn't do this. I've never even *been* to Israel."

"I'm not that mad at you. But as a friend, I'm telling you, that money has to go." He took a Tupperware container out of his backpack and scooped his leftover food into it, then sealed the container and put it back into his backpack. "Okay, Ross. I gotta run. I have Frisbee practice. Thanks for brunch," he said as he skipped out the door.

I sat there all alone, finishing my final few bites of broccoli. And when it came time to go up and pay our bill with my fancy metal credit card, I noticed in the reflective "marble" of the cashier's podium, that my hair looked very nice—nicer than usual. So, after I'd settled my debt, and exited the restaurant, I made an unsolicited Zoom video call to Lora Liamant.

She looked surprised when she answered, but I think she was more surprised that I was calling at all, rather than surprised at my appearance, or that it was me (oh, if she had deleted my number from her contacts (or something) and not known it was me calling when she picked up I would've blown my brains out right there on the spot).

"Hey!" I said to her.

"*Hi*, nice to see you," she replied cutely. She looked lovely. She was outside, on one of her family's many decks or patios, wearing sunglasses; she seemed tan. Not that she was ever pale—she had the natural complexion of a young Jamie-Lynn Sigler. She was really very beautiful. I couldn't help smiling at her like some kind of dummy or idiot.

"Sorry, I haven't been very much in touch," she went on. "I've been really busy."

"Oh I bet you've been getting busy." I don't think she got this epic and subtle zing that I dropped. But I couldn't help myself.

"I'm sorry about your parents, Ross."

"Oh, yeah. Thanks. I was just at Swingers Diner with André and he stormed out after I showed him how much money I inherited from them."

"Why did he storm out?"

"Well, he told me I was cursed for not donating all of my new money to the Minnesota Freedom Fund."

"Is it really that much?" she said as she walked inside, closing a creaky door behind her.

"No, I don't think so. I mean, it's a lot for a child to have. But I think a reasonable amount of money for like . . . a smart forty-year-old to have."

"Well, that sounds about right for you, doesn't it?" She gave a cheeky smile.

"Yeah, ha ha, you look great . . ." I said, without really realizing it; it just sort of came out.

"Thanks."

". . ."

"You too, Ross. I hope you're getting some sun while you're out there."

"It's all cloudy here. I'm going to be back soon. I'm hoping I can see you on sunny Roosevelt Island. I just got *Woody+* and I really want to use it with you."

"Is that some kind of sex thing?"

"No, no. It's a new streaming service. You pay $4.99 a month and they have every Woody Allen movie."

"Oh, yeah. That sounds nice. That sounds great. I've been meaning to watch *Interiors* (1978)."

"Yes! We can watch it together. It's his masterpiece, in my view." I don't know why I was saying this, I hadn't even seen it. "Even better than *Radio Days* (1987), which is my personal favorite, for sentimental reasons, of course."

"Of course," she said with a smile.

"Well, I'll see you soon. I have to get on a scooter and go home now."

"Bye, Ross. Thanks for calling. It was nice to hear from you. I mean it."

∼

When I got home, I was starving. Every time I eat eggs I just seem to get hungrier, for whatever reason. I went into the pantry and grabbed myself about a thousand calories of macadamia nuts, which have one of the best Omega-3 to Omega-6 ratios of any nut—they're typically very safe to eat. In the pantry, I scoffed at a number of weird fake health foods in there that Mom and Dad must've been buying before they died in that helicopter accident. Things like flax seeds and quinoa and overnight oats. They'd all have to be donated to people needy and hungry enough to want to eat things like that.

I walked out into the living room, munching macadamias out of my little blue bowl, and saw Emily sitting in on the couch flipping through one of the many graphic novels I'd enjoyed as a youth that were now being used as coffee table books throughout the house.

"What are you doing?" I asked her.

"I've never actually opened one of these. Are they yours or Dad's?" she replied.

"Well, they're definitely mine now."

"Uh huh."

"But I hope you aren't actually reading these things. What is that? Is that *Batman: The Long Halloween* (1997)?" I paused while she yawned at me. "Really," I went on, "you shouldn't bother reading something like that in print. I mean, I didn't know about real books when I was your age, so I could only read stuff like that. I didn't have a brother who *cared* about me enough to tell me what to read. But really, Em. If you want to be like me some day, you know, smart, like me, the kind of person who spends every waking moment contemplating art, culture, *narrative*, the *human* condition, the kind of person who has an intuition for *real* art, then you can't be reading smut like that."

"These aren't culturally relevant?"

"I think they've become *more* relevant lately, because our elites are trying to turn us all into children by forcing superhero content down our throats as much as possible. So if you want to watch one of those silly movies, fine, but I don't think you should ever *read* this sort of thing. If you're into action and explosions, heartless *low art*, why wouldn't you just watch the movie version where they spent $300 million to make cool explosions?"

"That makes sense," she put down the book and slid it back into its proper position on our coffee table. "What are you eating in that bowl?"

"I have a ton of macadamia nuts in here. Did you want any?"

"Sure let me grab a hundred calories' worth. So like three."

"Ha, I was just thinking the same thing," I told her.

"Oh these are unsalted," she said, as she plucked a few from my bowl and returned to her seat. "These are for the real macadamia nut purists."

"Oh, also, I wanted to make sure you were fine with going to high school in New York," I said as I sat down on the opposite wing of the couch, perpendicular to the segment she was occupying.

"That sounds good."

"So you're fine with moving back to New York with me? You don't have any friends or things that you'll miss here?"

"No, I'm sure I'll miss certain things, but I don't think there's anything urgent I need to stay here for."

I scooted over across the microfibrous sofa surface and gave her a small seated hug. "That's nice," I let go. "You're going to like it there."

"I've always enjoyed when I went to visit."

"Yeah. It's much better than what we have here. I need to go back in about a week to uh . . . quit my job. You know, let them down easy."

"Can I come?"

"Eh . . . why don't you finish out the school year here? It's going to be a quick trip. We can go back next month and look for a place to live."

"Okay."

"Well, anyway, don't worry about that right now. We have to watch *Interiors* (1978) right now. He made it in between *Annie Hall* (1977) and *Manhattan* (1979)."

"Okay. I didn't really like *Manhattan* (1979), *but* I'll watch it with you. Do we really have to watch it right now? Why do we have to watch it right now?"

"We just have to. Okay? Now hand me the remote."

Six

In an effort to seem spontaneous, low maintenance, unautistic, well adjusted, etc, etc, I flew back to New York a few days later without telling Lora. I kept my phone on "airplane mode" for about forty continuous hours before I landed, even though I was only on an airplane for about five of those hours. This "airplane mode" trick was so I wouldn't be tempted to contact her or check her whereabouts digitally. Etc, etc. It was a neurotic attempt to make myself appear less neurotic.

My dad, before he died, once pulled me aside for a talk about this sort of maneuver. "Son," he told me, "with girls, *women*, it's a lot like selling a car. You realize that, right? Except instead of selling a *car*, you're selling yourself. You're selling *Ross*. When someone comes up to the lot, do you know what I do? Let me tell you what I do. See, most people, son, most salespeople, they go up to the customer guns blazing, just full of energy, and they start rattling off factoids about different vehicles on the lot. This pisses the customer off. They'll almost always *rebuff* you when you try this, Ross, when you're too eager. I, on the other hand, I keep the *customer* wanting more. I walk up to him—or her—and I just say, 'if you need any help, I'll be at the front desk,' and start walking away. I just say my little line and start walking away. And before I can even take three steps in the opposite direction, the customer is desperate for me. The customer is begging me to come back. 'Uhm, excuse me, actually!' the customer will say. It works every time. You have to throw them off balance, Ross. That's the key. That's why I'm so successful at selling cars. And I think that can help you with your girl problems. What? You don't like that? Just give it a thought. It can't hurt." I had these words of wisdom in mind in the days leading up to my return to New York.

But at the LaGuardia baggage claim, while I was waiting to be picked up by a car I'd ordered on an app on my phone, I checked Lora's location on the *Find My Ex-Girlfriend* app and was shocked to see she was in, of all places, Santa Fe, New Mexico. I was livid. What could she possibly have been doing in *New Mexico?*

Fine! I would have to wait another few weeks to see her. Let this be a lesson. This is what happens when you try to do things without coordinated planning.

The trip wouldn't be total waste, however, as I still had to perform the courtesy of resigning from my job face to face. Yes, my *job*. My job which I've neglected to talk much about up until now.

~

It seemed like a smart thing to do, when I was eighteen, go to school to become a nurse. You go to "nursing school" for four years, and then immediately start making something resembling a hundred grand a year. Not a bad deal for a guy like me, right? It's a steady, stable, responsible career. With a narrow band of possible outcomes (almost all good, in the sum of all *possible world*, as Leibniz would put it). Low risk, medium to high reward. And plus I thought it would be funny in an ironic *Meet The Parents* (2000) sort of way, to be a male nurse, while at the same time, that the twenty-first-century women I'd be surrounded by would find it untoxically masculine of me to take on a job like Nurse, while still appreciating the sexiness of my salary. Which all proved more or less true. Of the three base needs humans have—health, status, and material comfort—becoming a male nurse gives you something like two and a half out of three.

So, after I graduated from one of the more prestigious private research universities in all of lower Manhattan (whose nursing program has a higher median starting salary than the allegedly more respectable majors like finance or computer science), I had no problem procuring a job quickly and locally at the Roosevelt Island Hospital. The interview, which might've posed a threat to a lot of people, was no match for my hyper-focused male brain and the many nootropic nutraceuticals I took the morning of.

Everything was going according to plan. I had a job, assisting Dr. Amos Bloomberg, a big-biceped Israeli American with a no-nonsense attitude. I had an apartment in walking distance from work with a view of the East River, I was making regular contributions, maxing out my *401(k)*, my *403(b)*, and of course, my *Roth*. Everything was going according to "plan." So, why then, was I, Ross, a few short weeks after my twenty-third birthday, so eager to make a dramatic departure from the career I'd made for myself?

The human body, it turns out, is a disgusting thing, on average. But before you become a full-time male nurse, you really only see your own nude body (which you're naturally sympathetic to) and the well-groomed nude bodies of a select set of exceptional women. These, to put it simply, are not at all representative of the sorts of parts you encounter as a nurse. And I know this sounds hackneyed and trite, and cruel and clichéd, but really, I didn't consider it at all before I started working and seeing these bodies in the flesh. There's so much you miss, by only exposing yourself to the images of diseased corpuses in books and in lectures, on projected PowerPoints, etc, etc. The real thing is so much worse. The smells, the jiggliness, the painfully tight gloves you have to put on.

I remember my first week on the job, this ridiculous old man was bused into the emergency room, panting in a frenzy after he'd swallowed a bunch of bleach and sleeping pills or something, all because he'd gotten an email saying he owed $730,000 in something called "back taxes." His wife was in the emergency room with us, crying, sitting in the bedside seat, sipping iced oolong tea from a plasticky bottle, while her husband lay in the bed, tubes flowing out of him, etc, etc.

"Doctor, please, is he going to be alright?" she kept saying to me.

"Ma'am, I am a nurse?" I replied.

"Well, well, what about my husband? Oh, you should have seen him when he came in, Doctor. He came into our living room, and he said to me: 'Honey, I just poisoned myself. I have to die now. Because the government is going to bankrupt me.' And then I saw that horrible email. It isn't true? Is it? Have we lost everything?"

"We've got the stomach pump, the saline drip, the charcoal, all out in full force for your husband," I said, as I handed her one of our cute little brochures for family and loved ones: *So, Your Husband Tried to Kill Himself After Panicking About Money.* "And no, it isn't true. This happens all the time. These sorts of scams," I told her.

"Now what kind of sick, sick . . . *animals* send an email like that? To an old man? Just to give him a heart attack?"

"From what I understand it's usually Indian guys, or Nigerians trying to get you to pay them like ten percent of what you allegedly owe in the form of iTunes gift cards."

She sat solemnly, thumbing through the pamphlet, until finally, in a burst of righteous anger, she asked me, "And just how exactly is any of this *legal?*"

This is the sort of thing you're forced to deal with. People like this, their crumbling physiques, their myriad medical maladies. But this brings us back to the *what else?* What would I *rather* be doing than putting my nursing skills to good paying use? Well, as it turns out, I've always had a fondness for politics, philosophy, public debate, in general. After my freshman year at a prestigious private research university in lower Manhattan, I lied my way into a summertime editorial internship ("Yes, I'm studying politics and journalism . . .") at Vox Media's Vox.com, authoring articles like "Why This Year is the Biggest Year Yet for JK Rowling, explained" and "Why you should stop eating beans, or maybe start" and "We asked a doctor whether swallowed gum really stays in your stomach for seven years. It doesn't." These were a nice start for a nineteen-year-old. A valuable foot-in-the-door of the Media World. I'm very proud of the work I did as a journalist, but its poor pay prospects meant I never really considered doing it full time.

The plan was always to use my nursing background as a launchpad for my career as a public intellectual (I really did earn a minor in philosophy in addition to my nursing degree), and then my career as a public intellectual as a launchpad for my career as a professional politician. Nurse, I had thought, would make for an interesting origin for my future political career—one of those new, likable non-lawyer professions for an elected official to have, like bartender, or Muslim.

It's not just some selfish desire, my political ambitions. The *marketplace of ideas* was sorely lacking minds like mine. Just this morning, before I went into the hospital to quit my job, I brainstormed a number of brilliant and wonkish policy ideas that would've made Ezra Klein proud.

Of course, as a liberal-minded guy, I'm very concerned with the issue of poverty. And to fix this, you have to be *compassionate.* You have to understand that poor people aren't to *blame* for being poor. It's not their fault that they make terrible decisions. They're just not smart enough (like I am) to be responsible with their money. So my first idea would be to make all lottery tickets fake lottery tickets. You have to give your social security number when you buy the ticket, and no one ever really wins. Instead, we just put the money into an exchange traded retirement account for the poor people buying the tickets. That way, when these poor people turned sixty, all the money they thought they were spending on lottery tickets, will actually have been invested for them, earning ten percent annual compounding interest. The average poor person who spends $600 a year on lottery tickets from ages eighteen to sixty would be presented with $292,111.09 at retirement. Not bad, right?

My second idea, would be to give every adult $1,000 a month, but only if they can pass a drug test showing they haven't smoked weed in the past thirty days. And if you slip up, of course you can always try to get it again the next month. People will be so eager to get that thousand bucks a month that they would stop smoking weed every day. And once they stop smoking weed, we would see joblessness, laziness, and mental illness rates plummet all across the country. Poverty solved. No one else (perhaps with the exception of Andrew Yang) is even *thinking* of stuff like this, let alone saying it aloud.

That's why it's so important that I get my face—and ideas—out there to start saving the country. And now you can see why the first step in this plan would be to quit my job as a white male nurse.

～

Before I left my apartment in the morning, I took some Horny Goat Weed and L-Tyrosine to help my brain synthesize sufficient levels of dopamine (via L-DOPA) to give me the *chutzpah* to resign midway through the day, offering an additional two weeks of my services (which I'd hoped they'd decline).

I set my Roomba to *on*, ran out the door and down the fourteen flights of my building's stairs. I was dressed in my scrubs and sneakers, as I've had problems with people stealing my belongings from the Roosevelt Island Hospital And National Nursing Association's locker room. The plan was simple. Find Dr. Bloomberg, get him alone, break the news.

I waltzed through the lobby, tapped my ID card on the turnstile, and saw Imani, a fellow nurse friend of mine (although she was an LPN, and I was an RN), already walking through the white walled halls carrying her clipboard and sipping a new limited edition beverage composed of iced coffee, caramel, blended up donut holes (called "Munchkins"), whipped cream, and 102 grams of sugar (which she must've brought from Brooklyn, as Roosevelt Island doesn't have a Dunkin' of its own).

Imani was my mentor in a lot of ways, being fifteen years older. She often joked that I was her "work hubby," and everyone would laugh. We definitely have great chemistry. Who knows what could've happened if we were ever *really* alone together.

"Ross! Ahh! He's back!!" she yelled out to me.

"Hi Imani," I grinned, "hope you didn't miss me too much."

She laughed and embraced me, wrapping her unempty arms around me for a huge hug. "Now Ross, don't you start trying to joke around too much with Imani. I know you must be hurting inside. If you need to let a good cry out, because of what happened, you know, to your parents, in that helicopter crash, Ross, I'm here for you, baby."

"Thanks, Imani."

I picked up my clipboard at the central dispatch desk. Aaliyah, the main secretary, was never a fan of mine, most likely because she and Imani had been embroiled in an age-old rivalry since long before I arrived on the scene, and by cozying up to Imani, I'd alienated myself from Aaliyah. She wouldn't even look at me when I picked up my assignments for the day.

To start, I had to go see a sixty-six-year-old man named Chaim Goldcoyne. He was sitting upright in the hospital bed in Room F8, dressed in gray gown and slipper socks.

"Hello, Mr. Goldcoyne, my name is Ross. I'm going to be your nurse today."

"Gr . . ." He let out a slight grunt.

"Now, I'm just going to take your temperature, if that's alright with you, Chaim. Do I have your full consent to do that?"

"GGHM."

"Sir, due to the *Yes Means Yes* laws in the State of New York, I'm going to need your unambiguous verbal consent to have your temperature taken."

"Yes," he said.

"Thank you."

I held the infrared thermometer a few inches from the skin of his forehead until it beeped. "Perfect," I told him.

"I'm always cold. I'm always freezing, doctor," he told me. "What can you do for that? A pill? A shot?"

"Well your temperature was 98.2 degrees. That's actually a bit high. The average used to be 98.6, but scientists have found the average temperature in humans has been declining for the past thirty years and—"

"Oh, just shut up. Please, shut up. You're giving me a headache!" He fell flat on the bed. "Just give me pills, doctor. I need pills!"

"Sir, I am a nurse. The doctor will be in to see you shortly," I said as I slunk out and went into the Nurse's Lounge, where I was greeted by Dr. Amos Bloomberg.

A word about Doctor B, who is mostly unremarkable. I've found doctors to be some of the most obnoxious and evil people on the planet. Far worse than lawyers or dentists. Did you know medical malpractice is like the third leading cause of death in the United States each year? Something like 250,000 people per year die due to medical malpractice. These are totally preventable deaths caused by *doctors*. Now, there are only 950,000 doctors in the United States. So you do a little elementary school math, and you get that for every one hundred doctors, twenty-six people a year are getting killed by doctors (which is to say nothing of the maimings and cripplings). Compare this to a much more maligned group—police officers. There are about 800,000 police officers in the United States, and they kill 1,000 people a year. Take your calculator out. That's only 0.125 people killed per one hundred police officers, versus 27.7 people killed by doctors per one hundred doctors. You're over two hundred times more likely to be killed by a doctor than by a police officer. But does anyone know that? No, of course not. They love doctors. They have no problem with doctors making a million dollars a year to commit murder. Doctors like Amos Bloomberg, the man who made my life a living hell for eighteen months.

"Hey dummy," he said to me, barely looking up from whatever he was reading.

"Hi Doctor Bloomberg," I said.

It seemed like an appropriate time to break the news to this guy. He was sitting at the conference table, sipping coffee from a Styrofoam cup, looking down at his Microsoft Windows tablet computer. I was about to clear my throat to begin speaking when he beat me to the proverbial punch. "Oh, uhh, Ross! You're back!" he said.

"Yes, sir, Doctor Bloomberg, sir."

"We need you to take one for the team, Ross."

"What do you mean?"

"Well, as you know, business is down. After, you know, the busy season, with the virus. So we need to spice things up around here. Do a little promo, Ross. We need to get these numbers *goosed*." He was still barely looking up from his little computer.

"Well sir, Doctor Bloomberg, sir. I have uh, actually been meaning to ask you—"

"So we need you Ross. All the nurses are gonna do a viral dance, Ross. To promote the new psych ward."

I just continued standing awkwardly in my scrubs, my legs tiring, semi crossed, one foot over the other, "sir, I wanted to talk to you about—"

"So what we're going to *DO*, Ross. And you're going to listen to me . . . because I'm the *boss*, and you're the *Ross*, is you and all of the other nurses are going to do a viral dance. You're going to put on strait jackets."

"Sir . . ."

"Just listen. Just listen. You're going to put on strait jackets. And you're all going to dance to Beyoncé and Jay-Z's 2003 smash hit "Crazy In Love" (2003), as a promotion for our new psych ward. And we're going to put it on Facebook, and it's going to be *big*, and it's going to save this hospital."

"Would you just *LISTEN* to me?" I yelled out. "I'm so sick of how you treat me around here. You and Aaliyah all the time. Bossing me around, making me dance, fix the printer, play catch with your son on Take Your Kids to Roosevelt Island Day. Screw this crap! I've had it! I am too smart for this. I am too good for this. I am *richer* than you, Doctor Bloomberg. You didn't even *ask* me, how I was doing after the death of my parents, or after my *acrimonious* breakup with my long-term girlfriend. And now you want me to *dance?* You think I'm going to debase myself, for *you* and for this *hospital*, that has done NOTHING but humiliate and degrade me? No, sir. You are mistaken. You are sadly, *sadly* mistaken," and then I uttered those two words that I'd been so eager to avoid ever uttering: "I *quuuuiiiit!*"

I threw my mask off and knocked over all sorts of little mugs filled with paper clips and rubber bands and large bottles of hand sanitizer on my way out.

From the distance, I heard Dr. Bloomberg say "I had no idea he felt that way . . ."

And to be fair, Doctor, neither did I. When I got home, I threw out that bottle of Horny Goat Weed as it seemed to make me act a little unhinged.

Seven

"Well, I've missed you, my gorgeous Ross."

"Thank you."

"You look amazing, better than ever. As if that were even possible. How long has it been?"

"I think almost five months."

This was Robert Crispane, the aging homophile who'd been serving as my pill-pushing "confidante" in the five years since I'd started studying at a prestigious private research university in Lower Manhattan. He was approaching seventy—a sort of wispy-framed cane-wielding geezer, unsteady on his toes, but well groomed, with a distinguished gray beard, always dressed in linen pants, cashmere sweater vests, bowties, things like that. There are a ton of guys like Bob Crispane in New York City. Creepy old men who give hot young boys (like me) whichever pills we ask for.

For years, I would go in and rant rather aimlessly. Scream for forty-five minutes straight. About politics, about philosophy, about how easy my life was. ("Yes, doctor! I really *am* the smartest, funniest, most handsome man who lives on Roosevelt Island!") I didn't have any problems that I needed help with for the first few years, it was really just about getting pills from this man. And also, I've always enjoyed going to therapy. There's something soothing about having an old man who has no choice but to listen to you.

Since I was a toddler, every psychiatrist I'd ever gone to had mostly just nodded and smiled, telling me how smart and right I was. So it remained unclear, then, whether anything he ever said to me was to be believed. And of course, epistemologically this intrigued me. Were they just telling me that because they knew (using their psychological training) that that was what I wanted to hear, or were they actually impressed and in agreement with my reasoning? It seems to me like an unescapable Cartesian conundrum.

But Bob Crispane, this man, he took it to another level, his adoration of me. It was a nonstop lovefest in there. The man simply could not get enough.

"So do you like my new office?" he said, grinning and then coughing into his hand. He'd explained over the phone that he had entered into a semi-retirement, fleeing to Fire Island, only coming back to this new dingier midtown office for two days every two weeks, to see his "favorite" (and you have to wonder if he really meant it when he told me that) patients.

"Uh . . . it's interesting. It's pretty nice, I guess. I like this chair."

"No you *don't*. It *sucks*. It's awful. I'm so sorry, Ross. This is *squalor*!" he said to me. Upon closer inspection he was right. The room was dark and yellow, with a number of switched-on dehumidifiers working overtime in the corners. Gone were the vast bookshelves of his old office, now replaced with decrepit fireproof filing cabinets.

"Ha, ha," I laughed nervously, "so what is this place?"

"It's a shanty . . . it's a *bagnio*!"

"No, I mean, like, how did you find this place?"

"I'm renting it from another doctor. Would you believe that?"

Yeah, sure, why not. I was eager to change the subject and start talking more about myself. "Well, I've missed you too. I know I told you a bit on the phone about what I've been getting myself into in the past twelve weeks since I turned twenty-three. But let's see if we can get a real 'breakthrough' today." Now, my health insurance provider and Bob were in agreement that I was only supposed to be receiving nondenominational talk therapy and simple psychopharmacological counseling, but ever since I'd read the Stanford Encyclopedia of Philosophy article about Jacques Lacan, I was desperate to force some real complex analysis out of Doctor Robert. "And because you've been unavailable to me, I've had to settle on far less scientific sources of psychological assistance."

"What do you mean?"

"Well, when I was at home, I found my mom's copy of *The Secret* (2006), and I thumbed through it, just because I remember hearing about it all the time as a kid, and because you were *gone*, because you had *abandoned* me, doctor—"

"I would never abandon you, Ross."

"Yeah, yeah, I know. But because I couldn't *see* you, I had to seek wisdom from *The Secret* (2006), and I think it might actually be kind of smart. That all these women were smart for reading it in 2006."

He leaned up a bit in his chair, "Do tell," he said.

"Well there's this idea of the *law of attraction*, that a person's thoughts can change real-life events. And we've talked before about how I'm obsessed with narrative, so I've started compiling this narrative of my past few months, a diary of sorts, but written with *intent*. Written to try to *steer* things in the right direction. And that's what I need."

He tilted his head confusedly at me.

"You might not be able to see this, but I'm a mess, doctor. I'm going absolutely nuts. I've been on the verge of blowing my brains out directly into the nearest East River. But I think it's all going to be better soon. I think I'm about to have everything resolved. I think I'm approaching a nice, neat ending of the *narrative*. And I'm constantly recording audio of my conversations and encounters. Have you seen this? My watch can just record audio. It's a huge privacy problem." I held up my blinking red wrist to show him that this was all being chronicled. "So I'm hoping I can *manifest* a happy ending for myself. Through this *predictive programming* I'm writing up."

"What are you calling it? *Ross Run? Ross's Complaint?*" He giggled gayly, scribbling something onto his little pad of paper.

"Well it's really more like *Ross Is Rich* now. But I like the names *A Portrait of the Ross as a Young Man*, or *Paradise Rossed*, or *My Year of Ross and Relaxation*, or if, you know, it sucks and makes no sense and I end up blowing my brains out directly into the nearest East River before it's all done, *The Sorrows of Young Ross*, or even *The Original of Lora*. But that's beside the point. And to address your suggestions . . . no, I don't really think I'm anything like those guys anymore. I think I'm totally different from these post–World War II horny male protagonists. I'm one of the *least* horny people, doctor. You know that."

"Yes, such a shame."

"You take a guy like *Rabbit*, doctor, and you read that today, in this world . . . this sick perverted world I'm living in, and you can't imagine *why* he would want to *Run*. I mean, he had it all. He had a house, a job, a wife, a kid. What was he running from? I can't believe that guy wanted to run. I would never run if I had a nice stable life like that."

"Why don't you talk about what you've been dealing with? The sorts of things you're trying to run from."

"Okay. Okay. Sure. If I had to give my current arc a *beginning*, I would say it started in March when I broke up with my Lora Liamant. And you know this part, but I'll summarize it again since it's part of the *narrative*. Recall, she had been smoking weed every day, and I really wanted her to stop smoking weed. So I broke up with her, and gave her this sort of vaguely threatening—but hopeful!—speech about how I wanted to marry her—because I did, and I *do*—but that I thought she still needed to do some . . . growing up. And that I didn't want her to resent me for limiting her while she figured out what she wanted in life. Which I thought was a mature thing to do, right?"

"Sure."

"So recall, that I thought she was going to be totally miserable without me. I thought she would flounder without my love, and come crawling back, eager to settle down, promising to change, etc, etc, and *I*, Ross, would have all the leverage, be able to make demands. But then, days went by, and then weeks . . . until one night, I woke up in the middle of the night, overcome by this horrible cucking sensation. And I realized she had been *moving* on, with the unsuccessful alcoholic brother of a famous network TV actor. And this caused a great crisis, in my mind, you know?"

"Why did that cause a crisis?" He leaned up a bit from his chair.

"Because this guy was a total Thirty-Year-Old Loser, a guy with absolutely no accomplishments despite being thirty years old. And because we men are told that after we break up with a woman that at any time at all, all we've got to do is call, and they'll be there, ready to take us back. They're not supposed to *get over* us so quickly. Especially not with such . . . *losers*. I mean we see stories of these guys beating their wives, and the wives keep coming back. The wives can't get over these guys. So why am *I* getting gotten over, doctor? Because I don't want her to smoke weed? That's really such a *crime?* That makes me *manipulative* and *controlling* and all these new dumb buzzwords people use about anyone who asks them to make the slightest accommodation in the context of a loving long-term relationship?"

"Well—"

"So then, on the night before my twenty-third birthday, I met up with this ridiculous woman. Do you know what I mean by ridiculous? It was just a total mismatch. And I was only doing it because I thought I had to preserve something about myself, something masculine, I suppose. But this woman was, and I cannot say this enough . . . ridiculous, but I went to dinner with her, and then I went 'to town' *on* her, back at my apartment. And of course, as sex so often is, it was disgusting, and foolish, and fleeting and humiliating."

"It really breaks my heart to hear someone like you hate sex so much, Ross."

"And *then*, after I finished showering, I got this phone call that my parents died in a helicopter accident in Turks and Caicos. It sounds nuts, doesn't it? That this all happened so quickly."

"Yes, very nuts. Before you keep going, I wanted to ask how you're doing with your little," he let out a slight moan as he stretched his back "hallucinations. Ah . . . Particularly the ones with references to popular culture from the late '90s and early 2000s?"

"What are you trying to say, doctor? That the 'black box' recording of the moments before the crash, in which I heard my dad fighting with the helicopter pilot because he wanted to play "Fly" (1997) by Sugar Ray into the noise-cancelling helicopter headphones wasn't real? That was just a hallucination?"

He smiled at me as if I were joking. And then I continued.

"So back home in Los Angeles, after the funeral, I found out that my dad, in his fearful finite wisdom, had taken out ten figures' worth of life insurance on himself and my mommy, which all went to me and my sister, whom I'm also the legal guardian of now. So now I'm extremely rich. *Extremely*."

"And how does it make you feel to have to take care of her?"

"Oh I'm grateful. I've known for a while that my parents weren't up to it, doctor. They're really sort of 'blue collar' folk, but Emily is like me, only smarter, because she's had a mentor (me) to help her."

"So you like helping people, telling them what to think."

"Yeah sure. We know that. And then I quit my job at the hospital, because it seemed stupid, and my boss was mean to me, and it was hard to have respect for a *boss* who had a lower IQ *and* a lower net worth than I did."

"And less sex appeal."

"Thank you, doctor."

"Of course."

"And the newest fiasco is this penthouse apartment I just bought. It's in Fort Greene, Brooklyn, in the lot where they had that pizza place with the child sex trafficking ring going on in the basement. Do you remember that? It was all over the news a few years ago."

"No."

"Well they tore that building down, and built luxury apartments for affluent orphans to live in. It's called *The Fort* because it's in Fort Greene.

And also it has a ton of security. That's cute, right? *The Fort.* Who knows what percentage of my penthouse purchase paid for that cute name from the marketing department at Flank Reality Incorporated Inc. But anyway, my sister and I are now the co-owners of a fortieth-floor penthouse in Brooklyn. And I feel terribly adult. It feels like Bruce's apartment in *The Dark Knight* (2008), have you seen that?"

"No."

"Well, what I'm trying to say, is that I feel like I've had adulthood *thrust* upon me, *FOISTED!* upon me, doctor. I'm a single parent, a homeowner, an heir, a cuckold, all in a few weeks' time."

"Well you're very mature, very responsible, certainly *ready* for this sort of responsibility. And from what I understand, this is what you've been *wanting,* isn't it? You would come here, week after week, whining about the orgies and loud music and new types of ways to smoke and drink that people your age were inventing and popularizing. So now you've gotten what you wanted, right?"

"But that's the problem, it all feels so *fake.* It feels rushed and cartoonish and ultimately meaningless. Such is the nature of the narrative."

"You know, we have an old saying," he groaned again, his voice getting creakier and creakier as he was sucked into the leathery loveseat in his sordid sublet. "If you don't want to grow old, hang yourself when you're young."

"That doesn't sound very good at all," I replied, "that sounds terrible."

"Well, it makes more sense in Yiddish . . ."

"Yeah, yeah, I'm sure a lot of things do. But all of this, the money, the maturity, the morality, this is all tertiary. I do *not* care about this stuff. At least, it's not a priority anymore. I've *won,* in these departments. What I'm really blowing my brains out about, is Lora Liamant. She's *really* got a hold on me. I'm really not thinking about anything else, at all, doctor."

"What is all this talk about blowing your brains out? Should I be concerned about this?"

"No, it's kind of like . . . a new catch phrase I'm trying out. But it is a good metaphor for how I feel. Which is to say, ridiculous. I feel ridiculous. I am a cartoon character. I am a Shylock drawing. I am sweaty and greedy and I spend every waking moment being terrified about money and women."

"Do you think it's because your—"

"Because my mother died? Yeah sure, why not. See, you psychiatrists always think we're going to scream and fight when you suggest that. But no, I'll admit it. Yes, I want to replace my mommy. I want someone to tell me I'm smart and amazing and handsome and cook and clean for me."

"Well, maybe *you* should be the psychiatrist."

I raised my eyebrows at him and nodded, as if to thank him for his clinical stroking of my ego.

"But back to Lora. The love of my life, whom I'm desperate to tame. It's making me sick to my stomach, doctor. What she's been up to. It's terrifying. For whatever reason, things seemed to have fizzled out with the actor's brother. And for the past few weeks, she's been . . . oy . . . getting . . . *town* gone to on her. It's heartbreaking. These twenty-first-century New York City women, doctor, you don't even want to *know* what they're getting themselves into. They just smoke weed and forget how to say no. They'll just go home with anyone who asks."

"And what's wrong with that?" he asked, unrhetorically, as if he actually couldn't see what the problem was.

"Because these men are *losers*, compared to me. How can she go from me, to these . . . these *himbos?* Do you know about *himbos?* It's like a bimbo but—"

"I think I've had a himbo or two."

"I'm sure you have. And I'm sure you had a lot of fun, in the seventies in plenty of downtown bathrooms, but this is the woman I want to *marry*, doctor. I want to have children with her. But she's humiliating me. She has sex partners like I have money, doctor. And by that I mean, a lot for our age, and too much to know what to do with. Except I know *exactly* what she's doing with them. And it's *sick!*"

"Why don't you show me what she's doing with them?"

"Ha, yeah yeah. That's funny. But seriously. How am I supposed to have children with this woman who's been getting absolutely *run through* by dating app retards?"

"How do you really even *know* she's doing that?"

"I just know it, doctor. I just feel it in my gut that she's cucking me like nobody's ever been cucked before. Which is not to say these are purely synthetic *a priori* ideas I have. There's proof *aplenty.*"

"Go on . . ."

"So, since I found about her little . . . tryst with the thirty-year-old younger brother of a fairly famous network TV actor, I've been obsessively monitoring her. Both on the *Find My Ex Girlfriend* app, which she never revoked my access to, and for the past week I've been obsessively checking the app where women post pictures of themselves and their food. I've made a Microsoft Excel spreadsheet that tracks her followers, and the people *she* follows, and I've found three "new" male "friends" in just the past week. The first is this gay guy, he's very clearly just a gay guy, named something stupid. He's from the south, I can't remember it, his name, but it's something stupid like Layne, or something. The second is a New England white guy, who, according to LinkedIn, is a 'Senior' 'Software' 'Engineer' at something called 'CarGurus.' I think she may be involved, you know, *involved* with that guy. And the third guy, who also seems vaguely threatening, to me, is some kind of swarthy Greek guy, who went to that art college in North-Central Brooklyn. Now, it would just be truly *sick* if she were seeing both at the same time, or had even *seen* both at all! It would just be totally degenerate, doctor."

"See, why would that be degenerate?"

"Well, because compared to *me*, any man is degenerate."

"That much I can agree with."

"How serious are you when you say things like that to me?"

"You're a beautiful boy, Ross. You're witty, and kind, and that nose . . . so Roman and masculine. It's like something generated by an algorithm . . ."

"If only these twenty-first-century women could see it the way you do."

He took a sip from a small coffee cup next to his chair.

"So I'm a totally defeated man, doctor. I have a raging Oedipus complex and a textbook case of castration anxiety. I'm doing reaction formation like there's no tomorrow, and my death drive is in *over*drive. The world is far too horny for my comfort. But I'm nearing the end of this nightmare. I haven't told you about my big ending. Well, here: Lora is coming over tomorrow. To my Roosevelt Island apartment. After weeks of me trying to get this coordinated. And it's going to be nice, but I've been blowing my brains out worrying about it. Because after how I've seen her behave, I'm not sure I'll be able to trust her in the context of a relationship. You know, since we're going to get back together tomorrow. And I'm looking forward to that, having her again, but you can imagine how emasculated I feel. How *foolish* I feel. So I need to figure out how to regain some integrity, some *leverage*, some awe-inspiring masculinity."

"You are perfect just the way you are, Ross."

"You think so?"

"I think . . ." He paused to reach into a little satchel next to his seat, letting out another pain-filled grunt, "I think I'm going to write you a prescription for thirty Vyvanse, and sixty Adderall. How does that sound?"

Eight

Emily was about five weeks into her freshman year at Brooklyn's Brooklyn Technical High School (she found Stuyvesant "creepy," Hunter College High School "disgusting," and the Mathcamps have always had a strict "no private school" rule, so *Tech* was her only real option. She also thought it was funny that Anthony Weiner went there). She'd been getting home late, well, not late, but later, maybe around five, because, at my request, on the days when school wasn't conducted over Zoom, she'd been checking out the exciting clubs New York's public high school system had to offer. The *Books N' Beyond* club, the *Linguistics* club, *Girls Who Code*, the *Rubik's Cubes* club, *Stock Market* club, *Orphan* club, etc, etc, etc, etc. All the things I wish I'd had access to when I was her age. I was really very proud of her.

But I was going nuts. Life as a single parent was taking its toll on me. Since Emily and I moved into *The Fort* at the end of August, I was up to my ears in expenses. Mostly going to Erik Prince's Academi Real Estate Management (Formerly Blackwater Development Group), my building's property / security manager. Amenities fees, mortgage payments (with rates this low, you'd have to be an idiot not to take out a huge loan for your penthouse), tips for doormen and delivery guys, etc, etc. And it's not like I was *doing* anything.

I'd somehow convinced myself that it was "productive" for me to "take care" of the house, buying kitchen gadgets and toilet trinkets, robot vacuums, special lightbulbs that allegedly increase your IQ. But really I was sitting around doing not very much of anything at all all day, which is not to say I wasn't *earning*. Emily gave me permission to park her cash next to mine in the WisdomTree 90/60 US Balanced Fund

(NTSX), and with a principal of $10,000,000, it was normal to see net worth swings of upwards of two hundred grand a day. If you've read the Wikipedia page for Tom Piketty's *Capital in the Twenty-First Century* (2013) like I have, you'll know that this is going on all over the world, heirs and heiresses reaping profits without lifting fingers. Not that any of this money is enough to prevent us (rich people, like me, Ross) from blowing our brains out directly into the nearest East Rivers.

I was sitting in the parlor, leaning on the army of my navy blue chair by the big corner window, looking out at Lady Liberty, trying to get some literature ingested—I'd started reading the new fourteen-hundred-page original manuscript of *Stephen Hero* (1904) that was just made public for the first time, but I was really struggling to make any progress on the thing, what with all my personal responsibilities and the book's juvenile prose . . . The furniture was beginning to piss me off; the home had come mostly pre-furnished, with a simple bring-your-own-mattresses policy. Which seemed good at the time, I didn't want to have to worry about picking out pieces of mid-century-modern furniture for months on end. But the stuff was junk. Not the sort of stuff you would want to sit in while reading.

I was set to see Lora later in the evening; we were to meet at my Roosevelt Island apartment, which had a one-year-lease expiring in April (it's still September) and seemed like a convenient place to indulge my lust and ambition without bothering Emily, who came home around four, dressed in black denims and white T-shirt, white sneakers, etc, etc.

"Hey, look at that," I said, "We're wearing the same outfit! It's almost like we're twins!"

"Ha, yeah, I guess that's true," she replied sort of solemnly.

She took her shoes off, putting them on the plastic rack underneath my new pinball machine ($10,000), and walked into the kitchen corridor, looking into the big Blomberg fridge. I ran around to the other side and started emptying the Maytag dishwasher.

Channeling Mommy: "Is there anything I can get you? Do you want me to make you a smoothie?" I said as I put a few bowls and cups into the flat flush cabinets.

"No, I'm okay."

"Do you want an avocado? I just got some ripe organic ones from Rite Aid."

"No, I'm okay."

"Is everything okay?"

"Yeah. I'm fine."

I felt like a real Mom of a Ross, in that moment, like I was really harassing my sister-daughter in a truly motherly fashion. But I'd always thought Emily and I were too close to have this sort of tension. Too similar, really.

I went into the master bedroom to shower (my second of the day, for Lora, although I'd probably take another when I got to my Roosevelt Island apartment), floss, oil pull, and rehearse funny and clever things to say later in the evening. Things like: "Well, sure, money can't *always* buy happiness, but it's not like we have a *controlled* experiment here! I mean, if my parents died and left me a bunch of *debt,* I think I would be even *more* miserable!"

As I was putting on my Levi's 501s (light blue), Emily knocked a few times on my door. "Yes?" I asked.

"Can I come in, Ross?"

"Yeah one second," I grabbed a pink T-shirt out of my closet. "I just need to put on my pink T-shirt."

"Is it on yet?"

"Yes, you can come in now."

I sat down in my beanbag and she stood in front of me nervously.

"Ross . . ."

"Yeah?"

"I need you to baptize me."

"What?"

"I need you to baptize me."

"Like, ironically?"

"No, in the name of the Father, the Son, and the Holy Ghost. It's not a joke or an ironic thing at all."

"Why do I need to baptize you?" I snapped back. "We're *Jewish*, Emily. I'm *Jewish*, and you're just like me, only better. So why would you want to be baptized? I was never baptized. Our parents were never baptized. No one in our family has ever been baptized."

"Well, it all started when I was going to all of those clubs you wanted me to visit. And then I went to see the Atheist Club, and the people there were not very smart, a bunch of boys, all obsessed with Hitchens and Harris and Hawking and Hume and the like, and then I went to the Jewish Club, and it was all the same people. And I realized if you could be an *atheist* and still be Jewish, then it isn't really a religion at all."

"Yes but—"

"And then I was reading this Harold Bloom interview with NPR, from 2005." She was talking increasingly quickly, losing bits of her breath, the poor thing. "He wrote some silly book about Jesus, and he talks about how he feels there's no God because of how poorly Jews have been treated over the past two thousand years. That he felt he lost the covenant, that he feels the Jews were never the chosen people, but he's making a big causation error. He's not thinking about a big event that happened two thousand years ago that might have caused Jews to lose their good fortune."

"Well I don't care very much for that guy anyway! You know he claimed to be able to read a thousand pages an hour, right? It's ridiculous! That works out to being able to read a paragraph in like one second. If he were actually that smart, he would've been able to come up with something more profound than just saying 'Shakespeare is epic.' So, please, Emily, don't talk to me about *Bloom*!"

"Well it's not really about him. I just thought you would like the reference."

"Well I *didn't*. I can't stand that guy!"

"But then I started reading the *Gospel of Matthew* (~70), and if you read it, it's really clear that Jesus *was* the Jewish Messiah, it was really literary how he fulfilled all the—"

"Yeah, yeah yeah. I've heard this all before, Em. I know all about *Matthew* trying to convince his Jewish audience to believe Jesus was the Messiah. You don't think all this 'the Jews are no longer chosen' stuff sounds awfully *self-hating*, Emily?"

"Come on, Ross, you gave something called *Operation Shylock* (1993) a *five*-star review on Goodreads."

"Yeah, but—"

"And then I read Chesterton's *Orthodoxy* (1908), and it just became even more obvious that Catholicism is the only real religion."

"Where are you reading this stuff? I can't read anything in this house. You're just going to the school library and reading Chesterton? Who told you to read that? I never told you to read that! That wasn't on my list."

"Ross, it's okay for me to read something that you haven't read."

"So *that's* what this is about. You don't want to be like your big brother anymore. You *hate* me. You want me *dead*. After everything I've done for you, all you do is resent me and want to be *different* from me."

"No, no. Stop it, Ross. You sound like Mom."

"Well what do you think *she* would think? About you giving up our traditions?"

"I don't see why this even matters. I'm still halachically Jewish, I'm still *ethnically* the same as you. If I told you I were an atheist you would cheer me on, tell me to pass the pastrami, but I just ask for one little baptism and you start freaking out. I mean, I at least *believe* in the TaNaKh now, isn't that an improvement? Doesn't that make me *more* Jewish than you and almost every other Jew?"

"Okay, fine. I'll baptize you. As long as you don't start getting all weird, I won't care. But why do *I* have to do it? How *can* I even do it? Doesn't a priest have to do it?"

"No. The Council of Florence says even a pagan or a heretic or a woman can perform baptism if they use the proper form."

"But still, why *me?* Why can't you go to a priest?"

"They'll make me spend a year studying in one of their weird programs, but if I die before then, I'll go to hell. I don't want that. I need to get baptized as soon as possible, Ross, so I won't go to hell if I die."

This was troubling to hear, especially coming from a thirteen-year-old. I personally didn't start having fear of death until I was nineteen, and I never got all religious about it, worrying about *hell* of all things.

She continued, "It's also doubtful whether they're even real priests anymore. The rite of ordination was changed in 1968, and they deleted every important prayer, and now they might just be guys dressing up in robes, pretending to have powers."

"I think I heard about that."

"And I want *you* to do it because you're my brother and I love you more than anything else in the world, and I don't know whom else I could even possibly ask."

"Well that's nice, I suppose."

"Okay, so you'll do it?"

"What do I even have to do?"

"You just have to pour water over my forehead and say, 'I baptize thee in the name of the Father, and of the Son, and of the Holy Ghost.' You can either do three separate pours, or one continuous pour. Both are valid."

"Uh . . . okay. And we have to do it right now?"

"Yes, and you have to believe that you're really baptizing me. You do believe that, right, Ross? That's your intention?"

"Yes, I believe it. But don't think I'm going to let you do it to me anytime soon. Or ever, really."

"I mean just consider the expected value of being Catholic and getting baptized, Ross. Even if there's only a tiny chance that it's true, it's not *rational* not to accept it. The stakes are too high."

"I'm the one who taught *you* about expected value!" I huffed.

We went out into the kitchen, and I stood there, confusedly, worried about the health of the mind of my sister as she read the profession of faith from the Council of Trent, saying things I'd never thought she'd say, things like *"I firmly hold that there is a purgatory, and that the souls detained there are helped by the prayers of the faithful"* and *"I affirm that the power of indulgences was left in the keeping of the Church by Christ, and that the use of indulgences is very beneficial to Christians."*

And when she was done, she stepped onto a stool, stuck her head over the kitchen sink, and with water from my "World's #1 Older Brother" mug, I baptized her in the name of the Father, the Son, and the Holy Ghost.

Nine

You know, deep down, I'm really just a romantic guy. This is one of the things people don't understand about me because they're too busy focusing on the more immediately obvious oddities, etc, etc. But it's true. Everything I do is for love. It controls me. Motivates every decision I ever make. And this, the preparation for my reunion with Lora Liamant, was nothing less than a labor of love.

I got to Roosevelt Island early, following the baptism, around 5:30, to make sure my floors were properly swept, my fridge was properly stocked, my bed was properly made, etc, etc. Of course, I'd already done each of those things the night before, but with Lora on the line one (I, Ross) could never be too careful. Another thing, worthy of note, Lora doesn't love luxury like I do—she finds my living environments too pampered, perhaps embarrassingly clean, but, even as I tried to leave some carefully curated messes (a stray sock sticking out of a drawer, a slightly dusty dining table), I still couldn't bring myself to will for her anything less than the best, even after everything she'd done to me.

Lora texted me around 6:00 to say she was "almost there," which I already knew because I'd been compulsively checking her location on the *Find My Ex-Girlfriend* app.

When she arrived at the Roosevelt Island air-tram station, I was waiting for her outside holding a pack of Smart Sweets low-sugar plant-based peach-ring candies (these have been a favorite of mine as of late). A lot of people aren't smart enough to know that New York City has a sky gondola that carries you, suspended by ropes and wires, two-hundred-fifty feet in the air, across the East River. From 59th and 2nd to "Tramway Plaza" on Roosevelt Island.

"Hi there," she said as she hugged me outside the station, "I didn't realize you were going to meet me here." She was wearing a grayish plaid patterned skirt with a large orange tee tucked into it. It was all very enticing.

"I got you these candies," I told her. "They have hardly any sugar. But they taste just as good as real candy. Like, they taste just like real candy. If you tasted them, you wouldn't know they weren't bad for you . . ."

She smiled—it was nice. She'd only gotten better looking since the last time I'd seen her. "Well that's perfect for you, isn't it, Ross? You get to trick yourself into having fun without any of the consequences."

I laughed and leaned in to give her a kiss on the cheek. She seemed to turn away slightly, as if to defend herself from me kissing her on the mouth (as if I were even trying to do that!).

We walked for eighteen minutes up the main street, to my building on the other side of the island, The Octagon, at 888 Main Street, which is a real place and a real address that you can look up if you don't believe me and think it sounds made up.

"We have a new Asian woman doorman. Luis, the old doorman, got fired for posting 'All Lives Matter' on Facebook in 2015," I said, as we walked through the lobby, waved to the new Asian woman doorman, and entered the elevator. "Oh, also, it's a mess in here. I'm so sorry." It was actually quite clean in there, but it was something of a joke between the two of us that I was always worrying about being perceived as filthy even after having cleaned for hours on end.

Inside, I planned to pull out every conceivable stop for her. "Did you eat? I can make you a grilled cheese, if you'd like."

"That sounds good, thanks. Are you eating bread and cheese now? Have you evolved?"

"Well . . ." I went into my refrigerator and pulled out the Whole Foods 365 Everyday Plant-Based Cheddar Alternative slices and the gluten-free Food for Life White Rice Bread (most people don't know white rice is *much* healthier than brown rice, which is loaded with arsenic) I'd bought the day before, "I haven't evolved, so much as *cheese* has evolved, although, I don't think they're legally allowed to call this cheese, because they'd get sued into the ground by all the dairy industry lobbyists and lawyers. You know . . . the dairy lobby, it's very powerful . . ."

She nodded understandingly and sat down on my bed.

I continued: "But this says 'bread' on it, and I've found it to be safe to eat, generally." I took out my carbon steel skillet from underneath the stove and began warming it up on medium heat. "The carbon steel pan is like cast iron, Lora, it has a really high *specific heat*, you know, the *joules* per *kelvin kilogram*, how much energy it takes to raise the temperature by a degree kelvin."

"Uh huh."

This is the sort of thing I love saying to women. "So you have to heat it up on the stove for a bit before it's ready to use. But it's worth it. I wouldn't gamble with using a nonstick pan, covered in Chinese carcinogens and endocrine disruptors."

She looked up from her phone, "Sorry, yeah. I like that pan. I like the orange rubber handle. That's cute."

"Yeah, it's all one piece of metal. So the handle needs rubber on it. Or else it gets . . . too hot."

" . . ."

"I have *oat milk* for you, if you'd like that to go with this grilled cheese."

"Sure."

I stood around the stove for a bit, while Lora sat in the microfiber upholstered kitchen table chair facing the window and the river and the view of Long Island City. The plant-based cheddar alternative was particularly well suited for sandwiches that could be described as "melts," the white rice bread was fine, not great, and so, for good measure, I slid a few pieces of pre-cooked pancetta onto the pan and added them to our sandwiches. I brought both plates and two cups of unsweetened oat milk onto the table to eat with Lora.

"This is nice, isn't it?" I asked her.

"It's lovely, Ross."

I felt happy. Happy and comfortable. Happy and comfortable and in control of my surroundings.

"So you're doing fine?" she asked. "What have you been up to in the past few months? Any new obsessions and cogitations?"

In truth, I'd had quite possibly the worst six months of my life. It'd been awful and Loraless. "Well, I've been busy. Busy in a macro sense. A lot of big things have happened to me, but my everyday life isn't very busy at all. I don't know if I told you, but I quit my job, over the summer."

"Really? You were always going on and on about how you were so much smarter than other guys our age, because you had a job. But now you're just like them?"

"Well, I mean, that's true. And I still am, better, because I'm still the type of person who worked hard and *got* a job. I just don't need one anymore now that I'm a millionaire life insurance heir. The other kids, the other people we went to school with, they were already millionaires, or at least, they lived like it, and so they never had to learn anything or work hard. I'm lucky, really. That my parents died *after* I was educated and employed."

"That's a neat way of putting it," she took her first bite of the "grilled" "cheese" I'd made her. "Where did they die again? St. Jacques?"

"Turks and Caicos," I replied plainly.

"And how about Emily? Is she handling it well?"

"I'm not sure. She's Catholic now, she says. She asked me to baptize her this afternoon. And I did it. I performed a baptism on my Jewish sister. I'm a bit worried about her, but I think she'll be fine. But I think the death has been tricky for both of us."

A breakthrough. When I mentioned my dead parents and sad sister she put her arm around me, and scooted her chair slightly closer to mine, nuzzling up against my side. This was pity affection, but as a desperate consequentialist I was willing to acquire my ends by any means necessary, etc, etc.

"Do you want to watch *Interiors* (1978) now? We've been waiting for months," she asked me.

"Yes."

"Okay."

"Did you watch that Khan Academy video I sent you about the Krebs Cycle? I think he did a really good job explaining it."

"Ross, why would I watch that?"

"I just thought you would be interested in knowing how our cells worked. . ."

"If I watched every video, and read every article you sent me, I would have a full-time job."

"Well I *did* have a full-time job, and I still had time to watch and read all of them."

"Fine. But why are you even giving me *activities* in the first place? What activities do I give you?"

"Everything I ever do is for you. And I mean that."

"That's not true. It always has to be what you want. Your books, your movies. Your luxury apartments. You think your way is better than mine."

She got up and started putting our dishes into my dishwasher.

"Wait. Wait! Just stop!" I told her. "Let me do it. You're going to do it wrong and they're not going to get washed properly, and then I'm going to get mad and then you're going to start crying and leave me here all alone. And I don't want any of that."

We sat half-upright on my bed, Lora comfortably in my arms, resting the weight of her head against my chest and shoulders, as I navigated the rather clunky *Woody+* user interface on my "smart" TV. It was perfect. I was free from the inescapable feeling of doom and temporal distress that had dominated my short adult life. I was rich, I was holding the woman I loved, and we were watching my favorite filmmaker's first foray into Serious Drama. It was perfect. Throughout the film I placed well-received kisses on Lora's cheeks and neck. I felt satisfied in a way I hadn't in a while.

"So what did you think? It was certainly *Bergmanesque*, but I have to admit, he seemed astonishingly assured in his first drama," I said, after it was done, plagiarizing a Roger Ebert quote that I'd read on the film's Wikipedia page.

"I liked it. You know I always love Diane Keaton."

I stood up and walked over to my desk. "Do you want to draw on my new iPad? I got the Apple Pencil, and they say it's good for drawing."

"Why did you get that?"

"Well, I guess partially because I don't really care about money anymore, and also so you can draw me nice little digital pictures while I'm in the shower."

Lora smiled.

"Okay, here, take this, I'm going to take a shower. So you have like five minutes."

～

I put my silver-lined anti-microbial bath towel in the dryer (to heat it up) and then locked myself in the bathroom, performing additional flosses and rinses of any spots I might've missed in Brooklyn, or any new uncleanlinesses I might've acquired during my F train ride over. After some scrubbing, I felt satisfied with my state of sanitation and hobbled nudely to fetch my towel from the dryer. I didn't seem to mind Lora seeing me stark and dripping.

"Okay, your turn," I said as I got dressed, pulling a pair of silk-like cotton underwear out of the dresser next to my bed.

"Look, Ross. You should know that I'm not in 'the mood' . . . *at all.*"

"You think I *am* in the mood? You think I'm just some *horny guy?* You think that's what this is about? Why would you say something like that? What a rude thing to say. After everything I've done for you tonight."

"Well you don't have to make me feel so *guilty* about it."

"Well maybe if I had a *brother* who was in *Zoolander 2* (2016) you would be in a different mood."

"Oh." She seemed sincerely sad, surprised, even. "I didn't know you knew about that."

"I know all about it. It had me all set to blow my brains out directly into the . . ."

"Come on, Ross, you and I were broken u—"

"It's fine, really. It's not your fault. Here, just take these," I handed her a 500-mg turmeric pill (contains curcumin, an alleged anti-inflammatory agent) and two 500-mg organic gelatinized maca root capsules (may boost libido in men and women), "and then a shower, and we'll see what happens. That way we don't have to interrupt anything later on, if we find ourselves, in . . . some sort of *mood*."

"That's fair," she took a sip from her stainless-steel water bottle and swallowed all three pills.

I looked at her digital doodlings while she showered. A little cartoon, Alvy Singer telling an LAPD officer via speech bubble "Don't take it personal." I was charmed. I loved Lora Liamant. She came out of the bathroom looking fantastic. It's no one's business what her unclothed body looked like, so I won't be describing it. Why would I want to? She looked good. Amazing, even, and had only gotten more attractive since I'd broken up with her, which I mentioned earlier. I would've preferred that she looked worse, even. She was approaching a point where she'd soon be getting so much attention from so many men, that poor Ross wouldn't stand a chance. It was going to be a nightmare.

"You're looking good," I told her.

She acted as if it were understood, etc, etc. "You too, Ross." I think she might've even meant it.

"Well remember, men peak at like fifty-five, and women peak at maybe twenty-two, so you really ought to lock me down while you still can."

"Thanks. What a terrible thing to say."

"I'm sorry. I've missed you terribly. I've spent . . . every minute of every day thinking about you and thinking about how I'd behave when I finally saw you again. You've missed me, right?"

Lora blushed as I ran my hand through her hair. "Of course."

"But you haven't been freaking out like I have?"

"It comes and goes. Sometimes I miss you more than others."

"Well this is urgent. This is of infinite importance. And I understand that I'm not 'fun' because I don't 'toke,' or 'light up,' or 'drink' 'beer,' but can't you see how silly these things are? That they're not actually fun or exciting? That if we don't get married soon, your life will just be terrible. No one who smokes weed and drinks alcohol has a job! Sure, it's fun for a bit, to throw the ping pong balls into the cups of beer, and then drink the beer, or whatever that game is, but isn't it *more* fun to have a house and a family and a stable career where you do the same thing every day and don't have to worry about surprises and spontaneity?"

"Ross, listen to yourself. You have to respect me, and the things I enjoy, and how I want to conduct myself. How would this ever work if you can't do that?"

"I will do *anything* you tell me to. I am *desperate* for your affection and approval."

"And this talk of marriage. You can't get married. You're only twenty-three."

"Oh, well I bet you would be more interested if I were *24* (2001–2010)."

"Ross . . ."

"Do you get it? Like the name of the show?"

"Yes. I get it."

"Just come here."

We fell into a passionate fit of groping and kissing. I had been studying up on *techniques* from some of the smuttiest grownup sources I could get my hands on, like *Cosmo* and *Teen Vogue*, and she seemed to be responding well. Lora, too, seemed to have some new tricks, which I appreciated, and then resented, naturally.

Then, at exactly 10:00, as we were finding ourselves increasingly enthused, my Roomba began its scheduled daily cleaning, which I'd (stupidly!) hit the snooze button on several hours earlier. It was hissing and whirring, running all over my apartment, sucking up whatever small crumbs it could get its jaws on. Oh, I was livid.

"Sorry, that's my . . . vacuum."

Lora laughed. But I was not at all amused. I jumped off the bed, fully nude and jiggling, and ran after the Roomba as it scurried all about the floor, evading my clutches, blindly bumping into everything in sight. I only needed to press its single dorsal "STOP" button, but it was dragging me all over town, eventually escaping to a robot-friendly hiding place underneath my couch. Fatigued, humiliated, I got on my knees, buttocks protruding into the air, and reached my arm between the floor and the sofa, finally managing to stop the thing. I let out an exasperated "Woo!" when it was all over, and walked to the sink to wash my hands.

"Sorry about that. This is what happens when you live in Gadget World."

"It's fine."

We picked up right where we left off. I really put in a tremendous effort, unlike anything anyone had ever seen before.

"That was great, right?" I asked afterward.

"Well . . . it's always fun with you, Ross."

We showered (together), and resigned back to my bed, where I fed her from a bowl of organic diced pineapple and some Shaloub's sugar-free monk-fruit-sweetened sorbet, glancing, intermittently, at something silly on my TV, I think *Sleeper* (1973), but I can't really remember. I dressed her in my long cotton socks, men's underwear (which looked very nice on her), and a large Japanese cotton T-shirt. I felt satisfied, relieved, wholly depleted of dread.

"Oh! I almost forgot." I jumped off the bed and ran over to my pantry where I picked up a package of Kirkland nicotine gum and held it up for Lora to see. "I got this for you at Costco!" I smiled. "I was reading about the best types of nicotine gum, and they say Costco makes really good—basically the best—nicotine gum for the price."

She sat up on the bed and looked at me confusedly. "Why would I want to start chewing nicotine gum, Ross?"

"What do you mean *why?* So you can stop smoking and vaping and gradually be rid of your nicotine addiction."

"I didn't tell you I wanted that," she shook her head around, disgustedly, as if *I* were the bad guy.

"Sure, but I did something *nice* for you, to *help* you. Why would you want to be addicted to something? And you're just being *mean* to me about it."

"Ross, it's just. This whole thing. It's like we're dating again. And you *know* I don't want that. I'm going to be single for a while, Ross. I'm having a lot of fun."

Oh. Oh! I had thought we *were* dating, after everything we'd just done together. My goodness. "Listen to yourself, Lora. It's not *good* to be single. It's terrible. You need to stop thinking your life is *Sex and the City* (1998–2004) *and* start preparing for the worst. Like, think of the potential catastrophic outcomes. You're totally dealing with an asymmetric risk-reward payoff here. I mean, you read *The Easter Parade* (1976), you see what happens when women get too cocky, stay single for too long. It's terrible. I'm trying to help you minimize misery."

"You didn't even read *The Easter Parade* (1976) until I *gave it* to you!" she said, her voice sounding strained, near tears. "You always do this. You always have some *reason* why my way is stupid and imprudent and risky and *your way* is smart and well-adjusted and *obvious*. We were having a nice time, Ross, and then look at what you did. You just had to bring rules, and scaremongering, and . . . and . . . product reviews into the bedroom. What kind of person looks up the best type of nicotine gum to give to his ex-girlfriend? I hate this. I hate this. I hate this. I really wanted to stay friends with you, Ross, and you just always have to do stuff like this. I hate it I hate it I hate it."

"Okay, okay, fine. Calm down. Sheesh!" I threw my hands up into the air and walked over to the bed and picked up the sorbet bowl to take it to the dishwasher. "Let's just brush our teeth and go to bed. To sleep. I'm sorry. I'm sorry. I'm a bad guy." Oy gut.

Ten

For a while there, with Lora, during our evening together on Roosevelt Island, things seemed to be going well. Didn't they? There was promise of a near future together. And then she whacked me over the head with that twenty-first-century bunkum about wanting to "enjoy being single" for a while. Which really meant she wanted to enjoy . . . no, no, I won't say it, it's too upsetting. But rest assured, I wanted nothing more than to blow my brains out and throw them directly into the nearest East River after she told me that she wasn't interested in resuming her role as my one-and-only. She also finally unshared her location with me on the *Find My Ex-Girlfriend* app, which meant I wouldn't be able to compulsively check her whereabouts anymore. The whole thing ended so poorly, I wondered if it might've been a mistake to see her at all. Perhaps if I'd waited a while before seeing her, she would've missed me in a more meaningful way.

The biggest change I noticed (re: Lora) was how much ground I'd lost with her. When we were first dating, every tick and oddity of mine charmed her. My strict schedules, my many supplements and gadgets, etc, etc. These things made me seem *cool* and *original* in her eyes. But during the most recent post-breakup "visit" we'd had, I could tell she found all of my idiosyncrasies to be not charming and cute and quirky, but rather neurotic and annoying.

"Fine," I thought to myself, a few hours after she left, "that'll be a clean break. I'll find someone new, someone *better*, who's fascinated by me the way Lora used to be." It was clear that if Lora was no longer impressed by me, things couldn't work between us; I would be left fawning over an attractive woman who was flaky and elusive and insufficiently obsessed with me. How could that be good? That would never do at all. My upbringing simply wouldn't allow me to love any woman who didn't treat me like her special little genius.

I spent a few hours search-engining things like "meet smart women," and "meet women who don't do drugs," and then finally "meet women clean," which yielded the most promising result. An ad. An ad for a new dating app, *Rawr* (formerly *Cleanr*) (pronounced "raw-er"), that mandated its members receive frequent and vigorous STI (sexually transmitted infection (formerly sexually transmitted *disease*)) screenings in the form of weekly blood and urine tests. This was *perfect* for me, as someone who finds condoms absolutely disgusting (especially in literature). The app required a ten-thousand-dollar security deposit (chump change), in the event that you *transmit* something ("something") to someone ("someone"). It was perfect for a man of my means, and it would allow me to meet literate women and become *intimate* with them (to a degree so many other apps couldn't guarantee safely . . .). It was so perfect, in fact, that if I didn't download it and put down the five-figure security deposit, I would've thought I'd imagined it entirely.

~

But as it turned out, the Roosevelt Island Hospital wasn't an approved location for the *Rawr* STI blood test, and so I had no choice but to have my blood drawn in Brooklyn, which wasn't terribly inconvenient, since I had to get back home anyway after leaving Emily unattended for almost eighty hours while I was being a pervert on Roosevelt Island.

"Hey! I haven't heard from you in days. How was Lora?" Emily asked from the kitchen when I walked back into our penthouse in Fort Greene, Brooklyn's *The Fort*.

I put down my backpack and kicked off my shoes. "Uh . . . we, well, we decided we're going to give each other a little space. For now."

"That was your idea?"

"I'll tell you about it later," I grumbled back on my way into my bedroom where I grabbed my passport and health insurance card to bring to the hospital.

Walking through the streets, I felt as if the teens in my neighborhood, out in groups, dressed coolly, enjoying one of the last nice days of the year, were staring at me, judging me, as if they knew I was on my way to the Brooklyn Hospital Center to have my blood drawn and tested for diseases that you get from being a pervert, in order to sign up for an app where I can meet women to be a pervert with without fear of giving or getting any of those pervert diseases.

"Hi, I'm uh, checking in for Ross Mathcamp," I said at the front desk of Brooklyn Hospital Center.

"Yes, we have you right here. If you'll just take a seat in the grownup waiting room, a nurse will come get you shortly," the secretary replied from behind a wall of glass.

After a few minutes, a woman named Jennette, dressed in loose-fitting floral nurse attire, called my name and escorted me into an examination room.

"Okay, baby, just take your shoes off and stand right there, on top of that scale, so we can weigh you." She fiddled with the sliding block on the scale for a moment and then wrote down my weight.

"You know," I smiled at her, "I used to be a nurse, I mean, I technically still *am* a nurse. But I'm taking some time off, since my parents died."

She made a sound like *aww*, then said, "Well I'll pray for them, Ross, and you, and your family. Now what is it you're here for again?"

"Doesn't it say on there?" I replied.

"Let me see." She looked down at her paper, squinted, frowned, then said, "Oh, you're here for that new *blood test*. I'll be right back." She shook her head disappointedly.

A cold breeze was haranguing my arms, just tickling me, making me uncomfortable, generally. My body descended into a shiver as Jennette came back into our little room, carrying a long tube and a hypodermic needle.

Joking, I tried to lighten the mood with a taste of my famous wit. "You don't have phlebotomists here? They make you do everything here?"

Jennette snapped back at me, "Look, boy. I don't know what kind of rich-ass hospital *you* worked at. But you're in Brooklyn now. Don't think I don't know what you're getting this test for. I see who made the appointment. I know you're here for that new nasty-ass app. You're here tryna get a test so you can have raw-ass gay-ass gay sex with other men. That's a sin you know. You're making a mockery of God every time you use your body like that, you know."

"Jennette, Jennette! I think there's been a misunderstanding," I pleaded. "You have me all wrong. I'm getting this test so I can have unprotected sex with *women*. The way God intended. Wouldn't you agree that condoms are totally unnatural and a mockery of God's creation? A *perversion*, if you will?"

"Oh . . . They got women on that app now? Okay, then. I'm sorry, honey. I had you read all the wrong way." She laughed to herself. "You know, since you mentioned you used to be a nurse and whatnot."

"That's understandable," I replied, and then we both shared a laugh together as she placed a flexible fabric bandage on my arm.

"We'll get these results to you by the end of the week, Ross. Good luck. I hope you meet someone special," she winked at me as I walked out. What a nice lady, right? Really, I mean it. She was lovely other than the brief few moments when she thought I was a gay man.

～

A few days later, I got word (an email) from *Cleanr Labs Incorporated Inc. (a Delaware Corporation)* that my urine and bloodwork had come back. That I showed no signs of syphilis or gonorrhea or any of the herpes simplices. No AIDS (obviously, I'm circumcised and straight). No HPV.

No chlamydia or trichomoniasis. I was given a clean bill of health, which was to be expected.

These spotless test results unlocked (for me) a digital carousel of uninfected women to finger and swipe through in the *Rawr* app's user interface. For the most part, women at my age (twenty-three) are extremely annoying. Constantly talking about their favorite early 2010s NBC sitcoms (whereas I'm partial to the good old days of *Frasier* (1993–2004) and *Becker* (1998–2004)), rap music, drugs, and allegedly "liberal" causes that the CIA had tricked them into caring about. And this is just how they advertise themselves on dating apps. Although, perhaps they don't realize how unoriginal they're being since they can't see what their fellow females are posting. Sort of an epistemic blindfold they're wearing, unable to spy on their competition—instead faced with countless men (men seem to outnumber women 3:2 on most of these dating apps), countless disgusting men with profiles describing their love for fishing and sneakers, or whatever it is that other men my age care about. I have no idea. I'm wearing the blindfold, too, I suppose.

I had Emily take photos of me seated at the head of our dining room table, wearing sunglasses, holding up an upside-down copy (as if I were reading it) of *Finnegan's Wake* (1939) to be used on my *Rawr* profile. With some other older pictures of me with my hair at different lengths (you want to keep these broads guessing, on the apps, you know) mixed in. My "occupation" read: "Nurse / Orphaned Heir," and my "Song of Songs" (the app's term for the musical accompaniment to your photo slideshow) was Lit's "My Own Worst Enemy" (1999), a personal favorite of mine.

Several swipes later, I'd made my first "match," with a woman named "Madison," age twenty-four, who seemed like the sort who would be interested in me. The sort of blotchy-skinned woman who enjoys irony and whose photo showcase showed her dressed in light-wash denims, surrounded by books. A plain-looking woman, by any definition, but her face had something smart about it that made it seem like she was well aware of herself. Which is to say, I could tell that she was clearly of above-average intelligence, just based on the way she was frowning into the camera. Also, her "Song of Songs" was "Seasons of Love" (1996) from the *Rent: Original Motion Picture Soundtrack* (2005), which I thought was very ironic and funny, at the time.

"Good afternoon, Madison," I wrote to her.

We struck up a conversation. I kept asking her if she went to Bard College, since she dressed and looked like she had gone to Bard College. She told me that she did not graduate from high school, which I thought was some sort of ironic dating app joke, but as I pressed her on it ("so what? You have a GED?" etc, etc) she finally wrote to me—and I quote this directly from my mobile device, i.e., this is an entirely real message I received from a real life woman named Madison—the following message:

> > Dude I've talked to a lot of dudes on here. It's something I like to do when I'm drunk. I've talked to dudes from all corners, mostly Columbia grads and professors, and purely because they're annoying and so very simple. You're one of the more annoying dudes.

What? *Me?* Annoying? Panicked, I made an apology, explained that I was "really not like that," etc, etc, that my parents had recently died, that I was a feminist (as the guardian for my thirteen-year-old sister), etc, etc.

> And I've never ingested any drugs or alcohol <

I added after my more sincere spilling of facts.

> > That's kinda freaky man

she replied, trying and failing to be clever.

> You a Jehovah's Witness or something?

No. But I should add that I *do* take amphetamines almost every <
day. But they come from a Jewish doctor, so I don't think that
counts as drugs.

> Oh, of course. As long as they're from a Jewish doctor . . .

Eventually, I lost control of the situation again, spending time texting
about my life insurance money, my credit score, my investing my money
in ninety percent stocks / sixty percent bonds, etc, etc, causing her to
say to me:

> You tell me all the things you would tell a potential landlord

and when I tried to deflect and diffuse:

> The defensiveness is really unattractive
> Even if it's half ironic

I don't know why this woman was being so mean to me on the dating
app. We'd both pressed the necessary buttons that signaled we wanted
to have unprotected sex with each other, right? So why was she acting
mean, and why was I acting defensive? Shouldn't that tension have been
alleviated by the dating app contract of "we both already *agreed* that we
want to have unprotected sex with each other"? My Madison was buck-
ing all the strict rules that I'd previously understood about dating app
women. I was desperate to meet her.

Hey <

I wrote back,

versation, up to this point. I don't think you were getting a fair
idea of what I'm all about. You should come over to my apartment on Roosevelt Island this weekend, and I should be able to
change your mind.

> Sure. Whatever, babes

she wrote back.

∾

The next Saturday, I was helping myself to a cold one (a cold shower,
which I had read can make you smarter, improve mitochondrial function,
and increase testosterone levels) in my professionally spruced Roosevelt
Island apartment. I had sprung for the *Rawr* (formerly *Cleanr*) app's professional housekeeping service (called "The White Glove Experience")
who, for half a grand, will come to your apartment and sweep and mop
and wipe and scrub all of the necessary (and many of the unnecessary)
surfaces a few hours before the woman you invited over for unprotected
sex is scheduled to arrive.

   In an effort to seem "cool" and "not uptight," I asked Madison to
arrive by 9:00, which seemed like the time a normal person would invite
a casual sex partner over. The ideal time was probably something like
8:37, but people really get freaked out when you give them jagged numbers like that, even though no one ever actually shows up *exactly* at the
nice round number you give them. In the hour or so I had to prepare
before Maddy's arrival, I went through my bathroom cabinet to make
sure there was nothing incriminating (weird skin creams, womanish
cosmetic supplies, etc, etc) that could make me seem vulnerable. A Lora
artifact caught my eye. A small transparent cylinder filled with plastic
toy sharks with a sticker that read "BUCKET OF SHARKS" that she'd
given me as a gift several months earlier.

"I got these for you at the aquarium," she said as she pulled them out of her bag one evening, back in February, shortly before the breakup.

"Are you high?"

"What do you mean?"

"Are you on drugs right now? Are you on like mushrooms, or something?" I asked her.

"Well, I mean, I had a bit of an edible a few hours ago . . . why?"

"What am I supposed to do with these plastic toy sharks? I just . . . you're just doing drugs and bringing *junk* into my apartment."

"So you're mad at me," she said.

"No, stop it. I'm not *mad*, I just, I just wish you wouldn't show up here . . . under influences. It makes me feel like you're bored by me. And I don't like having to deal with you on all these—"

I won't bother transcribing the rest of that; it was a suffocating memory to uncover (along with its associated trinket). I felt sick to my stomach, standing there in my bathroom with a dating app whore on her way over, realizing how much of a *mamzer* I'd been with Lora (a Ross in need of reform). I stashed the bucket of sharks away in my backpack to save for later, and sat on my couch, doing breathing exercises in an attempt to lower my heart rate before Madison's arrival.

Around 9:08, or some time similar, the "intercom" in my apartment buzzed and I pressed the button that signaled I was expecting a wanton visitor, and that she should be sent up immediately. I gave myself another few deep breaths, swallowed a 500-mg Phenibut pill, and walked slowly (not too eagerly!) over to the door when its bell finally dinged.

"Hey," I smiled widely at her as I opened the door, "you made it."

"Oh this place sucks," she said, taking off her shoes. She was wearing a dark green jacket, and a black sweater underneath, with tan pants. For the most part, I find it obnoxious when men describe women's breasts and butts and faces in prose. It's just . . . I mean, it feels like a waste of time. So I'm not going to get into that. But if you really must know, this woman was not special looking. Shaped homely, with light brown hair, she looked like a very cool elementary school teacher.

I walked over to the kitchen counter and picked up a grapefruit, which I had wanted to eat earlier but didn't, for fear of her walking in on me, in the middle of the act, so to speak, and then it would seem like I had planned it, timed it or something, which is an impression I wanted to avoid giving. "Do you want some of this grapefruit?" I asked, digging my fingernails in, breaking through the crust; from there it was a relatively simple peel job. "I like to have a grapefruit at night, before I have sex with strangers from the internet . . . but we can share this one. I'll let you have a few slivers, if you'd like."

"No, that's fine. I have to say, this place really is terrible, Ross. Even worse than I had imagined. And remember, I thought very little of you before."

"Why do you say that?" I sat down on my sofa while she kept looking around.

"Oh it's just *exactly* what I expected you to have. You're just so typical," she was opening my cabinets, going on tippy toes and inspecting my plates and bowls, crouching down to the lower levels to look at my pots and pans. "It's just psycho. You have an autistic apartment. Is this a carbon steel pan?"

"Yes, it's really good for—"

"Yeah, yeah. You're so boring, Ross." She walked over to my refrigerator. "Look at this, look at this fridge. It's just full of *pills*. And not even cool ones. You're taking exactly the things I thought you would be taking. Every guy really is the same."

I tore off another slice of grapefruit and plopped it into my mouth. "Where are all these men you're meeting? These men who are *just like me*? I don't know *anyone* like me. Why do you get to meet all these guys? I want to meet them. I would like to be friends with these people," I said, laughing slightly and nervously.

She walked back over to me pertly. "Actually, I will take a piece of that grapefruit, babes."

I handed her a segment and after she'd put it into her mouth, she took off her shirt (I had the heat on very high, for her sake, naturally), revealing a pale stomach and a number of tiny inexpensive-looking tattoos. "Your books are so *gay*, Ross."

Staring at her nude stomach, her arms, her chest, her bra, "What do you mean they're gay?"

"I hate this. Wow. I hate this. At first I thought this was alphabetical, you have *Great Expectations* (1982) by Kathy Acker next to *Great Expectations* (1861) by Charles Dickens. But then you also have your DeLillo next to your Deleuze. Oh I *hate* you. Oh this is so *annoying*."

"Is that how you pronounce that?"

She kept going through my bookshelf, which is actually very cool and smart, even if she didn't want to think so. "You're sick, Ross. You have *The Conscience of a Liberal* (2001) by Paul Wellstone, and *The Conscience of a Liberal* (2007) by Paul Krugman. And then *The Dead* (1973) by Joyce Carol Oates, and *The Dead* (1914) by James Joyce. Haruki Murakami and *Ryu* Murakami. *Zadie* Smith, and *Dodie* Smith. What is this? What is the joke here, Ross? That you only have books and authors whose names sound the same? And that's supposed to be funny in some kind of ironic way? Why is that funny? Explain to me why you're so much smarter than everyone for buying pairs of books whose names and authors sound similar, Ross."

"Those are just the books I was interested in." I got up to rinse my hands off after finishing the grapefruit.

"And what about this? You have *Calculus* (1967) by Michael Spivak, and then *An Invitation to Applied Category Theory* (2019) by David Spivak. What, you know category theory too?" She started flipping through the book. "Or is that just to impress girls you meet on dating apps? Tell me the definition of a functor, Ross. What's a functor, if you're so smart?"

"I'm planning on getting around to that . . . eventually, I mean, well . . ."

"OH!" She really scoffed here. The noise she made was terrifying. Followed by a sour contortion of her boring and maculate face. "And this, this is just appalling." She pulled out a stapled set of papers I had in a folder on the bottommost shelf. "You printed this. You printed this out yourself, Ross. This is Alexandra Bellow's PhD thesis from Yale. You've read this? What is wrong with you? Why would you have this? Just so you could have two Bellows?"

"Well," I sat back down on my bed while she continued snooping through my things, "I guess after reading *Ravelstein* (2000) I was fascinated by her character. Although lately I feel a lot more like a *Herzog* (1966), it's kind of funny actually, my—"

"Shut up, just please, shut up. Please."

"Why?"

"I just feel sorry for you, babes. You're just some gay Jewish loser, desperate to impress women. Just admit you're horny, babes. It's okay. Just say it. Say, 'I, Ross, am horny. And my horniness makes me do ridiculous things to impress women.'"

"I'm *LONELY!*" I replied, shouting semijokingly.

"You *should* be, babes. You're a pathetic character. I mean, you're terribly unlikeable. Let me just say, that you are one of the most transparent frauds I've ever had the displeasure of meeting on any dating app. You're just some guy who thinks he's smarter than everyone because he's rich and Jewish. And then you think that because you're 'ironic' or 'self aware' or whatever that you can't be criticized. You're such a cliché, babes. I feel like I've met you a thousand times before."

Now I was actually starting to feel hurt. "What? Why are you saying this as if you're so original? Some woman who lives in New York City who's depressed and mean, and has tattoos and does drugs and meets men on her phone and has sex with them after insulting them?

Why is *that* original? Why is that more novel than me having vitamins and a clean apartment and a collection of books?"

"Because"—she walked over and sat down next to me on the bed, grabbed me and kissed me on the mouth, then pulled away—"because you're a *hack*. You don't know math, you don't know *anything*, you're not as clever as you think you are, it's *weird* that you live on Roosevelt Island. It's not cute or funny. It's stupid. I feel like I'm getting dumber just being around you. Now say some more mean stuff about me."

"You're sick. I'm appalled at your behavior. Don't you think—"I said as she brought her thin lips up to my face for another kiss.

"You don't suffer, you don't struggle. Everything is just some joke, there's no *consequence* for men like you. It's all just some big ironic joke. And I hate you for that."

We just sort of stared at each other for a minute. Unsure of what to say. She put her hand on my pants and attempted to unzip. "So are you going to *nail* me now, or what?" she said.

"No," I replied disgustedly, shooing her hand away, "you're *mean*. Why would I want to *nail* someone who hates me?"

Eleven

Ever since that horrible woman came over, I haven't felt like myself. Really. Something's been horribly askew. I don't know if it's because of some kind of curse she placed on me—one of her (many) tattoos appeared to be some kind of pagan / occult symbol. And while I'm skeptical of religion and the existence of a benevolent and caring God, I have no doubt in my mind that people can find themselves cursed, afflicted, and tortured by spells of bad luck.

My parents were always superstitious, each in his or her own way. Mom, on more than one occasion, warned me never *ever* to be in the same room with a Ouija board. One such exhortation, from when I was eleven about to be dropped off at a friend's house for a sleepover, has remained memorable: "Believe you me, Ross, Ouija boards are nothing but trouble. They ruin lives. If I find out you and your little friends have been playing with Ouija boards, I will have you sent off to one of those camps in Utah for kids who kill their pets and swear at their teachers so fast your head will spin. Do you understand me? You will be sent off to a camp for kids with disorganized attachment disorders and fetal alcohol syndrome. Do you want that? No? Then don't play with any Ouija boards, tonight, or ever. If the kids try to take one out, go stand outside and call Daddy, and he'll come pick you up."

Dad had rituals of his own that revealed superstitious impulses. Having special shirts and underwear he'd wear to work when he was "slumping," which is to say, not selling a sufficient number of motor vehicles. He'd also repeatedly made clear to me: "Don't talk bad about people. Whatever you say about others will happen to you. Life has a way of catching up with you." Which, I don't really see why this would be true, but in my biased (so often fooled by randomness!) mind, it seems to happen quite often.

And this, moreso than my mom's warning against Ouijas, bounced around in my mind in the moments after Madison (the woman I met on the unprotected sex app) crudely stormed out of my apartment and called me "a truly, deeply pathetic guy" and a "coward the likes of which the world has never seen," and said that I would "pay" for what I "did to her." Despite my best efforts to seem unfazed by and unconcerned with the opinions of others (to an arguably pathological level), for the past few days I've found myself fixating on my near-sex-experience, and its resolution. How harsh the sound of her slamming my door was—it seemed she really put the full strength of her large left arm into pulling it shut, a final tantrum meant to torture me after I broke the news ("We absolutely will not be having sex, unprotected or otherwise. Now, I kindly ask you to leave") to her and sent her out into a car I'd ordered for her on an app on my phone.

And as an immediate consequence of her slamming shut my front door (due to my refusal to give her *every piece* of me . . .), my glass-encased *mezuzah* lost its connection to the upper right corner of my doorframe and fell to the floor, fracturing into three large pieces. "Well that's inauspicious," I said aloud in the voice I often use when there's no one around to hear me. "I don't even know what a mezuzah's for!" I exclaimed exasperatedly, again, to no one but myself.

But I knew I didn't like the idea of mine falling on the floor and breaking, especially because this had been given to me by my Bubbe, who told me to bring it with me to New York City, and touch it sometimes when I walked through the door, and then kiss my fingers after I touched it. And I actually *did* do this. Probably two or three times a week before that woman slammed my door shut and caused it to fall to the floor and break. But still, in the immediate aftermath of its breaking, I thought very little of it, instead focusing on trying to replay this negative interaction I'd just had with M (Madison).

For eighty-eight hours straight, I holed up in my apartment, lying around in bed, barely moving, only taking one shower a day, subsisting on nothing but low-carb protein bars and this new dissolvable "Greens" powder that claimed to contain a day's servings of vegetables (and fruits) in every scoop. I simply wasn't myself—my usual cool and unaffected self. During this seclusion, I accomplished absolutely nothing of productive value. Instead choosing to spend my time watching live (and some prerecorded) online "debates" between different video game players. Between video game players who wished to establish a genderless communist utopia, and video game players who wished to usher in an era of theocratic fascist authoritarianism. There were hours upon hours of these available on the internet on topics like abortion, women's suffrage, the right to own private property (including human beings), etc, etc, and despite my distaste for extremism (of all kinds), and lack of *skin in the game*, I found myself hypnotized by these videos. By the beautiful Socratic structure of it all. The left-wingers would say things like "and this exercise is not solely semantic, in fact, when we offer *prescriptive* definitions, we are actualizing our praxis by virtue of that very fact," to which the right-wingers would offer responses like "this is all just sick and demented. You need to be in jail. Locked up and executed by firing squad." It was enthralling.

And when I wasn't watching videos of debates, I was sulking silently in one of many contorted positions atop my bed, or perhaps sitting on the floor of my shower while water streamed onto my head, contemplating the futility of being Ross. Thinking about, how everywhere I go, I upset people, rub them the wrong way, and cause them to get angry with me. I found myself asking: "Is this all my fault? Am I just a bad guy? What if I'm wrong about all these firmly held beliefs of mine, and I'm simply alienating people for no reason?" Replaying moments from my early childhood and adolescence in light of this perspective. That perhaps I needed to become a totally different guy. The type of guy who goes on "benders" and vomits all over Las Vegas hotel rooms after staying up all night playing "poker" and doing "mushrooms." That maybe if I were just a little less risk averse (willing to *put myself out there*), then people would find me more agreeable. Less creepy and infuriating.

At 12 p.m., after three days inside, I came out of hiding, convinced of this perspective: that it was wrong to be Ross. I ran down the stairs of my building in a frenzy, in a truly manic mood, ready to do something drastic. I got out onto the cloudy autumn streets of Roosevelt Island and marched intently toward the Bread N Butter Market, one of a small handful of convenience stores located on the island. I walked up to the counter and the man began shaking his head at me: "No bathroom! No bathroom!" he kept saying.

"No bathroom! No bathroom!" I replied in agreement, raising my arms and straightening my fingers as if to signal, *don't shoot!*

"Here to buy cigarette," I added, leaving off the letter 's' in *cigarettes* because I thought it would help him understand me better.

"You? Cigarette?" he asked, nearly erupting with incredulous laughter.

"Yes, *me*, cigarette. Marlboro *lights*, in fact! One pack, please," I added, even though I didn't really understand what a "light" cigarette was or could be.

The man behind the counter handed me this golden pack of smokes, and I tapped my Watch against a proof of sale (POS) terminal until it buzzed slightly, giving me a haptic indication that my credit card had been charged for this pack of cigarettes. On the box, I read the words "LOW TAR & NICOTINE," which sounded reasonable enough to me.

Giddy from my edgy (it's truly subversive, I mean, basically the first thing anyone tells you as a child is never to smoke cigarettes, even if they're *light*) carcinogenic purchase, I skipped home, fantasizing about all the ways people (women) would soon be sympathizing with me once I became addicted to cigarette smoke. They'll look at me toking, taking long drags on a dart (who *knows* how many I'll have already had that day) and think, "Who is this mysterious man, who has the *guts*, to smoke? I bet *I* can fix him. He needs a good wife to take care of him, to save him, and turn him into a proper man." And soon I'll be back to my normal unaddicted self, but with the benefit of several months of nicotine-enhanced cognitive development, and the life experience gleaned from a brief excursion into vice.

It would be incredible. People would no longer think of me as some naive naysayer, bullying them for their substance abuse, but rather as a reformed addict, speaking firsthand from experience! I peeled back the lid on the cigs, took one out, and held it in my hand, already feeling cool, fiddling and fidgeting with it. It was going to be perfect. I put it back into the pack and the pack into my jacket pocket and waved hello to my doorman and walked into the elevator up to my apartment.

Calmer, now that I'd made my purchase and conceived of an escape hatch from my citadel of suffocating sobriety, I sat down on my green loveseat and again picked up the pack of smokes, pulling them out of my pocket and up to eye level. "Your golden ticket, Ross," I said to myself. "Why not have one right now? Smoke indoors, that way your whole apartment stinks of smoke and people think you're a laid-back *Bohemian*?" The idea wasn't half bad. I could smoke inside my apartment, hotbox the place, and then people (women) would come over and fancy me a carefree artistic type, living a relaxed island lifestyle of cigarette smoking and casual (yet passionate) ro-mance.

I plucked a single fag out of the box and with two fingers, held it up to my lips, miming my eventual first inhalation while watching an online video titled "HOW TO SMOKE A CIGARETTE (FULL TUTORIAL)" with over nine hundred thousand views. Empowering. I could really feel it: the entire world at my fingertips. But at about two minutes into the six-minute video, as I attempted to follow along, I realized I had neglected to purchase any lighters or matches from the man at the Bread N Butter Market. Typical, idiotic, forgetful Ross. You could have all the light cigarettes in the world, but without a lighter, they were useless! Perhaps I had a lighter, left behind from Lora or for candles or something. Or some matches taken from the maître d' desk at a fancy restaurant. I walked over to my "junk drawer," silently asking "please let there be something in here . . ." (although I'm not sure to whom) and instead only found a tangled nest of weird wires, several batteries of dubious levels of charge, and the three fractured pieces of my *mezuzah* which I couldn't bring myself to throw out after it had shattered several days earlier.

I just stared at it for a beat, then picked it up with my right hand, while holding the pack of MLs (Marlboro Lights) in my left hand. The poetry of it all was completely unsubtle—I wouldn't have believed it either if I hadn't physically felt these sacramentals in each of my sweaty paws. My parents immediately came to mind . . . their myriad warnings of "Remember, Ross, Mathcamps don't smoke" that I heard almost daily growing up. How at my seventh birthday party, they brought one of those guys with a hole in his throat to talk to me and all my friends (through one of those robot voice boxes pressed up against his throat hole) about how we should never smoke, and made us promise never to smoke or gamble.

They were really very funny, my parents. Funny, and wonderfully odd, often aware of these oddities in a way I haven't done an honest job of conveying. Choosing instead (regressively) to characterize them cartoonishly, as a couple of cretin monsters that made me into this retentive curmudgeon who hates anything resembling a good time. These were two people who cared about me and my sister and gave us everything we ever wanted. And in return, they asked only that we never smoke or do drugs.

Here was a brief moment of clarity, of being able to articulate, in words spoken softly by the voice in my head: that just because they'd never donated to NPR, didn't mean they couldn't love me. And that there was nothing fundamentally *broken* about me just because I was raised by a couple of small business owners who couldn't talk about "jazz" or identify the difference between a "Croque Monsieur" and a "Croque

Madame." That these were people who with their love and money and idiosyncrasy managed to rear two children who never crashed cars or shoplifted or pissed their pants after drinking too much beer. How many college professors, movie producers, hedge fund managers, or acclaimed authors can say the same about their children?

This moment, this limpid little moment of longing for mommy and daddy while staring at my *mezuzah*, was powerful enough for me to put my whole "it's wrong to be Ross" idea on pause, at least temporarily. At least until I replaced this messed-up *mezuzah* with a functioning one and ensured that that wasn't all it would take to make me feel normal again.

On my phone, I searched "jewish store" and found a shop called *Judaica Esoterica Warehouse*, which I'd never heard of before, but after reading the reviews which said things like "I make the trip over to Roosevelt Island just to come here once a month and say hello . . ." I figured it was probably more than sufficient for my needs.

The Judaica store was a twenty-seven-minute walk from my apartment, located at the northern tip of Franklin D. Roosevelt Four Freedoms State Park. When I arrived, I was surprised to see it was a three-story brick building, with a teal-painted gothic wooden door at its entrance on East Road, probably two hundred feet from the Queens side of the water, with tall wild grass and a chain-link fence separating the road and the river. Truly a weird-looking building, in the style of an old Quaker meeting house, but narrower and taller, with nine windows on each side (three on each floor). I walked inside, mumbling to myself to rehearse what I'd say to whoever was working there.

I'd anticipated something more like a Jewish Walmart, but this was more like a Jewish antique shop. Rather than organized aisles with hundreds of bins of Chinese-made tallitot, menorahs, dreidels, etc, etc, there were instead mismatched tables with half-melted Yahrzeit candles (one of which I'd be needing, but not quite yet), dusty books, silver rings, sandals, and other Israeli-looking things that I didn't quite recognize.

"Can I help you?" an older-looking Jewish woman asked after I'd been in there looking around for a few minutes, hunting for a single *mezuzah*.

I readied my rehearsed line "Hi, yes, uh, I need a *mezuzah*, mine broke, I have the broken one here because I wasn't sure if it would curse me to throw it out . . ."

"Ah, a *mezuzah?*"

"Yes, a *mezuzah*."

"Isn't that nice, such a handsome young man looking for a *mezuzah*. What a mitzvah! It brings me hope for the Jews, it really does. What's your name?" She was about fifty years old (but keeping it tight) with dark dyed black hair and a nose that, while large, looked good enough that you could've easily mistaken her for an Italian.

"I'm Ross," I replied. "Nice to meet you."

"Welcome, Ross. *Shalom.* I'm Rabbi Sikho. My husband and I own this store. I can tell you're Jewish, you have that Jewish look to you, Ross. But don't be shy. Please. You're home here. How did you find this place? This little . . . diamond in the rough we have," she said with a laugh.

"Well, Rabbi Sikho—"

"Please, call me Minrose, my first name. Or Rabbi, if you'd like."

"Well, Minrose, you see, I've been in something of a *spiral* ever since my parents died a few months ago, and a few months before that, I broke up with my girlfriend."

She made a concerned face. "Do you want to sit down, Ross? I have these new benches in from these hasids in Edison, New Jersey, who make these cute little upholstered benches."

"Sure," I said as we walked over to the back of the store and sat on a bench next to some rugs rolled up and leaned against the wall.

". . . and they're pushy, sure, the hasidim, but people seem to love buying these benches, so I keep a few in stock . . . you know?"

"Yeah, I know."

"But back to your little spiral, Ross."

"Yes, of course, my *spiral*. Well, I had this woman from a dating app over a few nights ago because I'm . . . you know, a sick guy."

"Ross, please, don't be so hard on yourself, you're on a journey, we all are. The Indians call it *dharma*, the Greeks and Carpatho-Rusyns call it *theosis*, but we're all trying, we're all going to end up in the same place some day."

"Well, I'll have you know, that I didn't do anything, sexually, with this woman from the dating app, and she was so incensed by this—the chastity of the night—that she slammed my door shut, and it shook my *mezuzah* off, and then it fell and broke."

"Well, at least something got smashed that night, huh, Ross?"

We both laughed at this.

"That's very funny, Rabbi."

"You know, I'm not *like* other rabbis, Ross," she leaned in toward me and put her hand on my leg. "You don't have to be afraid to tell me anything," she pulled her hand away and put it on my shoulder.

"Thank you. So am I in trouble? With this broken *mezuzah*? I've felt sick ever since it happened, and today I almost smoked some cigarettes, which my parents would've hated. And then I found the broken mezuzah again and started thinking about my parents and how they're gone and how much I miss them and how I didn't really appreciate them while they were here. And now I'm worried that I'm doomed or cursed or destined to a life of . . . forlorn misery, and that perhaps I was *already* cursed, and my parents dying is simply part of that curse."

She stood up and pulled on my arms, gesturing for me to stand. "Oh Ross," she said, wrapping her arms around me for a hug. "You're not cursed, Ross. I would be able to tell if you're cursed, and trust me, you aren't." She released me from her grip.

"That's good to know, Rabbi."

She appeared to be tearing up slightly, "You know, Ross. I lost my parents too, when I was young. It changes everything." She looked me directly in the eye and nodded her head. "Everything," she said.

I nodded and she continued. "Were they your best friends? Could you talk to them about anything?"

"No, but in death I've come to appreciate their perspective more."

"Isn't that always how it is, Ross? How does that old poem go?"

"What poem?"

"That old one. *They fix you up, your mom and dad. They turn your brain into their slave. They fill you with the thoughts they had, and add some extra, from the grave.* Is that it?"

"I'm not sure I know that one."

"You know, Ross," she said, standing up and walking toward the back office. "Oh, do you want a water bottle?"

"Sure."

"You know," she said, grabbing a little miniature water bottle, "if you want to hear from your parents, it's not exactly impossible . . ."

I took the bottle out of her hand and took a sip. "What?"

"I said, it's not exactly *impossible.*"

"No, I heard you, but I don't understand what you're saying."

"Well, Ross, I'm actually a *medium.* I'm quite good at talking to the dead—to their spirits. Especially if they were, you know . . . Jewish?"

"Rabbi," I was standing up now, "I'm sure you know much more about the *Mishnah* than I do, or whatever, but I'm pretty sure it's forbidden, like by Moses, to try to talk to the dead. Like I was raised pretty secular, but even I know about this rule."

"Ross . . ." She shook her head and showed a smile at me, "you know, there are six hundred and thirteen commandments in the Torah."

"I've heard that."

"And if we exiled people, or *stoned* them to death, every time they broke a tiny little one of them, well . . . then, well *our people* would've ceased to be any sort of people at *all*, a very long time ago."

"Uh huh."

"I mean, that's what being Jewish is about, Ross. It's about doing what you can to survive. Doing what you can to survive in a world where everyone hates you for what you are. You have to adapt to modern times. Simply ignore the parts of divine commandments that are no longer convenient to abide by. That's what religion is all about."

"That makes sense, I guess, Rabbi, I mean, I like to think of myself as pretty practical, for the most part. I'm basically *allergic* to dogma. You know, that and most other things." She laughed at this. "But I feel like . . . divination is a little different from eating a Chinese food dumpling with some shrimp in it."

"Believe it or not, Ross, there's a long tradition of women talking to spirits in Jewish culture. King Saul himself visited a medium in *Endor* to conjure up the spirit of Samuel. It's right there in the Bible."

"I didn't know about that, actually. But it's interesting that you bring this up, your status as a *medium*, because my mom, while she was alive, you know, was very very against any sort of occult trickery, Ouija boards, in particular, used to send her over the edge."

She grinned widely at this. "I can see that for her, Ross. But you have to keep in mind that people don't know what they want until you give it to them."

"What do you– "

"You should have seen the way my husband reacted when I came out to him as *queer*, Ross. He looked so . . . defeated . . . but now we have three kids together and have an abundantly happy partnership, and the sex just keeps on getting better . . . and we're just so damn happy!"

"I'm sure," I replied, scratching the wooden surface of the bench with my fingernail.

"What I'm trying to say is, your mom wasn't upset at all to hear from me. In fact, she reached out. She says hello, Ross."

I shivered and shuddered. "She's here . . . right now?" I asked.

"Yes," Rabbi Sikho replied. "But she's leaving. And your dad is coming over," the Rabbi was sitting across from me, staring into the distance in a mystical manner. "Your father says you look terrible Ross. He says you seem weak and unimpressive, and you're not honoring the family by being so sad and pathetic all the time."

"Ask him if he was murdered, and if I should avenge his death like Hamlet."

She nodded. "He says he doesn't know what that means, but that you need to stop feeling sorry for yourself and work on self improvement, that way you can win Lisa back. He says he and your mother both thought you and Lisa were very cute together."

"That's not her name . . ."

"I *swear* he's saying Lisa, Ross. Now he's telling me to tell you to quote 'grow a pair.'"

"Okay, fine. Tell him I appreciate it."

"He says you're lucky he didn't listen to you about the life insurance, and if he were alive right now and saw you acting like this, he would put you in something called an 'arm bar' and make you 'tap out.' He says you're making Jews look bad. You're embarrassing our entire race, he says."

"Is he mad?"

"No, it seems like he's having fun."

"Okay, I get it. I think that's enough. Thanks Dad, love ya man . . . I'm gonna go now, I'm gonna finish up in here and get working on becoming the sort of young man you'll be proud of."

"He says he loves you too and only pushes you because he knows you can take it."

The Rabbi gave me two hugs. One from my dad, and one from herself. "Oh, and I almost forgot," she stepped a dozen or so paces toward a shelf near a paned window. "You came for a *mezuzah*, didn't you?" she said as she grabbed one off the shelf. "Take good care of this, Ross. According to my seller, it once belonged to the brother of Ariel Sharon's mohel."

"I will. Thank you so much, Rabbi. I feel like you've given me so much to work with."

"Ross, please. It would be a *shande* if I didn't share my gifts with the younger generation. I could tell you were suffering when you came in here, so to see you now, with your brand-new mezuzah, with some advice from your parents . . . it brings me . . . a lot of joy, let's just say."

"I'm happy to hear that."

"And you know, if you ever want to get into any . . . *fun* with an older couple, I'm sure my husband would be *very* approving. You're definitely our type . . ."

"Uh . . . I think I'm alright. Thanks."

I'm still not sure how legitimate the signs and wonders of the psychic Rabbi were. There are of course, many things to consider. Can women even be Rabbis? Need she even be a Rabbi to harness necromantic powers? Was she communicating with the actual souls of my parents? With an evil spirit impersonating my parents? Was she simply performing a cold reading on me—or perhaps a not-so-cold reading, as I told her my full name, meaning she could've looked my parents up on a popular internet search engine when she went into the other room for a few minutes. But all of this was (and still is) immaterial to me

As I walked out of the Judaica Esoterica Warehouse, the potentially pseudepigraphal words of my father's poltergeist reverberated in my mind's ear. I *was* pathetic. A broken man. A man of inaction, cowering and fleeing from his own healthy desires. And worse than that, even, was the realization that I really had been living the life of a cheap stereotype of an urban J.

It was shameful the way I'd left things with Lora. So passive, so deferential of me. To let her walk out my door with nothing more than a peck on the cheek and a "we should do this again soon . . ." There was no confrontation, no expression of what *I* wanted, or what *I* felt entitled to.

All of this for no particular reason. You'll recall that my parents' death rendered me a man of myriad means. But my inheritance was being sidelined, socked far far away in a brokerage account accruing interest that'd never actually be used for anything. Inaction, my fatal flaw. You could inherit the whole world, but what use would it be if you're too meek to do anything with it while you're still alive? Well, obviously this would have to change. It would be a grave disservice to my deceased parents to continue on like this.

On my walk back home, I considered donating my pack of cigarettes to a beggar or vagrant, but then I realized first, that it would be wrong to hand out poison to a stranger, and second, that beggars and vagrants are practically nonexistent on Roosevelt Island anyway. So I took the pack of cancer sticks out of my pocket and hurled them directly into the nearest East River, where they fell and floated with a faintly perceptible plop.

Twelve

"And then . . . after all that, after that beautiful night we spent together, just as we're about to go to sleep in the same bed, she says to me: *'But don't think this means we're getting back together. Because we aren't.'*"

"*. . .*"

"Just think about how she said it. Think about the contempt for me with which she said it. And everything was going great, I was being a lovely host, I was being generous . . . in the bedroom, if you know what I mean."

"Yes, Ross."

"It was terrible. When Lora told me that, that she didn't need me anymore . . . But she also said she still loves me, that was clear, that we still love each other. So I've spent the past week or so since she left piecing this all together, and what's happened has become . . . obvious, to me. She's become much better looking, gotten attention from the younger brothers of famous actors, gotten a taste for Rossless life, of the attention she can wield with her looks, and she thinks she's *too good* for me. She thinks there are other people out there who have things to offer that I simply can't give her. And that's wrong, because I have basically unlimited potential, given my precocious intellect and even more precocious net worth."

". . . and those sexy legs."

"Sure, yeah. So I was up all night last night, I took some amphetamine salts, and I've cooked up this list of urgent actions to take. And I've identified the problem with me, the problem with Ross."

"There you go again doing my job for me."

"The problem, as far as I see it, is I am a Shylock, a shyster. A nickel nose? A yid? A hymie? Do you understand what I'm saying? That I am the archetypal weak and pathetic Jew? An anti-semitic cartoon character. And I'm sick of it, doctor. I'm sick of bringing shame onto my race. But I have a plan to fix it. I'm going to stop being such a cliché—become a better representative for my fellow *Members of the Tribe*. And in the process, win back the heart of Lora Liamant, restore my dignity, and, you know . . . establish myself as a real adult. I'm calling it The Goldberg Strategy. Which I think will make a great title for the book I'm writing. The Goldberg Strategy. Rolls off the tongue brilliantly, and features the sort of highbrow, lowbrow contrast that I seem to be obsessed with. Do you know about Bill Goldberg, doctor?"

"No."

"Okay, that's fair. People like you—snobs, like you, probably don't know about him. So I'll attempt to summarize. You're familiar with professional wrestling?"

"Heard of it."

"It was of great importance to my late father."

"Interesting . . ."

"So pro wrestling really took off in the late '80s, you know, you had the Hulkster, Macho Man, Jimmy 'Super Fly' Snukka, Jake 'The Snake' Roberts, etc, etc. And the brains behind all of this brawn was this guy Vincent Kennedy McMahon, who purchased, not inherited, but purchased—it's Freudian, Oedipal—the World Wrestling Federation—from his dad, Vincent James McMahon. And this WWF thing was really starting to take off in the '90s, so Ted Turner, who was making a killing off of CNN and the Atlanta Braves, decides to buy this small regional competitor called World Championship Wrestling. Blah blah blah, and by 1996, he's going head-to-head with Vince, throwing tons of money at his little wrestling project, and it becomes known as the *Monday Night Wars*, with WCW's *Monday Nitro* (1995–2001) going head-to-head against WWF's *Monday Night Raw* (1993—)."

"Uh huh . . ."

"And at first, Turner and this guy he'd hired, Eric Bischoff, were just poaching guys from Vince, just paying WWF stars to join the other side and play slightly different versions of their old characters, which was interesting for a bit. Until finally, he brought in this guy Bill Goldberg, who *really* put WCW over the top. This was his first real original invention. And it was all a scam, you see. Goldberg had the best body in the business, a truly monster physique, but he couldn't wrestle to save his life. So they would bring him in against some chump, get the crowd all fired up, and then Goldberg would throw him around a couple times, and then just tackle him—they called it 'The Spear'—and the match would be over in under two minutes. And they were actually able to do this a hundred seventy-three times. He had a one hundred seventy-three match winning streak, doctor. And people were so *stupid*, they didn't realize he wasn't actually a good wrestler. They didn't even realize their fake fighting was even *faker* than they knew. He was just an extremely jacked Jewish guy. Let me pull up a picture of him . . . Here, what do you think of this guy? And his muscles? Is that doing anything for you?"

"Oh, you know I only have eyes for you Ross."

"That's what I like to hear, doctor. But is this clear, what I'm doing here? How I'm *shifting my priors?*"

"Elaborate, just a bit more . . ."

"It's so clear in my mind. Consider Bill Goldberg versus Jon Stewart. Two of the most important men of my childhood. Jon Stewart's real name is Jon Stuart Leibowitz. He changed his name to seem *less* Jewish, and still, people think of him as the most Jewish guy. Bill Goldberg goes into a wrestling ring and just calls himself *Goldberg*, and somehow, when people hear that, and think of him, they think of this hypercompetent muscular man. Whereas Jon Stewart, despite the name change, the nominative rhinoplasty, if you will, was still the five-foot six nebbish making snide comments at a *desk* every night, making twenty million a year by being clever and mean and critiquing the *media*, which he also controlled somehow. So that's what this is, remove any schmucky schlemiel tendencies from my personality. Be like *Goldberg*, impressive, powerful, an intimidating representative for my Race."

"So you're going to start working out? You're going to become a much larger Jewish boy over the next few months?"

"That's funny. That's fine. That's part of it. I've made a list of all the things I need to do to become—or appear—*so* attractive, *so* competent, that Lora will be overpowered by me and my new offering."

"But Ross—"

"Oh I know what you're about to say. That love is never totally rational and reasonable and what might seem good on paper can't possibly be enough to *make* someone fall in love with you, or else every woman would be in love with the single most competent and handsome and wealthy man in the world, maybe *The Rock*, or something, you're thinking, you're planning on telling me. But you have it all wrong. That's not at all how you should be thinking about this, and it's a total misreading of what The Goldberg Strategy is all about. It's really all about overwhelming her, coming in like a ton of bricks, being so dazzling so quickly that she won't know what hit her, like Goldberg spearing the guy after two minutes and appearing invincible."

"Oh, I see—"

"So I totally ignore her for months on end, and then reappear, so handsome, so muscular, so physically fit, so compassionate, so well adjusted, so well read—so thoroughly *improved* from the Shylock she shooed away on Roosevelt Island that night—that before she knows it, she and I are standing in Las Vegas, telling each other 'We do.'"

"What made you go with this idea first, instead of say, finding some new woman to make her jealous? You think this is more clever, more *adult*? That's why you like it?"

"Well yeah, definitely. This is cased in self-improvement, and the end goal is marriage. I'd say it's awfully grown up. I'm probably one of the most mature patients you have. And don't even get me started on—"

"Fine, Ross. But what about after all this?"

"Probably start an organic baby food company, or run for some political office. I have a new ingenious policy idea that no one else even wants to *think* about. I was reading that twenty percent of police shooting victims with one gunshot wound died, versus seventy-four percent with five or more gunshot wounds. These numbers are from Chicago, by the way. So I'm thinking, doctor, that we just give the cops magazines with alternating real and rubber bullets. So they shoot one rubber bullet, one real bullet, one rubber bullet, one real bullet, etc, etc, etc, and then when they empty their clips, it's really only three real shots, at the *most*. I'm thinking we can get the police killings down from a thousand a year, to maybe six hundred. So why is no one suggesting this? This is why I need to get my voice out there, and save the country, the world."

"That's very cute. Like *you*, Ross. But even after all this, with the wife, with the baby food company, with the saved world, will you be *happy*? I'm not saying you *won't*. I'm just asking."

"I wish you could've seen me with Lora the other night, doctor. I was alleviated of every fear and anxiety. I was relaxed, I was at ease and comfortable with myself and my surroundings. And that's all I want. Lora alone would be enough to remedy my satisfaction deficit disorder."

"You're suffering . . . from an awful ennui, Ross. Too privileged to have anything to complain about, so you complain about everything. Too unstimulated to get any pleasure out of everyday life."

"Well that's why I have you prescribing me stimulants every month."

"I think this will be good for you. Self-improvement is always good. And a challenge, a powerful *want*, will have you getting out of bed, the inevitable obstacles will give you things to think about, and then you'll have to make choices. And live with them. It all feels like a very *adult* project, Ross."

"So you like it?"

"I *love* it, Ross."

"Yeah, but you love everything I say. Loving me pays your bills."

~

I got off the D train at Atlantic Avenue around seven, feeling "well adjusted" after my "therapy" session with Dr. Crispane. As I was exiting the station, I used the unlimited MetroCard I got as part of my agreement with the National Nurses Association union (which was weird since I walked to work on Roosevelt Island every day) to help out one of those guys who stands near the turnstile saying "Swipe? You got a swipe?" by letting him in, which made me feel really nice, and good, even though it cost me absolutely nothing.

I stepped out into the streets, tiptoeing around gratuitous globs of garbage and disposable face masks. It was a bit after sunset, not terribly dark, but colder than it should've been, which left me feeling vulnerable, as I was dressed in shorts, which I usually wear to my Crispane appointments in order to show off my boyish legs. About a block away from *The Fort*, on South Oxford Street, I saw a crowd of rowdy Puerto Rican-looking teenagers walking menacingly, so I crossed the street to the opposite sidewalk, where a pony-tailed Brooklyny-looking white guy (you know what I mean) approached me and said, "Give me your phone."

"Do you need to call someone?" I asked him. "They have those LinkNYC digital payphones everywhere. They're ridiculous. The city spent $300 million on them, and for what? For homeless people to watch porno? It's disgusting."

"What? No. I'm robbing you, man. Give me your phone, your watch, and your noise-cancelling wireless earphones." He took out a large "gravity knife," which are actually *illegal* to own in New York City.

"Okay, okay. You can put that away. I'm very young and weak, so you'd probably still have a great advantage over me, even if you were unarmed."

"Uhh . . . no. Just give me your phone."

"I'm going to, I'm going to. But it has a password on it. It'll only unlock if my face is looking at it. It's totally useless if it still has the

password on it. Unless you're going to use that knife to cut my face off
. . ."

"Oh I know all about the passcodes. Believe me, it has not been easy being a criminal lately, even with the defunded NYPD. First few times, I demanded people give me their wallets, but no one carries cash anymore, so the cards just ended up getting cancelled immediately. So those were total wastes of my threats and intimidations, you know? I just scared people for no reason at all. And that's not what I want."

"Yeah, I hear you, brother. That's a total lose-lose scenario. I have a lot of sympathy for you. It's getting harder and harder out there, for everyone."

"Yeah."

"So you want me to take the password of my phone?"

"Yeah, you're gonna want to go to settings, then click iCloud, first turn off Find My iPhone, obviously."

"Ha, yeah, wouldn't want me keeping *that* one on."

"Yeah, yeah. Okay, so now that that's off, then just go to General, Reset, and then click Erase All Content And Settings."

"Do you want my Watch, too?"

"Oh . . . it's one of those? No, why would I want that?"

"I thought you just said . . . sorry. Okay it's going. It's loading. Do you think it's safe for me to go now?"

"Can you just wait for it to finish, just in case it asks you for your password again?"

We waited for it to finish resetting itself, and when it was sufficiently wiped, I handed it off to him, and we thanked each other for making the process so painless.

Inside the apartment, Emily was sitting near the window, under a new lamp she must've just bought, reading some Walker Percy novel, which I resented, since he was nowhere to be found on the list of things I wanted her to read. Jarred, I went to the nyc.gov NYPD Crime and Enforcement annual "activity reports" for the past five years (since I've lived here), and found that on average, only four point three eight percent of robbery suspects were white during my time in New York. I mean, obviously with my understanding of statistics I knew I should've been skeptical of any man on the street, but I couldn't help but wonder why I didn't immediately run when that white guy approached me in the first place. I suppose I really had just internalized the pernicious stereotype that white guys with beards and ponytails and sandals are not likely to commit robbery. I took the online *implicit bias assessment* on Harvard.edu and it said I wasn't racist, so that was settled.

I guess I just felt bad for the poor guy who robbed me; had he just waited another few days, he would've been able to rob me and get the *new* iPhone, which I'd already preordered.

I went into the kitchen to grab a bottle of lemon-flavored bovine-collagen-infused water, and to let Emily know about an upcoming personnel change around the house.

"Hey, Em?"

"Yeah?"

"I just wanted to let you know, I invited my friend, Amanda Bauer, to come live with us, for a number of reasons."

"Is this part of The Goldberg Strategy?"

"No . . . well, not really. I wasn't even thinking of the GS when I invited her. I guess I realized there are a number of things that a brother can't possibly be good for. Things like makeup, and your period. You haven't gotten your first period yet, have you?"

"No . . ."

"Oh, boy. Well, from what I understand, it's got to be any day now."

"I know. I've been reading up on it."

"Well that's why I think it'll be good to have a woman around here. You'll like her, trust me. She's really been a great friend to me over the years. And her dad is a doctor, of sorts, so we'll be able to collect rent from her—from him. I already talked to Robert Shapiro about it this morning. He's drawing up the papers."

At the kitchen table I snuck a peak at Emily's pink maths notebook.

"Do you need help with this? What are you learning this week?" I asked.

"We just started taking derivatives. Doing the power rule."

"And you have no problem with it?"

"Not really."

"So you don't need anything from me?"

"No, I think I have it under control, thanks Ross."

"And you have a good grasp of what a derivative is? The instantaneous slope?"

"Yes."

"And you learned about the epsilons and deltas?"

"No, but I don't think I have to know that until I take Real Analysis."

I started walking back toward my bedroom. "Okay then," I said. "Let me know if you ever need me to help with anything then."

I felt terrible. I was phoneless, my sister hardly needed me, and I was quite possibly (probably not, but still) a racist for thinking my white male mugger wasn't a threat, initially. I recalled a time when Lora L. accused me of not caring about "doing good things."

"Well, I'm a nurse, right? That's pretty good, that's pretty *helpful*, don't you think?"

"Yeah, but you admit you just did that for the great pay. Do you ever do anything out of your own personal *goodness*?"

She might've had a point, and with my newfound fortune I was in a real position to take on some charitable endeavors—pro bono, so to speak. I fired up the website people go on to buy and sell used stuff and find roommates and prostitutes on my laptop computer and composed an advertisement in the services->education section.

FREE K-12 TUTORING FOR MINORITIES
Hello, I am a retired registered nurse and recent graduate of a prestigious private research university in Lower Manhattan. I am looking to give back to underprivileged communities (harmed by

the moronic education-policy-legacy of George W. Bush) by offering my tutoring services free of charge to any black children in
Brooklyn, Manhattan, or Queens. I would also offer my services
for free if you and your nonblack child are immigrants (or the children of immigrants) from a country whose average life expectancy
is below the United States' 79.11 years. This includes Uruguay,
Turkey, and Thailand, but excludes Cuba, Poland, and Slovenia,
among many others. Please do your own research on these figures
before contacting me.

I have a personal interest in literature and strong quantitative
training. I should be useful for any subject your child is struggling
with.

As soon as I pressed post, I felt satisfied with my activism and commitment to helping out the community. I knew I was doing the right thing.
And in the spirit of education, I went back into the living room with my
laptop to teach Emily a little more about the world she was born into.

"Hey, Em. Put that book down for a minute. I put together a
PowerPoint about the time Don Imus called the Rutgers Women's
Basketball team 'nappy-headed hoes.' It should take like a half hour. But
it's really important that you learn about this."

Thirteen

The real first step of The Goldberg Strategy, my new plot to radically self-improve within a radically small timeframe, was to renovate my physical capacity—the only metric by which I was unambiguously *below average*. IQ, net worth, pages read per year, nursing degrees, etc, etc, etc, all of these, I was in the top first percentile for. But my body, oh, my poor body, it was pathetic. People take one look at me and see nothing but a Yiddish Lilliputian. Consider that at 140 pounds (63.5 kg), I weighed-far less than the average (disgusting, but still) American woman, who weighed 166.2 pounds, and could probably best me in an "arm-wres-tling" match, which is just not good. There's nothing *Goldberg* about that.

And so, I found myself standing in shorts and sneakers atop the speck-led marbly rubber floor of *Mike Monad's Strongman Gym* in Pacific Park, Brooklyn. It was a rather "industrial" environment, on St. Mark's Place (in Brooklyn), with ceilings reminiscent of Home Depot or Costco, or IKEA. I'd chosen it as my means to muscularity because, of the four gyms within walking distance of my house, Mike Monad's Strongman Gym was the most personal, and the most willing to put its terrifying founder front and center. It was also right around the corner from Kith Brooklyn.

Mike Monad was a culturally Italian American south Brooklyn native with massive arms, huge shoulders, gigantic glutes, and gener-ously gelled hair—each of these features featured prominently in the many photos of him on his gym's internet webpage. The site was full of photos of Mike, dressed in his signature skintight meshy shirts (on this particular day, the day we first met, his was inscribed with the words "BIG LIFTS MATTER"), performing feats of strength in and out of competition.

"Ross! Good to meet you, buddy, you found the place okay?" he said to me as I walked out of the locker room for my 10:00 personal training appointment. Oh, yeah, another thing I've noticed about extremely jacked steroid-looking guys (like Mike Monad). I've found that they have much squeakier voices than they look like they ought to have, and they're also all always extremely friendly. And why wouldn't they be? They're enormous and masculine and have nothing to be bitter about.

"Yep, Mike. The directions you gave me over the phone were top-notch."

"Ha ha, that's what I like to hear. That's what I like to hear. "

". . ." I took a nervous sip from my glass water bottle.

"So tell me a little more about what you're trying to do, Ross. I know you're trying to get your girl back, but what does she want? Big muscles, or big strength?"

"Well, I guess I'd like to have more muscles and more strength. So I figured I'd come here and have you show me to how to lift weights—and by that I mean just lifting weights, to look and perform better, not like, doing Olympic style capital 'w' Weightlifting. I've read Mark Rippetoe's *Starting Strength* (2005) and I think those seem like reasonable exercises for us to do."

"Ha ha, sure, Ross. We got a lot of people coming in here who read that book. And—"

"And do they get jacked?"

"Bro," he smiled, "if you come in here, with a good attitude, and you stick to the plan, you'll have *phenomenal* results, bro. You believe in hard work, right Ross?"

"Absolutely, Mike. So let's get lifting, eh? Can we get lifting?"

"Whoa, whoa, whoa, Ross. I like your enthusiasm, buddy, I love it, but legally, for legal protection, Ross, I can't let you pick up a barbell today. Soon though."

He took me through a series of stretches and breathing exercises which taxed my beleaguered body. I was sipping every few seconds from my tempered glass water bottle, touching my toes (well, trying to), lunging all over, performing planks, etc. Mike Monad, bless his heart, told me I was doing "kickass" for my first warmup ever.

"Okay, okay. How you feeling, bro? Not too bad, right?" He gave me an enthusiastic smile.

"Not too bad." I felt terrible.

He asked me to grab two "kettlebells" and began instructing me on how to perform what he called "Romanian deadlifts."

"So you're going to want to push your ass all the way back, like this." He pushed his ass all the way back, keeping his knees semi-straight, and his back upright. "You should feel this in your hamstrings."

"Like this?" I asked him.

"No, not quite. Come over here in front of the mirror."

He brought me in front of a mirror so I could watch myself as I bent and squatted.

"See, your form is terrible, Ross. And that's okay, bro. That's why I'm here."

"That's why I'm paying you."

"Ha ha, exactly, exactly. Now watch how I'm *exploding* in my hips Ross. I'm taking off like *Superman*, Ross."

"Like this?"

"No, no. That's all wrong. Completely wrong and awful. But better. You're getting better."

We moved on to the "goblet squats," which asked that I held the kettlebell up to my mouth "like a goblet, or a big cup," and "squatted all the way down."

"How's this?" I attempted a set of six "goblet squats."

"Those are *great!* Those were *really* good, buddy. They're almost perfect."

After I'd grabbed my bag from the locker room, Mike Monad stopped me in the hallway for some final few words of wisdom. "Ross," he said, "I want to help you, bro. I want to help you get your girl back. But you gotta promise me you're gonna eat. Right now you're skinny,

Ross. You look like you eat like a *bird*, and that's fine—when you walk in here, you're entering a judgment-free zone. That's what the sign says, right? But you gotta eat until you're full, and then double it. I got some shakes that I sell, and they'll help you put on muscle. Just let me know if you wanna try some."

"I've actually already started eating like a pig, Mike. You should've seen me a week ago."

He laughed.

"But seriously, Mike," I went on, "I am going to be eating a *ton* when I get home."

He gave me a nice fist-bump style handshake, and said "Alright bro, I'll see you in a few days." That's the thing a lot of people don't understand about me. That I really get along superbly with guys like Mike Monad, guys who don't have psychiatrists and penthouses and nursing degrees. I grew up around people like that, normal people of normal intelligence. And I like them. I like them a lot more than my snobbier economic peers who only want to talk about things like "Žižek" and "David Lynch," as if those guys don't totally suck. I'm a man of the people.

I walked home and made myself a strongman smoothie. Chock full of essential nutrients and assorted anabolic add-ons. Creatine monohydrate, branched chain amino acids, egg-white protein powder (I can't have whey, I just can't. Even lactose-free whey protein isolates wreak havoc on my semitic stomach and skin. Everyone asks me if I'm lactose intolerant—and I don't know, maybe I am, but I know for sure that the lactose alone isn't the problem. There's something else in milk and dairy that causes me bodily harm. The lactose free products are just as deadly to me), L-Glutamine, a banana, some almond milk, blackberries, etc, etc. And it was lovely. That's the thing about smoothies that no one wants to talk about. You just put whatever you want into your brand new Vitamix A3500 and it's going to taste good, often even great.

I stood at the counter sipping my smoothie and prepared my InstantPot Duo SV to make four cups of white rice with coconut oil mixed in liberally. I'd spent a long time being skeptical of carbs, but in order to actualize my bodybuilding ambitions, I'd have to ingest about two hundred grams of carbohydrates per day. And the only nontoxic options for getting these carbs in my system (sans sugar) were white rice and sweet potatoes. Regular potatoes and bread and oats and other grains are all far too toxic, filled with lectins and mold spores that would make me wish I'd never been born.

~

I had about forty-five minutes to shower and brush my teeth and listen to the NPR hourly news report before a couple of college friends, Allie Miller, an avowed eco-Leninist, and Taylor Gonzales, an anarcho-syndicalist (who were a *couple*, I should add), were going to stop by to see my new penthouse apartment.

As I was about eight-elevenths done with the shake, my phone on the wall next to the door started to ring and so I answered it and said "yes, send them up," and within a minute or two they were standing in the foyer removing their shoes. Allie had dyed her hair gray and gotten an ironic lip piercing, which actually looked fine on her. Taylor—who is much more European and less Latinx-looking (blue eyes, strawberry hair, etc) than his name would have you think—was wearing a pair of painfully tight black denims and a yellow hooded sweatshirt that simply read "THINK!" in big bold letters.

"Look at this place!" Allie said. "And the neighborhood is great too. You're right down the block from that black-owned sex-toy store I've been meaning to go to."

"Uh huh," I replied.

"Really, Ross. How much are you paying for this?" said Taylor, kneeling on the floor of my foyer unfastening metal clamps on his leather boots.

"I don't know. Maybe like twelve grand a month? With the mortgage and the fees and everything."

We walked into the kitchen. "Oh, so you're rich now, Ross," one of them said.

"Do you guys want anything to drink? I have iced oolong, a ton of white rice."

"I'll take an iced tea," Taylor told me.

"I'm fine."

I poured the oolong. "And 'rich,' I mean, I don't know. You two are total wealth reductionists." You see, Allie was the daughter of a famous American political comedian, and Taylor's father was a former United States attorney general. "I mean, my parents left me a lot of money, but culturally, what did they know? They didn't go to college, they never learned about 'critical theory.' You two are way more *intellectually* privileged than I am."

They looked at me as if I'd just committed some social infraction.

"Do you guys want to go up to the roof?" I asked them.

"Sure. Is it safe to smoke up there?" Allie asked as we headed toward the stairs.

"I don't know what you mean by 'safe,'" I replied. "Like, will you go to jail? No. Probably not. Will you lose seven IQ points from the weed by smoking before you turn twenty-six? Yeah, probably. So is that safe? You tell me. I would say *no*. I would say it's not safe to smoke any*thing* any*where*."

They laughed at this as if it weren't gravely serious. I sat on a cushioned chair facing the sun, while they huddled onto a shady chaise lounge.

"Let me get back to this class as culture versus wealth argument I was trying to make. Take Lora, for example. She's gotten to live all over the world, gone to the best schools, had the best tutors, and gets to smoke weed and paint now."

"Where does she get her money from, again?" Taylor asked as he lit up his marihuana cigarette.

"Well her mom is descended from real New York royalty. A Mingott or a Welland or some famous family like that. And her dad was the ambassador to the Philippines."

Taylor took a big puff and held it, filling his cheeks. Allie interjected "She's Filipina?" and took the marihuana cigarette from Taylor.

"Well her Dad is half Filipino."

"Oh that makes sense," Taylor coughed a few times. "I always wanted to ask why she looked like that."

"Yeah," I said.

"Ross," Allie exhaled coughlessly, "you're almost making it sound like you're *mad* at your parents for not being smart or something."

"Well maybe I am. I've been thinking about it, and I was just an extremely gay kid. I knew nothing. My parents took me to New York in second grade, and we saw *Mamma Mia!* (1999) and they got me the soundtrack, and I was just extremely gay, listening to ABBA all throughout elementary school. First on my iPod Mini, then on my iPod Nano."

"Come on, Ross. You don't have to call ABBA *gay*," Allie said.

"I don't know how else you would describe an eight year-old listening to 'Dancing Queen' (1975) for several hours after school every day."

"Oh man," Taylor laughed, "I didn't realize you were listening to 'Dancing Queen' (1975). That is pretty fruity. It has *queen* right in the name, Allie."

"Yeah, I mean, what kind of parents would encourage their *son* to listen to that?" I said.

"I don't think it's that bad to let your kids listen to ABBA," Allie replied.

"I don't either, actually. I just think it was very *low-culture* of them to take me to see *Mamma Mia!* (1999) on Broadway. But I still like a lot of the songs. A lot of the best ones weren't even in it. 'Fernando' (1976), for example."

"Isn't that pretty gay?" Taylor exhaled some smoke through his nostrils. "I mean, it's a guy's name, right? The title of the song is just a man's name. Maybe if they called it—"

"No, no," I interrupted, "that's not what it's about. It's about a war, or something," I told them.

They just sort of stared at me the way people stare at you when they're high on weed. I continued, "I don't want to be too hard on my parents, I don't think that's fair. I don't hate them for being 'right-wingers,' or whatever, like you guys hate your parents. I think they did a good job letting me watch TV a lot. I think I learned a lot from that; Jon Stewart gave me a lot of what they couldn't. And I am pretty grateful that I learned about working people, *normal* people, with hundred IQs who fix and sell cars for a living."

Taylor interjected, "That's what I've been trying to tell Allie, Ross. That there's something really *American* about you. About this plan of yours to get Lora back by relentless self-improvement. It's only in a place like New York, or maybe LA, where people would even think of a scheme like yours, Ross."

"I don't know if that's fair," Allie ran her fingers mindlessly through Taylor's hair, "and I don't think we should be trying to like . . . *glorify* what Ross is doing. It's kind of disgusting, and *manipulative*. Rooted in patriarchal ideas of what a *man* ought to be."

"Ehhh. . . shut up, Allie. Not everything has to be like . . . a thing to get pissed about . . ." Taylor said.

"Yeah, come on, I don't think I'm doing anything wrong. I mean, my goals are unambiguously . . . altruistic. I want to help people. I was thinking the other day, that when I eventually run for office, I'm going to make it so *every* car has that breathalyzer that you have to blow into before it starts. I mean, it's pretty stupid, right? That they only give you that after you get a bunch of DUIs. You basically get a bunch of free drunk-driving passes before they install the breathalyzer on your car's ignition."

Taylor scoffed at this. "Give me a break, Ross. This just sounds like more technocratic think-tank Bloombergian bullcrap."

"Yeah it's just so . . . *neoliberal*," Allie added.

"This is the problem with you guys. Any time someone comes up with an actual *good* idea, you call it 'regressive,' you call it 'a tax on the poor.' And why? Because rich people can afford to order cars on apps to pick them up when they're drunk? Well maybe *poor* people shouldn't be drinking. And they *definitely* shouldn't be drinking and driving. So what are you mad about? I'm here coming up with ideas that'll save lives, and you guys get *mad* at me, but what are your big ideas? Let all the rapists and murderers out of prison? That's your big solution for everything? That's really going to help working people? They're going to love it when you unleash a tidal wave of marauders into their neighborhoods?"

"It's just that people like you—"

"Like me? What do you mean, *like me?* I am a *worker.* I am in a *union,* Allie! Just because my sister and I have an eight-figure net worth doesn't mean I'm not working class, at heart. You guys are lazily judging people based on their bank accounts."

They looked at each other and shrugged. They asked me about Emily, about how she was doing. I told her I was a bit worried about the Catholicism shtick, but that I couldn't help but *kvell* when I saw how smart she was becoming. I showed them some of the slides from the latest lesson I'd presented to Emily, about Charlie Sheen's 2011 "meltdown" which got him fired from the cast of *Two and a Half Men* (2003–2015) and replaced with Ashton Kutcher.

"Oh, I remember that. Everybody was talking about *tiger blood* and *winning* back then," Taylor said.

"Yeah, exactly. I'm trying to make sure Emily doesn't miss any of the cultural moments I was given access to as a kid. I mean, I don't want her to lose her childhood, you know?"

"That's sweet of you," Allie said, "and when does Amanda move in?"

"Tomorrow, actually."

"Doesn't she have a boyfriend?" asked Taylor.

"Yeah . . . but he's deployed, to Syria, or Ukraine, or something, so I'm not really worried about him showing up here and beating me up."

"Yeah yeah, that's cool. I get it. Allie and I actually just joined a polycule, too, Ross."

"What? What is that? Is that some kind of sex thing?" I replied.

"You know, it's like a network of people and their partners who are open minded, who understand that sex and love don't have to be so . . . *rigidly enforced.*"

"So you just cheat on each other? You just have sex with strangers, but it's okay, because you tell each other?" I asked.

"Yeah, basically. It's all about honesty, and trust," Taylor added.

"Well that's not why Amanda's coming here. I'm not interested in joining some kind of disgusting sex cult, like you people. I just want a responsible female role model for my *sister.* And perhaps someone to make the house a bit nicer. But you people, what you're describing is just sick. And that you thought I was even *attempting* something similar is just, is just . . ."

"Oh come on, Ross," Allie started, "it's so liberating, you know. I mean, of course we still love each other, but we're free to enjoy ourselves with other people we meet. I mean, we're still young, Ross. Why should we deprive ourselves of pleasure like that?"

"Because it's sick. It's a sick thing you're describing right now. You're sick. There's no reason ever to do what you're doing. I would sooner blow my brains out and throw them directly into that river right there, than ever join a 'poly' 'cule' like that."

They both looked me and laughed, as if *I* were the silly one, as if *I* were the one lacking some grasp of essential truths about life.

We talked a bit more about sillier things, sophomoric anecdotes from our freshman year in the dormitory at the prestigious private research university in Lower Manhattan. About roommates, about dining halls. Unnoteworthy reminiscences. They told me they had to go (so soon?). We walked back downstairs and I put Taylor's tea glass in the dishwasher.

"Oh," he said to me as he was stepping back into his sneakers, "Professor Lancet asked about you."

"What did he ask?"

"Just . . . how you're doing, I guess. Oh, and he said he needs a TA for the spring semester who isn't 'out to get him,' whatever that means. You should ask him about it. It'll give you something nice to do all day."

"Uh . . . okay, sure." I escorted them to the door, gave Allie a kiss on the cheek, and returned back to my kitchen table to eat my late afternoon meal of chicken (air-chilled), rice (white), and orange juice (not from concentrate).

Emily came in in a trendy and asymmetrical black rain jacket that made her look like a fashion-forward "international student," of sorts. She'd also begun wearing something called a "Brown Scapular" over the previous few days, which she told me would lessen her time in purgatory dramatically if she died while wearing it.

"What is that jacket? Is that from the Yohji Yamamoto Kids Collection?" I asked her.

"Mom actually got this for me before she died in that helicopter accident. I don't think it's necessarily for kids, it's just a Japanese women's size extra small."

She sat down next to me with a pod (is that what they're called?) of a dairy-free coconut-milk-based yogurt-alternative with blueberries at the bottom. "You're having chicken and rice?"

"Yeah, and orange juice."

"This is to gain weight to impress women?"

"Just one woman, really. But I figure if that doesn't work out it'll impress others too."

"And you think at some point, you'll be *good enough*? You'll have *perfected* yourself to the point that you'll be happy and satisfied?"

I took a big bite of chicken and chewed obnoxiously, making eye contact with Emily while she stirred her yogurt-alternative around until the blueberries were adequately dispersed. "I mean," I swallowed a mouthful of chicken and rice, "I guess . . . no? I guess I won't ever be 'perfect'? I'll always be trying to improve?"

"And that sounds good to you? Just freaking out all the time, trying to get a little bit stronger, a little bit smarter, a little bit richer, just to impress human men—and women?"

"Okay, Emily. Is this some kind of Catholic thing? I just wanted to eat chicken and rice, and now you're giving me some kind of Catholic lecture."

"Well I was getting to that. I wanted to ask you, in good faith, what you think happened to Jesus's body. Why hasn't anyone found it?"

"I don't know. They burned it?"

"No, that was forbidden in Jewish law at the time."

"They hid it?"

"Well why did so many people claim to see him after he died?"

"Why is that so important?"

She spooned a blue blob of fermented coconut milk up to her lips. "Why *wouldn't* it be important? If we trust the people who knew Him, who are telling us He kept saying He was God, and then performed feats and miracles that gave credibility to the claim, it's of *infinite* importance. It's eternal bliss versus eternal punishment."

"Okay, fine. Then what do you *want* me to think happened to his body?"

"I mean, He appeared to like five hundred people after He resurrected Himself, Ross. That's why all these people were going nuts back then, and were willing to be murdered for their belief that He was God. Have you considered that maybe the Bible is true, and it's time to become a traditional Catholic?"

I put my fork down harder than I meant to, and it made a loud noise, which I didn't mean for it to make. But I figured I would use the angry effect of it to make my point with gravitas. "You know, Emily. You're starting to get on my nerves. See, Jews never try to convert anyone. That's a Christian invention, trying to get everyone to join your little team, Em."

"Well if it's *true* and meant for *everyone*, why wouldn't I want to convince as many people as possible? Judaism is like your little secret club, with a racist god who only loves you if you had the right kind of mommy. Does that really seem aligned with your *enlightenment* values, Ross? A god who loves people more or less depending on their races? You don't even *do* any Jewish stuff. You're just proud of your race. Why would you be proud of something you had no control over?"

Oh, I wish she would give it a rest. It's so tiring, having to listen to this every few days. "Have you been able to convince anyone of this yet? With these talking points? Anyone at school?"

"No. All the other teens are mad at me because I said prostitution was bad and disgusting for everyone involved."

"Well maybe you should lay off some of that stuff, with everyone at school. People your age seem to love prostitution, it seems . . . Or maybe, join the Young Republicans Club or something."

"That's the thing, Ross. That *was* at the Young Republicans Club. They're all just libertarians now. They love weed, abortion, prostitution, pornography, in-vitro fertilization, you name it."

"Then what makes them Republicans?"

"Well, they hate taxes and seatbelt laws."

"Oh, yeah. That's right. Well, in that case, I don't really know what to tell you."

Fourteen

I was sitting in this Upper East Side "cosmedical" "spa" waiting room, surrounded by Westchester moms, social media models, gay guys, Belarusians, etc, etc, etc, shuffling in and out of the office, waiting to meet with Dr. Semigroup (MD, PSURG)—the founder, CEO, and staff doctor of *Lexington Avenue Pulchritude Development*—to have their ugly faces fixed up. And I was no better, really. I was there to alter my God-given body just like the rest of them.

On my Watch, I read an email from Robert Shapiro, with another important update regarding my wealth.

> You should've seen the deal I got you, kid. We sold daddy's dealership, the lot, the building, the inventory. The biggest thing, get this, was your old man's rolodex. People all over SoCal wanted to get their fingers on that thing, and when all was said and done, between the two dealerships and all the cars and the rights to those top notch salesmen your dad had trained, I managed to get another $10,000,000 and change for you and Emily. Do you realize how much that is? That's nearly 5X your EBITDA. Nobody not named John Elway gets 5X EBITDA for a car dealership. You're rich, Ross. You're so rich! You never have to worry about anything ever again. Thank me later.
>
> Love,
> Uncle Bobby

No matter how hard I tried not to, I couldn't help but coming into more millions, it seemed. With about $22 million between the two of us, invested in US equities earning an average of ten percent a year, Emily and I would have a combined $1,940,344,675.70 ($1.9 billion?) by her sixtieth birthday. As long as things in the future continue to behave like they did in the past.

And speaking of Emily, I'd noticed she was terribly bored lately, struggling to struggle with the middlebrow schoolwork her allegedly "specialized" high school was giving her. So I asked her to write a few thousand words, with a thesis of her choosing, about what Wikipedia called the "September 2007 University of Florida Taser Incident," in which a twenty-one-year-old student was "tased" for asking (then) Senator John Kerry if he was a member of Yale's "Skull and Bones" secret society. You'll recall, the incident went viral because Andrew Meyer, the student, shouted "Don't tase me bro!" right before they tased him. I remember watching it as a kid and feeling sick to my stomach, but it seemed like all the adults were laughing and making jokes about it. I was interested to see what Emily had to say about the whole thing.

But back to this plastic surgeon's office. I was scheduled for a "consultation." To evaluate what sort of work I would need done to make myself objectively attractive. I imagined my nose would present the biggest problem. My parents had both had nose jobs as teenagers, removing the bumps and crookedness they were dealt at birth. And I'm no psychoanalysis expert, but it seems likely to me, that growing up with this, this . . . *beak*, enduring taunts on the playground, etc, etc, all the while my parents' noses were positively goyish, must've traumatized me in some way, the same way a Chinese child adopted by whites must feel. But again, I'm no psychoanalysis expert.

A short-haired tattooed lesbian (a secretary, not a nurse) with a nondescript voice came into the waiting room, carrying a clipboard, and said something like "Ross? Dr. Semigroup is ready for you."

Dr. Semigroup, who was wearing a dark green cashmere sweater (with no white medical coat to speak of) and tan chino pants, shook my hand, and said, "Ross, right?"

"Yes, sir."

"I have your file right"— he tapped a few things on a tablet computer—"here." He squinted at the screen, and said, "Oh, oh, okay. Mhm, mhmmm . . . Definitely."

He pointed the computer at me and said, "Stay still, I'm going to scan your face. This thing has LIDAR. It's the newest model."

"Okay."

Within a few minutes he was projecting his scan of my face onto a television screen in the office, circling in red things he called "problem areas."

"You see, Ross. I do this all day. I do this all day for a living. And I studied physiognomy at Stanford, so I can tell a lot about you, just based on your face."

"Can you really?"

"Oh absolutely. And I don't want to be mean to you, Ross. But you have the classic *coward's* face. And you're not as smart as you think you are. I mean, you're a smart kid, I can tell by your face. You have the face of a guy who has a one-in-fifty intellect but thinks he's one-in-five-hundred. But these are minor details."

"Uh, okay."

"The good news is, I won't have to break your jaw."

"That's good."

Then he held up a fist threateningly and said, ". . . unless you piss me off."

We both laughed. "That's funny," I told him.

"We don't have to break anything, actually. It's all filler now. That's the secret about my job. I hardly ever have to do surgery anymore, unless I get a real monster in here. You know, burn victims, incest babies, that kind of thing, Ross."

"For sure."

"So you'll come in here, once every few weeks, yadda yadda yadda," he started manipulating the digital rendering of my face with great precision, almost seeming bored. "Suck some fat out here, even out your nose like this, collagen for the lips."

"I thought they don't really use collagen anymore."

"Oh, wow. You're *so* smart, I'm *sooo* impressed. Maybe *you* should be the doctor. But yes, it's a hyaluronic acid dermal filler. Congrats on using the internet before you came in here, Ross. Anyway, so we'll give you *hyaluronic acid* for the lips, maybe an eyelid peel, mhm . . . Can you grow facial hair?"

"Not really."

"And you're rich, right? And this is all to impress some woman? Did I read that email right?"

"Uh huh."

"Okay, so we'll throw in a beard transplant. You can always shave it if you don't like it."

"That's true."

"And what are you doing about the rest of your body?"

"I've been going to this gym in Brooklyn run by an Italian guy."

"Oh, okay. That's good. Do you need me to prescribe any human growth hormone? Test? Tren?"

"Is that safe? I worry about it affecting my fertility, or making me go bald, or something."

"No, no. You're rich now, Ross. You'll get the good stuff. The stuff Disney gives comedians to get them ready to act in Marvel movies."

"Oh, okay. Sure. And we won't get into any trouble?"

"TROUBLE? *Trouble?* With whom? With the Office of Professional Medical Conduct? With those losers? Those morons?"

"Yeah, I guess."

"Oh, don't worry about them for a minute. You think they and their wives aren't coming in here every other week for assorted tune-ups, Ross?"

"I don't know. Are they?"

"At *least*. Trust me, Ross. These people need me. Their lives would be ruined without me."

"That makes sense."

"Alright, let me go get all my needles."

I sat in this doctor's armless chair, looking around the consultation room, at his degrees, one of which was from my prestigious alma mater, another from the Albert Einstein (not a doctor?) College of Medicine. And then I noticed the blinds adorning the room's windows. They looked identical to the blinds in my childhood bedroom from ages six to eleven. They were a style called "cellular shades." Cellular shades resembled pleated shades (vertical cotton accordions) but were composed of "front" and "back" panels (cells?) that prevented heat from entering the room.

The summer after my eleventh birthday, my parents let me build a "gaming" computer, which is actually very common and totally natural for Jewish boys at that age. I'd spent the previous year extremely jealous over baby Emily, the attention she was getting. Everything was "Ross! Can you check on Emily?" or "Ross! Put on a show that's appropriate for the *whole* family" or "Ross, can you help figure out what's wrong with Momma's breast milk pump?" And my parents, to thank me for being a good sport about this new situation, let me order all of these expensive parts and put them together and use them to play video games with. I would lock myself in that room for hours on end, amusing myself on the computer. And my mom, who was certainly dealing with a lot, would come into my room, lift up the blinds, and say, "This room needs light! You can't be in the dark all summer, Ross!" This went on several times a week, through August.

One day, when I thought no one was home, I pulled down the blinds, and (illegally) downloaded a *.mkv* file containing *Vicky Cristina Barcelona* (2008), which had debuted at Cannes a few months earlier. Ten minutes of the film had gone by, maybe more, and I was sitting stunned at

Scarlett Johansson's sultriness (you'll recall that she was the most beautiful woman in the world, at the time). Stunned and distracted. So much so that when my mom burst into my room, swinging the door open, shouting "Why are those blinds down!?" I jumped out of my wheeled desk chair, crudely ripping the headphones out of my computer.

"Uh . . . nothing, just watching a movie," I replied.

"Well you look guilty, Ross. I know my baby, and you look guilty."

"It's nothing, mommy. It's just that I know you didn't want me putting the blinds down."

She walked over to the desk and looked at my monitor. "What is this? Why are you watching a movie with Javier Bardem drinking wine? You're eleven years old!"

"Uh . . . I saw an ad for it on Comedy Central."

"You saw an *ad* for it? Is this that new *Vicky Cristina Barcelona* (2008) movie that everyone's talking about, Ross?" With each question she grew more and more impatient.

"Yes," I responded meekly.

"Look at me when you talk to me, Ross. I'm your *mother*."

"Yes," I said more firmly, looking her in the eye.

"And how are you *watching* this movie that's still playing in theaters?"

"I . . ." I felt tears beginning to form, my eyelids grew heavy.

"Go on, go on, Ross."

"I downloaded it. Online."

She unplugged the monitor crudely, as women are wont to do, not knowing the intricacies of wires and cables that boys care about. "We told you, Ross. We told you, you could put this computer in your room, with no parental spying software, as long as you didn't illegally download any romantic comedies. But you didn't listen. We gave you *one* rule, Ross." She wedged the monitor under her armpit. "*One* tree you were forbidden to eat from, and you just had to do it. You just had to disobey your parents, who love you so much."

"Please, please! Don't take it! I'm sorry!" I was crying out.

Calmly, she carried the monitor out into the hallway, wires dangling from its backside, before returning to my room to continue admonishing me.

"Your father runs a business, Ross. You know he has very powerful enemies, people in this town who are out to get him."

"I know. I'm sorry! I'm sorry! Please."

"And how do you think it would *look*, if the FBI raided our house because our little *boy* was *stealing* movies on the internet?"

"It would look bad! I'm sorry, please. I'm sorry, just stop screaming at me. I'm sorry. I'm so sorry. I won't do it again I promise. Please, please, please, mommy, let me have my computer back. I'll delete it, I promise. I won't do it again, never ever. I'm sorry."

"Oh, Ross. I know you won't do it again. You won't be *able* to do it again. This is going to be very painful for you. And don't think I *like* being the bad guy. You *make* me do this, you *make* me act like this. I just want to be a fun mommy, and love you. I love you so much, Ross. But you leave me no choice but to do this. And it's going to hurt me a lot more than it hurts you."

I thought she was going to hit me (which she never ever did, I just thought she was going to, based on the odd way she was talking), but instead, she walked over to my window and ripped my blinds out using her bare hands. "See? This is what happens. This is what you deserve. This should teach you to download dirty movies over the internet. Now you don't have blinds anymore. Blinds are for good boys who use their computers for reading and playing games."

Oh, just thinking about that made me sick. Who knows how much sleep I lost because of the lack of blinds in my room from age eleven to twelve (I got new ones on my next birthday). I can only imagine how much taller and stronger and smarter I could've been if I had slept better during those formative years.

"Sorry I took so long," Dr. Semigroup said as he reentered the room. "I actually dropped a bunch of syringes on the way in here, and had to go back and get new ones that weren't all over the floor."

"No problem."

"Okay, pull your pants down."

I dropped my trousers (slightly) and bent over the examination table, "Like this?" I asked him,

"Yes, that's fine." He injected me with whatever Disney gives its comedians when they're cast in Marvel movies. "Now, are you alright with a little lip filler?" he asked me.

"Sure, I guess."

"Because you could use it. It could really help take your face to the next level. Also, you can pull your pants up now. And turn around."

"Oh, sorry." I sat upright on the exam table. "You know, I'm a registered nurse," I told him.

"So?" he replied.

"I just thought maybe you would find that interesting. Do I look like a nurse? In my physiognomy?"

"What kind of stupid, *asinine* question is that? How would I be able to tell what *job* someone would have based on his face?"

He picked up a tinier syringe and filled it with a filler, then walked over to me and proceeded to make pen marks all over my lips to mark the injection spots. "Look, Ross. This is going to swell up your lips. For about thirty hours. Is that okay with you? Have anywhere to be?"

I shook my head no.

"Okay, then let's give it a shot." He gently inserted the needle into my lip at the marked-off locations, dispersing dermal filler into my face. "Alright, that wasn't so bad right?"

"Let me see the mirror first, and then I'll tell you."

He laughed that horrible laugh of his. He really looked evil, standing there, towering over me in his cashmere sweater, helping people commit facial fraud for a living.

On the street, I felt terribly self-conscious having walked out of the office building that housed Dr. Semigroup. Especially with such massive, inflamed lips. Oh it was humiliating. Homeless men were making crude comments at me ("hey lip boy!" etc, etc), teens were taking photos of me (to be posted online and laughed at), and women wouldn't even look at me. I had no choice but to order a car for myself using an app (since taking the train would really be putting myself in emotional harm's way).

I stood on the corner of 53rd and Lexington, next to a skyscraping office building, bustling with International Bankers and their cronies, tapping in and out with their RFID badges. There was also one of those creepy Manhattan shopping malls under there, with weird stores like Armani Exchange and Auntie Ann's Pretzels. After a few minutes of waiting, my car arrived, driven by some kind of Indian guy, who kept staring at my monstrous lips in the rearview mirror. I put in my noise-cancelling wireless earphones to ignore him and pressed play on the latest episode of Nicholas Sandmann's podcast, *The Nick Sandmann Experience* (2019–).

Fifteen

The Fort, the structure that housed my penthouse condominium, featured a really rather intricate lobby, with twenty-foot glass windows covered in cast iron grates. Unvarnished concrete floors, conspicuous security cameras at every corner, and a bulletproof booth for the doorman (who dresses in camouflage pants and a black tactical vest) to stand behind and operate the digital turnstile gate separating his building's residents (for whom he took an *oath* to serve and protect) from the rest of Downtown Brooklyn's wandering riffraff. When I arrived after my cosmetic spa appointment, I had a feeling the building's automatic facial recognition wouldn't "recognize" my "face." As it almost always is, my suspicion was correct. The gate wouldn't open for me.

I walked up to the booth. "Hi, I'm a resident here, in PHJ," I told him. "I got . . . stung by a bee, on my face. But here's my driver's license, and Academi ID card, to show that I really live here and I'm not just lying to you."

"Sorry about that, Mr. Mathcamp, sir." He buzzed me in. "Oh!" he shouted to me as I was walking toward the elevator, "There's a note from your sister here, in the system. That Amanda is up there. Just to warn you."

Of course, Amanda hadn't been a serious romantic interest of mine for nearly five years at this point, but I still felt something resembling dread for any woman who wasn't my mom or my sister seeing me in such a swollen state. "Thanks for letting me know!" I called back in an attempt at politeness. I tapped my ID badge against the elevator's contactless badge reader and nothing happened. I did this three or four times with no effect whatsoever. So I walked back over to the doorman and asked him why my badge was useless.

"Didn't you get the email, Mr. Mathcamp, sir?" he asked me.

"No. What email?"

"The elevators are down. We have our best men working on it, but it may be another several hours, sir."

"How are they all out?"

"Uh."

"What about the service elevator? Surely that's separate."

"For security reasons, I cannot allow you to take the service elevator."

"Why not? Can't you just have someone watch me? Aren't there cameras in there?"

"Mr. Mathcamp, when you purchased your apartment here, you signed your name on a document that acknowledged that you wouldn't be allowed to use the service elevator under any circumstance, sir. You gave your word, Mr. Mathcamp, sir."

"Well, I live on the thirty-fourth floor, what do you want me to do? Do you have someone who can carry me? Surely there's someone extremely strong working here who could sprint up the stairs with me in my arms. Don't you have a private . . . like, group of firefighters here who can carry me up to my apartment?"

"No. You have to take the stairs."

"Okay, fine. I'm just going to do it. But I want you to know that I'm very upset, I'm just smart enough not to yell at you about it, because it's not really your fault."

"Thank you, sir."

I walked defeatedly over to the stairwell, tapped my badge, and opened the (extremely heavy, for me) door. I walked up a single flight, onto the first floor (*The Fort* starts its floor indices at zero, for whatever reason). It took me about eighteen seconds. I figured, given varying floor heights and my own tiredness, it would take me about fifteen minutes (nine hundred seconds) to scale the remaining thirty-three floors and be able to sit down and eat food with Emily and Amanda Bauer.

∼

Amanda Bauer and I first met in a freshman seminar titled "Thinking with Words," where she had announced to the class during our introductions, "Hi, my name is Amanda, I'm from New Jersey, I'm studying Evolutionary Psychology, and an interesting fact about me, is that my mom divorced my dad when I was ten, and they are now both living with other women. So I kind of grew up with three moms, if that makes sense."

Floor three.

I found this revelation totally shocking, and titillating, what would a woman who grew up with three moms be like? Her wry tone in relaying this to us, I found very humorous, it reminded me of something I would've said (at the time) in an attempt at "dark humour." After class, I saw her sitting on a bench in the park, where she was sipping tea from Peet's Coffee and reading some translation and commentary on Søren Kierkegaard. I opened the Facebook Messenger app on my phone from a nearby bench and typed in her name, adding the following message:

> Hi, I was just in your seminar. I am utterly fascinated by <
> you and your introductory anecdote. I'm sitting across
> from you in this park right now, where you're reading that
> Kierkegaard book. Don't be frightened, really. I'm not some
> kind of cowboy rapist [you had to be in the seminar to get
> this hilarious reference, although, I don't even remember what
> it referred to anymore. Maybe it was funny at the time, but
> who knows?]. Would you mind if I came and sat with you?

I watched her as she picked up her buzzing phone and smiled. She wrote back, simply:

> Come here

"Hey," I sat down next to her; she was wearing a denim skirt, with pale legs, very similar to my own skin's coloring, with German-made sandals that made her toes look terrible—stringy and shriveled. Most really pretty girls have pretty ugly feet, it turns out. But other than that she was breathtaking. The most beautiful woman I'd ever seen in my life, what with her pointy knees and skinny wrists, etc, etc. "How is that guy? His name has the cool 'o' with the line through it, so you know he's probably pretty smart."

(Now, this was the sort of "joke" I was in the habit of making at age eighteen, and in that valley of insecurity and horniness and confusion associated with the first semester at a prestigious private research university (like the one I went to), this sort of thing passed for genuinely clever, charming even. Even though now I can see how hollow and stupid a remark like that is.)

She made a girlish noise that signaled amusement, "I'm reading this book, *Fear and Trembling* (1843). I think he's writing beautifully. But I don't think I've read enough Hegel to understand any of these points he's trying to make."

"Yeah," I replied in a serious tone, "I haven't read it, but I've seen the movie with Johnny Depp, which was pretty cool." She laughed aloud at this. "I'm joking, you know," I told her. "The joke is that Johnny Depp was in the *film adaptation* (1998) of *Fear and Loathing in Las Vegas* (1971)."

"Yeah," she smiled, "I got that. That's really funny." I was so unbelievably charmed by this woman. You wouldn't believe how charmed I was. Very! Her laugh was humble and smart, her phenotype greatly resembled my own (I asked her flat out if she was of Ashkenazi descent later on in the conversation), and she had no shortage of original thoughts.

For weeks, I courted her, in that painful collegiate manner (poor baby Ross! such a coward!), reading Gogol, Sebald, Balzac, Baudrillard, etc, etc, comparing translations, compiling trivia, just to impress this

Jewish woman. It was in my mind that she was *just like me,* and that this—this perceived similarity—would make for a good romantic relationship. Any discernible difference was reconciled ("Yes, that's true. I mean, you *would* have to be an idiot or a monster not to call yourself a feminist. It's *definitely* a meaningful category!" "No, of course not. I was just kidding. I actually *hate* Woody Allen! I totally agree with you, Amanda. He's a pervert! Let's watch this week's episode of *Charlie Rose* (1991–) instead."). This went on for a while, until finally, right before we left for our university's Thanksgiving recess, we finally *saw each other nude,* so to speak, indulging awkwardly (poor baby Ross! So inexperienced!) in sexual acts with one another.

Floor ten.

While we were apart, I in Los Angeles, she in Paramus, New Jersey, I neglected to message her, call her, contact her digitally in any way. I wanted to, of course (recall, she was the most beautiful woman I'd ever seen in my entire life), but I was suffering from a prototype of the cucking sensation mentioned in Chapter Uno. As soon as I landed, I became acutely aware of a newly forged supernatural distance between my mind and Amanda's. I was being replaced; I could feel it. I had no appetite. ("Ross, I made your favorite food, steamed zucchini with olive oil and salt, and you've hardly even TOUCHED it! I can't believe I made you this nice *paleo* dinner and you won't even FINISH it! What kind of son would do this to his mother? Tell me, Ross. Tell me what I ever did to make you hate me so much. Why you hate your mother who only ever wanted the best for you.") I was in no mood for entertaining eight-year-old Emily ("Ross, can we play Connect Four? I think I figured out how to win every time, as long as you let me go first"), I was miserable. Preoccupied with Amanda, terrified to contact her for fear of seeming too eager, repulsively and zealously infatuated with her, etc, etc, etc, etc. And after a few days of not hearing from her, that horrible cucking sensation crystalized into a fully formed revelation—I was being replaced by her high school ex-boyfriend, a shaved-head tattooed rap-music-fan named Jeffrey Daniels.

"Ross, you've been very special to me. I can't imagine I'll ever not love you," she said to me, in my dorm room on November 29, after we'd both returned from some time with our families. "You're very important to me, but after you didn't talk to me all of last week, I went to lunch with my ex and—"

"Yes, yes, I know. I did the same thing." (No I didn't!) "I know what you're going to say. I agree. We should just be friends, for now." Oh, I was crumbling inside. I was in *shambles*; I was being replaced by an eighteen-year-old named Jeff Daniels. I felt so stupid, so cucked. And this was all because of my own sexual ineptitude and emotional cowardice.

She rolled off my comforter and onto the little gray antimicrobial rug I kept at the foot of my bed, "Well I'm glad we can be mature, can be *grownups* about this, Ross."

"What does he have that I don't have?" I burst out.

She looked surprised, "Well, he took me around in his car, and we went to the Garden State Plaza Mall, to Legal Sea Foods, to the AMC Garden State 16—"

"We have restaurants and movie theaters in New York! Chains, too!" I realized how nuts I must've sounded and brought my voice back down to a reasonable meter. "I mean, yeah. I'm sure it's not just that. I get it. I know how you feel. Missing home and the like."

"And we snorted cocaine in the parking lot of the Bergen County Zoo." She said it like that (*snorted cocaine*) to be funny, but she clearly wasn't joking or lying about what had happened.

Oh, I felt sick (poor worthless teetotaling Ross . . .). I collapsed onto my latex pillow and let out a characteristic groan. "Okay. Yeah, that's fine. I need to do some reading now. If you could leave."

And then I didn't talk to her for a year. What was I doing during that time? Not very much of anything, it turned out. Reading biology textbooks, Jean Rhys short stories (etc, etc), wallowing into the occasional clinically depressed dating-app strumpet, but mostly just feeling sorry for myself. Unlike now. Unlike this current Ross, who's wealthy and well equipped for post-breakup self-improvement. When I finally did run into Amanda again, on the Lower East Side of Manhattan, she was taking some guy to see *Crimes and Misdemeanors* (1989) (which I counted as a personal triumph). We had lunch sometime after that and I was pleasantly surprised with how easy it was to talk to her again, how much we had in common, and how much she'd moved earnestly in my direction (after putting down the Butler and picking up the Paglia) on so many issues, including cinema and abstinence from drug use. I was vindicated by the cucking. Ross had conquered his rude conqueror, etc, etc, etc, etc, and soon she became a reliable ally of mine, a confidant, a trusted member of my inner circle, and since we'd already seen each other nude, "things" between the two of us were free from any tension or jealousy, obviously. Why wouldn't they be?

Which is why I felt so comfortable inviting her to stay with me and Emily in our luxury penthouse. Because she'd embodied and adopted certain qualities that I appreciated in myself, but also, had experienced a lot of the adolescent debauchery that I'd abstained from, and would be able to testify to E (Emily) that Ross had it right all along.

Floor thirty-four.

Panting, sweaty, ridiculous, inflamed, I stumbled through my penthouse's front door. Inside, my sister Emily and Amanda Bauer were sitting on the couch parallel to the large window overlooking the East River, getting along like a couple of *yentas*. Just two women talking to each other about something other than a man. What a fun home indeed.

"Hey," I called out from the kitchen hallway, "I'm going to pour myself some orange juice. I just had to," deep breath, "walk up all these stairs. Because the elevators broke." I looked into the fridge, at all of the shelf-unstable supplements Emily and I (and now Amanda) were taking. CoQ10, *women's* probiotics (if you know what I mean), krill oil, etc, etc, etc, etc.

"Oh my gosh," Emily said. "Are you okay?"

"Yeah, it just took a long time. . . . Oh, you mean my lips. Yes, they should be fine. I just had them filled in by my doctor."

I walked over to the living room with my orange juice and sat down across from my female roommates. "So what are you two talking about?" I smiled. "I hope you're teaching her good stuff, Amanda, like how to make latkes, or knit things, or pronounce *Goethe*."

"Your sister is a *genius*, Ross."

"Oh, did you play her at Connect Four?"

Amanda smiled. "No, she was just telling me about the Catholic Church."

I threw my head back and let out a regretful sigh. "This again? Emily, don't bother Amanda about this stuff. She's actually quite proud of being Jewish."

Emily smirked at me.

"No, no," Amanda said. "She explained it so well, Ross. That if there is a God who invented reason and logic and mathematics and abhors contradiction and chaos, that it follows, *a priori*, that that God would establish an infallible authority on earth. Catholicism is the only religion that can't contradict itself, because of the papacy. There's really no such thing as *Judaism*, anymore, really, since no one can even agree on what it would entail."

"What?" I put down my orange juice on the glass side-table next to somebody's copy of *JR* (1975). "What, so you just think there's some guy who can never be wrong? Because he puts on a certain hat?" I said, raising a finger to scratch my eye, which had begun feeling itchy.

Emily chimed in, "No, Ross. I went through the First Vatican Council (1869–1870) with her—" (How long was I gone?) "—and showed her that the pope is infallible when he speaks to the universal church, as part of the ordinary magisterium, or when he speaks *ex cathedra*, in the extraordinary magisterium."

"And then she baptized me in your sink. I feel so . . . *regenerated*, Ross! I can't believe I never realized how badly I needed to be *baptized*. That the reason I've always felt so dirty wasn't due to mitochondrial fatigue or glutathione depletion-induced obsessive compulsive disorder, but because I was *stained* by original sin. All those years I spent taking four, five showers a day. One after another, just trying to get clean—that was really just my innate understanding that I needed to be baptized, Ross!"

Was I dreaming this? Why was this happening to me? Emily is a *kid!* A *child!* She's supposed to be doing normal kid stuff like practicing for AP exams, reading Oscar Wilde, and enduring miserable mawkish episodes of unrequited teenaged love. Not performing baptisms or learning Latin for the sole purpose of reading about how to avoid going to something called "hell." What kind of brother-parent am I if this is how she's turning out?

"Uh, okay. That's fine," I said. "I'm going to go to my room now to—wait—" I heard a faint sound and then saw, out of the corner of my itching eye, a small gray cat. "What is that?" I asked. "Is that a cat? Did you bring a cat into my house, Amanda?"

"Well, no," she said, bending down to pick it up, "I brought *two*, and they're kittens. But it's fine Ross. You're going to love these kittens. They're Manxes, Ross. That's the only Irish breed of cat. They're called Araby and Eveline—isn't that cute? Isn't that the sort of thing you would like, Ross?"

"It *is* the sort of thing I would like, but what—you expect me to have these things in my house? I just have to have these *animals* that make me *sick* living in the house?"

"They're very useful," Emily chimed in. "They kill mice and other pests!"

"Stop it, why would we have pests? Why would there be mice here? This is a heavily protected luxury condominium, not some . . . not some

. . . rotting barn! Don't mock me like that, trying to appeal to their utility. Just tell me you want them because you want something to pet." I sneezed into my arm. "See! See!" The human girls started laughing at me. "I'm already getting *sick* from them. But fine, fine. I'll just spend even *more* money on air purifiers and robot vacuums. Does that sound good? Maybe two thousand a month on air purifiers and robot vacuums? Does that sound like enough to you two? Because that's how much it's going to cost me for you two to have your little furry friends."

"Oh come on Ross," Emily started, "stop pretending you don't love spending money on toy cleaners. You enjoy their companionship just as much as we enjoy the cats'."

"Okay, okay, very clever. I'm going to go to my room now, to do some reading."

I went into my room to roll around my bed and groan about the burden of living in a religious and fur-filled household. And a less *Jewish* household, and not in the way I wanted. Soon I would be getting leered at for eating meat on Fridays, for going shopping on Sundays, for . . . well, there were probably a bunch of other things that Catholics did that I didn't even know about, that were sure to make my life on earth (which is all that really matters, right?) less convenient.

I was trying to nap, really. Really just trying to get a little shuteye, and then at 7:45, my HomePod and Watch started chiming and vibrating to remind me of my upcoming Zoom meeting with Drew Lancet, a philosophy professor from my alma mater. I jumped out of bed, flung open my curtains, removed my Oura Ring from my finger (for heart rate monitoring and motion detection to measure my sleep quality) and my Dreem headband from my head which used patent-pending EEG (electroencephalogram) sensors to measure my brain activity while I was sleeping. The Oura gave me an 85/100 sleep score for the two-hour nap, but the Dreem 2 (which sat much closer to my brain) gave me a paltry 56/100. Further tests would have to be done, it seemed. In the bathroom, I brushed my hair and teeth then sat down at my desk.

"Hello? Can you hear me, Professor Lancet?" I asked.

He looked grizzly, aged, droopy, depleted, disgusting. Dressed in a tight blue flannel shirt, nipples protruding. "They're killing me, Ross. They want me dead. These animals. And please, call me Doctor Drew."

"Who's killing you?" I never knew Professor Lancet to be all that nervous of a man, but he certainly *looked* like it, or had the potential to fit the frightened boomer archetype, with his curly receding hair, large shoulders, and short stature. But I'd always known him to be more pissed than petrified.

"They're trying to *cancel* me, Ross. Hello? Can you hear me?"

"Yes, I can hear you. I don't know what that means. I've never heard that before. 'Cancel.'"

"Erm, well, that's what they're calling it. This new generation, the next crop of students, Ross. These new kids. These children of the twenty-first century. They are totally illiberal."

"Can you just tell me what happened?"

He was making a number of exaggerated hand gestures. "You know I'm not some rank racialist, right? Some supremacist scoundrel . . ."

"Yeah, I mean, you have a black wife, right?"

"*Had*, a black wife, Ross. She's gone. That mutt, that . . . *whore!* She left me for dead. She believed all the *lies* about me. She's totally gone, run off with some sillier younger man, leaving me here, all alone, beaten within an inch of my life." He put his head into his hands.

"Well what happened?"

"It all started during a lecture in my Intro to Metaphysics class. Some idiot, some troublemaking muckraker asked me if we could derive any properties about *ghosts* from what Socrates says about the afterlife in the *Phaedo* (~400 BC). So I replied, and you know how I love wordplay, Ross. I said 'Ghosts? This is a *philosophy* course. Not one of your silly seminars in Critical *Wraith* Theory.' A B-minus quip, I figured at the time. But since I delivered it—with great charisma, I should say—I've been reported, blacklisted, excoriated on online forums, based on these," his voice sounded terribly pained "*trumped up* charges of 'racial insensitivity,' and *ableism*! They said I was mocking people with *speech impediments*, Ross. They see no humanity in me. Only a privileged oppressor exerting his power."

"That sounds terrible." It really did. "How did the class react when you said it?"

"A few white guys laughed, they got it. But before the class was even over, I was inundated with emails from two Pakistani American females demanding that I apologize and resign. This infuriated me. Oh, I was so stupid, Ross. I escalated it all, this whole mess, by looking up their fathers on the web and finding that they were highly compensated surgeons or lawyers, and telling the whole class that these rich women whose fathers made eight hundred large—in a bad year—were trying to accuse me of being privileged, and out-of-touch."

"So—"

He kept going. "This was my most miserable mistake, Ross. Soon a petition was circulating. Thousands of out of state signatories demanding my head on a pike. And for what? A harmless joke. So now I need you, yes *you*, Ross, to help me out."

"What can I do?"

"Your friend, Carlos. And Skylar, too. I need you to give me their emails. So he can write a letter, an open letter, testifying on behalf of my character. That I treated them and their brown skin with nothing but respect."

"And that's all you want from me?"

"Oh, Ross, you're not going to make me beg, are you?"

"I don't know what you're talking about, Doctor."

"Oh I see that sick smile on your face. *Fine.* I *need* you, Ross. I *need* you to come fill a slot as one of my PhD students, and work as a TA in my classes. There's no one like you, Ross. There's no one your age whom I can trust the way I can trust you."

"Yeah, I mean. Thank you. That wasn't very difficult, right? That must've been fairly uncomplicated for you to . . . you know, spit out."

Sixteen

My condition, post-adoption of The Goldberg Strategy, was profoundly unlonely. And this was not at all what I had hoped for. At all hours of the day, I was surrounded by normal people, having conversations with friends, etc, etc. And it was *tiring*. For years I'd fared well in New York (City) in part because I had (after my first year in school) always lived alone, and given myself plenty of time to be lonely. You need a little loneliness to get some good thoughts out, I've realized. But since my parents died (may they rest in peace) I was never alone. I was always either in the presence of Emily or Amanda or Mike Monad or some idiot young person or some creepy doctor, demanding that I speak with my mouth and deprive my mind of solitary moments conducive to insight.

A few days after my call with Professor Drew Lancet, I bought the *Dr. Chung's Number One Prep Book Brand* brand GRE prep book, had it shipped to my Roosevelt Island apartment (which still had another five months until its lease was up; I think this was November and it was up in April. What is that? six months?), and packed a bag for myself. At dinner that night, with Amanda and Emily, I told them, "I'm going to be splitting my time. Between here and my other apartment. It's just too much. Too many people and cats. That's okay with you two, right?" And of course it was. They didn't care. They didn't care about me or my goals or my strategy.

I decided it was prudent to take Professor Lancet up on his offer to do research under him. For years I'd wanted to pursue philosophy more formally, starting with a master's in mereology and logic, which Drew assured me over the videophone I would be allowed to work on. Doctor Ross Mathcamp, now that would command respect, wouldn't it? And I was desperately missing the excitement of the academy, the thrill of test taking most especially.

~

Locking myself in my Roosevelt Island apartment for a few weeks was a fantastic move (strategically). The revival of that collegiate loneliness (stuck on an island, blinds drawn, staring into screens and books all day with no women around whatsoever) reminded me of how much I missed Lora, infusing new life into the mission-at-large. Studying for the GRE was another great move, a wonderful confidence booster (as all standardized tests have always been for me). And so, the better part of the month of November was devoted to standardized testing.

Drew Lancet repeatedly assured me that they really, truly, just did not care how well I did, only whether or not I could pay for my master's degree. Is it really all that interesting for me to say that I took the GRE on a Dell desktop in the Roosevelt Island Elementary School (PS 217) library, on a Saturday morning, and that I scored in the 95th percentile for quantitative reasoning (I got like two questions wrong) and the 97th percentile for verbal reasoning (I got like four questions wrong)? My writing score? I don't really want to talk about that. But this was plenty, my hard work had paid off and I'd earned myself the privilege of paying a hundred grand for another two years (and then another free four, probably, when I start working on the PhD) of academic philosophy.

Where did this leave me in terms of Goldberg? I would say I was about two-thirds done, that I would be ready to see Lora around on March 8, the anniversary of my (idiotic! So stupid! But so necessary for personal growth!) original breakup. On December 1, I had already gained about fifteen pounds from my diet and exercise and hormone routine. My powerlifting stats were as follows:

Deadlift—69 kilograms
Bench press—46 kilograms

Front squat—46 kilograms

Back squat—60 kilograms

Overhead press—32 kilograms

For reference, these numbers are about eighty percent of what the average thirty-year-old white guy who's never lifted weights is capable of doing. Mike Monad would come around, complimenting my form, saying "let's get it!" and "okay, okay. I see you, bro. I see you. Getting brolic, brother" and offering high-fives as often as he saw fit.

My face was similarly improving. The dermal fillers had stopped causing swelling, leaving my lips at a consistently plump level. One could've easily mistaken me for a person of a vague (maybe twenty-five percent?) Latino ancestry. The injectable anabolics were working wonders, my nose was non-surgically smoothened out, and I'd begun using this tool called the Chisell 2, which was a chewable silicone block meant to strengthen my jaw and cheek muscles. And I was seeing moderate results; my face overall was becoming increasingly modelesque.

~

When I returned home after the GRE, I signed into my email for the first time in several weeks, and I was reminded of an offer I made on Craigslist to tutor YoC (Youth of Colour) free of charge. Recall, that I was concerned that I might've been racist after neglecting to flee from a white man on the street in Brooklyn, who turned out to be armed with a knife in hopes of coercing me into surrendering my phone.

In my inbox, I noticed dozens of responses to the free tutoring advertisement. After filtering through several Armenians (who are basically white, I'm pretty sure) I settled on a compelling email from a woman with an attractive sounding name:

Dear Ross,

I am currently working to help out a black family in Bedford-Stuyvesant, Brooklyn. They have a family of seven and need all the help they can get. Their oldest son, fifteen years old, could use some extra help in geometry. Please let me know when you're free.

Sincerely,

Isabel Turtleman

So I found myself buzzing the bell (I thought it was odd that there was only one button at the address Isabel Turtleman gave me) of this brown-stoned building in Brooklyn's Bedford-Stuyvesant neighborhood around 4:00 in the afternoon. It was terribly cold out, and my (already reliably cold and clammy) hands were crying out in pain, even though I had them wrapped in a $400 pair of high-tech gloves that I saw an ad for on Facebook.

"Who is it?" said a woman's voice over the speaker next to the buzzer.

"Hi, this is Ross Mathcamp. I'm here to see Isabel Turtleman."

"Oh, I'm Isabel! I'll come get you, Ross."

She opened the door for me and extended her arms for a hug. Her clothes were tightly pressed against her body, a pair of shorts seemingly cutting off the circulation to her sizable thighs, a crude cardigan (very likely from "Brandy Melville") struggling to contain her . . . chunky upper body. In my arms, she felt childish and annoying, no taller than 162 centimeters.

"Glad you could make it, Ross. I'll get you set up in the study room with Marcus."

"Okay."

"He's the one I emailed you about. For geometry tutoring."

"Yes, that sounds familiar," I told her.

This home was nicer and larger than my own personal penthouse (albeit with worse, more "urban" views). Something felt wrong about being in there, the elaborate "bauhaus" furnishings, the Jewish "help." I wondered if I was about to be tied up and beaten, initiated into some sort of sex cult—which is a thing that I've heard happens to a great lot of people when their net worths finally exceed ten million clams.

We sat down in the "study room" on the first floor, a fluorescently lit space with a large, light brown (maybe oak? I was never one of those guys who knew about the different types of wood) writing table in the center, next to a gray leather sofa positioned in front of a screen, which, I assumed, was for projecting lesson plans for . . . some sort of after school program that was hosted in this lavish building.

"Do you want anything? Glass of milk?" Isabel asked me as I sat down.

"No, I'm okay. Maybe a glass of water, actually, if that wouldn't be too difficult for you. If you have it. But if you only have milk, I'm fine with nothing." I took it as a great sign that she offered me *milk* of all things. It meant that the combination of my non-surgical rhinoplasty and my weightlifting regimen meant I no longer looked Jewish. I looked like some kind of muscular Anglo or Aryan who could not only *tolerate* dairy, but *enjoyed* it, drank it in the homes of strangers in order to fuel his powerful body.

"Sure, I can get you a water. Sparkling or still?"

"Still is fine. Thanks."

I put my phone down on the writing table and it started wirelessly charging. She walked back out into the kitchen while I sat there, growing increasingly confused about what this place was and why they wanted me there.

"Marcus! Your tutor's here! Get your ass downstairs!" I heard her yell out.

"I'm coming, I'm coming," replied a boy's, no—a young *man's* voice.

I smiled at Marcus when he walked in. He was about my height (with so much time left to grow!), dressed in tan pants and a pink pastel sweatshirt, with a cool youthful haircut.

"Nice to meet you, Marcus, I'm Ross." I extended my hand.

He smiled at me, "We don't shake hands anymore. After that whole thing, remember?"

"Oh, yes, of course. I never really liked it either. I just thought maybe you would want to do like a cool handshake."

"Why? Because I'm *black?*"

Uh . . . "No, no. Because, because you're . . . a teen. When I was your age I loved doing cool handshakes with my friends . . ." Did I?

He squinted skeptically at me and tilted his head in disbelief, then relaxed, broke into an infectious smile and said, "I'm just messing with you, Ross."

"Oh . . . ha!" I let out an earnest guffaw. "That's funny," I told him.

Marcus fished out a folder from his backpack and pulled out a packet labeled WEEK 16 PROBLEM SET. "So here's the homework for this week. They're all Regents exam problems. You know about the Regents? It's a test we have to take at the end of the year."

"Yes, I know about it. I took a practice geometry one from the New York State website before I came over."

We looked at the first question.

A cone has a volume of 108π and a base diameter of 12. What is the height of the cone?

"There's like . . . a formula for this, right?" he asked me.

I grabbed a Dixon Ticonderoga and started scribbling it out. "Marcus, you really gotta memorize this one. I'm twenty-three years old, and I still have the formula for the volume of a cone memorized. So I'm gonna write it down for you, and then we'll see." I didn't want to tell him that this formula would be printed on the last page of his test booklet, or that I had long since forgotten it until earlier that afternoon.

$V = \frac{1}{3}\pi r^2 h$

"Oh, that makes sense."

"Yeah, so now it's just algebra. You plug the radius—six. And the volume—108 pi—into there and solve for the height."

He pressed a few buttons on his Texas Instruments Ti-84 Plus Graphing calculator "Alright. I got nine."

"Nice. You got it, bud."

We went through a number of these. Parallelogram problems, trapezoid trivia, glimpses into trigonometry. "Promise me you'll memorize the 45-45-90 right triangle, and the 30-60-90 right triangle. If you can draw those, and label the ratios of the sides, then you're golden, Marcus. Then all you have to remember is *SOH CAH TOA*. That's it."

Frustrated, he turned to me, "See, no offense, Ross. I like you, I like how you explain things" (this makes sense, as I'm an intern alumnus of Vox.com), "but I just don't think I'll ever be able to do this stuff. I just think it's all fake, like, some old white guys just made up all these rules and patterns and force us to memorize it."

"No . . ."

"What? I said what I said. I don't like geometry. I like history."

"Marcus! Don't you appreciate that geometry is *provable*, it's *certain*. That these beautiful little rules weren't *invented*, but . . . but were *discovered*?"

"Not really."

"Well don't you care that these things are just *objectively* true? That no matter who figures them out, the answer will always be the same? Muslim or Greek, Newton or Leibniz, everyone eventually reaches the same conclusion. And we can test it, and it works?"

"No?"

"You can read two books by two people who witnessed the *exact* same event, and their versions will be totally different. No two people will ever agree on any *a posteriori* knowledge that comes from experience. But the rules of geometry just exist. Independent of our own minds. There's no wiggle room. Just objective *facts*. Right and wrong!"

"Yeah, I know. I get what you're saying. And I just don't like that, man. I'm sorry. I don't like that. I don't think we always have to be certain about everything. I don't know if it's possible to even know *anything* for certain. That's why I like history."

This poor kid was just lost. An epistemological nihilist—I felt sorry for him. "Well, Marcus, it's getting pretty late. I should probably head home."

"Why? Because you might get mugged in this *black* neighborhood?" He smiled at me.

"That's funny. I actually got mugged by a white guy. In Fort Greene a few weeks ago."

"Was he Latino? Middle Eastern?"

"No, I don't think so. I think he was just an actual white guy, not just a census white guy. White. Descended from Europeans."

"Oh, wow. I wouldn't have expected that. But I guess that's my problem, for making assumptions about people."

"Exactly, Marcus. Nothing good can come from making assumptions about people."

I packed my pencils into my backpack and got up to leave.

"Wait!" Marcus called out, as I was heading toward the door. "My mom wanted me to give you this." He handed me a hundred-dollar bill.

"Oh, wow. Thanks Marcus. But that's a lot of money, and you probably need it more than I do, right?"

"No. Here, take it."

"I really don't need it."

"Well my mom wants you to have it."

"I don't get it. Are you rich? How are you so rich?"

Marcus looked at me as if I were an idiot. "You don't know? My dad was the point guard for the New York Knicks from 2002 to 2006."

"Your dad is *Allan Houston*?"

"Yeah, you've heard of him?"

"How else would I have immediately known whom you were talking about, if I hadn't heard of him?"

"Oh . . . yeah."

"Well, why did you hire a free tutor? I was trying to do something nice, helping out a bla— I mean, underprivileged youth. Someone else could've taken this spot."

"I had no idea you were *free*. Our nanny Isabel found you. I'm sure she figured the less money we spend on the tutors, the more we could spend on the nanny, since she's . . . you know."

We both laughed. Laughed at poor, Jewish, Isabel Turtleman.

Outside, I was immediately accosted by the scent of one of the neighborhood's many famous fried chicken restaurants. Ever since I'd started training for strength, I'd been ravenous for things like chicken and yams. Anything I could get my slimy little fingers on, really. My newfound muscles demanded it, and as part of my commitment to helping small minority-owned businesses, I figured the least I could do was purchase a meal for myself, leave a nice tip for the Cashier of Colour, etc, etc.

"Welcome to Kennedy Fried Chicken, how may I help you?" said the woman at the counter.

"Uh . . ." I was looking at the menu, at its idiosyncrasies, its typos ("raised without antibodics"), bizarre puns ("The Clucker Tartarelson (RAW CHICKEN) Sandwich"). No one wants to talk about how there are over six hundred restaurants in New York City named Kennedy Fried Chicken, none affiliated with any of the other six hundred-plus locations, no two sharing the same menu. "How's the 'mixed chicken'? What exactly is that? It's mixed race?"

She ignored my very funny joke, "It's chicken legs, and chicken breasts in a box. With fries."

"Okay, that sounds fine. I'll get that."

I sat down in a booth, playing Pong on my Watch, waiting for them to call me by my name when my chicken was ready. From behind me, I kept hearing this obnoxious hissing noise. Like a guy going "Pssssstt . . ."

trying to discreetly earn someone's attention. At one point, I could've sworn he was loudly whispering "Ross!" This went on for a few rounds of Pong, until finally, my Watch's screen was overwhelmed by a text message from an old friend, Victor "Vic" Bowflex, whom you may remember as my driver to the airport from the morning after I heard about my parents' death. It read:

> Turn around bish

I looked behind me and saw Vic giggling. He tilted his head upward and said "YO!" then ran over to sit across from me in my booth.

"Hey, Vic," I said to him, only remembering his name because it had just appeared on my Watch a few seconds earlier.

"What are you doing around here?" he asked me, with his foot up on the seat of the booth, "smashing somebody?"

"No, not at all. I was teaching geometry to this kid. He's actually the son of a famous basketball player."

Vic looked greatly relieved. "Oh, that's right. That's good. I was scared I was gonna have to whack you."

"What?"

"Allan Houston, he just got divorced, bro. He's paying me to do private security, make sure his wife doesn't have any new guys coming over to his house and blowing her back out, you know?"

"That makes sense. So if I said I was doing that, that I was 'blowing her back out,' you would've beaten me up?"

"I prolly woulda gave you a warning."

"And that's only because we're friends, right?"

"Yeah, I would go *sicko* mode on anybody else, bro." He started doing karate hand gestures into the air.

A voice from the front called out "Rozz?" so I went up and traded my receipt for a "mixed chicken."

I brought it back to the table and sat next to Vic, who, after a few minutes, came back with a box of what the menu called "Demon Wings." We both dug in, so to speak.

"Vic," I asked him, ripping a sheet from the roll of brown paper towels they kept at every booth in lieu of napkins, "how did you meet Allan Houston?"

"Networking, bro. That's what this driving thing is all about. Making connections, meeting new people. Building my business."

An idea came to me, something I should've thought of months earlier. "I need you to do some spying for me, Vic. I have this ex-girlfriend, whom I broke up with because I wanted her to stop smoking weed. And then when I wanted to get back together with her, she didn't seem very into it. So for the past several months, I've been using every available resource to make myself as desirable as possible to her."

Vic nodded along, dipping a Demon Wing into some sort of white sauce. I continued, "And I think we need to start spying on her. I think that might be the next logical step."

"Get into her *head*, yeah, definitely," he smiled at me, "and you got time to help me with my money, right? My financial pre-dic-a-ments?"

"Sure. Of course. We can work on that. I love explaining things to people. It's one of my favorite things to do, Vic."

"Alright. Let's set up a time, bro. That's perfect. I help you stalk your girl, you help me figure out my loans."

"It's an obvious pairing of talents, Vic."

Seventeen

". . . yeah, exactly. At a Kennedy Fried Chicken, in Bed-Stuy, no less. The same guy who drove me to La Guardia Airport on my birthday, after my parents died. And he had mentioned to me before that he did Private Investigator-type work, but I never even *thought* to use his services to spy on Lora Liamant."

"The spying, Ross. It's a natural progression of your desire to *know* everything. Have you considered why you have that urge? Why you have the need to make everyone feel that you're smart?"

"I have an anecdote, for you, actually. This is from my youth. Perhaps this will give you some insight into my upbringing. So in elementary school, I was the only kid with a TV in his or her room, and as I've told you so many times, we didn't have books in my house. Books were out of the question. But my parents, who really tried their best after seeing me watching far too much of the thing, installed this complicated V-Chip based setup onto my television. The V-Chip, if you're not familiar, is an idea cooked up by Ed Markey, who's now the junior United States senator from Massachusetts, that let parents block certain programs on their kids' TVs. In the late '90s, early 2000s (think post-Columbine), there was this hysterical moral panic about kids watching violence in movies and sex on TV. And I was born right at the peak of the Clinton-era culture wars (over whether or not single mothers were brave heroes, etc, etc), which led directly into the Bush-era culture wars, which really shaped my entire early childhood. Fights about things like chat room pedophiles, hummers, mass murder depicted in video games, etc, etc, are deeply ingrained in my mind."

"Yes, you've talked about that a lot in here, Ross."

"Well, the V-Chip, or whatever it actually was that my dad bought and had connected to my TiVo, would only let me watch four hours of *fun* things a day, you know, Comedy Central, TV Land, Nickelodeon, Carton Network, these sorts of *fun* things. And then after four hours of screen time, I could only watch PBS, CNN, Fox News, MSNBC, CNBC, ESPN, ESPN2, which my parents thought was doing me this great favor, but really just led to me having a terrible fixation on politics and sports and that 2000s cable TV style of arguing and debate.

"Which brings me to my school experience, and this memory that came to me the other day, of my suffering for wanting to impress my third-grade teacher, Mrs. Margera. Who maybe looked kind of like my mom, but come on, that can't be that important, can it? You see, I had progressed beyond the other kids my age (whether that was due to the methylphenidate I'll let you decide) and because I was so *gifted*, I became something of an answer hog. To the point that Mrs. Margera would have to stop calling on me. It was a horrible feeling, a primitive cucking sensation, watching other kids spit and struggle to answer questions you knew the answer to. The occasion that came to me, so clearly and distinctly, was in an afternoon civics lesson, a few weeks into the rate limiting of Ross answers. Mrs. Margera had called on maybe four or five other students (all while my hand was raised!), none of whom could tell her who the Speaker of the House was. I sat there squirming and waving my arm around, and she wouldn't even look at me. She refused to make eye contact with me. Why? Because I was the best? I don't know. I was so upset—wondering 'why would she even expect us to know this? Who else has a TV in his room but me?'—that I ran into the bathroom and wept in a stall. Well, I also had to use the bathroom, but I did get into 'trouble' (as if that really means anything. But it was painful at the time. It felt very bad to be told I had done something wrong) for leaving the classroom without asking. But that's the thing! She wouldn't call on me! Not to say the words 'Dennis Hastert' nor to say 'May I please use the restroom, Ma'am,' nothing! I was cut off from her entirely."

"And with this, this anecdote, you're trying to show me . . . an early example of what, exactly?"

"Well isn't that supposed to be your job to figure out?"

"I want you to tell me in your own words."

"I think, Doctor, what happened there, and what I *think* keeps happening to me, is that I get punished for being the best at things. Resented, withheld, cucked, whatever you want to call it. In that class, I was the best, and it didn't matter. I couldn't get the attention of my woman teacher. And that's how I feel right now with Lora. That I was already the best guy, the best she could do, certainly, and she's going around, like that teacher, going from man to man, and not finding any answers."

"That's a bit of a stretch, Ross. A little literary, for my tastes."

"Is it? Well maybe it is. But I'm suffering, I am simply so *cucked* right now. Just think about it for a minute, what's going on right now. I'm sitting here paying you three hundred dollars an hour to talk about how I can impress this woman and get her to love me again. She has the sole focus of my brain—which is a good brain, a great brain, I should add—and as we speak, it's possible, *probable* even, that she . . . that she has a . . . a *mouthful* of some other man. Some idiot. Some actor's brother, or drug dealer, or 'Dee-Jay,' or 'Art Handler,' or Israeli soldier, or Pizza Man—all of them alcoholics. And I'm incensed by this. That we no longer live in a meritocracy. That all of the lovely evolutionary ideas I had had about sexual hierarchies no longer seem to apply. That being the smartest, most handsome, strongest, funniest, kindest, healthiest, *wealthiest* man means nothing now. That it can only get you a few weeks or months of attention from a beautiful woman before she moves on to a never-ending series of chintzy invalids."

"So you feel the game is rigged against you?"

"That is *precisely* how I feel. I feel that as a highly competent man in his early twenties, I am given absolutely no respect whatsoever. I am treated as a schlemiel. No matter how handsome I make myself, no matter how many black kids I teach geometry to, I will be seen as weak, as pathetic, a little Jewish bug to be laughed at. And that's why I have to do something bad. Something *abject* like hiring a Puerto Rican guy to help me spy on a woman. This is the kind of thing women want in a man. They don't want perfect. They—"

"So you want to get caught?"

"No, no. That would be terrible. I couldn't handle the confrontation of that. I just want to turn myself *into* the type of person who *would* do something as creepy and objectionable as stalking a woman. And, you know, naturally, it will be very cool and smart and *adult* when I do it, since I'm employing a professional."

"You're getting very worked up, Ross. You're acting . . . manic. What have you been taking?"

"This is just something that happens to me lately, since I've started lifting weights and getting injected with Trenbolone or whatever it is that that other guy gives me."

"You don't even know what it is?"

"You would be shocked if you met him, the other doctor. He's terrifyingly intimidating. He really *humbles* me when I go in there."

"Now you're making me feel bad, Ross."

"Oh, stop it. You know he can't give me what you give me."

"I'm flattered."

"What I need you to tell me now is, why everyone is so unhappy. You told me a few months ago that I was suffering from an ennui."

"It's pronounced *ennui.*"

"Sure, sorry. I never learned French. But anyway, for a while, I thought maybe you were right. That people my age were miserable because they were bored and lazy and took horrible care of themselves. But I'm none of those. I take excellent care of myself, I am highly ambitious, I am working toward a *goal*. And I am still miserable. So tell me, tell me what the problem *really* is?"

"Well, if I told you right now, just said it, just laid it out there on the line for you, well, then I'd never see you again."

By the time I got home (maybe 11:40 a.m.), the plumber I'd hired to install bidets in each of the many bathrooms in my luxury condominium was packing his things up and preparing to head out. He said a number of truly original things to me, but the battery on my Watch was depleted and so I was unable to record him as he was speaking. And any attempt to paraphrase him would surely do no justice to his brilliance. But rest assured, he offered a number of fascinating observations about finance, race, and "these sickos who think they're girls."

I thanked him for installing these gadgets to make my bowel movements more pleasant and sanitary, offering a hint of self-deprecation ("thank you so much, Ross (his name was also Ross), for taking care of this so quickly. It's the sort of thing that would've taken me all day, but for you it was nothing!") as I handed him something like seventy dollars rolled up into a tip.

As I was exiting my master bathroom, after trying out my new toy, I heard my roommate and onetime love interest, Amanda Bauer, shouting from her room at the other end of the hall. I stepped out of my room so I could hear her better.

"Because, mommy, it's the DEFINITION of lust. It's *pleasure* for the sake of *pleasure*, and that's disgusting. It's greedy and disgusting and makes a mockery of God's creation. I can't believe you're going to keep doing this even after I explained it to you. This just shows you're of bad will. Okay, I gotta go, I love you, we'll talk soon, buh-bye," she shouted into her phone.

"Oh, hey Ross," she said as she walked out of her room. She was wearing a dark blue dress with tights underneath; she looked quite slim, I must say. "Did you know the plumber's name was also Ross?" she asked.

"Yeah, that was fun. I've always thought I had a blue-collar name."

"Well I think it suits you perfectly," she said.

"Yes, it does, because I'm a blue-collar guy," I replied.

"Yeah, that's why I said that. Because you say that about yourself."

"Okay."

I started walking over to the kitchen with Amanda following behind, tiptoeing past Araby (or maybe Eveline, I can never really remember which is which . . .), one of Amanda's kittens, which was staring at me with its green eyes, as if I were somehow intruding on *its* luxury condo, as if *it* were somehow allergic to *me*.

In the kitchen, I opened the refrigerator in search of some supplements. "Have you seen my BroccoMax? You know about BroccoMax? It's got sulforaphane and myrosinase, super bioavailable stuff. You'd have to eat like three pounds of organic broccoli sprouts to get the benefits of just one BroccoMax. But I can't find them. There's too much stuff in here. All I see is girl stuff in here. What is natto? Why do we have so much *natto*?"

"It's fermented soy, Ross. But it's Japanese and actually healthy so it doesn't make you gay. Here, let me find your broccoli pills," she pushed me out of the way and stuck her arm into the fridge, finding the BroccoMax in a few seconds. "See, I knew I would find it. Women have better vision up close than men. You men, your brains are good at spotting lions from a hundred feet away, but girls—moms especially—are great at going into closets and refrigerators and finding things immediately."

I popped a BroccoMax out of the bottle and swallowed it with some orange juice I poured from a glass bottle. "I have to take broccoli pills now, because real broccoli doesn't have enough calories, and when I eat broccoli it fills me up too much," I explained. "Because, you know, I'm trying to gain a ton of weight."

"Yeah you're looking massive," she said as she took out a BPA-free carton of coconut milk from the fridge.

"Thanks. How about you?"

"I think I weigh about the same," she replied, "maybe I've gained a few pounds since I moved in but—"

"No, I mean, what have you been up to?"

"Well you heard me on the phone just now, right?"

"I heard a bit at the end but no, I don't think it was very obvious what you were talking about."

She sat down next to me with a bowl of low-carb grain-free cereal. "Well my mom just called me to say she's getting 'married' to her girl-friend. I mean, this is just retarded, Ross. She divorced my dad and moved in with some woman named 'Christine.' And now they think they can spend a few hundred dollars and redefine the oldest human tradition. And they want *me* to go to their 'wedding.' It's so retarded."

"What's gotten into you? Everything is *gay* this and *gay* that lately. You know, it's one thing when the plumber hates gays, Amanda. But you have a *bachelor's* degree . . . from a prestigious private research university. You should really know better than to be saying things like this."

"Well if anyone ever gets mad at me I can just tell them I have a gay mom, and then they usually let it go."

"I believe that."

"And it's not even just about the *gay* thing, I've been yelling at my dad too about getting quote 'remarried.' Since it says in the Bible that if you get divorced and remarried you're committing adultery." She took out her phone and started responding to a message.

"Doesn't it also say you have to honor your father and mother?"

"Huh?" She looked up from the phone. "Oh, yeah. It does say you have to do that. But also I *am* honoring them by trying to help *them* obey God."

"Uh huh . . ."

"But actually you may be right, Ross. When I was a teenager, I used to get into screaming fights with them about . . . who knows what . . . colonialism and 'economic justice' or whatever. You know, some truly pissy teenaged meltdowns—calling them racist oppressors, Zionists, bootlickers, landlords, all sorts of calumnies. But now that they're all on board with that stuff because the TV told them to be, I've become a hor-rible reactionary, screaming about the gay atheist agenda. So maybe I'm just a total contrarian, with no convictions whatsoever, who just likes fighting with her parents and giving them a hard time."

I stood up, brushing some gray cat hairs off my pantlegs, "Well at least you *have* three moms and a dad. I have no moms and no dads."

"Aw, Ross. You poor orphan. Why don't you come to lunch with me and my old babysitter?"

"Who?"

"Her name's Jordana. You're going to love her. She's insane. She's thirty years old and loves restaurants. A real millennial success story."

"Does she have tattoos? I really don't want to hang out with some thirty-year-old woman who has tattoos."

"I don't think so. Just come."

"Are you going to the city? I was just in the city, I don't know if I really want to go again. It's so dirty there. And the rain, I mean . . ."

"I'll get us a car. Just come."

~

Downstairs, a large 2018 GMC Yukon Denali waited to pick us up. Armin, the driver, spent the duration of the ride yelling angrily in Farsi into the front seat's "hands-free" "Bluetooth" speakerphone. I don't have any evidence of this, as I couldn't understand what he was saying, but I could just feel, in my gut, that he was mad at me and Amanda for being Jews. Even though I was wearing a surgical face mask atop my nose (which had recently been (non-surgically) altered to appear less J-ish), I still had this eerie sense that he knew *exactly* what I was deep down, and was yelling about *me* into the Bluetooth speakerphone. Something like "whom does this idiot think he's fooling! He thinks I don't know what he is! But I know what he is! We should just kill him, for being a Jew. Do you have time to kill him with me today? No? You're busy? Okay, then we'll wait until another time to kill him for being a dirty ugly Jew." But I can't speak Farsi, so I have no way of knowing exactly what he was saying or if he was really talking about me at all. Nevertheless, you can understand how something like this would be stressful to go through.

We arrived around 1:00; Armin dropped us off on the corner of First Avenue and First Street. It was raining slightly, but not really an annoying type of rain, the sort of rain you could stand in indefinitely without really being bothered—a drizzle, almost like snow, really. We sat down together under an awning, I in my waterproof anorak, Amanda in one of those puffy polyester-shelled winter coats. "Do you know where we're meeting her?" I asked.

"Here, she's meeting us here."

"Sorry, sorry. I should've been more precise. I mean, do you know where we're eating with her? Which of these many . . . uh . . . places . . ."

"Oh, no. She didn't say."

"Okay."

I sat silently playing with a "fidget cube" I'd recently purchased based on a Facebook ad that said it was "scientifically proven" to "help autism."

"Can you call her?" I asked Amanda.

"I'm not going to call her," she replied.

"Why can't you call her? Did you text her? We're just sitting here like idiots. Everyone is laughing at us."

"I just checked where she is on the app where you can see where your friends are and she's right around the corner. She's going to be here in like two minutes, Ross."

When she arrived, carrying a large umbrella above her head (even though it wasn't really raining in any meaningful way), I recognized her as Jordana Prince, a minor internet . . . um . . . "personality" from the app where people get into fights with each other about politics. I follow thousands of people on there (especially in the NY-DC-LA media cliques) and Jordana was one of them, and I'll admit that she looked "as good" in real life as she does on the internet, by which I mean, fine. But it's still worthy of note because these journalist-adjacent personalities

(Jordana was a publicist) are often horrifically disfigured in real life (especially if they're from Washington D.C.), hiding their ghoulishness by adopting "avatars" of themselves from very specific and flattering angles that couldn't resemble reality less. But what else would you expect from people who get paid to do nothing but tell lies?

"Amanda!"

"Jordana!"

"You look so good—so healthy, is this your boyfriend?"

"No," Amanda said, "this is Ross, an old friend. I live with him and his sister now. Ross?" She turned to me. "Can you say hi to Jordana?"

"Oh, yeah," I mumbled back, "that's all true. I'm Ross and Amanda lives with me and my sister in Brooklyn."

"Nice to meet you," she said, laughing slightly at my apparent nervousness. "Well why don't we all go inside and sit down to eat? We're going to this one right in here, it's the *Ruth's Chris Steakhouse's Test Kitchen*, super exclusive—they're actually a client of mine."

Jordana gestured in the direction of the restaurant, a few dozen feet from us, and I jogged cautiously to the door to be able to hold it for her and Amanda, but it (the door) was locked and I had to stand there for several seconds until Jordana arrived and tapped her wallet against a small black RFID reader to the left of the door, triggering a slight "beep" and the unlocking of the door.

"Thanks," I said.

The interior of the restaurant featured that very contemporary fast-casual look—lots of metal bars, black painted tabletops, high ceilings, backless benches, etc, etc, etc, etc. "You're going to love this place," Jordana said to us, "they're actually a client of mine, I'm not sure if I mentioned that."

At the center of the table lay a quick-response (QR) code that we used our phones' cameras to scan, which opened up the menus in our respective mobile web browsers. "I feel like we're in *The Matrix* (1999)," I said.

"The menu's great. It's all superfoods. When they became my client, you know, after all that controversy with their racism a few years ago, I told them they had to start adding *superfoods* to the menu. I basically only eat superfoods."

"Oh, I'm getting the Eggs and Brains," Amanda said, "these body-builders I follow say brains are one of the healthiest things for women to eat, especially if they want to have kids soon. Brains are super dense in DHA."

Jordana and Amanda spoke while I let myself get distracted by the music playing inside the restaurant. This particular song had been play-ing in the car when my Dad and I were looking for parking outside the Staples Center for *Wrestlemania 21* on April 3, 2005.

"Listen to this song, Ross," he said, as he turned up the volume on his yellow 2002 Ford Thunderbird. "Listen to the words, Ross. It's a beautiful song, son. It's a song about believing in life after love."

"I think I've heard it before."

"It came out right after you were born. But we had never heard anything like it, son. What she did with her voice . . . it was brand new. They called it the *Cher Effect.* Listen to how she says she needs love to feel strong."

"I don't really get what it means to believe in life after love, dad. I don't know what that means. It doesn't seem like a sentence that makes sense."

"You're young. You haven't gone through half of what she's gone through. It was stupid for me to even try to show you this. You're just a kid. You won't get it. For years, probably. No matter how much I try to explain. I'm sorry, son. Let's just go in and watch Cena take the belt from that smug prick JBL."

"Ross?" Amanda said, rousing me from my daydream.

"Yeah?" I replied.

"I *said*: Did you order?"

"Oh, sorry. Yeah, I got like a burger, or something. . . . So, Jordana, what is your job, exactly? You're a publicist?"

"Yeah, totally. I love talking about my job since it's actually so fun."

"I think you mentioned this place is a client of yours?" Amanda added.

"It is," Jordana replied, "and of course, like, it was always my dream to represent a company like Ruth's Chris's. Given like, their whole history, with the female founder and everything," I nodded along as she continued, "but the thing about being a publicist is, it's not all just feel-good feminist chain restaurant lunches or going to bars and planting stories in *New York Magazine*. This is a real job, with real work, you know? Like I spend a lot of time working on documents."

"What?" I asked. "What does that mean?"

"I spend a lot of time working on documents, you know, past statements, reviewing upcoming statements, negotiating the terms of fake celebrity relationships where the guy is gay and the woman is a lesbian but they have to pretend to be married to appease their conservative fan bases, things like that."

At this point a dyed-haired, heavily pierced, ambiguously gendered (I really couldn't tell) person wearing a black cloth facemask arrived to drop off three paper bags containing food for our table.

Jordana: "And what do you do, Ross?"

"Well, I was trained formally as a nurse, uh, but then my parents died, so I quit my job as a nurse, because they left me all sorts of money, and now I'm spending a bunch of the money trying to improve myself to make my ex-girlfriend love me again because I got really jealous when I found out she was dating the unsuccessful brother of a famous network TV actor."

"Oh, that's hilarious, Ross. Have you always talked like that? I've never met someone who *talks* like you," she took a bite out of her salad, which featured dragonfruit, endive, and generous portions of avocado.

"Well, they say words are like weapons . . . they wound sometimes."

"What is that from?" Amanda asked.

"Oh it doesn't matter what it's from," Jordana said, "it's how he *says* it. He's so weird! In a good way! You should be on TV, Ross. Do you want me to make you famous?"

"Uh . . ." I considered whether this was really the kind of person I should be entrusting my future with. "I mean, what do you have in mind?"

"Well I just want to get you out there. I want to discover you before anyone else gets the chance. We can do for you what we did for Jiv Johnson. Would you like to be the next Jiv Johnson?"

Amanda and I looked at each other and each asked Jordana some variation of "who is Jiv Johnson?"

"Oh? You don't know about him? We must not have reached Brooklyn with him yet. He's this totally imaginary guy we cooked up. And I mean *really* cooked up, like CIA-level stuff: deepfake videos, astro-turfed social-media profiles, body doubles going to every downtown party pretending to be Jiv, you know, basically anything you can think of for faking a human being's whole existence. And it *worked*, everyone is talking about Jiv, at least here in the city."

"Why would you even want to do that?"

"Well, to see if we could," she said.

"And it sounds like you *can*. And just imagine how much easier it'll be with a real guy," I offered.

Amanda shook her head, taking a paper-straw-sip from her apple cider vinegar-infused lemonade. "I don't like the sound of it at all. It's just lying to people—which is wrong, and you're also promoting degeneracy." She held her phone out to us, "look at all these photos and vids of this guy Jiv drinking beer and smoking cigarettes. You're telling kids out there that it's okay to drink beer and smoke cigarettes."

"Amanda, come on," I shooed the phone away, "have an open mind, here. I mean, I hate beer just as much as the next guy, but you have to admit, it's impressive that they've convinced thousands of people that there's a guy named Jiv Johnson whose life they ought to care about."

"Thank you, Ross," Jordana added. "You know, I just realized who it is you remind me of," she lifted a paper napkin up to her face and coughed into it. "My boyfriend's business partner looks just like you. It's like . . . unreal. You guys have to meet him—my boyfriend I mean."

"I think I've met him," Amanda said.

"No, no! That was the old boyfriend. We broke up a few months ago because we got into a big fight about Israel. We were always fighting about Israel," Jordana said, but it wasn't clear why they were fighting or which side she was on. "But my new boyfriend, he's amazing. He's just such a go-getter, you know?"

"Well I don't know who he is, but it sounds very cool that he has a business partner who looks like me."

"Oh yeah, duhh . . ." Jordana stuck her fork onto Amanda's plate to take a few bites of brain. "I didn't even tell you guys about their new product. It's seriously incredible. They're going to be so effing rich off this pubic hair company."

"Pubic hair company? What are you talking about?" Amanda asked.

"It's called *Nothing to See Here*, and it's basically a one-stop shop for pubic hair needs. But the big product, and you guys have to *swear* not to tell anyone about this."

"I swear," I said.

"Promise," Amanda added.

"Okay, okay. Ready? This is so cool. So it's a whole new *underwear* that just makes your pubic hair fall out. I've been wearing it for a week and it really works. I'm all smooth. And the other awesome thing is it's actually really comfortable underwear, so you just keep wearing it and you never have to worry about your pubic hair growing back."

Amanda and I looked at each other as if to confirm that we were each hearing this correctly. I, naturally, was very intrigued by the idea of the pubic hair company and its magic underwear, but Amanda seemed much less impressed.

"How could that be healthy? It sounds disgusting, like, even if it did work it would just cause horrible rashes and burns and undesirable irritations," she said, as Jordana took the container of brains and eggs and tilted it up to her face to create a more advantageous angle for spooning any remaining bits of brains and eggs into her mouth.

"Oh, Amanda, you're always *worrying* about this and about that. Be more like Ross here. Ross has the imagination of a boy. I can see Ross's eyes lighting up right now as he thinks about the pubic hair company. That look in Ross's eyes just tells me that this is going to be a hit product. It has Goop written all over it. And soon, all the other underwear companies are going to try to copy it, but they won't get to market fast enough. And I'm gonna be rich."

"Is there any way for me to invest in this?" I asked.

"Yeah! Let me get your info and I can forward it to Douglas—that's my boyfriend, Douglas."

"That sounds great. I'd love to see if they have like a deck, or something."

"Oh yeah, sure. Do you mind if we go outside? I want to smoke a cigarette."

Outside, a deranged man approached us stumbling, and said, "You need anything? I got everything. You need weed, mushrooms, LSD? Here, you want my business card?" and I said, "No, thank you," and he left us alone but continued walking up the street asking other people if they needed weed, mushrooms, or LSD.

We walked a few blocks south, and I thanked Jordana for taking us to lunch at such an exclusive restaurant, and how it reminded me of the time my mom brought me to a Romano's Macaroni Grill in Redlands, California, in 2004 after bringing me to a "pox party" at a total stranger's house in San Bernardino.

"What do you mean? A 'pox' 'party'?" she asked.

"Did you guys not have this? On the east coast? My mom and a bunch of others were on all these forums, freaking out about how the chickenpox vaccine was mandatory for elementary schoolers that year. So all these moms would drive their kids to strange houses to let them play with chickenpox-infected kids, drinking out of their cups, French kissing, etc, etc."

"And did you get it?"

"Yeah, quite badly, actually. I missed two weeks of school, I was in tremendous pain, the whole thing was really rather ill-advised. So much so that when my sister Emily was the same age a few years ago, my mom decided it would be better just to let her get the vaccine."

Amanda sat down on a bench in front of the bookstore. "I think she was trying her best. I mean, when I have kids, I'm definitely going to space out the shots, I wouldn't want them getting shot up all at once. You know we do more vaccines than any other country in the world."

"Yeah, that's probably true. But if she were so LA and obsessed with health, why did take me to Macaroni Grill? Eating cheese and PUFAs and gluten? She really poisoned me twice that day, if you think about it."

Jordana smiled at this, gave me a hug, and said she had to go.

Amanda and I walked into a nearby bookstore on Prince Street, browsed for a bit, not saying much, but enjoying each other's company. With the credit card built into my Watch, I paid for our books: *An Exorcist Explains the Demonic* (2015) and *Woody Allen on Woody Allen* (1993).

Eighteen

Vic Bowflex, my hired gun, so to speak, was scheduled to meet me at *The Fort* around 10:00. Outside, snow was beginning to flutter past my thirty-fourth-floor windows, creating a neat, Christmasy atmosphere. The snowstorm (the first of the autumn) left me worried about how exactly Victor was going to find parking in my neighborhood, but I had to remind myself not to fret so readily about how gallant motorists managed their machines.

For the first time in weeks, I felt full of energy as I opened my eyes. Before bed, the previous evening, I lay a lamina of Scotch Magic Tape over my lips, sealing my mouth shut, forcing me to breathe through my nostrils exclusively. What a delightful discovery! I woke up with an unsore throat, clarity of mind, and an inner nose free from any troubling . . . *buildup* (which had become something of a problem ever since my non-surgical rhinoplasty), and perfect 100/100 "sleep scores," on both my Oura Ring and my EEG Dreem 2 headband. In the kitchen, I prepared myself a breakfast of six slices organic turkey bacon (rated a three out of five—the best I could find—on the Global Animal Partnership's Animal Welfare Rating), three pasture-raised chicken eggs, one small sweet potato, and green tea (sencha).

By the time this feast was finished and its dishes tided, the time was only 7:00, and so I managed to slip back into my quarters (the "master" bedroom) without interacting with Amanda or Emily. In there, I showered, shaved, brushed my teeth, flossed, rinsed . . . relieved myself, etc, etc. Finally, I dressed myself in a pair of relaxed-fit burgundy trousers, navy cotton sweater (I'm allergic to wool), and sat in front of my desk's Philips GoLite BLU Energy Light Therapy Lamp (which was supposed to ameliorate the symptoms of seasonal depression by tricking my brain into thinking it was summer time) and read the latest David Brooks column that my favorite friends and left-wing podcasters were all making fun of online.

Through the hallway, I could hear Emily talking to Amanda. I stood up from my chair and poked my head out the door (slightly) to take a listen.

"So *today* is the Feast of the Immaculate Conception in the Byzantine Rite. It was yesterday in the Roman Rite," Emily said.

Boring! I walked back over to my desk to take in more of that blue light, do some breathing exercises, and think about Lora Liamant, her family, and their home.

~

The first time I met Lora's parents, saw her home, we'd only been together for a few weeks. "Remember, they're *older* so be very careful about the references you make," she said to me as we walked east down 27th Street in Manhattan, toward her parents' so-called "brownstone" in Chelsea. "Like, don't make any jokes about *I Hope They Serve Beer In Hell* (2009), because they won't know what you're talking about," she continued.

"Oh, relax. I'll be on my finest behavior," I replied. She made an excellent point about our parents' respective age differences. I, Ross, being the product of a petit-bourgeois teenage pregnancy, was constantly micromanaged by my millennial mommy. Whereas Lora, on the other hand, was the child of boomers, and had an *old* dad, who was mixed race and highly educated. An entirely different dynamic to what I'd been accustomed to. When you have old parents, they really don't care what you do. They don't have all that much power, they need you (to feed them soup, and teach them how to use the computer) just as much as you need them (to give you money).

Inside, I gazed uncritically at the collected art, standing nervously, pretending to feel comfortable. The Liamants were an art family (whereas my family was obsessed with *low culture*, which I've already lamented repeatedly)—Ted was a trained painter and mildly successful muralist (by which I mean, he was given money for it on two or three occasions) in his youth, before foraying into bureaucracy and diplomacy. Lora's mother had taught a number of art history courses at a prestigious private liberal arts college in Poughkeepsie, New York. But by the time I had arrived, they were both retired and living off of Lora's mother's family's millions. Although, Ted, from what I understood, still collected a great deal in "consulting fees." But in short, they are erudite and accomplished; they each have Wikipedia pages and have published books, something I remain impressed by and envious of.

The home itself was worthy of exhibition. Built in the 1920s by a prominent Freemason, it featured elaborate trapdoors, graven occult imagery, high ceilings, and abundant natural light. Not to mention its fair share of dusty heirlooms, books, sculptures, the previously mentioned paintings.

"You must be Ross," Lora's mother said, smirking knowingly at me, as if she were familiar with my archetype.

"Yes, I should hope so." I don't know what I could've meant by that. Maybe I was trying to say something folksy. Humble and *normal* like *"that's what it says on my driver's license"* or *"You guessed correctly! Feel free to collect your prize of one hug."* But I can't imagine she put as much thought into it as I did.

Lora showed me her childhood bedroom, old photographs, poems, her many notebooks filled with disgusting drawings of teachers, friends, lovers, etc, etc, from her youth, labeled with funny nicknames like "Obese Dave."

"Have you done any of me?"

"Well, I'm not so sure that would be a good idea. The Anti-Defamation League would publish a newsletter about me the second I captured your caricature . . ."

We laughed and shared a brief (but passionate) kiss. Looking back at this joke, it's clear that she was pandering to me, to my humor, to my insecurities. It's sad. On my phone, a message from Mom.

> Dad and I on way 2 Goo Goo Dolls concert. Luv U

From the first floor, Lora's mother called out, "Kids? Dinner's ready!" and so we walked back down the stairs, into the dining room, and sat down at a long table, where Ted, the man himself, was seated at the head, with three additional place settings in the first few chairs in front of him.

"Nice to meet you sir," I shook his hand and made contact with his half-Asian eyes. He was short, but muscular, spry, with a firm grip and stature (especially for a septuagenarian). Lora had mentioned once that Ted's mother, a Filipina immigrant, had trained him in Arnis (the national martial art of the Philippines) as a child.

"I've heard a great deal about you," I told him, sitting down at a chair on his right, leaving a space between us for Lora to sit in when she got back from the bathroom.

"Probably terrible things," he replied, taking a puff of some kind of electronic vaporizer device, with a blue light at the end that came to life each time he inhaled.

"No, not at all. You have a lovely home. And a lovely daughter. She looks so much like her mother."

"What the hell is that supposed to mean? Are you saying you'd like to do to my wife what you're doing to my daughter?"

"Uh . . . no, of course not. I mean, would you like to do to your daughter what you do to your wife?"

"Well," he shook his head disgustedly at the absurdity, "*I'm* not the one saying they look alike."

"Terribly sorry, sir. They couldn't be more different."

Lora's mother began carrying in a number of serving dishes. "Lora mentioned you were a very *healthy* eater, Ross. So I made quinoa. And scallops. I hope that's alright."

I smiled and nodded. "That's perfect." It was awful. Quinoa, while tasting terrible, is also one of the least healthy foods. I'd prepared for whatever this house was going to throw at me by taking a combination of turmeric, activated charcoal, and prebiotic acacia fiber supplements before I'd arrived. Scallops are fantastic, though.

Lora came out of the bathroom, hugged and kissed her father, then sat down between us. Lora's mother followed and soon we were all seated, all eating, together, as a family.

"So Ross," Lora's mother started, as she served herself some quinoa and scallops, "I hear you've just started working as a nurse. How is it?"

"It's . . . well, it's interesting. I mostly enjoy it, especially when I'm not getting sexually harassed by the doctors."

"Is that supposed to be a joke?" she asked.

"He's kidding, Mom," Lora butted in.

We went on like this for a while. I tried to explain my parents to them, how I have a sister who's ten years younger than I am, how my dad's family changed their last name to seem less Jewish when they arrived at Ellis Island, etc, etc. They were for the most part, unimpressed. With the two of them, Ted slightly more so, squinting confusedly at me every time I said anything, unsure whether to take me seriously.

I tried to talk politics. "So Ted, I saw that photo of you shaking hands with Madeline Albright in the living room."

He smiled and nodded at me. "Are you an Albright fan, Ross?"

"Oh, no, certainly not, sir. I was going to ask why you didn't have it hidden away with the photos of you with Gaddafi and Saddam Hussein." I'd done a great deal of research on Ted Liamant and his career in the State Department before I arrived.

"What?" Ted was enraged. "Are you saying Albright was on their level? Based on what? What exactly?"

Based on a few Noam Chomsky quotes I think. Something about Serbia. I'm still not really sure. Just that a lot of my smart friends who don't usually hate women seem to hate Madeline Albright. "Uh. . ."

Lora intervened, "Dad, stop. Ross is just being cheeky, right Ross?"

"Yes, of course. Making fun of all the silly young people," I desperately tried to clarify.

He seemed to calm down. "The world is a complicated place, Ross. I wish someone had told me that when I was your age."

After dinner, I offered to help with the dishes, expecting them to graciously tell me I was excused. "Well isn't that sweet," Lora's mother said, "if you insist, Ross, you can help dry. I'll wash and you dry."

She washed and I dried. I think she liked me. I hope she still does. I'm certainly much better (from any sane parent's perspective) than the (many, many) other men her daughter associates with.

As Lora and I were leaving, putting our shoes on near the downstairs door before heading back to my apartment for some quote "late night fun" (as her mother put it), I could hear Ted shouting "He's bizarre! And I don't like *bizarre!*" from the second floor. But I was so excited to be dating a diplomat's daughter that I didn't even care.

I was sitting at my desk, waiting for Vic Bowflex, when my bedroom landline phone began ringing, a call from the front desk. They needed me to come downstairs to personally verify that I had invited Vic into my home. Something about his FICO score being so low that he set off special security flags. . . . While I was down there, I picked up a package, from Robert Shapiro, my family's estate's attorney at law.

"This place . . . this place is crazy bro. This is like MTV's *Cribs* (2000–), bro."

"Thanks, Vic. But remember, my parents had to die for me to get it."

"Oh, I wouldn't care. I would kill my dad, *and* serve time for a place like this. I hate my dad, dude."

What was I thinking inviting this man into my home? Oh, yes. I needed him to help me earn back the respect of a woman. "Well, you probably wouldn't get very much money for doing that, so I wouldn't recommend it."

We sat down in the living room, and I pressed some specific combination of buttons (on one of the many remotes we had lying around) that brought down the screen for our projector. Vic took out his laptop, something that looked like it couldn't have cost more than $300 when it came out five years earlier. It was disgusting, to my eyes, as someone who takes a great deal of pride in having high-end gadgets.

"What's in that package you just got?" Vic was leaning over my shoulder as I sat down on the couch.

"Would you relax? Please! You're making me nervous, Vic." I ripped at the box with my fingernails.

"I woulda used my pocket knife, but they confiscated it downstairs."

"Good." I managed to rip it open. "This is my dad's old SEGA Dreamcast. It came out on September 9, 1999. That's nine nine nine-ty-nine, Vic. My dad loved this thing. He used to complain to me all the time about it. With tears in his eyes, he would turn to me and say 'It was superior to the PlayStation 2, to the XBOX, and most definitely the GameCube. It was the best. And they got *screwed*, Ross. They got *screwed* by Electronic Arts and the Ubisofts of the world, Ross. They made a superior console, but everyone abandoned them. Without games, a good console dies, Ross. Remember that. If you have the best product, but you depend on someone else to make it usable, you can get screwed at any moment.' And I would just sit there and listen to him telling me things like that. He was a very smart guy, Vic. He would read *Game Informer* magazine every month and tell me about the latest news in the world of video games."

"Oh, cool . . . yeah, my dad does construction."

Vic walked back over to his computer, pulled up his credit card statement, his checking account, and a photo of his collection of baseball cards. "Alright, bro, I need you to tell me how to get rich. Like a Jew, you know?"

"This is it, Vic? This is all the money you have? This checking account? This is like no money."

"Well, times are tough. I'm thinking, if I can just get two or three side hustles, you know, then I'll be able to get some passive income, and—"

"What? What are you talking about? What is Barcade? Why are you spending $300, $250, $400 every week at Barcade?"

"It's like a bar, where they have—"

"I know. Well, I don't know, but I can imagine what it is. But you have to stop. You have to stop going to Barcade. You have to stop spending money on things like that. On Barcade. On vinyl records. On dating apps. And you can't carry a balance on your credit card. You have a ten-thousand-dollar balance, at like a twenty-six percent APR. Do you know what that means? You're paying like two hundred dollars a month just in interest. That's awful, Vic. That's just giving your money away. To *international bankers*, if you know what I mean. I can't just sit here while you get shafted like that. I mean, you're keeping ten grand in your checking account at point two percent interest, while you have ten grand in debt going up at twenty-five percent interest. Does that make sense? Of course not. So here's what I'm going to do for you, Vic. I'm going to pay this off for you. I have no choice. It's making me sick just to look at. You're about to be debt free."

"Wow . . . thanks, bro. I don't even . . ."

"No, stop it. Sit back down. Don't hug me. Consider this an early payment for the private investigator work you're about to do for me. But seriously, you need a belt tightening, Vic. Don't they talk all about wealth at your protestant church?"

"Yeah, but Pastor Jeff says we just gotta donate to him, you know, ten percent, a tithe, and then we'll make it back double from the Holy Spirit."

"No, stop it. Stop giving that guy money. You can't afford to give that guy money. Maybe a hundred dollars a month."

"Okay . . ."

"Don't be sad, Vic. This is important. You're learning how to budget your money. And the most important thing, is to give less of your money away every month, to Jews, like me. In fees, taxes, all of this crap. That's what separates the mensch from the goy, so to speak. Whether or not you let nameless faceless bankers take your money away from you for no reason. So next, open up Vanguard.com. You need to open up a Roth IRA and put in the maximum contribution of six thousand dollars. I'll send you the money for it. Oh, I just can't stand looking at these finances right now. They're pitiful, Vic. But we're going to get them into shape. And then, you're going to help me stalk my ex-girlfriend so I can learn valuable private information about her and use it to make her love me again. Does that sound fair?"

Nineteen

For years, I used to sit in front of the television, howling at Jon Stewart as he played clips of the idiots (fools!) at Fox News while they mongered fear about an alleged War on Christmas that was already underway. Little did I know that I would soon (ten years later) be in the middle of a war of my own—on Christmas, no less.

". . . I'm sorry, Ross. But Amanda and I absolutely cannot have any sort of Christmas dinner with you or celebrate Hanukkah. Unless you accept the true positions of the Magisterium of the Catholic Church and receive baptism."

"What? These holidays are a *tradition*!"

"I know, Ross. But first of all, Amanda and I won't be indulging in any festivals of the *old law*. And as far as Christmas goes, it would just be . . . indecorous to celebrate with any heretics or nonbelievers."

"This is just a little much, Emily, I really can't believe you're doing this to me. So what do you want me to do? What am I supposed to do for the holidays?"

"Well, first of all, it's only for the religious holidays that we can't eat together. And second of all, I think you know exactly what I want you to do, Ross."

So I ended up spending all ten days (Hanukkah (eight days) plus Christmas Eve and Christmas Day) alone, eating the Trader Jacob's brand frozen latkes and the Trader Joe's brand frozen sirloin beef Wellington. I considered inviting Victor over, but I didn't want to deal with his own sillier, less articulate brand of Christian proselytizing.

The day after Christmas, Boxing Day, as it's called outside of the US, I looked in my mirror and was shocked, repulsed, horrified to see what my hair had grown into. I truly resembled the late Aaron Swartz. Racking my brain, it seemed I had gone over six months without as much as a trim. It was just so long, so unruly, I was so *aware* of it, coming down in long strands, tickling my eyelids, sticking out on the sides, curling upward at the base of my neck.

"Why didn't you tell me my hair was like this?" I asked Amanda in the doorway of her room, where she was lying atop her comforter, contorted, belly slightly showing below her shirt, listening to some Nabokov audiobook over the Bluetooth speaker on her bedside table.

"Alexa, PAUSE," she said, before turning to me. "What? I thought you were doing that thing where you weren't getting it cut until you accomplished something."

Perhaps she was right. But I can't imagine what I could have been waiting for. Some weightlifting record, some GRE practice test score, whatever it was, I'm sure I'd done it. "Well, perhaps you're right. But whatever it was, I'm sure I've done it. I'm going downstairs to get it cut."

"Okay, Ross. Good luck." I do love Amanda. Her patience for me. I ought to be less bitter about her conversion to Catholicism.

Across the street, thirty-four floors below my apartment, I walked into *Santa Barber's*, a reputable Dominican barbershop. Pasted in the storefront window, photos of the same man sporting several different haircuts, numbered one through thirty. "I'll ask for the thirty," I thought to myself, as I sat down in the upholstered armchair closest to the door.

"What you need, papi?" asked one of the Dominican barbers, carrying a pair of electric clippers, wearing an extraordinarily tight gray henley that highlighted his well-groomed pectoral and deltoid muscles.

"I guess a haircut."

"Twenny minute, papi. You wan smoke hookah?"

"No, I'm okay."

He looked surprised, "We got meent, we got grayb, we got regalar. Ees hookah," he lifted his fingers to his lips and pretended to blow puffs of smoke. "Tobacco, papi."

"Yeah, I'm okay. Thanks."

The guy getting his haircut in front of me was telling some kind of story, about his quote "child's mother." Saying things like "So I told her, so I said to her, if you want to play games, with our child and his education, then I'll play your *games*! I'll go *Milton Bradley* on your ass. If you want to be playing games like that," while his barber laughed and said "Exactly. That's exactly what I would've said, bro."

On the TV, a large brown Magnavox affixed to the wall, fuzzy softcore pornography played inconspicuously. No one seemed to care. It seemed to be a music video featuring topless women tongue-kissing each other, rubbing each other with oil, etc, while an obese tuxedoed man crooned along to a reggaeton beat. All this, in broad daylight, on the day after Christmas. Luckily, the women weren't much my type, so I wasn't really tempted to stare.

When my time had come, when my ("my") barber signaled for me to come sit in his chair, don his smock, and submit to his sharp objects, I had already begun to have second and third thoughts about whether it was wise for me to be getting my hair cut at such an . . . *ethnic* establishment. But it was too late. The barber (*el peluquero*) said a few words to me in what he thought was Spanish. I nodded along meekly, "Yep, sounds fine," but I knew I was about to endure something far from fine. For the next twenty minutes I was his chump. I was his . . . *victim,* and he was going to town on me with those clippers. Every time I thought he was finished, he found more hair to cut. By the end of it I was sporting a military-grade bona fide buzzcut. Disastrous! And what did I do to stop it? Nothing. I was just sitting there. A coward, watching my hair get ripped away from me. Never again would I step foot inside a Dominican barbershop. My hair (so delicate! so subtle!) needed fine-toothed treatment, careful cutting from highly trained women with scissors.

The guy (my abuser) cutting my hair that day could probably tell I was getting increasingly unnerved as he went shorter and shorter. At one point he even offered to call it quits ("You wan me stop?") but I

didn't have the guts to tell him how badly he was ruining me. "It's okay
. . ." I replied. When all was shed and done, I settled my debt, left him a
generous (if not sardonic) fifty-dollar tip (he almost certainly needed it
more than I did), and ran back home (across the street) to take a shower
and remove the (great deal of) excess hair that had slipped through
the polyester cape and onto my back, causing a circus of creeping itchy
sensations. Oh, poor bald buzzcut Ross. They shaved me. They really
shaved me.

At home, after I was showered, I stopped to look at myself in the
mirror once again. And you know, ever since my non-surgical rhinoplasty, lip fillers, cheek fillers, and jaw exercises, it seemed my face had
really grown into being worthy of a shorter haircut. Emily and Amanda
agreed.

"Really, Ross, I don't think it looks so bad."

"Yes. You look very handsome," Amanda said.

"Well, thanks, guys. That means a lot to me. I was feeling very upset
when I walked out of that Dominican barbershop. But a shower and a
few compliments from women can really do a lot for a man's confidence."

I went into the powder room (the smaller showerless restroom
closest to our front door) and double-checked my appearance in some
alternate lighting. They were right! I was nothing short of strikingly
masculine. Oh, I felt terrible for that poor Dominican man to whom I
passive-aggressively gave an exorbitant tip.

"Girls, what do you say we watch *Idiocracy* (2006)? I think it'll be
an interesting thing to pop on, particularly for Emily. She'll get a nice
opportunity to see the sort of sick things liberals let themselves joke
around about before she was born."

"I've always wanted to watch that," Amanda replied.

"Well, then. Let's go get something to eat, some lunch, some snacks,
and then we can tune in."

I took them down to the Whole Foods Market on nearby Flatbush
Avenue. "Get whatever you'd like from the buffet," I told them. And they

did. I take this sort of thing especially seriously, finding something artful and freeing about it. Thick paper to-go boxes piled high with seemingly monstrous concoctions of hot and cold foods. Just as any smoothie you make will be pleasant and palatable once blended, any self-serve Whole Foods Market medley is going to be a joy, a treat. Braised beef short rib, kalamata olives, pan-seared haddock. Oven-baked Brussels sprouts! Toss it in there. Don't worry, it's going to be great. What could be better, what could be more fun, more *balanced* than grabbing a little bit of everything on tap? What could be better than getting a hot new haircut, having a huge healthy meal, and watching a film from the mid-2000s with my family, all in the same afternoon?

What a peaceful Boxing Day, indeed.

Twenty

On New Year's Eve morning I awoke with a slight headache, some mild muscle soreness (from the deadlifting), etc, etc, but for the most part was enthused, because I'd been invited to a party at Don Morton's house, which was also a penthouse (although Don's parents were still very much alive). I had met Don Morton during my first semester at my prestigious private research alma mater in lower Manhattan. I took a few turmerics in the early afternoon, plus an ashwagandha, and a 30-mg capsule of long-lasting Lisdexamfetamine to make sure I would still be cognitively . . . *there* late into the night.

"Do you think I should bring something?" I asked Amanda in the kitchen.

"Probably. It would be rude if you didn't, even though you're both millionaires," she replied, taking a sip from a green drink in a glass bottle.

"The problem is, I can't in good conscience bring like . . . beer, I mean, that would be an abomination. And then snacks, like *corn*-based snacks, that's just as bad as alcohol, really. How about . . . Would people find it funny if I brought a ton of coins? Like if I brought like five hundred dollars' worth of quarters, rolled up, from the bank, and put them in a big bowl like chips for them to take."

She laughed sardonically. "That is funny, but I think the banks close early today. So you may not have time."

"Well . . . And you're sure you don't want to come?"

"Absolutely not," she laughed dismissively at me, "while you're hanging around with a cast of characters right out of *1 Corinthians 6:9*, Emily and I will be attending a Tridentine Latin Mass (TLM) celebrated by a priest who was ordained in 1965. Father Fred, he's called. And then we're going to have dairy-free hot chocolates and say all fifteen decades of the Rosary together."

"Okay, fine! Enjoy!" I threw my hands into the air and went back to my room with a full glass of water. It was unusual, for me (Ross!) of all people to appear at a shindig. But my female flatmates' conversion to Catholicism coupled with the confirmation of Lora Liamant's best friend Hannah Nenner's attendance (Don told me she RSVP'd to his Facebook invite), what choice did I have? It was so very *Goldberg*. Hannah would see me, my fun new attitude (Party Rocker Ross . . .), refined face and body, and word would get back to Lora. Perhaps even a few photos of the New Ross would make their way onto that app where people post pictures of themselves and their friends and their food.

I grabbed my finest fall jacket (the outside evening temperature was predicted to be a temperate fifty-one degrees), a green suede Harrington that I'd paid four figures for a few weeks earlier, a pair of Levi's 541 Athletic Fit Jeans (my legs have gotten quite muscular from all the squatting) in black, and a muted mauve jumper that the gay guy at Bloomingdale's SoHo said looked "utterly vicious" on me (and my new broad upper body). Yes, a good outfit indeed. Fitting for the smartest, strongest, richest Ross in all of Downtown Brooklyn.

And it was also quite important (for personal reasons) that I upstage, (outshine, etc) Don Morton in his own home. He's always been something a rival, given how similar we look, although Don (often called "The Don" by our "ironic" "self-aware" circle of 120-IQ friends) is Italian, and not at all Ashkenazi. More to the point, however, is that Don, alongside Lora L, attended the *Zuckerman Progressive Middle School for the Children of Extraordinary Parents*. Oh, that sounds fine, you might be thinking; they knew each other as kids, and went to the same fun middle school where instead of grades from 0 to 100, or A to F, you're given vague inanimate metaphors (Lora once told me, proudly, that she earned a "keep up the good work!" in United States history) from some idiot Oberlin graduate, you might be thinking. It sounds totally innocent and harmless, Ross, you might be saying. Wrong! Although I myself thought the same thing when I initially met Lora and found out she used to know Don Morton.

It wasn't until several months later that Lora admitted she had a quote "gigantic crush" on Don Morton in the seventh grade, which was completely unreciprocated, according to her. How dare he, how dare Don Morton hurt the feelings of little Lora Liamant. This, naturally, was a constant source of insecurity for me; I know how powerful those little pre-teen tenderness can be—most *especially* the unrequited ones. So I've made a habit of trying to eclipse Don Morton as often as possible.

At 10:00, I arrived at his building, *The Tent* which was a county fair / circus-themed luxury apartment building on the opposite side of Downtown Brooklyn. Its eighty thousand square feet of advertised amenities included a petting zoo (disgusting), a house of mirrors (scary, and confusing), an arcade (gets old), and a "discotheque," which hosted popular musical acts every Friday (waste of space, and doesn't even *fit* with the circus theme). I checked in with the front desk, had my hand stamped, and ascended the elevator up to Don's thirtieth- (four floors lower than mine, but his building was taller . . . oy) floor penthouse.

He opened the door for me. "Hey! Whoa! You got a buzzcut too. Nice man."

Oh, I was sick to my stomach. What a nightmare, to be *scooped* on the buzzcut by Don Morton. "Yeah, it got way too long, and I figured it was time for a change," I told him.

No one had arrived yet; he showed me around the place, a personal tour. It bore a disturbing resemblance to my own. Nearly identical appliances, floor-to-ceiling windows, similar soulless modern furnishings.

"Did you want to put those bags down?" he asked me after we'd seen every room.

"Oh, yeah. Sorry. I brought you these organic grain-free tortilla chips from this website I found. They don't have the usual confused texture of the average store-bought grain-free tortilla chips. People will just think they're normal tortilla chips, made of grain."

"Awesome man, thanks," he replied.

Don and I sat down in his "study," watching an online video of the *Anderson Cooper 360: 2004 Year in Review* (2004), laughing at the many *Jib-Jab* appearances. I told Don what (not why) I'd been up to, about my parents' death, my living with Emily and Amanda Bauer, my upcoming teaching assistant position and pursuit of a PhD.

"That's great, man. I'm sorry about your parents. But I'm glad you're being productive about the whole thing. The Drew Lancet stuff sounds super cool. I'm sure we'll all be watching *you* on TV someday."

"Thanks, Don. That means a lot, really. I feel like such a jerk, I've been talking all about me, and my exercising and my orphanism, that I haven't even asked what you've been up to."

"So I started this company, actually. It's called Urase but it's pronounced like erase. It's basically a way to delete things you've done on the internet. And we have this new tool, where we dig up people's old posts, like Andrew Kaczynski style, and basically we just send it to them, and tell them we'll delete it if they pay us."

"What kind of stuff?"

"Oh, you know. Standard embarrassments. Blackface Halloween costumes, out of context rap lyrics, edgy unfunny jokes, stuff like that. Just things that you were allowed to do like ten years ago but aren't now. We're bringing in like twenty grand a month."

"Are you worried you'll eventually run out of things to blackmail people with?"

"No, not really. Every year the amount of things you're allowed to say just keeps getting smaller. New people enter the workforce and get promoted to jobs they don't want to lose. I think it'll be profitable for a while. And if not, I can just move on to something else."

At that point a few people came in the door and began playing music over Don's "smart speakers." He didn't get up.

"And you're running this whole company? It's just you?"

"Yeah, me and Kyle, for now. It's not that fancy, really. Just a little JavaScript. You probably know a little JavaScript, right Ross?"

He was well aware I didn't know JavaScript. He was trying to make me feel bad for not being a coder. This guy, this *backstabber* couldn't help but put me down for my choice of undergraduate major. You'd never see me saying to people, "Oh, you know how to take someone's temperature and blood pressure, and then get the doctor to come in, right?" Of course not! That would be *rude*. It would be showing off that I was a registered nurse. We nurses have some honor; computer scientists like Don Morton just can't help themselves.

Smiling, I replied, "Nope, never learned," and got up to see what was going on in the rest of the house, as people started to pile in.

The evening had quickly turned into a real "scene," with a now sizable crowd of friends, nemeses, strangers, etc. Allie Miller, Taylor Gonzales, Myles Xavier, Mia Sophia, Tristan DePew, were all already there. Honor Levy, too, was there, but she wouldn't even look at me. Every time I tried to get close, she would run off into another room. I'm not sure what I did to her, but it felt sort of hurtful, I mean, we'd played together as children for crying out loud. The least she could do was say hello, but whatever, fine. . . .

"Whoa! Buzzcut Ross!" Tristan said to me as I went to get a red plastic cup full of water. "Yeah, ha ha," I replied. In the living room, I stood nervously, listening to the conversations people were getting themselves into.

"Well you know who *owns* Lowe's, right?"

"No, who?"

"Home Depot."

"What year was 9/11? '02?"

"Yeah, I think so. It was awful."

"Yeah it's true. Just take one."

"That's all it takes?"

"Yeah, just one pill. I pledged it on Kickstarter."

"And you don't get a hangover?"

Allie Miller, over Don's stereo speakers, was playing some song from the early 1990s that Pitchfork.com described as "Marxist Shoegaze," in which a French accented woman repeats the lines

Money's like a knife
Money's like a gun

for seven minutes and fifty-eight seconds.

In another corner, two people I didn't recognize were saying things like "what's going on with abortion right now is *so messed up*" but I couldn't tell if they thought there were too few or too many abortions going on. I walked up to them and told them my idea for how to fix the whole abortion controversy.

"Hey," I said, "I think I have the perfect idea for abortion. So my idea is like cap and trade, but for abortion. So everybody gets one abortion. Every man, every woman, and everybody in between" (you have to make it clear that you think there are infinitely many genders when you're talking to young people), "they all get one abortion. And it's free, and it's legal. But you can *sell* your abortion if you don't want to use it. Or you can choose not to sell. That way we can make the left happy by giving away free abortions, and the right happy by putting a cap on it. And then we also create a good market, with incentives and externalities. What do you think?"

"Are you serious?" one of them replied.

"That's disgusting," said the other, and then they got up and walked away from me.

Back in the kitchen, I grabbed a can of this new monk-fruit sweetened soda that Don told me about. He had both ginger ale and root beer, but I figured I would start with a ginger ale and see what happened as the night moved on. On my shoulder, I felt a woman's finger tapping me. "Ross!" she was saying; I turned around and saw Candy Catena, a former lover, whose father owned a number of luxury car dealerships in the Tri-State area.

"Hey, Candy! How are you?" The problem with this woman, was that she'd gained a great deal of weight since we'd met five years earlier. And what was I supposed to do, not care? You'll recall that in the six months since turning twenty-three, I used a small percentage of my inherited wealth to transform my body and face into those of a conventionally attractive adult man. But what had Candy Catena done in that time? Eaten, evidently.

"Oh, you know, same crap different day."

I laughed insincerely. "You can say that again."

"So what have you been up to, Ross? Keeping cool?"

"Oh . . . you know, just taking care of my sister, going back to school for philosophy next month. You heard my parents died in a helicopter accident, right?"

"Yes, duh! That's why I wanted to talk to you. You know my dad bought your dad's old dealership in Los Angeles, right?"

"No, I didn't. I knew we sold it, but I didn't realize it was to your dad."

"Yeah, so I basically got you an extra million dollars, after taxes, Ross."

"You're the one who told him to do it?"

"Yeah!"

"Okay, well I hope he does well with it."

"Do you think that's worth a New Year's kiss, Ross? A million dollars for one kiss?"

"Look, I, I . . . come on. It would've sold to someone else for a similar price. Don't do this, in front of all these people, Candy."

I walked away to go say "Hi" to Mia Sophia, ask her about her new business, where she goes to estate sales to buy rich dead people's clothes and then sells them to living people on the internet.

"It's going well. I'm making like, six hundred a week."

"That's pretty good. And that's after expenses?"

"Well, I use my dad's credit card to buy the clothes, so I don't really have any expenses."

"Cool."

In the middle of the room, where Don had set up a "dance floor," I saw Hannah Nenner doing an internet dance called "The Alan Dershowitz Shuffle" that had recently gone "viral," after this old schizo-phrenic guy who looked exactly like Alan Dershowitz (who had just recently become a recognizable face for a lot of teens) was seen doing it on the platform for the M train in Queens, New York. This was exactly the sort of ironic collegiate party exercise that I felt comfortable engaging in, and in fact, I'd been practicing several viral internet dances for the previous few weeks in preparation for this exact moment. I ran over to Hannah and joined her in the shuffle, waving my arms around, touching my knees, torquing my toes to the rhythm of the song, which was a cool rap music remix of the original video of that mentally ill old man humiliating himself.

"I didn't know you knew how to *dance* like that, Ross," Hannah said to me afterward.

"Yeah, it must be this ginger ale I've been drinking."

"Oh . . . that stuff. Do you smoke now?"

"What?"

"That's that new CBD ginger ale."

What! I looked at the can; she was right. It was "that new CBD ginger ale," indeed. I felt lightheaded, my pulse dropping. Don, Don Morton had screwed me again. "Oh, cool. I didn't even realize it," I said to poor soft-hearted Hannah, pressing a few buttons on my Watch to order a 2015 Toyota Corolla to bring me home before I passed out from being *drugged*. "It was cool seeing you, Hannah. Make sure you tell Lora how good I've gotten at dancing."

She laughed at that (as if it were funny), and I retreated out of the apartment, wounded (drugged!), heading toward the elevator to get to my car safely. Who can even remember what race the driver was, or whether he said anything funny? Not me. I was barely able to make it home, shower, brush my teeth, put on my pajamas and retainer, turn off all the lights in my room, and get inside my bed before I passed out from the negative narcotic effects of that CBD-infused soda I'd had.

When I woke up, it was terribly bright in the apartment. My mouth had this salty slimy texture, and my toothbrush seemed to be missing from the bathroom. "Emily? Did you take my toothbrush?" I called out. "I really need that toothbrush; my mouth is *disgusting* right now." I didn't hear from Emily. I walked into our Florida room and saw my Bubbe, in a hospital bed, with Emily sitting in a metal stool by her side, with Mom and Dad on a couch across from them.

"Ssh!! Be quiet, Ross. Emily is trying to talk to my mother," Dad said to me.

"Yes, sir. I'm sorry, sir."

Emily was leaning in very closely to try to discern head movements from our Bubbe. ". . . and do you believe in one Holy, Catholic, and Apostolic church, Bubbe?" she was saying, as our grandma nodded along, weakly.

"No, not this! Not this baptism business again!" I cried out. "Emily, stop that. She's an old woman. An old *Jewish* woman. And you're taking advantage of her in this weakened state." I ran over to the bed and grabbed the coffee mug filled with natural water that Emily was preparing to pour over our Bubbe.

"Ross, stop! She told me she agreed with the teachings of the church and wanted to receive the sacrament. Give that back, we don't have much time!"

After I emptied that mug down the drain, I grabbed all of the Poland Spring bottled waters out of the refrigerator and started throwing them out the window, and then I went into the utility closet and turned a switch labeled *THE WATER* from "on" to "off."

"What are you doing, son? Why would you do this?" Mom called out.

"Dammit Ross! Turn that water back on, right this second!" Dad added in.

"I'm doing this for her own good," I said, as I walked back into the room to explain to them what Emily was doing. "Mom, Dad, she's trying to make Bubbe *Catholic*. We can't allow that. We're proud Jews, aren't we?"

As I was saying this, my Bubbe's head collapsed against her pillow, and our Jamaican hospice nurse, Miss Lilly, appeared to check her vitals. "She ded, mon. I leef yuh alone now fu a beet," Miss Lilly said.

"Okay, this is sad, but at least she came out of this world, the way she came in, a Jew. Right?" I offered, after a brief moment of silence.

My Dad, now nearly twice as tall and large as he was before (how?), threw me to the ground and stood ominously over me. "You idiot. You *jackass*," he was saying. "Why would you do this? Why would you sabotage something so *nice* that your sister was trying to do for my mother? Because of you, and your stupid ideas, there's a good chance my mother is in hell right now. What would it have hurt, Ross, for you to have let your sister perform a baptism on my mother? You're so *arrogant*, Ross. You know your sister was always smarter, right?"

"I, I . . ." I didn't know what to say. I felt myself shrinking right in front of him.

"Look at you. You're weak," his voice grew louder. "You can only get joy out of sending other people to hell."

"Mom, Emily, are you going to let him talk to me like that?"

They both nodded their heads. He continued, "Of course they are. What are they going to do? Side with you? Face it, you're a villain Ross.

And you need to be punished. You've been a devilish human being. Get out! Get out of my house! Get OUUUT!!!"

He lifted me up by the loop on my cargo shorts, carried me over to the balcony, and tossed me out the second story window, out into our hot tub.

"Dearest parents! I have always loved you, nonetheless!" I called out as I fell to my death, a few seconds before I woke up (for real this time) in my queen-sized bed, in my penthouse in Fort Greene, Brooklyn. "Oh," I let out a deep breath, "that was just a dream. A nightmare," I said to myself, "a nightmare in which Mom and Dad didn't die in a helicopter accident in Turks and Caicos. But it wasn't real. They're still dead. What a relief!"

Twenty-One

If you ignore my poisoning, the New Year's Party was a big success. A photo with me, Ross, prominent in the background—showcasing my new (non-surgically enhanced) side profile—received over two hundred "likes" (including one from a certain Lora L . . .) on a popular photo sharing app, which I had to count by hand, since they recently stopped showing the number of "likes" that each photo gets, but you can still count by hand, so I'm not sure whom they think they're fooling.

And then we have the success with Victor. This Victor, this Victor who drove me from my Roosevelt Island to LaGuardia Airport on the morning of my twenty-third birthday, this guy has turned out to be an extraordinary asset in the pursuit of Lora Liamant. He's been following her all over town, sending me photographs of her going in and out of different Starbucks locations, drawing in the park, smoking cigarettes, etc, etc. The guy, this Victor—so grateful that I paid off his debt—even drove down to West Palm Beach, Florida, to investigate Lora at her parents' "January home."

He called me up while he was down there to tell me she wasn't doing anything of note.

"Okay, keep me updated. And while you're on the phone, here's a money tip, Vic. A Jew money tip. You know how Starbucks makes all their money?"

"From selling those CDs? I heard CDs are like a money thing, right?"

"No, no. It's the *gift cards*, Vic. Do you realize when you buy a Starbucks gift card, you're just giving them an interest-free loan for that amount of money?"

"Huh?"

"Yeah, let's say you buy a twenty-five-dollar gift card. They collect that *immediately,* at no cost to them. They just have your twenty-five dollars without losing any cups of coffee. So they're free to invest that money in a hedge fund and make thirty percent a year on it. So they're really selling you a twenty-five dollar gift card that expires after one year, for . . . I don't know, eighteen dollars? It's called the time value of money, do you understand?"

"Yeah, I do, I think I do."

The next day, when I was on my way to my local University for a meeting with Dr. Lancet, Vic (the guy just doesn't quit) sent me some screenshots of Lora's profile on a popular "dating" app (you know, that boring one, the one your parents have heard of). Oh, these made me sick to my stomach. Old photos of her from before she became truly beautiful (which was after I broke up with her) in silly poses, weird angles, just sad to see. And then that bio, her little sales pitch, which really had me (a wicked guy who was born with a jealous mind, etc, etc) ready to blow my brains out directly into the nearest the East River. "Cheerful, tiny-titted man pleaser," it read. I don't even know what she could've possibly meant by this, only that I hated it. The idea of her pleasing any man not named Ross Elias Mathcamp. Oh, even now, I feel sick just typing it. Just a horrible thing for a Ross to have to see, especially right before a doctor's appointment.

As I swiped my new violet radio-frequency-enabled photo-ID card against the philosophy building's digital turnstile, I saw Dr. Lancet rounding a corner, furiously heading for the exit. "I'll be right back, Ross. I just have to . . ." he let out an exasperated sigh, ". . . deal with something."

"Okay, I'll wait in your office."

Inside, I helped myself to some snooping around his desk, shelves, folders, etc. Peeking at the books. His Aristotle, his Heidegger, his Coulter. So stimulating, invading someone's privacy. On his desk he had several galley proofs for still unpublished books, things like *It's Just Evolution: Why Women Want You to Act Like an Ape* by Vince Corkheim, *The Racial Papers: The REAL History of Group Differences in IQ* by Archer Rusmlay, etc, etc. I was going to look around on his computer but I waited too long, and the screen went black, locked itself, and was immune from my charms from then on. So I sat back down in the wheeled chair on the visitor's side of his filthy desk and—daydreaming about Lora Liamant— awaited his return. It was going to be perfect, she would say things like, "Oh, Ross. This is incredible. To propose marriage to me on the one-year anniversary of our silly breakup. I missed you so much this whole time, I never want to be apart from you again," and "You were amazing before, Ross. But now that you've improved yourself so much with all your millions of dollars, you're just the best guy ever. Let's get married right away so we can live adult lives together." Yes, yes! Things like that. It was perfect. Everything will be worth it soon enough, I thought to myself as Drew Lancet came back in carrying a styrofoam box stuffed with some kind of Indian (or similar, you know, one of those countries over there that likes to get creative with the sauces and spices) food.

"Sorry about that, Ross. I've got this dammed parasite and it leaves me *ravenous*." He took off his coat and hung it up on a tall hook on the wall behind him. "Now, where were we?"

"I don't think we were anywhere. You were leaving as I came in."

He opened up his street food box. "Yes, I remember now. That's right. And I called you here today to talk about tomorrow. Not literally tomorrow, but next Wednesday, your first recitation for my *PHIL-102: INTRO TO THOUGHT EXPERIMENTS*. It's a fine class, one of my favorites."

"Yeah." I cleared my throat. "I took it in the spring of my first year."

"That's right, well, good. Then here is the syllabus," he handed me a thick paper packet, "take some time to look it over later, but I'm sure you know what sorts of things I'd like them working on. You know, ask them problems of identity, the Ship of Theseus. Of morality, does it exist? The

Euthyphro dilemma, and be able to raise objections, counterexamples, really *moderate* the discussion."

"That sounds simple enough."

He put his plastic fork down and shook his head at me. "Oh it's harder than it looks, believe me. These kids are idiots. They don't care about *truth*, only narrative. I'm telling you, Ross. They will deny anything they find inconvenient, and then call *you* crazy. It's called gaslighting."

"What are you talking about?"

"They are gaslighting me. Haven't you heard this expression?"

"No, I guess not. But I'm sure it's real. It sounds very 'academic,' I suppose . . ."

Drew continued digging into his container of chicken and rice, feeding me bits of gossip ("Did I tell you about the time I saw Peter Unger's roach? We were in the locker room at the hotel spa for a conference once, and, well . . ."), wisdom ("*Always* show up late on the first day. You want them to think they're about to get off scot free. You know, that old myth about the teacher not showing up after fifteen minutes meaning class is automatically cancelled. So you'll throw them off balance, *and* you don't have to work as much"), and humor ("That reminds me of an old joke, Ross. About how stupid economists are. Truly some of the dumbest people in all of academia, and that's saying something. It goes like this: A financial economist and defender of the *efficient market hypothesis* is walking down the street with his buddy. Suddenly, the buddy tells his economist friend 'Look! There's a hundred-dollar bill on the ground,' to which the economist replies, 'No there isn't! If there were a hundred-dollar bill on the ground, somebody would've *taken* it by now.' So you see the point I'm trying to make, Ross? That all of this stuff, all of this theoretical grad school . . . *theory* will leave you feeling awful stupid in real life. So less thinking, more action! Act, act, act!").

There was something intimidating—something macho and Aristotelian, even—about Professor Drew Lancet that inspired me, made me feel capable (even more than usual). And as I tumbled out into the streets after our meeting, I reminded myself of how much I enjoyed the experience of snooping on him, of the power and sense of *access to information* that it gave me, so I walked about twenty blocks north up to Lora Liamant's parents' townhome and decided to break in (using my illicit and surreptitious copy of her house key that I'd had made at Home Depot before the breakup, just in case) and look around for clues that could help me make myself more desirable to her. Nervously, with a pounding heart, I inserted my cloned key into the old money lock. I took a few steps inside, looked at myself in the mirror, felt sick, saw some shadowy statue in a dark denny room, then ran out before I could get caught. Outside, on the steps, I caught my breath, thinking things to myself like "Wow, you really just did that! Incredible!"

I walked back down to street level, did a minute-long timed breathing exercise on my Watch (to help bring my heart rate back down to street level), then made a video call to Lora Liamant. She didn't answer the first time, but then I called again as I kept walking toward the train station, and she answered. People usually answer video calls if you call them twice.

"Hey, Ross. Is everything okay?" she said to me. She was sitting in the bedroom of her Palm Beach house, with a towel wrapped around her hair, wearing a robe, showing a little bit of skin.

"Yeah, I was just in your neighborhood, thinking fondly of you, and figured I'd give you a call."

"That's sweet. I like that hat you have on." I was wearing a "beanie" from a brand called "Neff" which the teenaged salesman at Pacific Sunwear assured me was very hip and cool.

"Thanks, the teen salesman at Pac Sun assured me it was a cool brand." I was positioning the phone high above my head, so that the glass was parallel to my (newly chiseled) face. This was allegedly the best angle. And my arm wasn't even getting tired, due to all the strength building exercises I'd been up to.

"That's funny. Well, you look well."

"I think we should see each other. You know . . . when you're back, I mean. You're in Florida for the month, right? Otherwise I would've been much more frightened to walk down your street."

She let out a little laugh, the sort of laugh you let out when you're alone and read something clever, much quieter than the sort of laugh she would let out in person or in a group of friends, it was like, a smile with noise, maybe. "I think we could do that," she said, getting up and walking to a different room.

"I've missed you so much, really. I went to a New Year's Party at Don's and drank a CBD soda, I can tell you all about it when I see you."

"Hello? Ross? Can you hear me?"

"Yeah, I'm talking, I can hear you."

"Ross? Are you there?"

"Yes, I'm here."

"I can't hear you. I'm going to hang up. I'll be in touch. I'll text you after this, just in case you can't hear me either right now."

On the train, some light texting back and forth between me and Lora. I felt at ease, excited for everything to work out. So at ease, in fact, that I even neglected to take an afternoon dosage of ashwagandha and bacopa monnieri from my backpack.

That Wednesday morning, that morning of my first 11:15 philosophy recitation, I was a real wreck, of the nervous variety. And you may not have noticed it, but I've actually displayed a number of neurotic tendencies throughout the book, but this morning, before my *debut* (so to speak), I was incorrigible. I tried every trick to help myself relax and regain any ounce of available self-confidence. Binaural beats, the Sam Harris meditation app, supplements galore. I even opened up my Joovv Max light therapy machine (which I had bought for my half-birthday), an eighteen-inch by fifty-one-inch slab of red-light emitting diodes that supposedly triples your testosterone, or helps you sleep, or something. I stood nude in front of this four-foot-tall sheet of red bulbs for thirty minutes, making sure my scrotum was absorbing as much light as possible (the instruction manual said targeting the scrotum was "crucial" for the machine to work).

There was a decent chance it had worked, because I'd felt something resembling relaxation (might have just been the New Gadget Placebo Effect), but then I worried that I would be tired, passive, and ineffectual as a recitation leader, so I took an additional 10 mg of amphetamine salts (I had taken an initial 10 mg when I first woke up) and an 800-mg capsule of phenylpiracetam, which is this drug that you have to buy on weird websites because it was never approved for use in the United States (because it was invented by Soviet scientists to help their cosmonauts endure extended periods of isolation in outer space). But it's used to treat dementia and epilepsy now and is generally considered (by people on the internet) safe for use as a nootropic. In the kitchen, Amanda, who was in the midst of perfecting a new banana bread recipe, said she would "pray for me" on my first day, which I suppose I appreciated.

"Thanks," I said to her, as I walked out the door, fidgeting with my phone, keys, and wallet, and pressed elevator buttons, waved to doormen, swiped MetroCards, etc, etc, etc. Underground, I inserted my noise-cancelling wireless earphones and relistened to the audio of Doctor Drew Lancet's lecture from the day before, nodding along and mumbling schizo noises like "mmhmm," "mmhmm," "definitely," to myself, which no one seemed to find odd or out of place.

I got to the philosophy building's second floor conference room at 10:00, which was far too early. Professor Lancet advised that I show up late in order to make myself seem important, busy. So I ran back down the flight of stairs and walked to an art supply store that was forty minutes north of there, bought a box of dry erase markers, then walked indifferently, lazily back to my building of employment, arriving just after 11:25, out of breath from sprinting up the stairs, creating a sense of urgency.

"Sorry, sorry I'm late," I looked out at the dozen or so students staring at me, "I hope you guys enjoyed the ten minutes I gave you for free this morning." An Indian American boy laughed insincerely at this. I opened my backpack to grab the markers, and accidentally let a bottle of Bee Propolis slip out onto the floor. "Oh, ha, ignore that. Those are just some pills that I'm addicted to." More students laughed at that. "My name, which you should already know," I grabbed a red marker and began writing "Ross Mathcamp" on the board, "is Ross Mathcamp? You should just call me Ross, usually." I spun around and sat at the chair at the head of the table. "Uh . . . a fun fact about me, I suppose, is that I am a Registered Nurse, and both of my parents are dead. Why don't we go around the room, introduce ourselves, everyone can, uh, give fun facts like mine."

The first kid, a smart-alecky Jew, who resembled young Ross (although clearly less clever), said, "I'm Levi, and my parents are both alive, and happily married, and still sexually active," which people laughed at, even though it was just a cruel derivative of my intro. They continued, counterclockwise around the table. The Indian boy, Pranav, had "never seen anime," a white woman, Markie, was "part Cherokee," a redheaded white guy, Max, said he once "fired a shotgun at his uncle's house," etc, etc, etc.

"Okay," I cracked my knuckles above the table for everyone to see, "that was fun. Let's try to do a little philosophy." I noticed Mercedes (who was "an undocumented immigrant") using her smartphone under the table, but I neglected to say anything. "I'll start. I would like you to tell me, why racism is wrong. And I'm assuming most of you are atheists, and my question is this, why is it wrong to be racist?"

Markie interjected, "Well because it simply hurts people. That's wrong. You don't need to believe in God to know that it's wrong to hurt people."

I was prepared to parry this utilitarian objection, "Okay, so Markie is making a utilitarian argument. That racism is *wrong*, objectively, because

it hurts people. But if we could quantify the amount that it harms people, then we could also quantify . . . the amount that some other group
benefits from it. Imagine, a world . . . with two ethnic groups, 'A' and
'B.'" Some students were jotting notes down as I spoke. "Let's say ethnic
group A despises group B, and there are only like . . . a thousand members of group B, versus like a billion of A. And it's just super culturally
ingrained, that everyone in group A really hates the members of B. And
another interesting cultural fact, is that B is known for horrible clinical
depression. All one thousand members are pretty much medically inca-
pable of feeling happiness. So in this scenario, if some member of A, let's
call him 'A' Dolph," a few chuckles, "decides to kill every member of B.
So now, everyone from B is dead, and the total number of smiles, is *up*,
people are *happier*, and more satisfied as a whole now that the members
of this minority group have been wiped off the earth. So was that morally *good*, Markie? He increased the total utility of this universe."

She looked at me horrified, perhaps near tears. "But you just made
that up!" she said.

"I agree that it's disgusting, and would be wrong. But a reasonable
test of an objective moral fact is that it's true in all conceivable worlds,
no? That it ought to be true *independent* of any one individual's feelings or
beliefs?" A few people began writing things in their notebooks. "Okay,
anyone else? Would you like to give an explanation of why racism, or
any hatred, really, is objectively wrong?"

A boy Antwon (who played drums) offered, "Because all people are
created equal?"

Another predictable response. "How do you justify that, Antwon?"

"I mean, it's like, obvious. Right?"

"I don't think it's obvious. Unless you invoke some supernatural reason for it to be true. But I look at this room, and I see people of different heights, genders, hair colors. They certainly look very different, and
have different abilities. So why should I believe that they're all equal?
Just, rationally, why should I?" I was at ease, finally. Drew's talking

points from the notes he gave me were coming in most excellent handy. "The point I'm trying to make here, is that if you believe in moral absolutes, moral realism, which a lot of young people seem to, about rape and race, then you're invoking some objective standard outside of our own minds. Which in itself, is a definition of lowercase-g god."

They continued debating this, even after I laid it out for them. It was a mostly unimpressive bunch, tepid tykes who didn't know their Kant from their Kripke. At one point, after I'd stepped back for a while and allowed them to bicker amongst themselves, I had to intervene, "You're fighting about the definition of the word *nothing*. You're using it in two different ways. Here, I'll show you. Let's say you say 'Nothing is heavier than the universe' and then you say 'my phone is heavier than nothing, therefore my phone is heavier than the universe, by the transitive property.'" They liked that example, the poor kids. They needed more coursework in set theory, theory of language, metaphysics, etc, etc.

With a few minutes left, Levi, who humiliated me during the introductions, cleared his throat and said, "What if you just believe nothing is right or wrong? Just inconvenient, or mean. But not objective. That everything is relative and in our heads."

"That's fair, Levi," I replied, "and this gets to the *metaethical* category of moral nihilism. That it's impossible to know what's right and what's wrong, and that it's pointless even to think about. I think most of Dr. Lancet's contemporaries hold this view. But it's very tough to live your life this way. We don't seem to be programmed for it." I was just reading the notes he had given me, making slight paraphrases. "Okay, that's it for today. I hope it wasn't too bad."

I stayed behind, pretending to write things in my notebook until everyone had long left, then went into the faculty bathroom and vomited repeatedly.

Twenty-Two

Oh I'm just a moron. You'll see; today was terrible. Sorry. Sorry. Let me calm down—I'm ruining the suspense distribution of the story. Pretend you're me (Ross), waking up on a normal Friday morning. And you don't have class today (such is the nature of Fridays) and so you sleep in until almost 8:00. And while you're eating breakfast and reading the latest Andrew Sullivan newsletter, you get a call from "BLOCKED NUMBER," and answer it, because you have an obsessive compulsion to answer your Watch anytime anyone calls you, and you think it may be a call from Lora, or Lora-related in some way. And so you answer it. And so I answered it.

"Hello," I said, pausing, waiting for some sort of beep or click or pre-recorded message telling me I'd won a stay at a Hilton, or was eligible for cheaper car insurance, or a cure for my back pain, etc, etc.

"Ross," a man's voice on the other end said to me, "I'm sorry. But this is for the best. You'll see what I'm talking about soon enough. You don't want to end up like me. Certainly not like me. I can't let you end up like that. Never like me. I'm doing you a favor. A huge favor right now, Ross."

Click! Well, not literally a Click! since phones on Watches don't have Click! noises like old phones used to. The guy, the manly voice on the other end just hung up. Without saying "bye" or "goodbye."

Amanda Bauer walked into the kitchen with her pink slippers (fuzzy) and asked me if we could turn up the heat. "You're like my Jewish slumlord, Ross," she started saying. "I'm paying you a grand a month. The least you could do is turn the heat up a bit. Especially given that this home is eighty percent female."

I told her that fine, we could turn it up a bit. She smiled at me, blew an ironic kiss, and asked me if I wanted a freshly baked sweet potato. "Absolutely," I told her. "I am just starving, constantly. Come get me in my room when it's ready."

In my room, I clicked on an article from my alma mater's local "news" "paper" by some Scarsdale idiot, with the headline PHILOSOPHY DEPARTMENT CUTS TIES WITH BIGOTED GRADUATE STUDENT. "Oh, boy," I thought to myself, "I hope it's that Palestinian girl who's always wearing that T-shirt that says 'kill all men' and screamed at the pregnant Chelsea Clinton that one time." But when I clicked it, oh, when I *clicked* it . . .

> PHILOSOPHY DEPARTMENT CUTS TIES WITH BIGOTED GRADUATE STUDENT
>
> By Abigail Govestein
>
> With white supremacy on the rise in America, reaching heights never before seen, one would expect our campus, located in the heart of the city Manhattan, of all places, to be an oasis, an escape, for students to feel safe to pursue thoughts without fear of hatred and evil. This is what students hope for when they come to school here.
>
> That dream was put to an end on Wednesday, when a TA

Oy . . . I knew I was in trouble at this point.

> in PHIL-102 went on an unhinged screed. One student, who chose to remain nameless, for fear of death threats, and other trials and tribulations which she has already received, described the TA's outburst for us.
>
> "It was really weird. He came in, and asked to say why racism was bad. And I was just like . . . of course it's bad. Then he told us if you don't believe in God you can't believe that racism is wrong. Which isn't true, 'cuz I don't believe in God and I know it's wrong."

Another student, Kaitlyn M, 20, a sophomore studying Crime, said that the TA seemed "nervous" and "on something, uppers, generic brand, for sure."

This follows controversy from the previous semester with the same professor, Drew Lancet, who was himself accused of making insensitive comments in one of his Freshman lectures.

When asked for comment, Professor Drew Lancet, himself no stranger to controversy, offered this: "I thought I was doing a kindhearted thing, inviting a former student of mine who has just recently lost both of his parents in a tragic accident. It's now clear that this job was too much, too soon for him. I condemn racial hatred, in all forms. Hate of this kind cannot be tolerated on our campus. We in the philosophy department extend our best wishes to the troubled TA and hope he will get the help he so clearly needs."

It's good to see him get out on top of this issue of white supremacist rage, and make a strong case that *hate* has no place on our campus.

For tips, corrections, or just to say hi, send me an email at:

You didn't have to be a high-IQ Ashkenazi male nurse to see that I'd been bamboozled. That it was all a big trick. That I'd been used as *bait*. Given a sheet of talking points designed to infuriate those vulnerable weak-minded children. In my email inbox, a more formal dismissal:

Dear Ross,
Given your actions during Wednesday's recitation, the Philosophy Department, in accordance with University Policy . . .

I stopped reading. What could this tell me that Abby's article didn't already say? My phone rang, again, while I was rolling around my bed groaning about how my academic future, like so many other things, was taken (ripped!) away from me by cruel forces outside of my control.

"Hello?" I said into the phone, after I answered it.

"Ross. That was me, calling earlier. Now I know you're probably upset."

"Yeah?"

"Don't you see I've done you a favor?"

"How?"

"Now you can *cash* in! Go on speaking tours, the podcast circuit, talk about how you were a victim of the mob."

"I already have fourteen million dollars. I don't want to do that. Why would you do this? Why wouldn't you ask me first?"

"Well I didn't tell that reporter," he paused, then laughed "oh it makes me smile just calling that idiot woman a reporter. I didn't give anyone your name. It's up to you, you can do whatever you want now."

"I just wanted to be a philosopher, a grownup philosopher," I told him.

Amanda came into my doorway to tell me that my baked sweet potato was finished cooking. "Okay, bye," I said into the phone. "No, not you, I was on the phone," I said to Amanda. We walked over to the kitchen; I was making Jewish groaning noises, slouching, dejectedly drooping my face. "They fired me, they fired me, Amanda."

"What do you mean they fired you?"

"Here, look, read this ridiculous article about me. I was tricked. I was tricked into angering my moron students and now I've been completely crap-canned." I AirDropped her the article and gave her a minute or so to read it.

"Jeez, Ross," she shook her head, "that's terrible. Did you really say that stuff?"

"No . . . well, it wasn't like that . . ."

"Well, you should eat." She plated a potato from the pan on the counter above the oven. "You'll feel better if you eat something." As she reached up to the top shelf of the refrigerator to grab my ghee, I snuck a small peek at her bare leg beneath her robe, which was getting pulled upward, slightly.

It occurred to me that she felt very maternal at this moment. Serving me food, consoling me after a terrible day at school, but this is possibly because at twenty-three years old, she was the same age as my own mother was when I began kindergarten. I'm not sure that she looked as good as my mom did at that age, though. Not that she (Amanda) wasn't a beautiful woman—she certainly was.

"Thanks," I said as she put the clarified buttered sweet potato in front of me. "Hold on," I ran into my room to get the paper Professor Lancet (that Judas!) had given me for use in class, "here," I put it down on the table, caught my breath, and sat down back before the sweet potato, "look this over. These are the sorts of questions I asked them."

"Oh," she said, "this is just an argument against, or perhaps for, moral absolutism. He just tricked you into using the only thing that young people feel morally absolute about."

"They're also morally absolute about rape, it turns out. Rapists and racists are the only two things they find utterly disqualifying."

"That's funny," she reached a fork over my plate and scooped out some of my baked sweet potato, peeling back the skin, "oh this is a great sweet potato. I did a great job."

"The ghee, I think, is really good."

"And you come down where, Ross? On the moral absolutism question."

"Oh, I definitely think there are moral absolutes. We've talked about that, that I do believe in God. One, to be exact. But I think it's reasonable, logically consistent that some people don't. Although, when you hear the word *nihilist* you picture some scary guy dressed in all black who wants to shoot up his high school."

"Yeah, that, or some immoral pleasure seeker. Doing drugs. Sleeping all day."

"That's the girl version of a school shooter."

She laughed at this, and pushed up her glasses. "So if you do think there exists some right and wrong outside of ourselves and our little monkey brains, why do you throw such fits whenever we bring up Catholicism?"

I chewed for a moment, "I guess, I guess I don't necessarily ascribe things like *all-loving* or *all-powerful* to God, or even any personality at all really. I don't see where that's *demanded* of me, logically. And I imagine we have very different ideas about which sorts of morals are encoded into the fabric of the capital-U Universe."

"Yeah, but it's like, you take all the evidence. You take the hundred thousand people who witnessed the Virgin Mary's miracle at Fatima in 1917, you take the Resurrection, the words of Jesus, all of that together, and then what are you left with? Did you know in 363 this Roman emperor Flavius Claudius Julianus—we call him Julian the Apostate—he ordered his men to rebuild the temple in Jerusalem, and every time they tried, fire would shoot out of the ground, earthquakes would erupt, and they could never do it."

I grinned at the thought, "This sounds like pretty obvious Christian mythmaking, Amanda."

"No, it's true. The historians who wrote about it were pagans who hated Christians. And that's the other thing, what do you have to lose by being Catholic? Did you know that in Judaism, if you're a bad Jew, you only have to spend one year, at the most, in hell, but most rabbis don't even believe in hell at all."

"Yeah, I remember looking that up once. Can you get me some oat milk?" (I usually would prefer coconut milk, but you'll recall I've been trying to gain weight, thus the oat milk here.)

"Sure," she walked back over to the refrigerator. I caught a waft of her perfume as she stood up. "Here," she put it down in front of me.

"You're going to be mad at me," I took a sip of the oat milk, "about something that happened in a dream. I know women are always taking things that happen in dreams very seriously."

"We can't help it, Ross."

"But I had a dream, on the morning of January 1, that Emily was trying to baptize our grandma right before she died, and that I stopped it, and then my parents were so upset and they were yelling at me, and my dad sentenced me to death by drowning and threw me out the window."

"And you don't think that's a sign of anything important?"

My voice raised itself. "I was *drugged*!" I yelped, before realizing it was an uncouth outburst. "Sorry. I was a man under the influence," I added calmly.

"Yeah, yeah."

"But in the dream, I was very concerned about my Bubbe losing her Jewishness. It felt like I was the only one who cared about preserving that. This thing we've kept up for five thousand years and never abandoned despite great pressure."

"Is that even something to be so proud of? Some group membership that you have through no control of your own? It's racial pride, really."

"I think we're allowed to do it though, because of the *shoah*, because of the *pogroms*, they said we're allowed to do nationalism and ethnic pride as part of our reparations."

"What does it even mean for you then? Are Emily and I not Jewish anymore?"

"No, I think . . . I'm not sure. Even if you say you aren't, you're both still gossipy, annoying, pale, smart, funny, neurotic, argumentative—"

"Okay, Ross."

"Sorry, sorry."

"It's okay. You can't help it. It's your *genes*."

"Yeah."

She picked up my plate and put it in the dishwasher; her hair looked very . . . gentle and wavy as she leaned down to put the fork in the silverware section. "Do you want to go to Sheepshead Bay later?" she asked me. "There's this new non-dairy frozen dessert place that uses coconut milk and allulose and it has no net carbs and is supposed to taste like real ice cream."

"Sure, I'll go."

"I just have to go get dressed."

"Sure."

Back in my room, I read and refreshed the comments on the article about me. About my "white nationalist views." About how I was "probably a rapist, too." About how someone needs to "find this guy's name and address, FAST."

Amanda put on a cream-colored sweater and a pair of black (what looked like) snowpants, which gave me a brief moment of pause, but must have been fashionable in some sense that was beyond my comprehension. She zipped up her coat and grinned widely at me as I held the door for her out of the apartment and pressed the elevator button.

"What?" I asked her.

"What do you mean 'what'?"

"Oh, I thought you were smiling at me," I said.

On the way to the Q train, we saw a woman, a mother and her young daughter, about Emily's age (wearing matching pink hats), stopped on the sidewalk. The mother was screaming, yelling things like "This is the *last* time I bring you to Brooklyn. Do you understand that? We are *lost*, and it's all your fault. And it's because you do nothing, nothing all day but stare at that phone. And now we're *lost* because of it."

"Should we go back and help that woman?" I asked Amanda underground.

"How lost could they really be, if she's right next to this station with like ten different trains?" She tapped her phone against the turnstile and waited for it to turn green and tell her to go.

"Yeah, that's fair," I said as I swiped my unlimited monthly Metrocard for Nurses that still hadn't expired.

We found two seats on the train; Amanda's knees kept bumping into mine every time it stopped. "It's the next one," she said at Neck Road.

I walked in front of her, down the steps at the Sheepshead Bay station. I made a joke about going to the Baskin-Robbins next to the subway stop. About how they serve a very 1990s/2000s type of ice cream, the sort of ice cream Emily was born too late to experience, which Amanda understood entirely, then said, "I'm impressed with your posture, Ross. It's really gotten a lot better since I first met you."

"That's good, then. That means I've made myself more impressive to women, and therefore to Lora Liamant, since she's a woman."

"Yeah, yeah. Sure. The place is just a few blocks from here." She pointed in the direction and began leading the way, through weird streets, Russian roads, avenues named after the latest letters in the alphabet, etc, etc. "And what makes you think these are the sorts of things that matter to Lora Liamant?"

"Well what else would matter?" I asked.

"I don't know . . . the structure of your thinking. Your goals, interests . . ."

"I'm so desperate and defeated, you know, despite my superficial improvements, to my nose, lips, cheeks, muscles, whatever, that I'm willing to concede a lot this time around. Like, I imagine I'll be so ecstatic to see her again that I won't be a nagging . . . uh . . . nagging nelly about all of the things she drinks and smokes."

"Okay," she nodded half skeptically (but not at all sardonically, as if to say *I believe you, I guess*).

We were standing in front of an unlighted storefront with a sign that said CHIKURIN: JAPANESE DESSERT

"Is this it? This is the place?"

"I think so," she said.

"It's closed."

"No, it can't be closed, the app on my phone says it's not closed." She jiggled the door a few times, then put her eyes up to the window. "It's . . . it's closed."

"It's okay, we can just go to Whole Foods—"

Amanda began stomping her feet and making fists with her fingers. "No! It's not okay," she said. "It's not fair that apps just lie. Everyone just lies, Ross. Do you see this? We came all the way over here, just to get lied to. We just live in a world of lies now. Everything is fake."

"Amanda . . ."

"Everything is fake, Ross. Fake meat, fake milk, fake noses, fake lips, even this, I wanted to get fake ice cream with you, to make you happy, and now we can't even do that, because of fake business hours on fake apps. At what point do we have to say we don't want to be lied to anymore? It's not fair."

"I think you're being a little pessimistic. It was a fun idea; we can just come back another time."

"No, not at all. Come on." We turned back toward the station. "You know they tell you the IUD insertion isn't supposed to hurt, but it's the most painful thing I've ever felt in my life? These doctors lied to me about pain, and for what, so I can then *lie* to my body into tricking itself into thinking it's already pregnant? We just live in *Liar World*, Ross. And the only way out is to be Catholic. That's the only thing we can do to save ourselves from nonstop trickery and deceit."

"Now I'm starting to think this whole . . . excursion was a way for you to trick me into being Catholic. Although, trickery, in my mind at least, is definitely a *Jewish* trait."

She laughed, "It's just frustrating. I'm sorry, Ross. I'm sorry for being a dumb woman and having dumb woman emotions in Sheepshead Bay."

"That's okay."

We boarded another train, toward the northern, less Russian parts of Brooklyn. I kept saying things like "Don't worry, really. You've been a good friend to me today." The Q train was completely empty except for Amanda and me and these two men who seemed to be on a first date of sorts, taking turns saying things to each other like "I don't respect divas, but I'm entertained by them," and "I just think she and Gavin were perfect together, but I like Blake, too," and "have you seen *The Spy Who Dumped Me* (2018)? It seriously changed my life." Amanda, too upset about being denied her dessert, didn't seem to be paying them very much attention.

At home, in our building's lobby, we ran into Emily, my thirteen-year-old sister, who lived with us, on her way out as we were on our way in. "Why don't I ever see you anymore, Ross?" she asked me, to which there was . . . not much of a good answer.

"Sorry," I replied. "Probably because I'm lazy and selfish and haven't thought to make time for you lately. You know, with all of these . . . scenarios that I've gotten myself into."

"Well I'm going to my night class. Maybe I'll see you two tonight," she said as she walked out the door.

"She's taking a night class? Where?" I asked Amanda in the elevator.

"At Long Island University's Downtown Brooklyn campus."

I walked into my room and lay on my bed, picking up where I'd left off earlier, before Amanda had come in to tell me that my sweet potato was fully baked. On my computer, I read more horrible things about myself. It occurred to me to send the link to the article to Lora, who would have some sympathy for my unfair media treatment, so I did, adding, "Look at this ridiculous article the media vultures wrote about me. I'm entirely innocent, really. I'll tell you all about it soon." My hope, really, was that she would see me as some kind of sexy villain, an expectation I would then later *subvert* by mentioning (casually) my pro-bono tutoring of a black boy in "Bed-Stuy."

At around 6:30, my Watch buzzed with a message from Amanda

> Can you come in here?

and by *there* ("here"), I assumed she meant her bedroom, so I brushed my teeth (they were due for their early evening / late afternoon brushing anyway) and walked over to her bedroom at the other end of the hall, where she was lying (staring at her ceiling) on her bed dressed in thin pajamas while some minimalist instrumental arrangement (most likely by Roger Eno (her favorite)) played tinnily on her laptop's speakers. I looked more closely and noticed she was crying; she was an elegant crier, which seemed to be an awfully advantageous thing to be, evolutionarily.

"What's wrong?" I asked her, sitting at the end of her bed, at a Respectable distance.

She sat up and let out a groan like "Oaahagghguuhhhhghhghh. My boyfriend died, he's dead, Ross."

I never met him, or learned his name, but was always faintly jealous, and wondered what he could have possibly offered her. "What? What happened?"

"Well, you know how he was in Syria, right?"

"Yeah."

"And how he was training a group of moderate rebels?"

"Yeah."

"Well, a bunch of the moderate rebels were actually Salafi jihadists with connections to Al-Nusra, and they killed him. They killed my boyfriend. It's going to be on the news tomorrow."

"When did you find out?"

"This morning. His mom called me. But I didn't want to tell you because I knew you were upset about losing your job as a teaching assistant for a freshman philosophy course."

"Come on," I said as she scooted closer to me.

"Well, now what am I going to do? My life is ruined, at least you got millions of dollars." She grabbed a tissue from the side of her bed and blew into it.

"You're young, still so young. I wouldn't be so negative about it."

"Am I? I don't even know what that means anymore, Ross. Everyone keeps telling me that I'm *still young*, but I'm going to be twenty-four soon. My parents got *married* at twenty-four. And bought a house. How am

I supposed to buy a house? How is anyone our age supposed to buy a house? I don't have a job, I'm now a *widow*, and then what? What am I supposed to do? Just be a loser like everyone else our age? Just never get a job or get married and have children and—"

I put an arm around her. "It's okay, really," I said, and then . . . oh, this is sick. And then, I don't know what happened. You know. It was like . . . one thing sort of led to another, and well, before I knew it, her body was coming closer to mine, and then our heads were touching and then . . . we were . . . well, you know, making love to each other, I suppose. It was sick. Which is not to say it was disgusting, or unpleasant, despite being *sick*. It was certainly better than our previous attempt in my "dorm room" (poor, nervous, teenaged Ross, talking the entire time . . .) several years earlier.

After we retreated to our separate showers, I returned to Amanda's room, where she was sobbing on top of her bed. I lay next to her, limply letting my hand graze the side of her leg.

"I'm sorry, Ross. That was awful."

Awful? "Why are you sorry?"

"The whole thing, it was so devilish of me," she sniffled. "I took advantage of your dumb male impulses. The food, the perfume, the dainty damsel tears. I'm so sorry, Ross."

"Well, I mean, I don't think . . ."

"I can't believe I did that. That was a mortal sin. Now I have to go to confession as soon as possible. If I get hit by a car or if Jesus returns tomorrow, I'll just end up in hell, with you, Ross."

"Is that true? But we'd already done it before."

"Not since I was *baptized*, Ross. You idiot. What, you think God just cares about body counts? And not *sin* counts? He lets you fornicate as long as it's with someone you already fornicated with once?"

"I don't think He cares at all."

"Ohhhhhh, I'm so stupid, I don't know why I thought that would be a good idea. I got tricked, by the devil and his lesser demons into indulging my lust. I should've just said the Rosary for five hours straight and never made you that sweet potato."

"I mean . . ."

"It could never work between us, Ross."

Twenty-Three

Things became . . . tense, around the house after I accidentally "had sex" with Amanda Bauer. Somehow ("somehow"), Emily found out about . . . about the whole . . . ordeal and kept begging me to get married to Amanda Bauer and become Catholic and have children with her (Amanda). "Please Ross, please, please, I want to be an Aunt," she kept saying to me.

This, this tension, along with a brief bear market (Emily and I lost four million dollars in February after the stocks crashed and then the Federal Reserve raised interest rates (why?), causing the bond market to crash, which normally wouldn't have cost us *that* much money, but you'll recall that I had placed all of our money into a leveraged ETF (exchange-traded fund) holding ninety percent stocks and sixty percent bonds, which was supposed to give me an average annual risk adjusted return of about fourteen percent, due to the uncorrelation of stocks and bonds), is why I'm skipping (marching?) directly to March. Offering you mere glimpses (summaries, not scenes) of what happened during the year's briefest month. March, you'll recall, was the scheduled finale of my plan to reunite with Lora Liamant. Display my new Ross to her. To go, in her eyes, from *mon*ster, to *ma*cher, from from *Silver*stein to *Gold*berg. March—the month of my uncucking. That's what this was all about, wasn't it? All of the pills and products and adventures. All of it coming to a concluding climax in the month of March. I would see her, dazzle her, hold her, and have her. That was the plan.

Is this doing it for you? Building up the suspense sufficiently? Evoking anything? Shaking your stolidity? No? In that case, perhaps a little more summary is in order.

I was spending a great deal of time at my Roosevelt Island home, in the leadup to March 8, the anniversary of my initial breakup with Lora L. I had heard from Vic B (my Puerto Rican American private-eye) that she was "spotted" repeatedly with some new gentleman. But I knew it couldn't have been terribly *serious* in any, like, meaningful sense of the word. Since she was always complaining about me (Ross) while we were together, finding little things to asperse about—and I was near perfect, a well-read handsome stable genius, with very few flaws. So what could this new guy have had that I didn't? Not very much at all, I imagined, and so I was assured that there was nothing *serious* (Serious!) about whatever new fling or tryst she'd gotten herself into. I'd come to terms with it; it was an acceptable loss. Enjoy, Lora, a little bachelorette party detour on the road to our future together.

Lora responded to my invitation ("Hey, would you like to get together on Monday") with a lack of alacrity ("Well . . . I'm not sure if that's so great an idea"), which was to be expected—she had no idea how superb I'd made myself. But after some coaxing ("please, it's really important. I need to see you, I need to talk to you about something that we can't do over the phone, and I will blow my brains out right into the East River if you won't see me. . . . Just kidding, but seriously, I do need to see you and I'll be very upset if you won't"), she accepted the invite.

Of course, I can't imagine Lora remembered the significance of the date, March 8 (she was always the more fun-loving masculine one; and interestingly enough, Amanda's told me that from her experience studying EvoPsych, that that trite trope about men forgetting things like birthdays and anniversaries is based in biological reality), so I'm sure she thought it would simply be an outing, a day together, free from broader symbolic significance. Etc, etc.

Then I had to get out of that safehouse I'd been pent up in. I had to isolate myself, give myself a period of loneliness on Roosevelt Island. Away from Em and Amanda et al. Because well, the thought that I'd already been living with a woman who, with some nontrivial probability, harbored romantic feelings for me *was* exciting (and worth taking seriously), but ultimately a distraction from all of the prepping I'd done to impress Lora and regain my dignity, or rather, *her love for me.* And so I had to go to Roosevelt Island, make myself feel terribly alone, cucked and miserable, so I wouldn't lose focus vis-à-vis my grand Goldberg stratagem. My plan to see her, dazzle her, hold her, and have her.

Additional preparations were made. I made a list of things my mother always valued and began addressing them. First, I began wearing my ten-pound weighted posture vest for two hours a day, making sure my back stayed straight and upright at all moments in the presence of Lora. By leaving this heavy back brace on, and then removing it right before seeing Lora L, a weight would be literally lifted from my shoulders in her presence. Next, I purchased a pair of "elevator shoes" from an advertisement I saw on Facebook to make myself appear about two inches taller than I really am, had my teeth professionally whitened at the *Lexington Avenue Pulchritude Development* office, and finally, I bought myself this new supplement, a digestive-enzyme probiotic combo containing glutease (for digesting gluten), lactase (for digesting lactose), and bacteria from the fecal matter of a particular family in Sweden who has a long haplo-history of tolerating milk extremely well (just in case), which would allow me to eat a meal of New York–style pizza (with all of its bread and cheese) in the presence of Lora—something she'd never seen me do. All of this, so perfectly planned, so perfectly crafted by me, the artist. It would make an excellent story for my great-grandchildren. My mother would've loved to see her baby boy, so tall, so broad shouldered, so conventionally handsome, eating slice after slice of cheese pizza with no side effects or complaints.

March 8

As I walked down the steps to the F train at the Roosevelt Island Main Street stop to prepare to meet Lora in "midtown," I had a moment of great inspiration, and wrote the following little limerent limerick into my phone, to be presented to Lora after she accepted my modest proposal:

I'm fixing a hole in my heart . . .
My love and I . . . one year apart
But after a year
Of trembling and fear
I can't wait to have a new start!

Oh, she would love it (she did a year of elementary school in Ireland) —I thought to myself, giggling at its campy rhymes as I sat down next to a teen wearing large over-ear headphones. Underground, it was hotter than usual, for whatever reason, so I slunk out of my jacket, so as to prevent my armpits from getting too sweaty, letting out a deep breath when my arms were finally free, earning odd stares from the many Queens residents all around me. Whatever—I thought to myself—this was part of *growing up*. No longer caring about what people think of you. No longer being afraid of being laughed or looked at by strangers or being recorded and put on the internet for more strangers to gawk at. And besides, I was still *very* handsome and wealthy.

On a lime green bench in the parklet in Herald Square, hidden between food trucks and decorative gazebos, there she was, impossible for me to miss, Lora L, doodling into a notebook; it nearly brought me to tears, just the sight of her sitting there dressed in floral spring skirt, hair dark and straight, skin tanned from a winter in Florida, etc, etc, I really was about to cry. An unprecedented feeling of contentment washed over me, a sensation of total painlessness. I sauntered toward her (she was looking down at her notebook and didn't see me until I was a few feet away) and said "Lora!" aloud when I was within a few feet of her. She stood up and gave me a friendly hug. "Ross! You seem so different . . . in a good way, though."

"Well, I did get a buzzcut about two months ago from this Dominican guy, and my hair is still a lot shorter than you've ever seen it."

"That must be it," she grinned at me.

We caught up as I led the way to *Muff's Pizza* on 47th Street. I filled her in on the things I'd been up to, making minor adjustments to details (here and there) to make myself seem as competent and mature as possible.

"Yeah, so there I was," I told her, "watching that poor old woman, *of color*, being mugged by this white guy. So what choice did I have? But to say 'Sir, stop! Take my phone instead!'? And the funny thing was, the new phone came out like a week later, so it didn't really bother me." Oh, she loved this story of my bravery in the face of an armed white robber.

To make myself seem adventurous and desirable: "Yeah so I met this depressed woman on a dating app" (I didn't tell Lora which one) "and she was just totally obsessed with me. She would've done anything to be with me. It was sad, but, you know, that's kind of the cost of these new technologies," these sorts of anecdotes made me seem as changed on the inside as I was on the outside.

"Okay, this is it, get whatever you want," I said when we arrived at the restaurant, one of those tiny pitzerias (this is how real New York Italians pronounce pizzeria) with a counter and two tables, stone floor, etc.

"Really? You're eating pizza now?"

"Oh, that? All that food stuff I used to go on and on about, so silly. So childish. Order whatever you want. They have a special, two cheese slices and a soda for nine dollars . . . not that I care about *deals* anymore."

"Thanks, Ross," she said as she walked up and ordered that deal with a diet cola to drink. While she was up there I stayed behind to take two chewable *GoyishGut* digestive enzyme / probiotic supplements to help me vanquish the slice without any hiccups.

"And I'll have, two pepperoni slices, and a non-diet cola, to drink."

I grabbed a handful of napkins and sat down across from her, on a wooden chair at a wobbly table.

"You can actually fix any wobbly table, you know."

"Really?" she asked.

"Yeah, by the *mean value theorem* there necessarily exists a point on the floor that'll balance the table, since the floor is a continuous surface. But this is stupid, dumb math stuff, don't worry about that." She laughed, flattered. "What have you been up to?" I asked.

"I actually just got into an MFA program, for painting. And then I think I may want to be a Kindergarten teacher, since they only work half days. But not for a while. Maybe in like five years."

"Oh, that's cool. I'm thinking of getting an MBA, *uptown*, you know, since I got kicked out of the other place."

"What do you learn there?"

"I think they teach you how to shake hands, how to have a good handshake. How to Make Deals, stuff like that."

"Is that really all they do?"

"Yeah they teach you how to make motivational speeches, spreadsheets, stocks, things like that. I actually lost . . . well, Emily and I, but I'm in charge of her money, but anyway, we lost like four million dollars last month." I took a sip of soda. "But it's mostly back." Wouldn't you want to get back together with a man who could lose four million dollars and talk about it casually between soda sips?

"So what else do you do all day? Now that you're out of a job?"

"Well, I've been reading, going to the gym, with this steroid guy who has a huge ass," she laughed, "and I've been writing this thing . . . sort of a roman à clef."

"I think it's *pronounced roman à clef.*"

"Yeah, yeah, sure. You would know better than I do."

"Can you pass me a napkin?"

"Sure."

"Well, anyway, I hope I'm not in it. This thing you're writing. At least not too much. Or, I hope—"

"I don't think I've seen enough for you to really *be* in it. But your influence is certainly there, like it is with everything I do."

I worry I'm not doing Lora justice. Accurately conveying how much she meant to me on this March 8, detailing her many qualities that delighted me. Her sultriness. The ease I felt in her presence, the joy that she brought me. My prose may be too weak, too *young* to articulate what it meant for me to be in the presence of the woman whom for the past year I'd spent every minute of every day thinking of, dreaming of how to spend the rest of my life with her. I'll attempt a simile. That should do it. Something about how my heart was like a . . . like a . . . *car* that only she had the keys to; how she really had a hold on me, etc, etc, etc, etc. Lora . . . Lora . . . Lorita, light of my life, fire of my loins. My sin, my soul. Lo-ree-ta . . . Etc, etc.

She smiled. "Well, I'd love to read it. Whenever you're comfortable."

We walked outside, into the clouds, the humidity, where I'd arranged (paid him a quarter of a grand, in advance) for a man without a home named Dennis, whom I'd met a few weeks earlier, to be waiting for me on the sidewalk next to Muff's Pizza.

Dennis was one of the smartest men without homes I'd ever encountered. He told me he was once enrolled in a prestigious New York City law school, when, on spring break in Peru, he was exposed to ayahuasca and decided to become a vagrant street artist, abandon his lofty corporate ambitions and embrace "bohemia." It sounded very hackneyed, banal even, when he explained it to me, but when I was talking to him on the street that day (a few weeks before *this* March 8 encounter), it occurred to me that he could be useful for crafting the image of a new and improved, unmiserly Ross.

"Hey! 'Scuse me, mister! You got a dollar or something?" Dennis shouted, as Lora and I took our first few steps outside of Muff's.

"I'm sorry, sir," I replied, "but I don't carry cash. *However*, if you'd like, I'll take you to Rite Aid, and let you get whatever you'd like." I turned to Lora, "You're okay with that, right?"

"Sure, of course, that's so nice," she replied.

It occurred to me, while we were in line at the nearby Rite Aid— Dennis, bearded, haggard, tattered, carrying a cartful of sodas and snacks and alcoholic seltzers—that this was actually a horrible thing disguised as a nice thing. Lying to Lora, buying Dennis inflammatory drug store snacks, etc, etc. I was buying poison for a vagabond to impress a woman. And then *lying* about it. And pretending it wasn't all planned and scripted ahead of time.

"That was really nice of you, Ross," Lora said, again, after we'd wrapped things up with Dennis.

"It's, you know, the least I could do . . ."

I promise, at this moment, she looked at me, stared at me, with some combination of respect and desire.

"Hey," I interrupted our Moment, "I really need to show you something, do you have time to come to Roosevelt Island? It's only . . . you know, a few stops from here."

"I would like that," she said.

Lora led the way, Ross (me) staying a few steps behind to admire her as she navigated the city streets; I used my Watch to pay for her subway fare, and we sat together, shoulders grazing, for the five or so stops from Herald Sq. to Roosevelt Island, making small but pleasant talk. It was going quite well until we stepped inside the Octagon.

As I replay this moment in my mind, and in the security camera footage from the discreet Blink XT2 Outdoor/Indoor Smart Security Camera with cloud storage included that I have hidden inside a fake potted plant pointed at the front door to my apartment, it's even more painful. A slow motion catastrophe, playing at point five ex in my mind. Here:

I jogged up ahead of Lora, out of the elevator, reaching my corner before her, inserted my key, and held the door in anticipation of her

MATTHEW DAVIS

arrival. And here, here is the precise moment of my undoing. When we walked inside, I instinctively removed my elevator shoes, causing me to lose nearly three inches of height right before her eyes. This, this shoe removal ruined me. Neatness being my fatal flaw, etc, etc. If only I hadn't done it right in front of her, shrunk in real time—if only I could've *waited* a minute or so, for while she wasn't looking or was in the bathroom, the rest of our time together would've gone much differently. At the time, however, none of this was obvious to me.

"I'm just going to use the bathroom," Lora said to me.

"I put the seat down for you, before I left, in anticipation that you might come. Not because I was . . . doing anything involving the seat being down, you know."

Lora smiled and walked into the bathroom, closing its wooden white door behind her.

Then, in a mad dash (planned all along), I tuned my television to a montage of memories Lora and I shared together subtly set to Gershwin's *Rhapsody in Blue* (1924). Us standing together in the mirror, pictures of us on the beach from our trip to Cancún, in bed dressed in pajamas, etc, etc. And then, I took my position, knelt on one knee, facing the door, waiting for her to exit the bathroom.

She opened the door, turned the light off; I took a deep breath, and started the montage using the Remote app on my Watch. The look on her face was electric and terrifying.

"Lora," I started, "There is no one in the world who makes me feel the way I feel when I'm around you. I don't ever want to be away from you ever again for as long as I live. I want to spend every second of every minute of every day in your presence. The past year without you has made me feel so lonely, so miserable, so *stupid*, so often. I am a *joke* without you. I am a *coward* without you. Never in my life have I felt like more of a man than when I've held you in my arms, gently fingering your flaxen hair. You are special. You are amazing. There is nothing you could ever do to make me love you any less. I want to spend forever

259

with you, two times over. And I know I don't deserve it—don't deserve you, but I'm here, groveling, begging for your hand. So what do you say? Will you make me the happiest Ross on the face of Roosevelt Island, Lora? Will you marry me?"

She squinted her eyes at me as if I were a combination of not only crazy, but also retarded, "What?"

"What do you mean, *what*?"

"Ross, what is that? What is that in your hand?"

"This?" I waved the box around a bit. "This is the most expensive diamond ring they have at Costco. I thought you would like that I went to Costco for a ring."

She walked over and sat on my sofa. I stood up and sat in one of the kitchen table chairs.

"I *do* like that you got it at Costco," she said. "But what did you think I was going to *say*? You thought I was just going to say yes?"

"Well, I imagined you'd need a *little* convincing, which I'm prepared to do. You know, we can have a long engagement, or a short engagement. We can fly to Vegas tomorrow and be back by Friday. Whatever you want. I am totally at your mercy."

"Ross, we're twenty-three years old. Why would we get married?"

"Isn't it obvious? We're just suffering without each other. What *good* is it having 'freedom' and 'fun' when we're just enslaved by our own loneliness? Don't you see it?"

"No, no, not at all. I don't see it like that at all," she took a sip of water out of the stainless-steel bottle in her backpack. "I'm a *kid*, I'm supposed to be doing *kid* things, not getting married to millionaires."

Ross, panicked: "Well what if we don't have to get married. Just let's be together again?"

"Ross, you should know I've been kind of seeing someone."

"Oh, sure. I know about that, but come on."

"What do you mean you *know* about it? How would you possibly know it?"

"Uh . . . I mean, I just assumed that you're never uh . . . celibate for more than a month at a time."

"See! This is what I don't want to have to deal with. You're so . . . *judgmental*. Every move I make is autistically inspected and scrutinized by you, like you're my dad, or guidance counselor, or *licensed clinical social worker*. I don't want to live in *Adult World* yet, Ross. I know you do. I know you care about buying bonds and taking pills and going to sleep at the same time every night. But I'm not ready for that, I'm not even *close*, and that's why this won't work. And even the *gifts* you got me were so . . . neurotic, Ross. All the fancy soaps and shampoos you used to get me, like, what am I supposed to think of that?"

"You're supposed to think they're nice gifts from a nice guy. Nice girlie gifts like lotions."

"Come on Ross. You have to move on. You can't just sit around doing nothing, waiting for me. A slave to inaction. You are a great guy, a very special guy, and you'll be able to make someone else very happy. Just not me."

At this point, the Gershwin had really begun to swing uptempo, strings and horns blasting high-energy sounds while my TV showed screenshots of messages between Lora and me—saying things to each other like "I want you so bad," and "What we have is forever," etc, etc. Lora got up and walked over to my refrigerator, opened it, and helped herself to a slice of Applegate Farms Organic "Uncured Capicola."

"What are you doing?" I asked her, my eyelids growing heavy, tears beginning to form.

"Just getting a snack . . ." she said.

And then, well, I just sort of lost it, I suppose. "No, no. You don't get to do that. You think we can just be *friends* after all this? You think you can just *reject* me like that, and then *still* help yourself to my Italian lunch meats? No, No! NO! You don't get to break my heart and then walk over to my kitchen and take my *gabagool* like it's yours. You have forfeited that privilege. You have forfeited so much, Lora, I can't even begin to tell you how stupid the decision you've just made was." Tears were now streaming down the sides of my face. "You think you'll be able to just keep smoking things, drinking things, going to bed with one penniless loser after another? You're going to get *sick* from sleeping in the bed of guys who don't wash their sheets twice a week like I do. You know that, right? I'm twenty-three and have millions of dollars and I'm a genius and I succeed at everything I do, and I was offering to *share* that with you, *relieve* you from a life of stress and heartbreak. I was offering stability, a chance to lock yourself into a happy relationship with someone who really cared, oozed love for you, and you pissed on me. I am drenched in your disrespect right now. You *dumped* on me. You treated me like *dirt*, Lora. And I feel sorry for you. Because sooner or later you're going to look terrible, from the diet, and the lifestyle you live. And you're not going to be *able* to find anyone half as fun or as competent as me—Ross! You realize I'm only going to keep getting better, more wealthy, more strong, more knowledgeable, more impressive. All you have are your looks, which are destined to wither. Just think, there are probably like a million sixty-year-old men you would be willing to date. But there are *zero*, and I mean *zero*, sixty-year-old women I would be caught dead in a bed with. This game favors *me*, and you were *still* too stupid to accept the golden ticket you were given on a silver platter. I mean look at this, look how many pushups I can do." Red-faced, I dropped to the ground and began doing pushups . . . "That was thirty pushups, Lora. I could've done more but I think you got the point. That I've made myself a physical specimen. And I did that for *you*, I put my body through hell for *you*. And you just don't care. I can't believe you don't care. This is over. We are not friends. I have never been more insulted in my entire life. You selfish, treacherous whore. You monster. You wench. You are a despicable person, and you deserve nothing but misery from this point forward."

I was breathing fast and heavy, I sat back down, staring silently at the floor while Lora packed up her bag and retied her boots on her way out. It occurred to me that I'd made an absolute fool of myself. Stupid, impatient Ross. Lora looked back at me in the doorway, made a face expressing pity, embarrassment, at me, and said, "Goodbye, Ross," resignedly.

"Wait!" I said as she opened the door, "I'm sorry. I meant *none* of that! I don't know what I was thinking. Can I have just one kiss? Just one? Please?"

(In which I, Ross, come to an understanding)

It couldn't have gone worse for Ross. To come close and still take a loss. A hapless schlemiel, who can't close the deal, and always ends up feeling cross!

Oh, I wanted to blow my brains out. And throw them directly into the blah blah blah. Even my limericks had begun to suffer. That one up there just isn't as smooth (or as clever, really) as the one I'd prepared for Lora. I felt more miserable than ever. Her comment about my alleged inaction really rubbed me the wrong way, too. After she left and I'd finished nervously vomiting cheese into my spotless toilet, I resigned back to my bed where I rolled around sobbing for several hours, saying things like "Why, why, why!?" and "I hate myself! I hate being Ross!"

I fantasized about how nice things would've been had I been born eighteen years sooner, like my parents were. Back when people had *standards* and women knew how to respect *nice guys* like me, Ross. In one of my many Moleskines, I started writing a draft of a letter to Lora.

> *Dear Lora,*
> *This is Ross's sister (Emily). Ross said you were 'literally killing him' and he took a ton of pills and now he's dead*

No, no that would never work. There was no *end game* there. Another attempt:

Dear Lora,

It's me, Ross. I don't know what I was thinking. Saying those horrible and dis-
gusting things to you. I'm well aware that I've made a fool of myself, have totally
lost all credibility, etc, etc. I'm sorry. I'm terribly sorry for hurting you. For
everything. I never wanted to do that. I don't expect you to want to talk to me for
a long while, but just know, that you were right, and I was wrong. Please let me
try again.

No, no! Even worse. Such a groveling and pathetic voice. What would
that get me? Admitting I was wrong, *debasing* myself, and then still telling her to go ahead, keep cucking me over and over again. I tore that out
and crumpled it up into a little ball, then threw it into the corner near
my garbage can.

What I really needed to do, was put my *thinking cap* on. Think like
someone who isn't constantly being humiliated and emasculated. The
Goldberg business was moronic. It was so *low culture*, so *not me*! I was
pretending to be someone I wasn't. My nature was not to be handsome,
muscular, and confident. I had to be more Elder of Zion than professional wrestler. Start using that *yiddisher kop*. Stop fighting biological
determinism. I was a Jewish guy, deep down, and the only way to solve
this problem, this Jewish question, was with a final Jewish solution.

I asked Victor to find out who this "new guy" Lora had been seeing
was. And then, while I was in the middle of scheming evilly, I thought of
a new ingenious political policy idea.

So right now, student loan debt cannot be discharged in bankruptcy
proceedings in the United States. With the idea being, that once you get
a college degree, you can never get rid of it. And this is only accelerating
the infantilization of my generation, and the one before me, and the one
after me. It's a disaster, and no one has any good ideas for how to solve
it fairly. My idea, which came to me in a moment of Jewish scheming,
would be to let people get their loans forgiven, but under the condition
that if they're ever caught putting their college degree on their résumé

again (after forfeiting it in bankruptcy), they go to jail. Would that not work? Why wouldn't it work? It seems like a great idea.

Anyway, back to *Ricky*, my umpteenth idiot replacement. I can't believe Vic found so much about Ricky. It's really incredible that Vic is so good at this and yet still so poor. One would think he'd have found a creepy Jewish guy sooner to help him finagle his finances. But anyway. Ricky. This Ricky, this Richard Sood, was (and I mean this, this is all true and real) an eighteen-year-old high school senior. With tattoos, tiny studded ear piercings, a short haircut, and at least two different skateboards. Vic and I also had good reason to believe that he liked smoking weed (big surprise!), but we didn't have any hard evidence of that. This was her new "Ross." A teenager with a "health food" clothing brand, which was just T-shirts with printed cartoons of broccoli on them. My first instinct (after discovering this, and being acutely aware of the rottenness and evil in me) was to call the police and send Lora to jail, or make her register as a sex offender (not for the sex they were having, since the age of consent is seventeen in New York, but for the lewd photos Lora almost certainly was sending him—and receiving from him! That's child pornography, for crying out loud!).

But there were two problems with this plan. First, there were no police officers left in New York, after everyone decided to fire them. And second, by the time Vic and I realized this Ricky was a threat, he had already turned eighteen, meaning our case would be thin at best.

So my *new* plan, my new and improved foolproof fabrication was to make *her* (Lora L) realize that this guy didn't care about her, didn't value her, had nothing to offer, at least not compared to Ross (ME!).

To accomplish this, this revenge homewrecking idea, I would use not power, not muscle or intimidation, nor a sexy decoy to distract him with, no, none of that. Just money. Just a few thousand of my many millions. I called up Robert Shapiro (my family's lawyer and personal friend of my dead parents) and explained the situation, how I'd been cucked horribly and left feeling miserable. He understood completely and liked my idea. He drew up the following contract: Ricky, for the next ten years, would receive a $106,000 per year stipend to fund his clothing line from an S-Corp (owned by me) called "Ricky's Gay and Dumb LLC," in addition to free housing in the city (not county) of Los Angeles. The only condition being that he never again speaks to Lora Liamant and has to live in Los Angeles. If he spoke to Lora Liamant or moved back to New York from Los Angeles, I would get to take his money, his car, his house, his parents' house, etc, etc. Did I mention he was poor? Yes, he was poor and nonjewish and had tattoos and rode a skateboard. He was the *anti-Ross* incarnate.

The mechanism (of delivery) was simple. I would ambush Ricky and Lora in a public place, present this Ricky with $10,000 in cash (on the spot, to show I meant *business*), have him sign the papers, and then share some choice words with Lora (something like "Are you happy? This guy doesn't *value* you. He just agreed never to see you again. Just for some money. An amount of money that meant very little to me. I hope you're happy, Lora. I hope you feel good about choosing *him* over *me*. I hope it was worth it."—Yes, something like that would work well). And what would Ricky, idiot Ricky have to say in the face of an intellectual powerhouse promising him wealth beyond his wildest dreams? What *could* he say, other than "Whoa, that's cool . . . yeah, I'll take the money. Bye forever, Lora!" His stupid tattooed hands would be tied.

Finally, after I'd destroyed Lora's new love (and showed her how loyal a hungry dog *really* is), I would seek the services of a hypnotist named Phillip Bouffard, whom I saw an ad for on the F train. Phill B would induce hypnosis, and command me to be totally disgusted at the thought or mention of Lora Liamant. I would be free. *I* would be the one going out on the town, yucking it up, while *she* sat around, abandoned and scorned.

I ran through the plan a few more times in my head, and it was so deliciously wily that I caught myself giggling and repeating aloud, with increasing volume (alone in my nighttime luxury island apartment), "Ross Mathcamp: one-fifty IQ *genius*!"

~

A few days later, on March 16, after eight days of indoor alternating between manic scheming and depressive Jewish groaning, I finally stepped outside and took a walk through Roosevelt Island's Octagon Park, past the rotunda attached to my apartment building. On a stone wall, I read the engraving on a plaque that I'd never noticed before, honoring the building as a historic monument, explaining that it was previously home to the NEW YORK CITY LUNATIC ASYLUM (which you can look up if you don't think it sounds real).

By the water, I took a deep breath, stared at Astoria, and felt utterly at ease, stretching my young legs out as far as they would go. A ferry on the Manhattan side of the Island sailed past me and rang its loud horn. I felt utterly at ease. Birds chirped in a nearby hedge. The sweet scent of springtime island grass wafted toward my face. I felt a buzzing on my wrist, a notification from my Watch to tell me the latest price of Bitcoin. I felt utterly at ease.

On my way back inside (twenty minutes of sunlight was plenty), I received a phone call from Victor Bowflex, telling me that he had used his parabolic microphone to eavesdrop into Lora's thin-walled brownstone, and determined that she would be meeting Ricky in Lower Manhattan's Stuyvesant Square in an hour, I mean, one hour after the moment he (Vic) called me, if that makes sense, 12:00 noon. This was perfect. "Okay, Vic, head over here. I'm ready this time. Let me just go brush my teeth, get my briefcase, and I'll meet you outside The Octagon," I panted into the phone, rushing to get ready inside.

I don't know why I said briefcase on the phone; the legal documents were in a three-ring binder, and the ten thousand dollars in cash was in a Reebok *Mike Monad's Strongman Gym* duffel bag that I had no use for. When Vic messaged me "here bish," I scuttled to the elevator and out of my lobby's front door, into Vic's brand new "Crystal White" Cadillac Escalade.

"You like my new whip?" he asked me.

"It's nice, Vic. Can you afford it?"

"Yeah, it's only nine hundred a month, and I make an extra two dollars per ride when I pick someone up now. Cuz it's so nice," he told me.

"I don't know, Vic. I just wished you had asked me before you did this." I dropped my things onto the seat next to me and pulled the door closed.

Vic shook his head and let out a slight verbal grunt crestfallenly, "I knew you were gonna say that, bro." He perked up, "but I had these two Russian girls in here the other night. And I had this thing *rockin* bro."

"You had it rocking, Vic?"

"Yeah, bro. I had it going like," he started shaking spasmodically, miming a washing machine, etc, etc.

"Alright, that's fine. You're free to do that. You know, as an adult, or whatever. But now I'm *sitting* here, in the backseat, and now I know you were doing that right where I'm sitting right now. So why would you tell me that, Vic?"

"Third row, bro." He adjusted his mirror and smiled at me. "We were in the third row, and you're in the second."

"Oh, okay," I said, "I guess that does make it better."

Vic sped down the East Side Highway, turning around occasionally to tell me things like "this car's simply a *beast*," and "we're gonna show that guy who's *Ross*." As he was driving, I looked over the documents one last time. Feeling unassured about lines like ". . . penalties include, but are not limited to forfeiture of your housing, equity, and garnishment of future wages . . ."

After several loops around Stuyvesant Square, I spotted Lora sitting on a bench through my binoculars. I felt terrible. I felt the kind of hate you can only really feel for someone you really love. The kind of hate that's free from any semblance of indifference. This was my enemy, in other words. She did things that hurt me and my mind was made up—I was going to cause more misery. "I'm gonna get out," I told Vic, "just drive off. I'll call you soon. I want to be alone for this."

I hopped out of the car and walked nervously around the park's perimeter (I was outside the gate and wearing a dark hooded sweatshirt, New York Yankees fitted cap, and sunglasses, so there's no way she could've noticed me) to the opposite end from where Lora was sitting. I was a wreck, dominated by a sense of impending doom ("Am I really going to do this?"). It must've been pretty similar to how Lee Oswald or John Booth felt in the final moments before they murdered those presidents.

While I was sitting on some steps on the corner of 15th Street and 2nd Avenue, in the middle of delivering a miniature motivational speech to myself ("You can do this Ross. He's a skateboarder. You're smarter than he is. You're richer than he is. You have the element of surprise"), the bells of several nearby churches began ringing to announce the twelve o'clock hour.

But that wasn't what shocked me. What shocked me was not what I heard, but what I saw. As I sat on these steps, I watched in awe as a young couple walked out of one of these churches, the woman carrying a baby, and the man carrying a compacted stroller which he proceeded to unfold and help his wife place their baby into. Without really thinking about it, I stood up and approached them.

"Excuse me," I started, "is this your baby? Like you two are the parents of this child?" I asked.

"Yes? Who else's would it be?" the woman replied.

"Oh, it's just that . . . you guys are so young," I said, laughing slightly.

"The median woman in America has her first child at twenty-six, and we're twenty-five. Why don't you mind your own business, pervert?" the man said before they continued walking past me.

Dejected, I returned to my seat on the steps, fascinated by these two. They looked like college students, about my age, but wearing wedding bands and pushing a stroller. These people had a child together, but in a good way. They looked like respectable, normal people, like they had a kid on purpose and had normal jobs and could afford to take care of it and give it a reasonably nice life. These were attractive people—not nerds or fat-faced-middle-America-megachurch-Protestants. These were people who dressed well and appeared educated (you could just tell based on their facial expressions and from the way they were walking that this was a medium-high IQ couple, the sort of people who've heard of Hegel), but with a baby in their mid-twenties and living in Manhattan (unless they brought the stroller in from a different borough). But this really shocked me, to see that there were people my age, people like me, creating life instead of destroying it. That I had been running in degenerate circles. That despite all my muscles and money, I was a loser. That there were still people in the world who were happy and fulfilled. People who spent the past year doing things infinitely more important than scheming or seeking revenge.

Fumbling through my bag, I found my binoculars and held them up to my eyes to get another look at Lora. My stomach softened at the sight of her. Something serious and conclusory went through my head. It felt as if I'd been holding my breath, that feeling when you're so close to concocting an original thought that you forget to breathe, or rather, *neglect* to breathe, deciding you have to use all available energy to focus on crystalizing this budding original ideation. I watched as Ricky came by on his skateboard, and I saw the excited look on Lora's face when she watched that innocent aged young boy attempt assorted "tricks" on his "board." She was happy. She was utterly at ease. And it further occurred to me that this whole thing, this whole mess I'd gotten myself into, this Lora Liamant infatuation had run its course. That not only was she happy without me, but that I (Ross) might very well have been unambiguously *in the wrong*. That I was the villain here, that I was the *other* guy from "Two Princes" (1992). That I had to move on in earnest, that it was high time I leave this poor girl alone, that the real Lora Liamant was the friends we made along the way, etc, etc, etc, etc.

I walked a few blocks west, cursing myself ("You acted so foolishly, Ross! You missed the whole point! It never would've worked out between you! You're too different. You wasted countless mental man-hours trying to stuff a Lora-shaped peg into a Ross-shaped hole!") for letting myself be so consumed by lust and pride and shortsighted greediness. My mental model of the past year was suddenly so clear and accessible, as if I'd just rid myself of some horrible burden obstructing the faculties required for rationally abstracting human interactions. I'd spent months cogitating on superficialities, prioritizing the dumbest aspects of my identity, lying to myself and the world around me, etc, etc. It was clear what I needed to do.

I turned toward the direction of the park and the bench on which Lora sat, and tearily, meekly waved goodbye, moreso to this idea of Lora Liamant, the mission of Lora Liamant, Lora Liamant my White Whale, etc, etc than the actual twenty-three-year-old girl wearing heart-shaped sunglasses a few hundred feet away. Smiling slightly, I caught myself saying aloud, "Well, it was a learning experience . . ." before pulling out my phone and composing a message to Emily and Amanda, which I hoped might smooth things over.

Carrying my duffel bag full of cash / blackmail contracts, I walked west into a nearby Whole Foods Market and bought a "low-glycemic lemonade" flavored with monk fruit and cayenne pepper that intrigued me with its fancy holographic packaging. But despite its great potential, this sweet, sour, and spicy treat failed to deliver a satisfying ending . . . I mean . . . taste.

On the Q train, on my way back to the penthouse I'd purchased in Brooklyn with money from my parents' untimely death, I picked up the velvet jewelry box containing the three-carat diamond engagement ring I'd splurged five figures for at Costco a few weeks earlier. "That was smart of you, Ross. A brilliant, well-hedged move—basically an infinite Sharpe ratio, given their excellent return policy," I thought to myself as I slid the box into my right pant pocket.

Inside, I set my bags down in the foyer and took a look at myself in the mirror next to the door. "Girls? I'm home!" I shouted. "Oh, wow, it's really hot in here," I mumbled to myself. "Are you sure it needs to be this hot in here? It's actually a really nice day out," I continued in the louder voice. "Actually, it's fine, let me take off some of these clothes I was wear-ing to disguise myself."

I walked into the living room and saw my sister sitting on the sofa, playing with one of the two cats that lived with us. "Hey Em, is Amanda around?"

"Yeah I think she's in her room," Emily replied.

"Okay, thanks. Did you see the message I sent you guys?"

"No, we've been trying to use our phones less in here."

"Oh, you should check it," I said as I walked over to Amanda's room and knocked on her door.

"Yes?"

"It's, uh, Ross?" I said.

"Oh, come in, Ross."

Amanda was sitting down, leaning forward over her desk fiddling with what looked like some sort of necklace or bracelet. "Do you need something?" She didn't look up at me. "I got this jewelry kit, but I'm not sure I like it. It feels way less *lindy* than sewing."

"Oh, did you see the message I sent you and Emily?"

"No, we've been trying to use our phones less in here."

"I heard about that," I said, still standing in her doorway. "Well, can you look?" I waited as she picked up her phone and read the message I'd sent nearly forty minutes earlier.

> I'm coming home now. Everything's wrapped up, re: Lora L, <
> you won't hear about her anymore. I'm sorry I haven't been
> around lately. I've been awful. The Roosevelt Island lease
> is expiring at the end of the month. And I'm feeling gen-
> erous and contemplative. I'd love to watch *The Passion of the
> Christ* (2004) with you two, if you'd like. I've never seen it
> and it seems "culturally relevant." But anyway, I'm really
> very sorry for how silly I've been. You two deserve better.
> Please, let me try again.

Amanda, upon reading this, stood up from her seat and approached me for a hug. "You look terrible, Ross," she said. "You look tired and full of shame."

"I know. I've been sleeping poorly and I haven't been lifting weights or eating four thousand calories a day lately."

"Let me make you something. Would you eat kale?"

"I like kale. But you have to cook it really well. If you don't cook it—"

"Yes, yes. The oxalates, they're terrible for you. Come on. Let's go to the kitchen."

In the living room, Emily stopped me while Amanda continued into the kitchen. "Do you mean it this time, Ross?" she asked.

"Mean what?"

"That you're sorry."

"Yes."

"You're going to live here and be good and we're going to be a family?"

"Yes. We're going to be a family. I think you'll be happy with my behavior for the foreseeable future. It's going to be really nice."

As I was hugging Emily (I was really doling these out, it seemed), my phone buzzed with a message from Victor.

> U make her cry?

To which I replied: "No," and began walking back toward the kitchen.

"Can you help me open this jar, Ross?" Amanda asked as she handed me a jar of rendered organic pork fat. "You just have to try the kale cooked in this pastured pork lard, Ross. It makes it taste so much better."

"I believe you," I said, using a dish towel to get a better grip on the jar.

"Here, it's open."

Back in the living room, I sat down next to one of my cats and felt my Watch buzz with another message from Victor.

> What happened? U chicken out?

Emily pressed play on the movie I'd agreed to watch, and Amanda came over with my bowl of sautéed kale. I looked at her (Amanda) and felt warm, comfortable. I tapped the engagement-ring-box in my right pant pocket and smiled. The kind of smile you smile when something smart comes to you.

No, not at all <

I typed back to Victor, looking up at my home, at my family, at the *Icon Productions* logo on the screen.

Just realized it wasn't worth the money. <

#Acknowledgements

So many people helped make this book happen.

My parents and brother for helping me be not only Jewish but also Catholic. Teaching me about pills and the value of family.

Elizabeth Priegues, Patrick Reid, Jameson Fitzpatrick, and Fernanda Amis for teaching me how to write and telling me I was ready for a novel.

Honor Levy, Dasha Nekrasova, Eugene Kotlyarenko, Tao Lin, and Sheila Heti for reading this book and advocating for it while it was still just a PDF on my website taolin.org.

My homeboy Sean Thor Conroe for standing on business and sending the PDF to our amazing agent Julie Flanagan.

My amazing agent Julie Flanagan for legitimizing me even after everyone told her not to.

My editor Stephan Zguta for being the only editor who wanted to buy it out of the hundreds we sent it to.

The famous artist Jon Rafman for making a delicious Jewish cover (for free).

Woody Allen.